FORT ENTERPRIZE

Kevin Emmet Foley

Hellgate Press   Ashland, OR

Fort Enterprize
©2016 Kevin Emmet Foley

Published by Hellgate Press
(An imprint of L&R Publishing, LLC)

Hellgate Press
PO Box 3531
Ashland, OR 97520
email: sales@hellgatepress.com

Editor: Harley B. Patrick
Interior design: Sasha Kincaid
Cover design: L. Redding
Cover image: Oil painting of Decatur Boarding the Tripolitan Gunboat during the bombardment of Tripoli, 3 August 1804 by Dennis Malone Carter. Courtesy Naval Historical Center, Department of the Navy, Washington Navy Yard.

Library of Congress Cataloging-in-Publication Data is available from the publisher on request.

Printed and bound in the United States of America
First edition 10 9 8 7 6 5 4 3 2 1

In Memory of
Lee Roy Howard
United States Marine

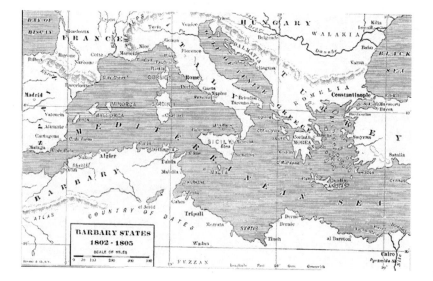

BARBARY STATES
1802 - 1805
SCALE OF MILES

PROLOGUE

Barrington hung against the limestone wall oozing fetid water as lice crawled through his long matted hair and over his naked body. In the darkness he heard rats scurrying across the slimy cobbled floor. His hands were held over his head, clamped in thick iron shackles that bit cruelly into his wrists. When his back grazed the damp wall Barrington screamed out in pain from the scores of lashes he had received after he attacked the driver.

They were trudging down a hill dragging the wooden sledges loaded with boulders for the breakwater the bashaw's engineers were constructing in the harbor. The harness ropes dug into the bare shoulders and chests of the American seamen, considered slaves by their captors and, worse, beasts of burden. The drivers enjoyed making sport of their misery, forcing Barrington and the others to race the heavy sledges to the waterfront.

Despite the cool winter air, sweat glistened on the emaciated bodies of the Americans. The men in the harnesses closest to the sledges were covered with a fine white dust churned up by the men at the front of the miserable procession.

The only sounds were the buzz of insects, the grunts of the Americans and the high cackling voices of the Arab drivers, who stood atop the sledges brandishing cat o'nine tails.

Barrington watched as the man in front of him, an able seaman named Simms, stumbled and then slowly dropped to his knees on the rocky road, no longer able to pull the sledge. The driver, angry that his wager might be lost, leapt down from the sledge and raced to the fallen man. He stood over Simms, lashing him with his cat and screaming incoherently at the stricken sailor who lay face down and unconscious on the road.

Perhaps it was the scene of torment before him, one of the countless he had witnessed since he and the others had been captured. It might have been the months of captivity or the crushing work performed without respite day after backbreaking day that suddenly pushed Barrington over the edge.

Without thinking and before his shipmates could stop him, Barrington dropped his harness and strode forward, seizing the driver from behind. The Arab was a head shorter, but wiry and agile. As he struggled, the American violently shoved him to the road. The man's white turban flew from his head as he fell and the back of his bald skull crashed into the sharp edge of a rock, blood splattering earth. The driver was dead.

Barrington stood over the guard, chest heaving, his skin blistered by the desert sun, beard filthy and gone the whiteness of snow from the constant exposure to the elements and the darkness of the Bashaw's dungeon. Simms stirred and Barrington began to help him to his feet when a truncheon struck his shoulders and he collapsed.

Presently Barrington was jolted out of semi-consciousness by the rumble of the dungeon's thick wooden door. It swung open and he saw the silhouette of a turbaned figure in flowing robes backlit by the harsh sunlight flooding the reeking chamber. Barrington blinked his eyes against the pain and then watched as the figure entered the cell and stood before him.

"'Tis a terrible fix you've got yourself into, laddy," a voice said. Barrington recognized the accent of the Scotsman. He said nothing in reply as he hung, chained to the wall, squinting at the face he could not quite see.

More forms materialized from behind the voice. Turkish janissaries unlocked the shackles and Barrington, free, dropped to his knees before being dragged to his feet by two of the biggest soldiers clad in scarlet tunics, turbans and white pantaloons.

"You oughtn't to have murdered that poor guard," the voice sneered as Barrington was dragged past. "He was the son of the bashaw's cousin and well thought of in Tripoli. More's the pity for you, I'm afraid."

Barrington was hauled through a bright courtyard and out a barred gate into the streets of the city. Seeing the filthy, naked American, a crowd of merchants and passersby began hurling mud, filth and abuse at the prisoner. The janissaries made no effort to stop them, although one of the huge Turks cuffed a boy who had inadvertently spattered his spotless trousers with a handful of sheep dung. The crowd grew, and now keening women in black veils joined the mob, stoning Barrington who covered his face with one hand and his genitals with his other.

They approached the city wall where Barrington could see stone stairs led to a rampart fifty feet above. There, a group of Tripolitans had gathered. As the prisoner and guards mounted the rampart, Barrington recognized the Bashaw Yusuf Karamanli, a great hirsute ogre in a jewel-studded turban. Above a thick beard the bashaw's eyes were black as pitch, glimmering as the American stood before him. Yusuf was seated on a plush velvet divan surrounded by his courtiers and six black slaves, each armed with a savage looking lance.

The cold morning wind raked Barrington's battered body as he glanced to his right at the shimmering Mediterranean Sea. There, at anchor, was the bashaw's fleet of corsairs, their marauding suspended for the winter. The sailor stood, hands at his sides as the bashaw eyed his bruises and welts and said something in a guttural voice to his attendants who responded with laughter at whatever joke Yusuf made.

Barrington ignored them. His thoughts were on his little red house in Rhode Island overlooking Narragansett Bay, his wife Martha and his five children. He had not seen them in more than two years when he had shipped out as a first mate aboard the frigate. A warrant officer, the twenty dollars per month he received was more than he ever earned aboard any merchantman. Barrington was also promised a share of any prize should his ship capture enemy vessels.

But now what was left of his ship lay in blackened ruins on the rocks in the harbor. She had burned to the waterline nearly a year before directly below the bashaw's castle. Shortly after that, a flotilla of U.S. ships and gunboats had bombarded the city and Yusuf's castle, destroying or severely damaging many of the bashaw's corsairs and feluccas as well as scores of buildings throughout Tripoli.

Barrington smiled to himself as he thought of how the fat, hairy Karamanli must have raged over the losses.

"His Excellency wishes to know why you are smiling," the Scotsman said. Barrington turned his head to look at Tripoli's Grand Admiral, Murad Reis. The man's complexion was fair, his wiry red hair tied off in a pair of queues, hung from beneath a turban of deep blue satin. His beard was cropped short. He wore green silken robes that fluttered in the breeze like a ship's pennant. A hoop of solid gold hung from his left ear and his teeth were flawless as he smiled at the American, almost sympathetically.

Barrington pointed at the charred bones of the ship he'd once sailed aboard and replied, "I am amused that the Grand Admiral wasn't able to protect the greatest prize ever taken by Tripoli, even as she lay anchored below the ape's hooked nose."

Reis's face went white. His crystal blue eyes glared at the American and he silently damned Barrington's impudence.

"What is it the slave says?!" demanded the bashaw in Arabic. "I don't like his look!"

Reis glanced at Sidi Mohammed Dghies, Tripoli's foreign minister and the only other member of the royal courtiers who spoke English. The man was old and feared Murad Reis so he averted his eyes.

"This Christian dog insults the bashaw and his family!" Reis roared in Arabic as he pointed at Barrington.

Yusuf's oily eyes darkened. He had been sitting placidly, hands over his enormous belly, fingers like hairy brown sausages locked together, but now he bolted up with startling quickness and grabbed Barrington by the hair. He dragged the prisoner to the edge of the rampart where two Turks seized the seaman by his arms.

At the foot of the city wall, a throng of Arabs was looking up at him. Excited chatter rippled through the mob as men below pointed and smiled evilly. The American now understood he was about to die. Barrington felt a sudden bolt of terror, but not just at being thrown from the parapet. There, halfway down, a row of iron hooks protruded from the wall, their points aimed at him, waiting.

The bashaw stood beside him wearing a sadistic grin while Barrington tried vainly to break free of his captors. If he was to die he would try to leap clear of the vicious hooks. But the janissaries held him fast and even began to laugh as he struggled.

"Dam'a C'ris'an," Yusuf growled as he pointed at the hooks.

With that Barrington felt himself thrown from the wall, falling toward the upturned faces. But before he hit the ground among the spectators the iron hooks snagged his body, impaling him through his shoulder, his side and through the calf of his right leg. He screamed in anguish as the mob roared its approval. Nathaniel Barrington hung from the vicious hooks, his blood splashed across the whitewashed fortress wall, excited Tripolitans throwing stones at his tortured body.

At first the American struggled but he slowly realized that to fight would make the excruciating pain worse. So Barrington hung from the hooks - for five days and nights...alive. On the sixth day, the pain disappearing, a peaceful vision came to Barrington. It was of Martha and his children. They were all smiling at him and he smiled back at them for one last time.

A full week after he'd been thrown from the parapet, vultures were picking the American's body clean. The townspeople of Tripoli had returned to their business no longer interested in the rotting corpse of the American sailor dangling from the city's wall.

1

LOGAN COUNTY, KENTUCKY
July 19, 1850

The day is intolerably hot and, vexed, I once again wonder why it is father has sent me on this burdensome errand. I would much prefer to be back home in my native Virginia engaged in leisurely pursuits with my friends than here, traveling to this loathsome backwater in search of some forgotten military officer. Cockfights, balls, riding, horse racing, hunting, these are what I am missing as I ride along this damnable rutted road, bouncing inside a stagecoach with two greasy drummers both of whom stink to high heaven.

"You *shall* go and you *shall* record for posterity what he has to tell you!" father had commanded me. "The man was a hero yet no one remembers his name!"

I could ask why this duty should fall to me but father's response would be because the hero in question was the uncle of my late mother. He would explain once again it had been mother's dying wish that "Uncle Presley's story" find its way to some publisher for the edification of the reading public. My elder brother, Thomas, is in charge of running father's plantation and my three sisters are all engaged in gentile womanly pastimes, so father approached me one warm June afternoon as I sat idly in a rocking chair overlooking our estate.

"What were you doing at university but preparing yourself to become a writer of books and such?" father asked. "At least that is what you claimed you were doing. Surely you would find Presley's exploits wonderful fodder! If you choose not to do this, then you may work as an overseer in the fields at your brother's direction. I shan't watch you while away your time on endless games and debauchery!"

Working under Thomas, ten years my elder and a stringent taskmaster, was an appalling notion. So here I am.

The stagecoach rolled to a stop and I found myself standing in a dusty crossroads called Russellville in the rolling hills of central Kentucky. There were a few ramshackle houses, a store and a tavern but little else to recommend the place. I was parched with thirst so I entered the tavern, an ancient log structure that might once have catered to Daniel Boone himself.

In the dark, stuffy interior I saw the landlord drawing ale for a customer so I called the same for myself.

"Where you hail from, sonny?" the landlord asked genially as he drew my pint. He was a short man with a mop of black hair clad in a stained leather apron.

I took a long draught of the lukewarm brew. "Fauquier County, Virginia," I replied as I set the mug on the bar.

"Oh, the cap'n's home county!" he replied a broad smile revealing very few teeth.

"The captain?" I asked.

"Yes, sir. Captain O'Bannon. Everyone in Logan County knowed the cap'n!"

"Indeed!" I replied excitedly. "He is the fellow I seek! Is he hereabout? I was told he was but no one in my family has had any intercourse with him in some years. My father told me this was his last known domicile."

"Domicile? Sure 'nough 'tis…" The tavern keeper replied. His tone now turned suspicious. "Why is it you want 'im, anyhow?"

"I am a relative of his. A great nephew to be precise. I wish an interview with him."

"What fer?" the man asked with a scowl. "He's old and he ain't none too well."

I decided it would be best to enlist the man's assistance even though my mission was none of his business, so I continued.

"You see, sir, my mother was his niece. She died two years ago but she was adamant that Captain O'Bannon's history be recorded, perhaps in a book about his life. I am an author…or, I hope to be one someday, so I wish to hear first hand of the captain's deeds and perhaps write a book about them."

"Y' know what he done, don't ya?"

"Not exactly, no," I replied with a look of embarrassment. "I…I believe he served in the war with the Barbary pirates years and years ago…I know that much."

"Oh, he done more than that…much more," the innkeeper remarked cryptically. "But I fig'er he should tell you that if'n he's able. Like I say, cap'n's health ain't good."

"Where might I find Uncle Presley, er, I mean the captain?"

"His plantation is about two mile or so up the north road there," he replied as he pointed through the dirty window. "It's called *Derne*."

"Indeed," I replied as I picked up my valise and portfolio containing my writing implements and paper. "Strange name."

"Not really all that strange 't al'," the tavern keeper said as I took my leave.

From a livery stable I rented a small gray gelding that had enormous difficulty understanding basic commands. I finally got the nag under control and half an hour later, I passed by a wide field of tobacco. It was approaching three o'clock in the afternoon but I saw no field hands and wondered why. I soon spied a dozen Negroes sitting in the shade of an oak tree alongside the road singing one of their spirituals and clapping their hands in time to its rhythm. This was an odd sight, but even more unusual, there seemed to be no white overseer to direct their work.

This was perplexing because, in the fields of Fauquier County, Negro slaves toiled dawn to dusk with only short breaks for feeding and watering.

As I came near, the Negros saw me. Several of them smiled broadly and waved cheerfully as though they hadn't a care in the world. Frowning, I half raised my hand to acknowledge their greeting.

After another mile, a lovely white clapboard frame house came into view. It sat well off the road, pleasantly shaded by stands of hickory and elm. A well-tended lawn and gardens fronted the house, which I now saw was expansive. It appeared as though its owner had added rooms over the years.

I dismounted and unlashed my belongings as a Negro boy appeared from a red barn nearby. He smiled and waved. "I'll take 'im, sir," the boy said as he trotted up to me and reached for the reins. A soft breeze blew through the thick leaves of the shade trees as I mounted the porch stairs and crossed to the wide front door. Before I could knock, a light skinned Negress opened the door and stood before me. She looked to be in her middle years and wore a calico dress of excellent quality. Her hair was swept back and she moved with casual grace.

"Good afternoon, sir," she said with a bow of her head and a smile. "Welcome to *Derna*. Whom may I say is calling?"

I was taken aback. Our house Negroes wore hand-me-downs and they were not very well spoken, nor did they carry themselves particularly well. By comparison, this black woman seemed almost gentile.

"Um, my name is Mr. Harrison Oswald," I replied. "I am Captain O'Bannon's great nephew."

She didn't reply, so I continued.

"His niece, that is, Margaret O'Bannon, was my mother."

"Was?" she asked. This truly startled me for I was completely unaccustomed to a Negro questioning me.

"Well, my mother died. Two years ago…"

"And the captain is unaware of her death?"

"No. Yes, I mean, no, he likely does not know my mother passed away," I replied as I felt myself becoming impatient. Who did this servant think she was? "See here, woman, I would really like you to announce…"

She slowly closed her eyes and held up her hand for silence. "The captain is resting at present, Mr. Oswald. I won't disturb him just now. Kindly seat yourself on the porch and I shall serve refreshment there."

With that, the Negress turned and walked into the house leaving me standing before the front door, mouth agape.

In all my life, a slave had never addressed me so.

2

A short time later the Negress reappeared with a tray. On it was a tall glass filled with tea over shaved ice. There were also sugar biscuits. As she bent next to me I noticed she smelled of lavender soap, another startling discovery, since our slaves seldom bathed. She placed the tray on the small table next to my wicker chair and returned silently to the house.

I sipped my tea and marveled at the ice, a luxury seldom seen at my home in the middle of July. Tired from my journey, I must have dozed off because I was startled awake by singing. The Negroes I had seen in the field earlier came trooping up the drive, their tools casually resting on their shoulders, chanting a gospel melody. I consulted my pocket watch and saw that it was just a little past five o'clock. There were at least three hours of daylight left so I wondered why they were quitting their work so early.

A tall buck saw me on the porch as he and the others passed by. He touched the brim of his wide hat. "Afternoon, sir!" he called out. I nodded at him.

"Supper time," a voice declared from the door. I turned and saw the Negress. I began to rise, but she held up her hand. "I mean it is their supper time."

"It is early, is it not?" I replied, confused.

"No. Captain O'Bannon's hands begin work at eight o'clock and retire for the day at five o'clock. They don't work on Sunday, and only half of a day on Saturday."

"But slaves usually…" I started to reply.

"They are not slaves," the Negress interrupted. "Nor am I a slave, Mr. Oswald. The captain freed us years ago when he arrived here. We are all paid a weekly wage for our labor as well as room and board. We may leave or we may stay."

I was truly astounded. Kentucky law permitted slaves so why on earth would a man pay good money for what he could have at no cost? It certainly must have hurt my uncle's income considerably. Reading my thoughts, the Negress said, "The captain will explain."

Shadows had by now crept across the lawn and the breeze had become noticeably cooler. The Negress walked to the side table and picked up the serving tray. "Won't you come in now and meet Captain O'Bannon?" she invited. "He wishes to make your acquaintance, Mr. Oswald." As she turned she looked over her shoulder. "You may call me Miss Lily. I am the captain's housekeeper."

Following Miss Lily, I entered a long hallway. Dappled sunlight spilled in through the wide Palladian windows and there was the pleasant aroma of pine oil in the still air. I could see the house was immaculate. As I passed through the main hall I noticed fine furnishings were arranged in the parlor and dining room. A stairway to my right led to the second floor.

Paintings were hung throughout the hallway. I paused before one of the pictures because it was different than the portraits and landscapes featured in the other works. It was an image of a hatless young man with flowing black hair standing atop a rampart clutching a standard at the end of which flew an American flag. In his other hand, the figure held a bloody sword. There appeared to be a battle underway, with turbaned figures and soldiers fighting to either side of the young man, white smoke hanging in the air.

"That's the captain," Miss Lily explained as she stepped up beside me and pointed at the gallant figure with the flag and sword. "In 1805."

I frowned. "Where…"

I turned to see her gentle smile. "The captain will explain."

She moved on and I followed. At the end of the hall she stopped, turned toward me and held her hand out toward a room to her left. "Captain Presley Neville O'Bannon will receive you now, Mr. Oswald."

I followed her gesture and entered a paneled study lined floor to ceiling with bookshelves stuffed with hundreds of leather-bound volumes. It was dark within as the shades were drawn, so I let my eyes adjust.

"Welcome, Harrison!" a baritone voice declared. "Miss Lily told me of Margaret's death. I am so sorry. She was my favorite niece, a kind and lovely young girl."

I turned and saw Uncle Presley seated in a leather chair, a shawl drawn around his shoulders. He appeared to be a man of perhaps seventy-five years, his thick head of hair gone to gray, his lean, clean-shaven face framed by long side-whiskers reaching his jaw line. He was still handsome, and although his face appeared pale and waxy, his green eyes were clear beneath bushy black eyebrows shot with silver. I could immediately see the vigorous young man Captain Presley O'Bannon had once been.

I bowed. "Captain O'Bannon, sir, I have heard so much about you."

He slowly pushed himself up from his chair and, despite the shoulders stooped by age and illness, he stood at least six inches taller than me, well over six feet. He held out his hand and I took it. His fingers were long and his grip cool and firm. His eyes met mine as he kindly placed his hand on my shoulder. "I trust your mother did not suffer in her passing."

"No, sir, not very much. She became ill with a fever," I replied sadly, remembering mother's sunken eyes. "The physicians were able to make her comfortable with medicines and she died rather quickly."

He nodded his head knowingly and patted my shoulder. "I am afraid my days are numbered as well, Harrison – may I address you informally, sir?"

"Of course, Uncle," I quickly replied.

"You may call me Presley, or Pres as my shipmates did," he replied taking his seat and drawing the shawl up over his shoulders. "In any event, the doctor tells me there is little he can do. I have perhaps six months to live."

"Uncle Presley...Pres...surely there is something..."

He was shaking his head. A smile slowly creased his face, his eyes wandering to the cold fireplace. "No," he replied, and closed his eyes. "I am ready. It is time. I learned years ago not to fear death. Nor to fight it. It comes to all of us. Some see it earlier than others as with your dear mother. But I am an old man. I have lived my life and I am fortunate that it was full. I am a terrible host, sir," he said suddenly with an apologetic smile that revealed a few missing teeth. "May I offer you a dram of sour mash whiskey? It is one of the singular pleasures of Kentucky."

Without waiting for an answer he rang a little silver bell and Miss Lily shortly appeared with a tray on which sat a crystal decanter, glasses and a carafe of water.

I sat in the chair across from Presley as he poured and handed me a glass. I sipped the liquor, which was indeed refreshing. Presley eyed me over the rim of his glass. "You look very much like Margaret," he said. "You have her eyes and her mouth. I last saw her when she and your father visited us here," he cast his eyes to the ceiling. "That would have been along about 1835, shortly before my own wife passed."

"I am sorry about your loss, Uncle," I quietly replied. At the words, his green eyes briefly misted over and the hand holding his glass trembled for a moment before he cleared his throat.

"Yes. Well, sir, what brings you to *Derne?*" he asked.

"I am embarrassed to say, Presley," I replied as I shifted in my seat. "You see, I have aspirations to be an author but I have never had much of anything to write about. My mother always thought yours was a fascinating story and wished it told, perhaps in a book. My father had me educated at Charlottesville, so he insisted I come visit you and record the events of your life."

The captain's shoulders began to shake. He covered his mouth with his handkerchief and he closed his eyes. I was at first alarmed, because he appeared to be in the throes of some kind of a seizure. Then I realized he was laughing. "Oh, dear God, that's a fine joke!' he managed to say through his handkerchief. "Events of my life! Very good! Very good!"

My embarrassment was giving way to annoyance, but Presley held up his hand. He dabbed his eyes and continued. "I am sorry, Nephew," he chuckled. "It is not you…it is me. You see, my life's events may be summarized in one word, and that word is Derne. I am very sorry to say your journey was for naught because my life was otherwise extraordinarily ordinary."

My expression must have turned to one of puzzlement because Presley stood again and ambled slowly to the fireplace. He reached up and took down a sword that hung above the mantle. He drew the curved blade from its scabbard and held it out to me. I took it and saw that is was made of fine steel, its hilt bejeweled and filigreed with gold and silver.

"A Mameluke sword," Presley explained proudly. "Presented to me by Hamet Karamanli."

I held out the handle to him and he took it. Presley gazed lovingly at the sword for a moment longer then slid the blade into the scabbard. I sipped my whiskey and looked earnestly over at my uncle, embarrassed.

"Captain O'Bannon," I began in a soft voice, "I am afraid I don't know anything about Derne. My mother often mentioned a battle, but she never told me much of anything about it and," I looked down at the floor, "I am ashamed to admit I was never much interested in learning."

The ticking clock on the wall filled the brief silence.

"You must be hungry, Harrison," Presley finally declared. "Supper is served in a few minutes. Why don't you find Miss Lily. She will show you to your room and provide water and towels. We can talk some more after we dine."

3

We sat on the porch watching the sunset splash vivid crimson and orange light across the dark blue evening sky while birds chirped and fussed in the nearby trees preparing themselves for the night. The breeze had died, but it was cool so before she permitted Presley to sit on the porch, Miss Lily insisted a thick woolen blanket be draped over his long legs. She had served us hot tea and then retired to the kitchen, where we could hear the clatter of china and silver and above that, Miss Lily's voice singing a sweet tune as she worked.

My uncle was staring out across the lawn and gardens while he rocked meditatively in his chair. I stayed silent and sipped my tea, not wishing to disturb his thoughts. After many minutes, we heard a screech in the nearby woods.

"A barn owl," my uncle explained. "He visits me most every evening about this time."

As though in answer, the owl screeched again and then was silent. "The Indians say that the presence of an owl foreshadows death," Presley observed. "I have read much about the Indians. That is my passion. Reading, I mean."

"Mine as well, Uncle Pres," I replied brightly before adding, "when I am not otherwise, um, engaged."

"Ah, I understand," he smiled. "When you are behaving like a young man! Sport, gambling and, dare I say," he raised his bushy eyebrows, "the gentle attentions of the ladies?"

I shot him a sheepish smile.

"We can speak freely, my boy," he continued. "I was a young man once, a marine officer aboard the ships sent by President Jefferson to the Mediterranean to deal peace or death to the bloody Mohammedans. During my service I spent many a pleasant evening with my fellow lieutenants in the company of lovely Spanish and Italian ladies in the ports of Cadiz and Naples."

"But, Pres, I thought you were a captain."

He chuckled again. "No, no, I was never a captain of the Marines, I'm afraid. I resigned because the commandant would not promote me after Derne. I think he was jealous of my fame. Anyway, the folk hereabouts took to calling me Captain O'Bannon when I arrived in Kentucky and I, well, I never corrected them. A silly vanity, but no harm I suppose."

I nodded and he continued.

"So, Harrison, you wish to know about Derne, eh?" he asked. "I was just thinking when we sat down that no one has asked me to recount my story for many, many years…I mean, the tale of the *entire* enterprise." His eyes now shifted and he was once again looking thoughtfully out over the lawn that had all but disappeared in the falling darkness.

"Mother sometimes mentioned a fellow named Eaton," I prompted him.

At the sound of the name, Presley pinned me with his green eyes and then slowly broke into a wide grin. "General Eaton!" he exclaimed. "Now there's a fellow whose story has been heard by everyone!" He paused and gave me an apologetic glance. "Well, almost everyone. General William Eaton! If you didn't ask him about the enterprise, he was sure to tell you anyway! I understand he made a nuisance of himself in Washington what with all his talk about Tobias Lear's treachery. And then there was the business with Aaron Burr later on." He shook his head sadly. "But I was a soldier, trained to follow the orders I was given and to carry them out to the best of my abilities. People never really seemed interested in that. I suppose I am not the raconteur the general was...or perhaps I was more humble about what I did...what we all did."

"What *did* you do, Uncle?" I asked earnestly.

A long moment passed. His face was hidden in shadows as we spoke, but he presently leaned forward in his chair and light from a nearby window revealed his clenched eyes and mouth. He began gasping, so I bolted from my chair. "Miss Lily!" I cried out. "Come quickly! It's Uncle Presley!"

I heard quick steps in the hall and then she was there, kneeling by his side tenderly stroking his head. "Shhhh," he whispered, "it will pass. It will pass."

He was clutching her hand, which must have been painful, but her face remained placid as she now moved her other hand to the side of his face. I could see whatever seizure he had experienced was slowly releasing its grip. His face began to relax and he seemed able to breathe again. Miss Lily looked up at me. "This happens once or twice a day," she explained. "It's the disease."

"Can...can you make him comfortable?" I asked, my voice strained with worry.

"I have laudanum...please, help me take him up to his bedroom."

An hour later, Uncle Presley lay asleep. I thought his breathing sounded shallow, but his face was peaceful so Miss Lily turned down the lamp and we left the bedroom together.

"Would you like more tea?"

I said I did so she led me to the kitchen where she brewed a small pot. I watched her delicate hands and movements and was once again amazed that any Negress could seem so completely refined. She poured the tea in small porcelain cups, one for me and one for herself. As we sat at the kitchen table in companionable silence, it occurred to me that I had never shared a moment like this with a Negro. It was almost as though we were equals.

"The doctor tells me he has a wasting disease in his organs," she remarked sadly. "The best they can do is help him with the pain."

I said nothing for a long moment. "How long have you been at *Derne*, Miss Lily?" I finally asked her.

"Since Presley arrived here in 1810 with his bride, Miss Matilda," she said. "I was born here. My parents were slaves that came with the plantation when Presley's wife inherited it from the estate of General Daniel Morgan. You know of him?"

Dan Morgan was legendary in Virginia, the Revolutionary War hero whose many exploits included dealing the British a crushing defeat at Cowpens in South Carolina.

"Every schoolboy in the Old Dominion knows of General Morgan!" I declared, "Even dense fellows like me."

Lily nodded, returning my smile and continued" "I was a young girl then and," she looked about, "this house was much smaller. The captain added many of the rooms; the study you saw today, for example, and he bought more adjoining acreage over the years."

"What does he produce here?"

"Principally tobacco. But also corn, cotton, wheat and some barley," she smiled proudly. "It's a very, very productive plantation. And it is all run without slave labor."

I was stung by this observation and felt myself getting angry with her. She saw my dark look and reached over to pat my arm.

"Young man, Harrison, please take no offense," she said in a kindly voice. "But you should know it is your uncle's opinion that, in the near future, slavery will be abolished forever. He believes it is a wicked and reprehensible practice that beggars any nation permitting it."

Now I was truly angry. My father owned several thousand acres in Fauquier County and our slaves were crucial to its success. How dare this nigger woman lecture me on a necessary institution peculiar to the

Southern states? And what the hell was Presley O'Bannon thinking? He was a son of Virginia and surely understood what slaves meant to us!

Her liquid brown eyes met mine, and she continued to pat my arm for a long, silent moment. "Do you know how and where your uncle formed his opinion about slavery?" she asked.

I shook my head curtly in response, my lips pursed.

"In the war with the Barbary pirates," she replied quietly.

"But…but what does that have to do with…"

"When he is feeling up to it," she interrupted me as she rose from her chair, "the captain will explain."

4

I awoke early and after I had breakfasted I looked in on Uncle Presley. He was asleep. I was pleased that his breathing was now deeper and rhythmic. It was a fine morning, so I decided to take a ride. I found the Negro groom at the stable behind the house and he happily tacked up a big white mare for me instead of the gelding I'd rented.

"Y' enjoy ridin' her, Missa Harr'son," the boy explained as he cinched off the girth. "Dolly here know'd the plantation and she very obedient."

Indeed the mare proved to be a wonderful mount as we toured the grounds in the coolness of the morning. Uncle Presley's farm was set among low hills and broad fields. I found a trail that led through a dense hardwood forest. After a half mile, I came upon a vast field of corn that promised a bumper crop come autumn. I turned Dolly back onto the trail that led up a hill. At its crest was a clearing that offered a pleasant view of Uncle Presley's sprawling white house, barn and its outbuildings, and, in the distance, his verdant fields where the hands were at work. The vista was altogether pleasing. Then I thought again of the sick old man in the house below, and the moment passed. I remounted and rode back to the stable.

"Good morning, lad!" Pres welcomed me as I entered his study. He placed the book he had been reading on a side table. "I understand you were out for a ride. I trust it was enjoyable."

"Indeed, Uncle, very," I replied. "*Derne* is most impressive. I rode to the top of the hill to the north."

"A wonderful place for a man to sit and contemplate life," he smiled. "I often go up there…well, I used too. I can't ride anymore, but in years past, I sat on the top of that hill and thought about how fortunate I have been."

I made no reply to this, so he continued, his eyes wandering to the nearby window where he could look out over a garden of flowers. "My days as a boy in the Virginia woods, as a Marine officer, my beautiful late wife, Miss Lily and, of course, the enterprise. I have been blessed."

"Are you feeling well this morning, Pres?" I asked.

He glanced over at me with a thin smile, said, "Never well, these days, I am sorry to report, sir. As you saw last evening, this disease has its evil talons in my guts. I am told I can expect the seizures to become more frequent and more painful, if that's possible. Thank God in heaven for Miss Lily and laudanum."

His eyes met mine. "As you may have ascertained, Harrison, Lily is more than a mere servant to me."

I frowned in my confusion.

"A year after my dear wife died, Miss Lily and I became, well, more than friends. We became companions, if you take my meaning."

I must now have looked completely shocked, but he smiled indulgently and continued.

"I was lonely and in a deep sadness over my loss. I had stopped working, riding, reading…I had stopped living, Harrison; I stopped caring about everything. I spent my days in the house grieving and drinking too much," he cleared his throat. "Miss Lily saved me. Brought me back to life, you might say."

There was nothing new about a white man communing with a Negress. Indeed, my own first carnal experience had come with a slave girl named Pixie in the woods behind our home in Fauquier County. But Uncle Presley was in love with Miss Lily and it now dawned on me that she was, for all intents and purposes, his wife. That was an altogether different circumstance and, in Virginia at least, altogether forbidden.

I shifted uncomfortably in my seat at this bit of news. Presley watched this and smiled.

"Yes, I know," he said quietly. "But, you aren't here to discuss social mores with me. You wish to know about the enterprise."

I nodded absently, still reeling from uncle's revelation about Miss Lily. He seemed not to notice.

"Fauquier County, Virginia," he stated. "Like you, that's where I grew up. Wonderful place for a boy. I hunted and fished and explored. My father was very indulgent with me. He allowed me to go to school when I wished, but he also instilled in me my love of reading."

I pointed at a violin displayed on a book shelf and said, "Did he teach you to play?"

"He did, though my fingers won't let me fiddle anymore," he replied, flexing his hands. He nodded at the violin and said, "That particular instrument has had quite a history. Anyway, I wish I could have remained a boy, but one day father told me I must find some gainful employment," he chuckled at this recollection. "He knew the county tax collector was looking for an assistant, so he offered him my services. You see I was taller and stronger than most and you needed those attributes as a tax collector far more than you needed a head for numbers."

I pictured young Presley riding from farm to farm, shop to shop, tavern to tavern with a ledger book, meeting with unfriendly receptions.

"I didn't like the work," he continued. "It was boring and I was a bit of a firebrand so I often exchanged fists with reluctant taxpayers. That didn't help county revenues."

I laughed out loud at this and he joined me. "One day I encountered a military officer at a tavern seeking recruits for a new service called the Marine Corps. He was dressed in a dashing uniform that I knew the ladies would find attractive. I was not familiar with what Marines did, so the officer explained that they were assigned to navy ships to prevent mutinies."

"Like constables?" I interrupted.

"Yes and no," he replied. "You see, the Navy was a new force. American ships mounted as many as forty-four guns and were crewed by three hundred or more sailors, many of them from England, France, Portugal and other such maritime nations. When the American frigates were at sea, mutiny was always a possibility. Marines were aboard each ship to keep order. During battle, we would stand guard against gun crews abandoning their posts. In close combat, we fired from the decks and rigging on the enemy."

"So you joined?"

"Naturally!" he barked out with a laugh. "The recruiting officer made the service sound a great deal more exciting than collecting taxes from angry landowners! He was also impressed with my size and the fact that I was well read and spoken, so he recommended to the commandant of Marines that I be given a commission."

His eyes roamed to the window and over the sunlit garden, his face relaxed, and I saw the fleeting shadow of a young Marine lieutenant. He paused for several moments, and then he abruptly looked back at me, the old man reappearing.

"I dreamed about it last night," Presley began. "About the enterprise, I mean. I saw General Eaton in his white Arab robes and headdress riding his horse through the endless desert once again, waving his scimitar, leading our bizarre little army toward the Tripolitan stronghold at Derne. But I get ahead of myself. You see, the bashaw…"

"Bashaw?" I interrupted him.

"The regent….um, the prince of Tripoli," he explained with a flutter of his hand.

"So the ruler of Tripoli, then?"

"Yes, the ruler, but answerable to Selim, the Sultan in Constantinople, as were all the tyrants of the Barbary," Presley continued. "The bey, dey and bashaw of Algeria, Tunis and Tripoli; they were all beholden to the Ottomans and required to pay this Selim fellow annual tribute." Presley glanced again out the window, and I could see his mood darken.

"And America was required to pay these regents tribute," he continued, his voice tight. "We sent our diplomats and emissaries to try to reason with them but it was no use. Theft and murder were their stock in trade. They only respected the flags of the nations that paid them their blood money. Any other shipping was fair game, sir. *We* were fair game"

"We?" I asked, incredulous.

"Oh yes, Harrison! We! The United States of America!" Presley replied. "It is difficult to believe, I know, but after our own merchantmen were plundered and our own innocent seamen thrown in Tripoli's dungeons and then tortured, we were left with little choice."

This was history I had never before heard. How was it possible that America could be so ruthlessly coerced? Presley continued.

"We had no Navy to fight the sons of bit....," he looked over his shoulder. "Those people! America was shamefully forced to pay tribute until Congress finally understood that the only way to deal with the dogs was to bring them to heel."

"So the Navy was founded?" I asked.

"Yes, sir. Keels for six frigates were laid," Presley proudly replied. "The first real American war ships. And it was to the Barbary Coast I sailed aboard *Adams* in 1802."

"And it was there that you encountered this Eaton?"

Again, Uncle Presley seemed to become distracted. A minute passed and then another.

"William Eaton was America's consul in Tunis," Pres replied. "He was a kind of diplomat who looked after our interests, always negotiating with the tyrant there and doing whatever he could to protect American and European merchantmen."

Presley sat back in his chair and said, "A remarkable man, really, as I came to learn. He graduated Dartmouth College, fought in the

Revolution and then on the Georgia and Ohio frontiers. He was an expert swordsman and he could shoot and ride better than any man I ever knew."

I was impressed for certainly my uncle had seen some of the best rifle and horsemen in his time.

"He also had a gift for languages," Pres continued. "Along with French, General Eaton could speak the Arabic and several derivations of it. Maybe his most important trait, though, was his ability to organize and lead. I never really had those skills."

"So Eaton was a military man then?" I asked.

Pres suddenly broke into a grin. "He should've been! It was he who devised the enterprise and convinced President Jefferson to approve it! But no," he shook his head, "William Eaton was not a general….at least not officially, shall we say."

Miss Lily appeared at the study door. She was smiling as she crossed her arms over her bosom. "Oh my word!" she declared, "You have him talking about the enterprise." She looked mischievously my way. "I hope you have plenty of time, Mr. Harrison Oswald!"

"Quiet woman!" Presley replied in mock anger, "I was just getting to the part about meeting General Eaton!"

Before he had finished speaking, she had her fists on her hips and was scowling at him playfully. "That will be quite enough Lieutenant O'Bannon!" she scolded him as she hid a smile. "Oh, I *am* sorry…I meant *Captain* O'Bannon! It is time for your nap, sir!

Presley looked my way, bemused. "After a broadside like that one, Harrison, I am compelled to strike my colors and surrender to the tender mercies of my foe." His eyes met Miss Lily's and the two gazed tenderly at one another.

To my complete surprise, I found myself smiling at the scene before me.

As he reached the door, Uncle Presley turned back to me pointing at the bookshelves. "I have several volumes about the struggle our naval forces waged with the bast…I mean Barbary pirates. You may wish to peruse them, Harrison. We learned much about the nature of the Mohammedan in those days that I hope is not soon forgotten."

5

MERCHANT SCHOONER *INTEGRITY*
March, 1803

Jeffery Talbert scanned the horizon, a frown etched into his forehead. The fog had lifted at dawn and now the convoy was nowhere to be seen. As the crew trimmed sails, Talbert checked the compass again. *Integrity* was on a south-southwest heading, the same as the convoy had been. He looked aloft and called to the lookout, "Any sign, Swanson?!"

"No sir!" cried the lookout, who stood on a small platform atop the mainmast.

"Keep your eyes peeled, if you please, Mr. Swanson!" Talbert replied. "We must find that convoy!"

Worried now, he bit down on the stem of his pipe cracking the clay.

He tossed the broken pipe overboard and looked once more at the empty sea before him.

Talbert had joined the merchantman convoy in Leghorn having filled his hold with casks of French wine, bolts of Italian fabric and cases of fine Swiss porcelain. He had no trouble finding buyers for the hogsheads of Virginia tobacco and oak lumber he'd brought from America, so this voyage promised to be one of his most profitable ever.

Shepherded by the American sloop-of-war *Enterprise, Integrity* and the five other merchantmen convoyed out of Malta in fine weather bound for Gibraltar. There they would re-supply before making the crossing to their ports in America, the warship escort no longer necessary.

During the night a fog bank dense as chowder enveloped the ships. The convoy and, worse, the *Enterprise* had disappeared. Talbert now found himself alone, twelve miles off the Iberian Peninsula.

The day wore on with no sign of the convoy, but by late afternoon Talbert began to feel confident he would reach Gibraltar unmolested.

"Daniel!" he called out merrily. "Kindly tap one of those casks below and bring us all a taste of that fine Bordeaux!"

"Aye, sir!" Daniel replied eagerly as he scurried to the hold with a wooden water bucket. Just a lad of seventeen and fair-haired, he was Talbert's cousin, taken aboard the *Integrity* to apprentice and maybe one day command a merchantman of his own.

The *Integrity's* fourteen-man crew heard the order and gave their captain a huzzah. Talbert, a portly man of forty-five, doffed his old fashioned tricorn hat and elegantly bowed to the crew in acknowledgement.

Among the most popular of New York's merchant-owners, Talbert never had difficulty signing crews for *Integrity's* trading voyages. In stark contrast to many other owners, he made sure his crew wasn't overworked, that they had plenty of good food to eat and grog to drink, and that each man received a fair share of the voyage's profits. Mindful of the abuse he had suffered as a young seaman, Talbert forbade floggings aboard *Integrity*.

"Captain Talbert!" cried the lookout. "Off the stern!"

Talbert spun around and felt a cold knot in his gut. There, out of the haze, five miles distant, a sail appeared. He snatched his telescope and scanned the approaching ship. Even at this distance, he could see the ship was painted a garish bright yellow. He silently handed the glass to the first mate who joined him at the stern rail.

"It's *Meshouda*," Jeremiah Mead said flatly.

Sweat broke out on Talbert's forehead, his worst fears realized.

Unaware of the alarm, Daniel approached the captain. "Your wine, sir!" he declared. Talbert absently grabbed a goblet the boy offered, gulped the Bordeaux, then looked about at the crew that had gathered around him.

"Lads! We need every inch of sail!" Talbert cried as he pointed to the distance. "That's *Meshouda* bearing down on us!"

The crew needed no further instructions as they scrambled to their posts. Talbert looked at Mead who was already peering at a chart. "Jeremiah?"

"I think we can make Malaga, sir," the mate said pointing at the Spanish port on his chart. Once close to the harbor, the pirate ship would be forced to veer off, unable to attack in a neutral port.

"We'll have to outrun her, then," Talbert replied, wiping sweat from his face with a handkerchief. "If we can keep our distance, perhaps we can lose her in the dark if we don't make port."

"Aye, sir," Mead replied. "Three points off the beam!" Mead called out to the helmsman. Both men were aware of *Meshouda's* reputation for speed, and laden as she was with cargo, Talbert and Mead knew *Integrity* would need luck to reach the Spanish harbor.

Over the next three hours the distance between the ships closed, but so did the distance between *Integrity* and the Spanish coast. By seven o'clock, the sun was setting and the *Meshouda* was a quarter mile from her prey, her twenty-eight cannon, painted a lurid red, bristled obscenely from her gun ports, ready to send shot ripping through the *Integrity* if she dared try an escape. Talbert could see the Tripolitans gathered on her bow pointing and chattering excitedly, their sword blades gleaming. Mead approached the captain. "We won't make Malaga, sir."

"Then we must hold them off until dark, Mr. Mead!" Talbert barked. Their only hope now was to try to outmaneuver the bigger ship and that required speed. But as the sun continued sinking the wind slackened. Weighted down as she was with cargo, *Integrity's* sails fluttered and she gradually slowed to a crawl. Talbert thought fleetingly of priming the carronade on his rail, but firing at the oncoming brig would prove fatal to all hands.

Meshouda, with more sail and lightly loaded with her guns and the hundred or so pirates on her deck, closed in as Talbert and the crew of

Integrity stood helpless on the deck. The bearded Tripolitans, clad in loose fitting white blouses and baggy calf-length trousers, turbans, and colorful sashes around their waists, grinned as they began casting their grappling hooks. In minutes, they had the ships lashed together and, carrying their swords, muskets, hatchets, and pikes, the pirates streamed over the rail of the American merchantman.

"I shouldn't resist were I you!" called a voice from above. "It will go easier that way for all hands! My fellows have been at sea a good long while now and they're in no mood for a confrontation. Or I should say, they *are* in the mood for a confrontation and you shall not like the consequences if you choose to fight!"

Talbert, accustomed to hardship, had silently watched the *Meshouda* come alongside with a sense of resignation. He had done what he could to protect his ship and his crew, but bad luck intervened. There was nothing to be done but surrender and hope insurance would cover the loss of his ship and cargo.

He looked up onto the deck of the brig for the source of the voice and spotted the red haired Scotsman standing at the rail in flowing golden robes. The Tripolitan Grand Admiral, Murad Reis, stared back at him wearing a mirthless smile.

"Do as the bastard says, men!" Talbert called out to the crew who needed little encouragement. Each man was surrounded by a dozen cutthroats who were stripping them of their outer clothing. The captain looked up at Reis. "Is that necessary?!" he asked angrily. "You have my vessel and you have my cargo, too! Let the men keep their clothing!"

In response Reis held out his hands and gave the American a helpless look as though he had no control of the Tripolitans swarming *Integrity's* deck. Presently there was a howl, "No! God, no! Cousin Jeffery…. help me!"

On the bow, young Daniel was stripped naked and thrown over a barrel. He was held firmly by a gang of leering pirates as one of them opened his trousers.

"Stop that buggery, damn you!" cried Talbert. As he made a move toward the bow, he was seized and held by several laughing pirates. "Reis, for the love of God! Tell them to leave that lad alone!"

"Your God! Not mine!" Reis snapped. "As I say, captain, my men have been at sea for many months! Best leave them to their perversions, sir!"

Daniel was whimpering now as another pirate took his turn. The rest of Talbert's crew stood by staring at the deck, unable to watch the gang rape of their young shipmate. Talbert could stand no more. A short man, the captain was also stout, much stronger than he appeared.

He suddenly flung off the pirates who held him and snatched a pistol hidden within his coat. He managed to cock the weapon but before he could pull the trigger, a pirate plunged his scimitar into the captain's back. Talbert cried out, his eyes wide in shock as the point of the cruel blade emerged from his belly dripping gore. The pistol clattered to the deck unfired. He went to his knees as another pirate swung his blade and beheaded Talbert.

Integrity's crew watched the brutal murder of their captain and, panicking, began struggling with their captors. As he grappled with one pirate, Jeremiah Mead's throat was cut by another, his blood spurting across the deck as he fell clutching his neck. Two of *Integrity's* sailors tried to leap overboard, perhaps thinking they could swim the two or three miles to shore. One was cut down by a scimitar and the other was skewered on a pike by a giant black pirate wearing a purple turban. He lifted the flailing sailor over his head as his mates gave a cheer of approval.

"Enough!" bellowed Reis in Arabic from above. "Spare the rest of the Christians, you fools. We want them for ransom!"

The bloodshed ended as suddenly as it began, but not the suffering of Daniel. He was raped again and again by the marauders while Reis inspected *Integrity's* hold. The Scotsman soon emerged on deck with a satisfied smile as the last of the dead men was dumped overboard.

Reis ordered his first mate to sail the schooner and his prisoners to Tripoli with a prize crew of four sailors. He decided that where there was one American straggler, there could be more, so he would continue his hunt for another defenseless merchantman.

As the gaudy *Meshouda* cast off in the twilight, *Integrity's* survivors lifted the slack body of Daniel and gently carried him to the hold where their captors chained them to the hull by their ankles before setting sail for Tripoli.

⚜ 6 ⚜

WASHINGTON
April, 1803

"You mean to say Morris accomplished nothing in the year he has been there!?" Thomas Jefferson snarled in a rare show of anger. In the president's hand was the commodore's newest "plan" for subduing the Tripolitans, which he had just read.

Navy Secretary Robert Smith shifted nervously in his seat. Never before had he heard the president raise his voice. The usually soft-spoken Jefferson's face was nearly as red as his hair.

"God damn that man to hell!" the president cried as he threw the papers down on the table and rose from his chair. Tall and lean, Jefferson strode over to the window that overlooked the unfinished palace grounds. What should have been the lawn was a muddy swamp churned up by wagons delivering building supplies. Smith knew Jefferson was gathering himself, so he waited several long minutes, silent.

Jefferson's personal secretary, Meriwether Lewis, appeared and placed several sheaves of documents on the president's desk. Lewis bowed toward Secretary Smith, and left without saying a word. As the door closed, Jefferson turned and faced Smith.

"I am sorry, Mr. Secretary. Please excuse me," the president said quietly. "I am experiencing one of my headaches and now...*this*," he pointed at the offending report that had arrived an hour earlier. "Apart from calling on European ports and convoying merchantmen, Morris' squadron appears to have taken no offensive action since arriving in the

Mediterranean. Is that possible? My God, it seems he's burned more powder firing salutes in Naples than he has against the tyrant Yusuf!"

Jefferson felt himself becoming angry again. He took a deep breath and sat down. "He says here he 'interpreted' our orders to mean that his ships would blockade Tripoli when conditions were right. I am not sure I understand that, sir. Were his orders not to blockade Tripoli regardless of conditions and force peace with the bashaw?"

Smith nodded his head. "Those were the commodore's orders, Mr. President. They were clear and certainly not subject to interpretation. We have received letters from our counsels in Spain, France and Syracuse that Commodore Morris and his squadron have enjoyed a leisurely autumn and winter, with extended calls at Cadiz, Toulon, Malta, and elsewhere." Morris glanced at the notes on a sheet of paper. "This fellow Eaton, our agent who was recently run out of Tunis, has been most strident in his criticism of Mr. Morris. He has also been shopping to Congress his own plan to win the war."

"Small wonder what with this so-called 'action plan' of the commodore's," Jefferson growled as he picked up the papers and glanced down at them. "After fifteen months of doing nothing Morris now wants to refit his flagship! Does he really believe I would permit him to take another pleasure cruise at the republic's expense?!"

Smith cleared his throat. "I believe part of the problem resides with Mrs. Morris, sir."

"Mrs. Morris?"

"Yes, sir. She, well sir, she accompanied Commodore Morris to the Mediterranean," Smith said. "She brought the couple's baby boy and her maid servant with her aboard the flagship."

Jefferson glared at his Secretary of the Navy. "And you permitted that Mr. Smith?"

The secretary cast his eyes at the floor, his face flushed. "I am afraid I did, Mr. President. I thought perhaps it would relieve Commodore Morris of concern and help him keep his mind on the war with Tripoli." Smith looked up at the president's steely blue eyes. "Apparently, Mrs. Morris is in command of the flagship. I am told the tars aboard *Chesapeake* refer to her as the Commodoress."

Jefferson couldn't help himself. He broke into laughter.

Smith, confused at first, finally flashed a rueful smile.

Jefferson wiped his eyes with a knuckle, said, "Well that explains much, does it not, Mr. Secretary? A woman aboard an American fighting ship that we learn does no fighting! Rather, it calls on those delightful ports you mentioned, where I am quite certain the local aristocracy feted the commodore and his commodoress at every opportunity. That is so much more enjoyable than actually confronting our vicious enemy in his home harbor and showing him we mean business! We really must call this gentleman and his lovely wife home so they won't miss the Washington social season."

This was more like the Jefferson Smith knew. "Yes, Mr. President. I shall relieve Commodore Morris at once."

"Have you anyone in mind to replace him?" Jefferson asked.

"I do, sir. Captain Edward Preble," Smith declared. "He has been ill of late but I understand he is well now and ready for service."

"Preble," Jefferson mused. "Have I not heard his name before?"

Smith replied, "You'll recall he was the captain who commanded *Essex*. She was dismasted in a storm some years ago but he made repairs while underway and sailed the ship around the Cape of Good Hope convoying merchantmen to the Dutch Indies."

"Yes!" Jefferson exclaimed, excited now. "I remember! *Essex* was the first American naval vessel to sail the Pacific. As I recall, all the merchantmen returned with their cargoes unharmed."

"That is correct, sir," Smith said. "But Captain Preble contracted malaria during that voyage. He suffers the effects of the illness from time to time."

"Has he fighting experience?" asked Jefferson. "We don't need another Morris in the Mediterranean."

"I don't think you need to worry about Captain Preble, sir," Smith said. "He fought the British during the late war, survived one of their loathsome prison ships, and returned to fight them again. He is the man we need for this assignment. I quite nearly chose him ahead of Morris, but, as I say, Captain Preble was ill at the time."

"Very well, Mr. Smith. Please keep me advised," Jefferson said as Smith rose to leave. "And please see to it Mr. Morris is court marshaled for his damnable insubordination."

"Sir," Smith replied with a bow.

The president retired to his bedroom, where the drapes were drawn and he could close his eyes against the searing pain of the headache. His thoughts turned to the nagging problem posed by Tripoli, Algeria, and Tunis, the regencies along the Barbary Coast of North Africa. For centuries their corsairs had wreaked havoc on trade throughout the Mediterranean. Small, speedy ships with long prows driven by their distinctive lateen sails were sent out by the Barbary rulers to prey on commercial shipping. Their crews were armed to the teeth and ruthless when they captured hapless merchantman from any country on which they'd chosen to declare war. No nation was immune to the threat. Once taken, ships, cargo and crews could be ransomed or a European ruler might decide to simply pay annual tribute to the regents in order to buy peace so his trading ships could sail the Mediterranean unmolested.

Jefferson also knew from his days in Paris that there were no bounds to the avarice of these pirates. As ambassador to France, he had watched King Louis pay the Barbary regents for "permanent peace" and then saw how the tyrants broke their treaties with impunity as they demanded still more tribute, "presents" and bribes in the form of gold, jewels, trade goods, grain, and, worst of all, guns and powder. And the king always agreed to pay.

Louis and his ministers had their own cynical reasons for agreeing to the extortion. France could afford the tribute while many smaller

European kingdoms could not. Thus King Louis had a competitive commercial advantage. His merchantmen could trade anywhere in the Mediterranean while those of countries like Denmark and Sweden fell victim to the marauding corsairs.

Paying tribute deeply offended Jefferson's sensibilities. He believed it stained the honor of any nation used in such a disgraceful way. America, he knew, should negotiate peace from a position of strength. He recalled how, as George Washington's Secretary of State, he had championed the building of a navy soon after the founding of the republic. But the new nation, burdened as it was with war debt, simply could not afford one. President Washington had little choice but to buy peace from the Barbary criminals or let merchantmen suffer their depredations.

In the fall of 1793 everything changed. The British negotiated a secret treaty between Portugal and Algiers that would benefit England in two ways. Portugal would ally itself with Britain against France and the Portuguese men-of-war blockading the straits of Gibraltar would be removed. It was like uncorking a bottle as Algerian corsairs streamed into the Atlantic hunting American merchantmen. This also served England's purposes because it effectively eliminated America as a trading competitor. Finally shaken from its lethargy by England's duplicity, Congress agreed a navy was needed to deal with the Barbary rulers, so six frigates were commissioned.

Jefferson shifted his weight. He reached for the cool damp cloth Lewis had thoughtfully placed on the nightstand and pressed it to his eyes. He felt the headache receding, so he rose from the bed, washed his face and ambled back to his office at the other end of the presidential palace that was still under construction. The president stepped over piles of lumber and buckets of paint and around workmen in the unfinished hallways.

"Are you feeling well enough to work, Mr. President," asked Lewis as Jefferson entered his office and strode to the window. "You look pale to me, sir."

"Thank you for your concern, Mr. Lewis," he replied as he glanced at his pocket watch. "I am expecting a gentleman shortly. A Mr. William Eaton. When he arrives, kindly show him in."

Lewis looked puzzled as he scanned the paper he was holding. "I am most sorry, sir, I don't seem to have..."

"No," Jefferson interrupted. "That's quite all right. I privately invited him to visit me. He's an old friend I wish to see. Alone if you please, Mr. Lewis."

"Certainly, Mr. President," the young man replied, bowing and stepping from the office.

Out on the avenue, Jefferson could see the world bustling by. Occasionally a pedestrian would stop and point at the new "President's House" and make some comment about it to his companions. Jefferson smiled to himself and finally sat down at his desk to continue his ruminations.

America's new navy had been tested in the Quasi War with France and had acquitted itself well enough against the battle tested warships it encountered in the Caribbean. Only one American ship had been lost. The brig *Retaliation* surrendered to a pair of French frigates off Guadalupe by her commander, Lieutenant William Bainbridge.

Distracted as it was by the entanglement with France, the new navy had been unable to defend American shipping in the Mediterranean so President John Adams was forced to buy peace with Algiers, the most powerful of the Barbary regencies. As Jefferson had feared, word of America's inclination to bargain reached Tripoli's regent, Yusuf Karamanli, who promptly declared war on America in a most unusual opening of hostilities. He had the flagpole cut down in front of the American consulate in Tripoli.

7

"Mr. William Eaton, sir," Lewis announced as he held the office door open.

Jefferson looked up from his paperwork as Eaton entered and made a deep, courtly bow to the president. Jefferson, who disliked such ostentatious displays, rose and held out his hand. "Welcome, sir," he greeted Eaton. "May I offer you refreshment...a glass of sherry perhaps?"

"You are most kind, Your Excellency," Eaton replied with another bow.

Jefferson gestured to Lewis, who disappeared. "Mr. President will do," Jefferson corrected his visitor. "'Your Excellency' brings to mind my days at the court of King Louis and I certainly don't wish to end up as that poor fellow did!"

"Certainly, Mr. President. As you wish," Eaton answered in perfect French as Lewis reappeared with two small glasses of sherry. Jefferson gestured to a pair of easy chairs and Eaton took one while Jefferson sat in the other. Lewis placed the wine on a small table between the two men and silently left the office.

"Your health, Mr. Eaton," Jefferson replied, also in French.

"And yours, sir," Eaton amiably replied.

As they sipped the sherry and exchanged small talk about Eaton's voyage from Tunis, the president studied the agent, who was dressed simply in a black jacket and waist coat, a plain white shirt and cravat, and black breeches. Trim and of average height and build, Eaton appeared to be in his early forties. He wore his sandy blond hair in a queue, his side-whiskers framing a somewhat round and boyish face whose most outstanding feature were Eaton's piercing blue eyes. When he smiled, Jefferson could see he had fine, straight teeth. His manner suggested no discomfort in casually conversing with the most famous and powerful man in the country.

"I understand you speak the language of these scoundrels," Jefferson remarked.

"I do, sir," Eaton replied with a nod. "I have always been able to quickly grasp the fundamentals of another language. I must say, Arabic is more difficult than any of the romance languages or the Indian dialects I have learned. But these Barbary savages are even harder to comprehend than their language," he added.

"Yes, President Adams sent you to Tunis," Jefferson replied. "And I understand you were, well, you were expelled by the bey."

Eaton blushed for a moment and then carefully set his sherry glass on the side table.

"Simply put, sir, I do not believe we can reason or negotiate with these pirates," Eaton began, his voice taut. "God knows I tried. But the bey and his ilk are truly heathens with no honor and no respect for civilized behavior. They torture and abuse their Christian captives, they enslave our sailors and force them to perform inhuman labor, and they cast innocent ladies and even young girls into seraglios for their perverse pleasures."

"Go on," Jefferson invited before sipping his sherry.

"When President Adams first sent me to Tunis, I was unaware of the magnitude of their viciousness, greed and dishonesty. I am a simple soldier, Mr. President, so perhaps I was naïve. Even though they are Mohammedans, sir, I took these regents for gentlemen. But I discovered that, even as we paid the negotiated bribes, their demands for more gifts and more money never ceased. And if we failed to act on their every whim, they threatened our consuls with violence. And every time we give them what they demand, they want more. I did not understand them at first, but after many months, I now know them for what they are. I believe I expressed myself too candidly before the bey so I was invited to leave his regency or be thrown into his dungeon."

"I never believed that we should allow our nation to be so used," Jefferson interjected dryly. "We sent the navy to the Mediterranean, Mr. Eaton, but our resolve to fight the bashaw appears to have been lacking."

"I should say so, Mr. President!" Eaton declared angrily, forgetting where he was and with whom he was speaking. "Excuse me, sir, but Commodore Morris was criminally derelict! He seemed only capable of convoying merchantmen but not attacking these villains in their home ports! And I cannot tell you how mortified I was when I learned Bainbridge allowed his ship to be used as Bobba Mustapha's transport barge!"

Jefferson winced at the recollection. Two years earlier, William Bainbridge, the same officer who had lost *Retaliation* to the French a few years earlier, was commanding the *George Washington*, a twenty-four gun sloop-of-war. Ordered to deliver gifts to Bobba Mustapha, the Algerian dey, Bainbridge was tricked into sailing his ship into the Algiers harbor right under the guns of Mustapha's castle. The dey immediately saw his advantage and ordered the *George Washington* loaded with tribute and treasure destined for his master Selim in Constantinople. Bainbridge had little choice but to comply or see *George Washington* reduced to kindling. Gold, jewels, African slaves, the dey's ambassadors, and even a menagerie of wild animals boarded Bainbridge's ship. Humiliated, the American captain sailed for Turkey.

"An American man-of-war fully armed and crewed usurped for such a disgraceful purpose *and* forced to fly the Algerian colors," Jefferson declared absently, sadly shaking his head.

Eaton said nothing. Finally, the president took the last sip of his sherry and looked at Eaton.

"I am removing Commodore Morris and appointing Edward Preble to command our naval forces in the Mediterranean. Have you any other suggestions as to what else we might do, Mr. Eaton?"

This was the opportunity the consul had been waiting for. He eagerly sat forward in his chair as he addressed Jefferson. "I do, Mr. President, I do," Eaton replied, unable to hide the excitement in his voice, his penetrating blue eyes bright. "There is a man I know, Hamet Karamanli, the brother of Yusuf, the Bashaw of Tripoli."

"Yes?"

"Sir, Hamet Karamanli is the eldest surviving son of the late Bashaw of Tripoli, Ali, and the rightful heir to the throne of Tripoli. Yusuf, Hamet's younger brother, tried to murder him but Hamet escaped to Egypt. Yusuf seized power and took Hamet's family prisoner. He now holds them hostage in Tripoli."

Jefferson could not imagine where this Barbary family melodrama might be headed, but he stayed silent. Mistaking the president's silence for acute interest, Eaton eagerly continued.

"Now, sir, if I may," Eaton stood and went to Jefferson's desk where he snatched up a sheet of blank paper and a quill and began drawing. "This is the coast of North Africa, and this is Alexandria in Egypt! Here is Derne, on the Tripolitan coast, nearly eight hundred miles from Tripoli. Derne is the second city of Tripoli and is strategically important because it anchors her easternmost border. Yusuf Karamanli has a garrison there but I believe it can be attacked and defeated!"

A little bewildered by Eaton's enthusiasm and a little annoyed at his untoward familiarity, Jefferson smiled thinly and joined Eaton at the desk where he patiently looked at the map the consul had drawn.

"You mean an attack from the sea?" Jefferson asked.

"No!" Eaton declared, nearly shouting in his excitement. "By land, Mr. President, by land! Together with Hamet and his exiled followers, I will personally lead a company of American soldiers on an overland march from here," he stabbed the point of the quill on the spot representing

Alexandria, spattering ink on the president's sleeve, "to here, the fortress at Derne!"

Jefferson looked up at Eaton, dabbing the ink on his sleeve with his handkerchief. The counsel stood poised, eyebrows raised, waiting for an affirmative reply from Jefferson who asked, "And what is the distance of this march?"

"I make it five hundred miles, more or less," Eaton declared proudly. "We will attack from land, sir! The defenders will never expect us. Once we take Derne, we will unify the disaffected people there, attack Benghazi and then Tripoli itself, depose Yusuf and install Hamet as the new and rightful bashaw. We would have our ally in power and a permanent peace with Tripoli!"

Jefferson stared at his guest. "An audacious plan, Mr. Eaton…"

"Fortune favors the bold, sir!" interrupted Eaton.

"But I fear it is impossible at this time," continued Jefferson. "We cannot send American soldiers to North Africa. Congress would never permit it. And while I have not been to that part of the world, a five hundred mile march across the Sahara Desert, well, that just seems…difficult."

Eaton stared at the president as though Jefferson was a dull schoolboy. "Sir, not only is such a plan possible, I can assure you, I will be victorious…"

Jefferson held up his hand. "Mr. Eaton, sir, I shall discuss the feasibility of your proposal with my cabinet in due course. Mr. Smith believes it has possibilities, however, for now we will put our faith in Captain Preble. I understand he is tenacious and daring. We shall soon see."

8

GIBRALTAR
August, 1803

Meshouda sailed languidly into the harbor on a light southerly breeze and dropped anchor among scores of other ships lying in the shadow of the great rock. With her yellow paint, sailors on neighboring vessels pointed at her, some laughing at the outlandish appearance of the brig. Others, familiar with her bloody reputation, fearfully eyed the vessel.

The crew was busy securing *Meshouda* as the grand admiral made his way down a rope ladder and into a boat that had been lowered for him. In ten minutes he was on the quay, walking with his body guards past rows of men-of-war and merchantmen flying every imaginable flag.

Murad Reis wore crimson robes and a vivid blue turban, a scimitar on his waist and a pair of pistols in his belt. The bejeweled scabbard that held his sword glimmered in the morning sun. Three Tripolitans, wearing their own hangers and carrying pikes, followed him closely, wary of those who came to close to Reis.

Reis seemed not to notice the occasional angry look. His beard was tied off in a point as were his mustaches. He smiled amiably at those who met his eye and occasionally pointed out something to his guards that caught his interest among the vendors' stalls along the quay.

Presently, a small, dark man in a green naval uniform strode up to the grand admiral. He wore a bicorn festooned with silver insignia and had his hand on the hilt of his sword. One of the guards, who towered over most everyone on the quay, stepped quickly in front of Reis. The man in the uniform stopped in his tracks. "Reis!" he called out. "Tell this man I wish to speak to you!"

Reis, completely hidden by the guard, now stepped around him and stood before the uniformed man. "Ah, Captain Fazzelli! How nice to see you again," the grand admiral replied in his Scots-accented English. "And it's Grand Admiral, if you please. What can I do for you, sir?"

Fazzelli's face was rigid. He glanced up at the guard.

"I want payment for my merchantman, *Admiral* Reis," he spit the title. "The one you stole from me last spring."

"Oh, no, Captain Fazzelli, that's not possible," Reis replied with a patronizing smile. "Tripoli is at war with the Kingdom of Two Sicilies, as you know. Your ships may be taken as prizes. Sad to say your little schooner was, let's see….ah yes, it was sold to a merchant captain in Morocco some weeks ago since your king refused to ransom her. So sorry," he added with a cheerful wink.

A crowd gathered around the scene, voices chattering in a dozen tongues rising to a din. Fazzelli glanced to his right and to his left looking for any ally but saw none.

"Reis, you took my merchant ship!" The captain angrily declared. "Only war ships may be taken as prizes!"

"Our law is different in Tripoli," Reis calmly explained. "We take the ships of our enemies, be they man-of-war or merchant."

Fazzelli saw he was getting nowhere. "I have my warship here," he replied pointing at a sloop flying the gold and red flag of the kingdom. "When you sail, I'll be waiting!"

"Avast there!" Reis cried out in mock fear, holding out his hands before him as though to ward off the captain. "Ye cannot sink me in a neutral harbor!"

"I can attack you on the open sea, you thieving bastard!" Fazzelli snarled. "You can't stay in Gibraltar forever."

"I'd be careful with idle threats," Reis warned, still wearing his genial smile.

There was laughter now among the onlookers. Fazzelli, red-faced, frustrated and helpless, suddenly shoved his way through the crowd and disappeared. Reis looked about, shrugged and continued his walk along the quay. Presently, he turned up a side street and entered a tavern. His guards waited outside the door. While alcohol was forbidden to believers, it was one vice Reis had never forsaken.

He ordered rum and took a seat, his back to the door lest others from the *Meshouda* pass by and see him enjoying his liquor. The innkeeper silently placed the bottle and a glass before the grand admiral. The few customers who occupied the dingy tavern stared at Reis' outlandish costume before resuming their drinking. The Scotsman poured and shot the hot liquor back quickly.

"I would appreciate it, sir, if you would accompany me back to the U.S.S. *Constitution*," said an American accented voice behind Reis. The grand admiral ignored it and gulped back his second drink, his eyes watering. After a long moment, he felt a large hand on his shoulder. "I am speaking to *you*," the voice said, now menacing.

Annoyed, Reis turned and found himself looking up at a very tall American wearing a crisp blue uniform with red facings, his chapeau bras casually tucked under his arm. The man's shoulder-length black hair was swept back off his high brow, his long, handsome face accented by jet black side-whiskers, his clear green eyes staring down at Reis.

"And who might you be, laddy?" Reis asked with a condescending cock of an eyebrow.

The tall soldier did not answer, but instead reached down and grabbed Reis' robes at the shoulder, easily pulling him to his feet with one hand. "You'll accompany me to the *Constitution* now," the American commanded. "Commodore Preble wishes an interview with you."

"Take your hands off me, boy!" Reis cried as he tried to pull away. "Abdul! Kamel!" He called out to his guards. They did not appear and now the tall soldier was shoving Reis through the doorway and out into the street. There six armed soldiers, wearing blue uniforms, white britches and black hats held the three Tripolitan body guards at bay with fixed bayonets.

"What the hell is happening here?!" demanded Reis. "Who are you?!"

"I am Lieutenant Presley Neville O'Bannon of the United States Marines," the officer declared as he placed his hat on his head. "Commodore Preble is aboard his flagship on the quay down yonder. I will explain one last time, sir. He wishes an interview with you. You can now accompany me there walking or, if you wish, my men can carry you there unconscious. What'll it be?"

Reis shot a murderous look at the American. "I'll go with you but nay put your hands on me again, Paddy!" he snapped. He turned to glare at his guards who cringed knowing their punishment would be a brutal whipping of their bare feet for allowing Reis to be so roughly accosted.

The marines formed up, three on either side of the grand admiral, O'Bannon in the lead. As they marched down the quay, passersby familiar with Reis and his reputation watched the procession with wide eyes. O'Bannon led them up the *Constitution's* gangway, saluting the quarterdeck as he came aboard. Sailors scurried about, intent on their labors, some on their knees scouring the deck with holystones while others were repairing sails and rigging. Naval officers wearing black bicorns, blue coats, white britches and calf length boots strode the deck observing the work and chastising laggards.

The lieutenant removed his hat and knocked on Preble's cabin door beneath the quarterdeck.

"Enter!" called a voice from within.

The cabin was spotless and smelled of tar and oil, its floor painted in a black and white a checkerboard pattern. A neatly made bunk was arranged along the bulkhead to the left and to his right a table and chairs were set up for dining and meetings with officers. A bookshelf beyond the table contained volumes, charts, maps and navigation instruments. Lanterns hung from beams and Preble's cluttered desk faced the door, sunshine pouring through the gallery windows behind Preble, who was presently engrossed in the paperwork before him.

The marine officer stood before Preble's desk at attention and snapped a salute. "Lieutenant O'Bannon reporting as ordered, sir! I have the man you wish to speak with."

"Very well, lieutenant, bring him in," Preble finally ordered without looking up from his desk.

A moment later Murad Reis stood silently before Preble who did not acknowledge his presence, occupied as he was reading the document before him. The grand admiral seethed at the humiliation, the tall marine officer next to him and two armed guards behind.

"Peter Lisle, is it?" Preble finally asked without looking up. He pronounced the surname liss-ell.

"It rhymes with guile," Reis corrected, "but I no longer go by that Christian name."

"No?" Preble replied, now peering at his visitor. "Why is that?"

Reis ignored the question, asked pleasantly, "What may I do for you?"

Preble gave a faint smile as he looked over his visitor. Reis could see Preble was of average height, but very lean, his short gray hair thinning.

"Peter Lisle. Born 1764, Edinburgh, Scotland," Preble continued, looking down at the paper before him. "Served as a tar aboard HMS *Response* before deserting in Boston to join the crew of the American merchantman *Betsey*."

Reis said nothing.

"*Betsey* was captured by Moroccan pirates in 1784. Peter Lisle was taken prisoner," Preble continued. "*Betsey* is now *Meshouda*. And," he looked up, "Peter Lisle is now Murad Reis, grand admiral of the naval forces of Tripoli. A remarkable story of advancement, I must say."

"I am a remarkable seaman," Reis replied smugly. "And, of course, I married well."

"Indeed. The bashaw's daughter, I understand," Preble said.

"One of my three wives, actually," Reis declared. "Polygamy is among the great benefits of converting to Islam, praise be the Prophet. Another is that one Muslim may not enslave another."

"Turned Turk, eh? A conversion of convenience?" Preble asked curtly. "Do your religious laws permit the murder of innocent seamen and stealing their ships and cargo?"

"If they are Christian and at war with my nation, yes."

Preble rose to his feet and stepped around his desk to face Reis. He clasped his hands behind his back as he spoke. "I am glad you are here in Gibraltar," Preble began. "You can carry a message back to your master. We are going to be bringing the war he declared against America to the bashaw's doorstep very shortly...."

At this, Reis chuckled. "I am sorry, captain, but we have seen you Americans at war. Commodore Morris showed your flag just one time at Tripoli in the many months he was in the Mediterranean and then only to negotiate. I almost took him prisoner, but thought better of it. Instead, I made him give me a gift of ten thousand dollars." Smiling, Reis shook his head dismissively. "If words were cannon shot, you fools would have defeated Tripoli long ago!"

"I brought you here to warn you, Lisle," Preble said, taking a step toward the admiral. "I order you to stop your depredations now or be prepared to suffer the consequences when we reach Tripoli. Return there and tell the bashaw we are coming. There will be no more words, no more tribute, and no more gifts. If he does not wish to see his city reduced to ruins, he will release all Americans he is holding and he will make permanent peace with my country. Follow?"

Reis met Preble's gaze. He was beginning to understand that this particular American was much different than those he had met before. The others seemed bent on diplomacy and winning peace through any method other than battle. This one seemed...warlike.

"Very well," Reis replied with a slight bow. "I will convey your message to my father-in-law. But whether he complies or not is his decision, not mine."

The American commodore stood staring at the admiral for a long minute. Preble decided that he'd heard quite enough from this damned peacock who pretended to be his equal. The commodore pointed out the gallery windows at the *Meshouda*, which lay anchored two hundred yards off *Constitution's* stern.

"*Encourage* him," Preble said through clenched teeth, "or I will see to it that floating whorehouse of yours is raked with hot shot when I meet you in combat. And after we have you in chains, I will personally deliver you to Washington. We have a noose at the end of a yard waiting for you there. You understand me, Lisle?"

The assassins slipped over the side of *Meshouda* and began swimming. Each was naked save for a breechcloth and the dirks carried on belts worn across their chests. They made their way silently through the harbor, past the sleeping ships toward the brig *Siena*. The harbor was calm, almost glassy as the two swimmers approached their quarry.

A pair of sentries aboard Captain Fazzelli's ship leaned against the rail, smoking pipes and quietly talking as the assassins climbed the anchor chain hand over hand. They reached the fo'castle without making a sound and split up, one moving down the starboard rail and the other along the port side toward the two guards. One lantern hanging at the waist cast pale yellow light, the night moonless and still.

The guards placed their muskets against the rail and turned their backs to the deck, leaning out as they admired the lights of the waterfront.

The assassins converged near the main mast and, after some furtive hand signals, pounced, covering the mouths of the sentries as they cut their throats. The two guards struggled and then collapsed to the deck.

Breathing hard the assassins waited a moment to see if the noise of the murders had alerted anyone. The deck was dark, the only sounds muffled coughs from the sleeping crew below.

The younger, more nimble of the two held up his hand telling the other to wait. He then made his way aft, toward Fazzelli's cabin. Unlike the bigger frigates, the sloop had no quarterdeck, so the assassin slipped down a passageway onto the gun deck and found the aft door leading to the captain's cabin. There was no guard. He moved quickly, placed his hand on the latch and entered. He heard loud snoring to his left. Ambient light from the ships anchored nearby filtered through the gallery windows. The assassin saw his victim sleeping soundly on his back, still wearing his green uniform jacket, several empty wine bottles scattered on the floor.

He approached, blade at the ready. Despite his drunken sleep, Fazzelli must have sensed the intruder because his eyes popped open. Before he could call out, the dirk was buried in his throat, blood spouting from the gaping wound. Still, the captain was able to reach his cutlass, which he swung blindly at his attacker. The blow was lucky, catching the assassin on the underside of his wrist, severing all the arteries.

The attacker fell on his victim as blood pulsed from their wounds. Fazzelli's attempts at alerting the vessel were swallowed up as he choked on his own blood and the assassin's blade. Finally, the *Siena's* captain lay still.

Feeling himself fading, the assassin stumbled to the door where his companion was waiting. He motioned at the wound on his wrist and then to the main deck. The other assassin nodded quickly and mumbled "*Allahu akbar*" before he disappeared. The wounded Tripolitan slid to the deck, crimson pooling around him as he lay down to die.

An hour later the *Meshouda* weighed anchor and quietly slipped out of Gibraltar's harbor.

9

The officers of the squadron assembled in Preble's cabin for a war counsel. It was their first formal meeting with the new commodore. Preble eyed them as they took their seats and once again silently cursed their youth. Only William Bainbridge, the commander of *Philadelphia,* was older than thirty. As they settled, Preble stood.

"Gentlemen," he began, "I have been sent here to lead the fight against these damned savages and fight we will."

The young officers, most whom had served and become disillusioned under the desultory Morris, glanced at each other at the welcome news.

"Mr. Bainbridge," Preble continued, looking at the *Philadelphia's* captain, "you will make ready and sail immediately to Tripoli. Mr. Smith, *Vixen* will escort *Philadelphia.*"

"Sir!" acknowledged Lieutenant John Smith, the schooner-of-war's commander.

"When you arrive there, Mr. Bainbridge, blockade the harbor until the remainder of squadron joins," Preble continued. He now pointed at a map on the table. "Our consul in Tangiers informs me Morocco is taking note of Tripoli's success in preying on American merchantmen and may follow suit."

"Sir, it was my understanding we had a treaty with Morocco," interrupted Lieutenant Stephen Decatur, commander of the schooner *Enterprise.*

"We do," Preble replied. "But I do not wish to have a threat to our rear when we begin our exertions against Tripoli. Therefore, the remainder of the squadron will sail for Tangiers as soon as we can make ready. I wish to learn Muly Soliman's intentions and if he is thinking war, disabuse him of that notion forthwith."

Preble crossed his arms on his chest and eyed the officers, one at a time. "I do not know any of you personally but I am aware of the reputations of each of the officers in this squadron," he said, looking at Bainbridge with the last word. "I believe most of you are too young and, frankly, too inexperienced for the rank and responsibility you hold. However, in the weeks to come I will give each man here a chance to demonstrate to me he is worthy of his position through his seamanship and his conduct in battle."

Bainbridge was stung. His boyish face red, the tall captain stood. "Sir," he began, "I think I speak for all of us when I say that we have proven our…"

"*Any* officer falling short of *my* standards will be removed from command!" Preble thundered.

Flustered, *Philadelphia's* captain took his seat. The cabin was silent.

"Sir, if I may," said Smith, breaking the awkward silence. "Lieutenant Wallace, the commander of marines aboard *Vixen* has taken ill and was removed to the British naval hospital this morning. The physicians say he has a fever. He will recover, but it will take some weeks. I require a marine officer, sir."

"Is that fellow O'Bannon available?" Preble asked Captain Hugh Campbell, commander of *Adams*, the frigate to which the lieutenant was assigned. "He assisted me yesterday in locating that reprobate Lisle and bringing him here."

"Yes, sir," Campbell replied, "I can make Lieutenant O'Bannon available to *Vixen*. I have another officer who can command the marines aboard *Adams*."

"O'Bannon is most impressive, I must say," Preble said.

"Indeed he is, sir," Campbell replied. "His marines love him and the tars, well, they respect him, sir. A few days after we weighed anchor on route to Gibraltar, a few of the British enlistees were making immoral advances on some of *Adams'* midshipmen…"

"We have far too many of those bastards in our ranks," Preble angrily remarked. "I'll have none of their buggery, by God!"

"No, sir," Campbell continued. "As I was saying, Lieutenant O'Bannon learned about their behavior and challenged the ringleader, a man named Gibbs, to a boxing match on the fo'castle."

Several of the officers now wore grins, having already heard the story.

"It being Sunday, of course much of the crew was off duty. Many of them assembled for the event. There was some wagering and a few dollars were raised for a purse. This Gibbs is a rather imposing man in his own right, but O'Bannon put on quite a display of pugilistic skill."

Campbell recalled O'Bannon, stripped to the waist, his arm muscles rippling, ferociously smashing Gibbs' face. The American sailors, crowded in the rigging and along the rails, cheered lustily as the big Englishman finally collapsed to his knees, blood pouring from his mouth and nose before O'Bannon laid him out cold with a roundhouse blow to the head.

Preble was now grinning along with the rest, the first smile any of the officers had seen on his face since meeting him.

"Well, sir, Lieutenant O'Bannon thrashed this Gibbs something tremendous," Campbell went on, "and perfect order was restored aboard *Adams.*"

The commodore slammed his open palm on the table, "By God, that's my kind of officer!" he laughed. "Very well, gentlemen, I mean to bring an end to this Tripoli business by spring. Please return to your ships and prepare them for battle."

Three days later, *Vixen* plunged through the seas a half mile ahead of *Philadelphia*. Despite the roll of the ship, O'Bannon was drilling his marines in musketry on the ship's waist.

"These are the conditions you'll fight in!" he called out over the wind. "I want to see every one of you load and fire your weapons from the top!"

The dozen marines tried to stand to attention, but were thrown off balance every time *Vixen* hit the bottom of a trough.

"Kineally, you first!"

The marine saluted and made for the mainmast's shroud. He slung his musket, and carefully scaled the rigging to the platform atop the mast. There, he braced himself, expertly loading his musket despite the wind and roll.

"Excellent, private!" called O'Bannon. He pointed at a small raft made of planks *Vixen* was towing fifty yards aft. "Now hit the target!"

The marine aimed and fired. Through his spyglass, O'Bannon saw a splash next to the raft. "Miss!" he called. "Reload!"

Kineally obeyed the order, but this time he held his fire until the raft reached the top of a swell. The ball hit the target squarely. "Very good, private! Butler, you're next!"

So the exercise went until O'Bannon was satisfied his new command were each able marksmen in less than ideal conditions. He had two men secure the floating target then assembled them once again on the pitching deck for inspection and generally liked what he saw.

Their uniforms were hand-me-downs from the disbanded Continental Marines, threadbare and, in some cases, patched, but clean from the daily brushing O'Bannon insisted they receive. Their black hats were cylindrical, with one narrow brim pulled up against the crown and fastened there with a black cockade. They were supposed to wear leather stocks around their necks to protect them from sword blows, but O'Bannon thought these unnecessary and turned a blind eye if his men didn't wear them at sea. Their blue jackets featured gold buttons and red facings. Their britches were white, and their black knee-length boots brilliantly polished. The muskets were smoothbore flintlocks, short and accurate only to a hundred yards but suitable for close combat between ships or putting down a mutiny if it came to that. Each man wore a sheathed bayonet on his belt.

O'Bannon made a note of the few deficiencies he found and then dismissed the company.

"Very good gunnery, Pres," Lieutenant Smith observed as he approached O'Bannon. "Let's hope they can shoot like that when we meet the Tripolines."

"Your Lieutenant Wallace has them well trained," O'Bannon said with an easy smile. "That's no easy trick loading and firing from up there in weather like this."

Smith nodded toward the *Philadelphia*, the majestic frigate under full sail bounding through the whitecaps, her crew scurrying up and down the masts, over her yards and through the rigging. "I do believe the bashaw will soil himself when he gets a look at her thirty-six guns primed and ready!" he told O'Bannon.

"Yes, and about damned time, too," O'Bannon remarked. "All we ever seem to do is talk to 'em."

"I think Commodore Preble is done talking," Smith said as a pipe sounded. "First dog watch."

The off duty crew and half the marine company now assembled at the scuttlebutt amidships, where a midshipman supervised distribution of the second grog ration of the day. Nearby the purser and cook prepared small barrels called kids containing the evening meal. The schooner's sailors then broke off into messes of six to eight men, taking their kids of salt pork and corn meal mush below where tables were lowered from the beams. O'Bannon joined the *Vixen's* off duty officers in Smith's small cabin.

Only a few days out of Gibraltar, the ship's five officers enjoyed a supper of boiled beef and fresh vegetables accompanied by Spanish wine. They ignored the roll of the ship as they ate, their plates prevented from sliding off the table by brass rails.

When they finished their meal, O'Bannon fetched his fiddle from his berth and brought it back to the cabin where he tuned it and began playing jaunty backwoods tunes he'd learned as a lad in Virginia. His impromptu performance produced smiles among the officers as well as the crew, for the music carried to the gun deck where the tars, relaxing after their meal, smoked their pipes and tapped their feet to the rhythm.

The roar of cannon shook *Vixen* just as the ship's drummer began beating to quarters. In less than a minute, the officers and sailors were at their places preparing for battle. O'Bannon joined Smith at the bow, where the lieutenant was glassing the horizon. Five hundred yards behind them, the bow chasers of the *Philadelphia* roared again, the twenty-four pound balls evilly hissing past *Vixen* toward their target, a vessel a mile away. O'Bannon and Smith watched as the shot splashed into the sea well short of the ship.

"That's a xebec," declared Smith peering through his glass, "though I can't make out a Tripolitan ensign." The naval officer turned his attention to *Philadelphia* and watched as signal flags were raised.

"Captain Bainbridge orders us to pursue and engage," Smith declared.

⚜ 10 ⚜

I n minutes, the lighter, faster schooner had set all her sails and was cutting speedily through the waves that crashed over her bow. The crew stood by for their next order. O'Bannon had assembled his marines at the waist. Six men would stand watch over the gun crews to ensure every man did his duty, while the other six would be ready to fire on the enemy when *Vixen* closed.

The xebec was making a desperate try to escape the Americans. She was still out of range, but Smith soon saw the Tripolitan ensign before her captain struck the flag and raised a Moroccan pennant in its place, a common ruse employed by the Barbary pirates.

"Cast loose your guns!" called Smith and the order was repeated up and down the deck by her ensigns and midshipmen. The crews manning the twelve cannon unlashed the carriages that secured them and placed them on their breech lashings, designed to take up the guns' recoil.

Vixen was rapidly closing as Smith called the order to roll out and prime the guns. Despite the swells and the spray, the crew obeyed without hesitation. Smith watched through his glass as the xebec's crew prepared their own cannon for battle. It would be a test of gunnery. In the heavy seas, the Americans would have to time their fire so the guns were level with the target - but so would the Tripolitans.

Now within a few hundred yards, Smith ordered the short barreled carronade on the bow rail loaded with langradge, a heavy canister filled with broken metal, iron bolts and grape shot.

"Fire!" the lieutenant cried when he saw the gun was ready. The report was deafening, the thick smoke carried by the wind, blew across the aft deck obliterating Smith's view. When it cleared, the lieutenant could see a dozen enemy sailors sprawled on the corsair's deck.

"Reload and fire at will!" Smith cried to the gunner on the bow. He now turned to the helmsman, "Bring us alongside! Ready port guns!"

The carronade sent another deadly hurricane of scrap iron across the enemy's deck, shredding sails, rigging and men. O'Bannon, judging the distance to be under a hundred yards, ordered his marines to take aim. From the waist, the marines fired in unison on the lieutenant's command, aiming at the Tripolitan ship's gunners. Three dropped as they tried to prime their weapons.

It was time for *Vixen's* cannon. With the enemy ship abreast and off her port side, Lieutenant Smith waited for the right moment, when his ship rose on the crest of a swell level with the enemy vessel and hesitated for a split second.

"Fire!" bellowed Smith over the wind.

The volley from the six port guns was devastating. The balls crashed through the xebec's hull blasting splinters and iron shards through her crew. Even as the enemy prepared to answer the broadside, the well trained Americans were reloading their guns. Several of the marines scrambled into the rigging and two men braced on the top began firing down onto the corsair's deck.

Reeling, the Tripolitans finally loosed their own salvo, but the shots were ill timed and aimed and went sailing harmlessly over *Vixen's* deck, punching holes in the sails but otherwise doing no damage. Smith saw several sailors appear on the xebec's deck with grappling hooks. The Tripolitans' preferred method of combat, he knew, was to close with the enemy and board for hand-to-hand fighting.

O'Bannon saw them too and ordered his marines on the deck to fire at the would-be boarders. Several of the pirates dropped while the others scrambled for cover where they could find it, abandoning any notion of boarding *Vixen*. One of the marines on the top managed to light the fuse of a grenade with a punk and tossed it toward the enemy helmsmen. O'Bannon watched the blast cut the man down. As he collapsed, the helmsman yanked the wheel down and the xebec slowly but steadily turned to port, away from *Vixen,* exposing the ship's stern.

"Fire!" called Smith to his port gunners.

The enemy ship shuttered under the raking fire, the cannon balls crashing through her gallery and ripping lengthwise through the vessel destroying her steering mechanisms. In less than a minute, the schooner's guns had fired another volley into the crippled xebec as the marines maintained a steady tattoo of musket fire, killing or wounding more of the pirates. Thick black smoke began billowing from the enemy ship's main hatch and shattered gallery windows.

Smith realized *Vixen* was in danger. "Heave to!" he called to his helmsmen. "Get away from her!"

The American turned to starboard and slowed as the xebec, now downwind, sailed swiftly away in the opposite direction.

O'Bannon watched the *Philadelphia* approached. From two hundred yards, she let loose her own broadside. Despite the wind, the shockwave of the frigate's starboard guns sent a shiver through *Vixen*. At least half the balls struck the xebec, several hulling her near the waterline.

Surviving pirates were leaping over the side as the enemy ship seemed to stall in the waves, the blaze from below igniting her tarred sails. The crews of both American ships gathered at the rails to watch as the flames finally found the xebec's powder magazine. She exploded in a massive fireball, the ship's deck, masts and sails disappearing in a ball of flame and smoke.

"Sweet Jesus and all the Saints!" cried O'Bannon in awe as the corsair's mainmast trailing its burning sails and rigging was propelled skyward like a rocket out of the blast. The heat of the explosion enveloped *Vixen* before debris began falling around and on her. The helmsman was doing his best to escape, but shattered planks, torn rigging and pieces of bodies littered the deck.

"Secure!" commanded Smith as what was left of the corsair sank beneath the swells.

Philadelphia now lay off *Vixen's* stern. The chase and battle had lasted more than three hours but to O'Bannon and the others it felt like three minutes. The sun was setting as the signal flags were hoisted on the frigate. "Well done little fox," Smith read aloud to O'Bannon and his officers who'd gathered around him. "Recover survivors; on to Tripoli."

11

As the wreckage of his xebec was disappearing beneath the waves, Yusuf Karamanli was at that moment eating a ripe apricot, his thick lips wrapped around the fruit, a loud sucking noise nauseating the Dane who sat on a pile of pillows across from the bashaw of Tripoli. Karamanli pulled the fruit from his mouth, eyed it carefully, then began sucking on it again, juice dripping onto his thick black beard as he made satisfied noises in his throat.

Finally, the bashaw set the apricot pit on a silver plate and leaned back on his pillows. His enormous belly swathed in red silk robes, he wore a blue velvet fez on his head of black curls streaked with gray. He adjusted himself and farted loudly as he looked about at the courtiers who had joined him for his latest negotiation with Denmark's consul, Nicholas Nissen. The ministers and advisers sat patiently on pillows arranged about the floor of the ornate, carpeted hall overlooking the harbor and the sea beyond.

Nissen, a lean, bald man of fifty-one years, waited for Yusuf to get comfortable and speak first. He knew he should say nothing until the bashaw spoke or risk one of Yusuf's childish tirades. The odor produced by the bashaw's fart, meantime, made him still more nauseous.

Yusuf was presently working at his teeth with a pick made of silver, his hooded eyes assessing the Dane.

"This is about the Americans again," the bashaw asked without preamble.

"Yes, Excellency," Nissen replied in Arabic. "The crew of the merchantman captured by Murad Reis. *The Integrity*."

"What of them?"

"I would like to have those men turned over to me so they will be no trouble to Your Excellency," Nissen said. "Surely you wish not to waste more money caring for them, feeding them and so forth."

Now in their sixth month of captivity, the survivors of the American merchantman's crew were chained up in the bashaw's dungeon when they weren't hauling rocks from his quarry to the waterfront. There were a dozen or so American seamen, Nissen had recently learned.

Yusuf's face revealed nothing as he digested the Dane's words. "The Christians are my slaves," he finally declared, his tone vexed.

"Yes, I am aware of that, Excellency," Nissen replied. "But there aren't very many of them and because they are merchant sailors, I believe I can negotiate a large ransom for the crew and their ship from the vessel's insurers if you will just allow…"

"That will take too long!" interrupted Yusuf impatiently. "I do not like dealing with these insurance people! They are too greedy and too slow! Governments are better. The American president pays me more and he pays me faster."

The Dane was nodding. He knew the bashaw. There was no arguing the point with him.

"Very well, Your Excellency," Nissen acknowledged with an indulgent smile. "I would be happy to begin negotiations with the American government, but that will take time, too. I have also heard that Morris was replaced. A man named Preble is now commanding the American Navy in the Mediterranean."

Yusuf waved a plump brown hand dismissively. "Americans! Children! Fools!" he declared. "Tell this Preble I want fifty thousand American dollars for the merchant crew and one hundred thousand dollars for the ship. I shall keep the cargo."

Accustomed to Yusuf's outlandish demands, Nissen merely nodded. He would pass the amount of the ransoms along with the names of the *Integrity's* surviving sailors to the American consul in Algiers.

"And what of the American crew, Your Excellency?"

Yusuf smiled cruelly.

"They shall eat stones."

Murad Reis had sailed *Meshouda* into port that morning, then gone to his palatial villa near the waterfront where he stripped, bathed in rose-scented water and was serviced by his three wives simultaneously. As he dressed in fresh silken robes he marveled again at how a dirty guttersnipe from Edinburgh, the son of a chamber maid and some unknown aristocrat, could have achieved and acquired so much in so little time. He smiled to himself as he walked to his father-in-law's neighboring palace. He passed Nissen, who was just leaving the bashaw. The Dane shot Reis a dark look but said nothing.

The Grand Admiral found Yusuf alone with a naked slave girl of twenty or so. She was a blonde Swede taken off one of that kingdom's ships but never ransomed. The girl was massaging the bashaw's feet. With her mouth.

Murad Reis tried to ignore her as he spoke to Yusuf whose eyes were closed, his hand buried in his robes. He seemed to be fingering himself.

"I am worried about this, Preble, Babu," Reis said. He was permitted to address Yusuf by his wife's pet name for her father when the two men were alone as they were now. "He has several warships at Gibraltar and he promised me he was coming to make war."

Yusuf's head lolled to the side as the girl moved to his other foot. He grunted in reply to Reis, so the admiral continued.

"He had me aboard *Constitution*. She is formidable...forty-four guns she has," he observed. "There were at least two other American frigates there and five or six sloops and brigs."

Yusuf grunted again. Reis felt himself getting impatient with the bashaw. After a long silence he continued.

"Preble told me there will be no more ransom and no more tribute. I think this American means what he says"

One eye popped open and peered at Reis. The other eye followed, and the bashaw was now staring at his grand admiral, heavy eyebrows meeting in the middle of his forehead. He yanked his toes out of the girl's mouth and shooed her out of the chamber.

"That woman Morris said the same thing! And Dale before him!" Yusuf replied angrily, recalling the two former American commodores. "But they paid me what I demanded. You must make Preble understand that he will pay me too!"

"There is a new American president, Babu," Reis said. "Jefferson. He has never been in favor of buying peace with tribute as his predecessors were. I don't think Preble can agree to pay even if he wanted to."

Yusuf's face flushed and his lips trembled. Reis sighed, knowing what was about to come.

"You will *make* him, Grand Admiral!" Yusuf cried as he awkwardly rose to his feet and began pacing the chamber waving his arms, his eyes wide with rage. "You will meet Preble's ships in battle and you *will* crush his arrogance! You will sink his frigates and take his men as slaves! *Then* we shall see how strong this Jefferson is! You will bring that Preble dog here and he shall crawl before me and I shall piss on him and ride him through Tripoli backwards on an ass! *Then* Jefferson shall pay me. He shall pay me twice," Yusuf thrust three fingers in the air for emphasis, "nay, *thrice* what I demand!"

Yusuf was panting from the exertion. He collapsed back on his divan and continued to glare at Reis, waiting for a response. The grand admiral thought of the American fire power he'd seen at Gibraltar, of the determination in Preble's eyes. He knew capturing or destroying one or more of the American war ships was pure fantasy.

But he also knew there was only one answer Yusuf Kalamani, the bashaw of Tripoli wanted to hear.

"As you wish, Your Excellency."

12

*P*hiladelphia trimmed her sails as she approached the coast, *Vixen* trailing a mile behind. Small trading vessels spied the Americans and warily hugged the shallow waters of the shoreline three miles away, well out of range of the two American war ships.

Bainbridge ordered *Philadelphia* to sail east, parallel to the coast. The helmsmen immediately brought the frigate into the wind and her sails billowed.

The captain glassed the shore and shortly the city came into view glimmering pale white in the late morning sunshine. He could see scores of corsairs, xebecs and feluccas riding at anchor in the harbor guarded by the gun batteries mounted on the ramparts of the bashaw's castle and the city walls. The inner harbor was protected by a breakwater that appeared to reach a quarter mile out into the sea with gun embrasures arranged at intervals of two hundred yards.

As easily as Bainbridge could see Tripoli and Yusuf's stronghold, he knew the bashaw could see *Philadelphia*, but just to make sure he had the tyrant's attention, Bainbridge ordered all guns rolled out and primed with powder but no shot. When the gunnery officers signaled their weapons were ready he cried "Fire!"

Thirty-six cannon fired simultaneously, their thunder reverberating across the sea as thick white smoke from the guns hid the frigate from view.

"*That* woke up the bastard!" smiled O'Bannon, who was watching the display with Lieutenant Smith aboard the *Vixen*.

Philadelphia emerged from the smoke, plowing through the light seas, her crew on the deck cheering the opening salvo. From the bashaw's palace came answering reports, but nothing like the roar of the great American guns.

For the next three days, the frigate and schooner patrolled the Tripolitan coast on the lookout for any shipping heading into or out of the enemy port. Bainbridge knew as they waited for Preble and the rest of the squadron that blockade duty could become boring and bored crews were lazy, unprepared crews so he ordered extra gunnery practice. This would sharpen their marksmanship while reminding the bashaw he was at war with America - finally.

Vixen chased down several trading vessels sailing toward Tripoli under neutral flags. Smith ordered their captains to sail elsewhere or risk having their ships and cargos destroyed when the American squadron attacked.

On the fourth day of the blockade, Bainbridge watched as *Vixen* pursued what appeared to be a Tripolitan merchantman out to sea. The smaller American ship disappeared from sight to the north shortly before noon, just as a triangular sail came into view on the western horizon.

The captain ordered the American flag struck and replaced with a French pennant so the mystery ship would draw closer. Two hours later, the xebec was a half mile off the *Philadelphia's* bow. Bainbridge called for the Stars and Stripes to be raised again and gave chase.

The xebec was one of Murad Reis' fastest. Its captain realized he had been tricked and made for the harbor.

"Cut him off!" Bainbridge ordered. The helmsman obeyed, steering the frigate at an angle that would put her on an interception course with the smaller vessel.

The ships closed, but not fast enough, the corsair passing three hundred yards in front of *Philadelphia*. Bainbridge's ordered the two bow chasers fired but the shots flew harmlessly through Tripolitan's sails.

"Sir…the reef!" cried Lieutenant David Porter, Bainbridge's second-in-command, pointing at a chart. "There are shoals here at two or three fathoms!"

Bainbridge felt the cold sweat break out on his forehead. He'd forgotten about the reef. American charts of the North African coast were faulty so in Gibraltar a British pilot who knew the waters off Tripoli briefed the squadron's officers on what to expect. Bainbridge snatched the chart from Porter's hand and read the notes the pilot had made on it. He looked at the spot that approximated his ship's position and, there, the pilot had made some circles and penned the words *Kaliusa Reef* alongside.

The xebec's captain expected a volley from the frigate's port guns, but pre-occupied as he was, Bainbridge had forgotten about the enemy ship. The vessel, its helmsman familiar with the shoals, speedily sailed off toward the harbor as Bainbridge ordered the *Philadelphia* brought about.

"Mr. Avery!" Bainbridge called to his navigator, a civilian warrant officer. "What is our pos…"

The *Philadelphia* suddenly shuttered, throwing officers and sailors to the deck. A man working in the rigging tumbled into the sea. There was a high pitched screech and sickening grinding sound from below as the *Philadelphia's* keel ran up onto a reef of sand and rock, her sails pushing her higher onto the submerged perch.

Bainbridge was on his back. He'd been thrown forward, his head striking the helm. Bleeding from his nose, the captain rose unsteadily to his feet and looked about desperately as the frigate ground to a stop and listed five degrees to starboard. The majestic American man-of-war *Philadelphia* was grounded two miles off Tripoli, within sight of Yusuf Kamanali's palace.

All morning through his spyglass Murad Reis watched the big American man-of-war with trepidation from the city wall. He knew, even if Yusuf didn't, there were enough guns aboard the American warship to reduce Tripoli to smoldering ruins. When the rest of the squadron arrived, he thought to himself, the Americans would position themselves within range of the city to do just that if the bashaw didn't agree to peace.

Then, to Reis's astonishment, *Philadelphia* began her pursuit of his corsair. He thought the American captain would come about as he neared shore, but instead the fool sailed straight for the reef protecting the harbor. Reis roared with laughter as *Philadelphia* ran aground, her three tall masts shaking violently. Scarcely believing his good fortune, the grand admiral dashed to *Mashouda*.

The sailors and officers of *Philadelphia* sweated through the afternoon, trying everything they could think of to dislodge their warship. They'd backed the sails, then they tried towing her off with the boats, men straining at the oars as officers and midshipmen urged them on.

Like hyenas sensing a mortally wounded lion, Reis' corsairs began slinking out of Tripoli's harbor, their decks jammed with armed men. Certain the frigate was prepared to defend herself, they slowly surrounded her, staying just out of range of the American ship's guns.

Bainbridge stood distraught on the quarterdeck watching as the enemy closed in. His cannon were useless. Because she was listing, *Philadelphia's* starboard guns were pointing toward the sea and her port cannon were aimed skyward and impossible to depress low enough to hit targets. Thirty marines along with most of the ship's crew had taken up arms and positions around the ship's rails and were waiting to repel boarders as the last of the boats that attempted to tow the frigate were brought back aboard.

Glassing the American vessel from *Meshouda*, Reis saw the frigate's cannon could offer *Philadelphia* no protection.

The marine officers and sergeants were looking up at the quarterdeck, waiting for Bainbridge's orders to fire as the noose tightened and enemy ships packed with boarders drew closer. The captain looked at the thirty officers, warrant officers, senior mates and midshipmen gathered around him on the quarterdeck.

"We must surrender, Lieutenant Porter," Bainbridge finally declared. "Dismount the guns and drop them overboard."

Porter, the ship's second officer, a strapping young man from Boston, stared in disbelief at his captain.

"Sir!" he cried. "We can't do that!"

"No, sir!" agreed the ship's sailing master, an old mariner who had fought in the Revolution. "Surrender to these sons of bitches without a fight?! That's...that's treasonous in my book!"

"I don't care about your damned book!" Bainbridge snapped at the warrant officer. He stepped back and looked at all of them. "I am not going to risk the lives of three hundred good men in a battle we've no means of winning. You - all of you - will follow my orders or I will have those who disobey hanged! Now do as I say! Instantly!"

Porter, his face taught with rage, glared at the captain. Finally, he turned to the others. "Do as you are ordered!" he commanded.

The marines cast all the ships muskets and pistols along with the weapons' powder and shot overboard. On the main deck and below on the gun deck, the twenty-four-pound guns of the *Philadelphia* were unceremoniously levered overboard by gangs of sailors, who swore bitterly as they worked. In the magazine deep within *Philadelphia*, a ship's carpenter began drilling a hole in the hull to flood the compartment and destroy the precious gun powder. Elsewhere, other carpenter's mates were drilling holes to try to scuttle the frigate. On the quarterdeck, midshipmen tore the pages out of the ship's log and signal books and burned them.

When Bainbridge was satisfied he'd done all he could to make sure armaments and intelligence wouldn't fall into the bashaw's hands he called Porter again.

"Strike the colors!"

Some of the junior officers and midshipmen wept as they hauled down the flag while tars and marines looked on with expressions of shock and anger.

Cheers went up from the surrounding enemy ships when the crews understood the Americans weren't going to fight. The corsairs closed in, lowered boats and soon pirates were crowding the *Philadelphia's* decks, some pushing the American captives to the rails, over the side and into the boats that would ferry them to shore. Others were searching the ship for plunder. Bainbridge had hidden the ship's money, some twenty-five thousand dollars in gold coins, but the pirates found it in a locker and brought it up to the main deck.

Reis was rowed over from *Mashouda* to accept the surrender. His boat was lashed to the American frigate and he climbed up onto the deck of *Philadelphia*.

The grand admiral wore simple white robes and a yellow turban as he met the shamefaced Bainbridge on the quarterdeck.

"Welcome to Tripoli!" Reis cheerfully declared holding out his hand. Without a word, Bainbridge gave his sword to Reis who was looking about with a broad smile on his face. "I have been admiring your beautiful man-of-war from afar all this week. I was imagining how I might put her to good use never believing for a moment I would *capture* her...yet, here we are!"

Bainbridge ignored the taunt. "I want my men..."

"Your men are the prisoners of Bashaw Yusuf Karamanli! So are your officers! So are you!" barked Reis. "What you want counts for nothing here! Ye made a grave mistake allowing yourselves to fall into our hands, laddy. Now you will find there is nay mercy for Christians in Tripoli."

13

"Where the hell is *Philadelphia*?" Lieutenant Smith asked as he peered at the horizon. *Vixen* chased the unknown ship for a day before losing her in the dark.

O'Bannon glassed the sea behind *Vixen* with his own telescope, but he saw nothing. "Odd," he remarked. "I wonder if Captain Bainbridge was called back to Gibraltar."

"Or maybe Leghorn?" suggested Smith. "That's closer. It would be an easier rendezvous."

This made sense to O'Bannon. Leghorn was a British naval base on the island of Malta used by the Americans, a couple of days' sail from the North African coast.

Vixen lay off Tripoli harbor, light winds pushing her to the east through choppy seas. O'Bannon scanned the harbor as they sailed past. He saw the usual traffic moving in and out of the harbor, fishermen and small commercial vessels, the bashaw's corsairs tied up along the quay or anchored. In their midst, he suddenly made out the masts of a much larger ship.

"*What* in the holy hell...." O'Bannon hissed. "Look! Is that... is that..."

Smith peered through his own glass.

"*Philadelphia*! Good God!" Smith cried. "What has happened?! Why is she anchored there?!"

"Has Captain Bainbridge captured the city?!" O'Bannon wondered aloud.

"Impossible," Smith replied. "The only way she could get into that harbor…"

"Is if Triploline pilots took her in," O'Bannon completed the lieutenant's thought. "Do you think they…captured her? Is that possible?!"

As if in answer, a small cutter flying a white flag of truce appeared from behind the breakwater. In half an hour it came along side. The cutter was manned by three Tripolitans. One of them stood up in the stern holding a speaking trumpet and addressed the officers.

"Americans! Murad Reis, grand admiral of the war ships of His Excellency, Yusuf Karamanli the bashaw of Tripoli begs to inform you that Captain Bainbridge, his crew and his ship have been captured!"

Stunned, Smith and O'Bannon could only stare down at the man who delivered his incredible message in thickly accented English.

Smith picked up his own trumpet. "I do not believe you!"

"Please to listen, sir!" the man replied. "Captain Bainbridge sailed his ship onto the reef!"

"Oh my God!" cried Smith. "Kaliusa Reef! He ran aground!"

"Sweet Jesus and all the Saints," muttered O'Bannon.

The man in the boat continued: "Murad Reis wishes to speak under a flag of truce to the captain of your ship! At His Excellency's palace!"

By now *Vixen's* crew not tending to other duties were gathered at the rail to hear the news. There was a buzz among them as Smith turned to O'Bannon. "What do you think, Pres?"

"You should stay with *Vixen*. I'll go. If an officer is taken prisoner by the bastards, it oughtn't be you," O'Bannon replied. He now consulted his pocket watch. "It's half past two. I'll go ashore. If I am not back by sundown, sail. I reckon Leghorn would be your best port. When the squadron gets here I'll somehow get word to the commodore you've gone there."

Smith was nodding as he saw the wisdom of O'Bannon's plan. If Smith were captured, *Vixen* would not have a commander. The lieutenant's second in command, a twenty-year-old ensign, was far too inexperienced to take charge of her.

"Alright, Pres," he replied. "But be careful."

The Tripolitan cutter entered the harbor, O'Bannon sitting in her bow. At the foot of the breakwater he saw slaves wearing rags pushing rocks off sledges and onto barges as their Tripolitan guards directed their labors. They slid past *Philadelphia*, anchored alongside a smaller vessel that looked like a merchant schooner, *Integrity* lettered on the ship's stern. The man who'd spoken on the trumpet steered the cutter to the quay, where she tied up. Four Turkish janissaries armed with lances, muskets and scimitars were waiting while a crowd of onlookers gathered around gawking at the tall American officer who stepped onto the quay.

The Turks motioned O'Bannon to follow. They led him along the waterfront back toward the mole. After ten minutes, they approached several of the rock-hauling sledges and the pitiable men laboring around them. At first, O'Bannon thought they were Europeans. Then one of the men, manhandling a rock off a sledge, caught site of O'Bannon's uniform. He cried out to his mates and motioned to the approaching marine.

"He's one of ours!" cried the man excitedly. Several others looked his way and waved frantically. "We're saved!"

O'Bannon now understood he was looking at the unfortunate crewmen from some American ship.

"What in God's name...?!" O'Bannon cried as he turned to the janissaries. "What's the meaning of this?! Those men are prisoners of war, not bloody slaves!"

The Turk spoke no English so he merely peered back at O'Bannon, who turned to the Americans. They were fifty yards away, being held back by their guards as O'Bannon was held back by the janissaries' crossed lances.

"Lads! I'm sorry you are in this fix!" O'Bannon called to them. "I'm here to talk to the Scotsman! We will free you as quickly as we can!"

There were cries and moans from the bedraggled crew as they realized the officer wasn't there to rescue them. "Dear God in Heaven, sir! You must help us!"

"Aye!" another called out. "They don't feed us! They be keepin' us in some dungeon and they been makin' us work like this hours on end...all we get is a drink of water and a bite o' rancid bread!"

"We will do our best, men! Believe that and be strong! We will deliver you from this!"

The Turks were now pulling him away, back toward the city. O'Bannon was flush with rage and grief at the plight of his countrymen, powerless to do anything but parlay with the damned pirate. He felt hot tears of frustration in his eyes as they marched him through the filthy streets past dilapidated shops and houses of dun-colored stucco. Women cloaked head to toe in black burqas and men in smudged robes silently stared as the procession passed by.

They shortly turned into an alley that led to a tall wooden gate. As they approached, it swung open and O'Bannon and his guards entered a wide cobbled courtyard shaded by olive trees. They mounted stairs that led to a roof commanding a view of the harbor and the Mediterranean beyond. O'Bannon could see the bashaw's gun emplacements that lined the waterfront, protected by embrasures of whitewashed stone.

"Paddy!" called Murad Reis with a smile. He was leaning back on a pile of pillows under an awning that shaded him from the afternoon sun. Beside him was a small table holding a silver pitcher and fluted crystal glasses. "It's good to see ye again, lad!" He motioned O'Bannon over to his seat. "Where's your captain? I asked for him, nay you!"

"Lisle, you son of a bitch!" O'Bannon growled. "You release those Americans or you will suffer ten times what they're enduring!"

Reis ignored the threat. Instead, he gestured toward the harbor. "What do you think of my new flag ship?"

O'Bannon, trying mightily to control his anger, remained silent.

"A most remarkable event occurred two days ago. Your Captain Bainbridge sailed his frigate onto the Kaliusa Reef," Reis observed. "Did he not know it was there? Damned poor seamanship by the commander of an American man-of-war. But a fine gift for His Excellency! All we had to do was wait for high seas to tow her off the reef."

O'Bannon waited.

"After all that talk about fighting by your commodore in Gibraltar, I thought Bainbridge would have more forcefully protected his ship after she ran aground. But he just threw his cannon over the side and struck his flag," Reis said, looking at O'Bannon. "Are all American officers such cowards? It seems as though they are. First you sent Dale here and then Morris. They were afraid of fighting us, the cowards. Are you a coward, too, Paddy?"

O'Bannon took a step toward Reis, but two of the janissaries seized his arms.

"What is it you want, Lisle!?"

Reis rose and pointed to the quay. "Look down there. My divers salvaged all the *Philadelphia's* cannon save three or four."

O'Bannon saw the guns lined up on the quay, workers cleaning sand and debris from their barrels.

"We're going to remount them," Reis went on, "and then add another dozen guns to her. I'll carry five hundred of my best fighters. With that frigate, Tripoli will *own* the Mediterranean."

Reis resumed his seat and poured orange juice from the pitcher into two glasses, offering one to O'Bannon. The marine officer, thirsty as we was, refused. Reis shrugged and sipped his, then sat back.

"Three hundred thousand dollars for the crew and officers," he stated without preamble. "And I'll throw in the crew from that merchantman yonder as a gesture of goodwill to your President Jefferson. My father-in-law has already placed a price of one hundred thousand on the merchantman."

"What else?" O'Bannon demanded.

"We need more powder and shot for our guns. A lot more. Also, muskets, pistols and ammunition," Reis replied as he gestured toward *Philadelphia*, "for my new flagship, of course. I'm renaming her *Fatima*, after my first wife, the bashaw's daughter. I think I will paint her…light blue, the color of Tripoli's early spring skies."

O'Bannon stared in disbelief at the Scotsman. "You've got balls, Lisle, I'll give you that!" O'Bannon said. "You want America to provide arms so you can plunder *more* American ships?!"

Reis couldn't help but smile at the irony of his demand.

"That's not going to happen" O'Bannon said. "But I will give Commodore Preble your message anyway."

Still smirking, Reis rose from his seat and waved O'Bannon off. "Mark me, Paddy. Ye go back and get my ransom money and arms, there's a good lad. If you fail, your men will suffer worse than those wretches ye saw at the breakwater."

O'Bannon broke away from the Turks holding him and snatched Reis' robes. The Scotsman's red turban flew off his head. O'Bannon pulled the man's face close to his own.

"Soon," he hissed, "we will meet, boyo, and you'll learn for yourself whether I'm a coward or not."

The biggest of the Turks yanked O'Bannon away and shoved him toward the stairs. The marine placed his hand on the hilt of his sword and faced down the four guards. Reis yelled something at the Turks and they backed away. One of the janissaries picked up the toppled turban and handed it to his master.

"Put your filthy Christian hands on me again and ye die!" Reis cried. "Now get back to your ship and do as you're told!"

The janissaries led the seething O'Bannon through the streets but before they reached the quay, they guided him down an alley. One of them stooped and used a big iron key to open the gates of a warehouse. He pointed at the interior, but sensing a trap, O'Bannon hesitated. Then he heard American voices from within.

"It's Lieutenant O'Bannon!" somebody cried.

There were shouts of excitement, so O'Bannon stepped into the gloom and found himself in a windowless room crowded with the crew of *Philadelphia*.

Several of the warrant officers pressed forward and one of them, a man O'Bannon knew as Nathaniel Barrington spoke to him.

"Sir, Mr. O'Bannon, are ye here to free us?"

O'Bannon looked at the anxious faces and shook his head. "No lads, I'm afraid that Scotch bastard won't release you until we pay ransom."

There were more cries and moans of anguish.

"How long will that take?" Barrington asked.

"I don't know. But Commodore Preble is on his way here and I will tell him what the Scot wants." O'Bannon looked around. "Where are your officers?"

"We don't know," Barrington replied. "They separated us when we came ashore. They put us here."

"Did you really run aground?"

"Aye," Barrington replied. "We couldn't get her off the reef. So Captain Bainbridge surrendered her."

Several of the men spit at the words and O'Bannon heard muttering and somebody say "bloody coward."

"That's enough!" O'Bannon said sharply. "Mr. Bainbridge had his reasons for doing what he did! Now hear me. We will sail as fast as we can and intercept the squadron. Then we will return and do all we can to free you as soon as we can. In the meantime, remember, you still serve in the American Navy."

14

At that moment in Gibraltar, where he returned a day earlier after successfully putting the Moroccan emperor in his place by simply appearing with his war ships off Tangiers, Commodore Preble was completing an optimistic report for the Secretary of the Navy, Samuel Smith:

"My dear Sir," he concluded, *"you and President Jefferson may rest with perfect confidence that we shall have peace with Tripoli by spring."*

He sealed the letter with wax and pressed his seal on the envelope. He gave it to his steward who would see to it the letter was placed in the hands of the captain of *New York*, a frigate ordered home for refitting.

The next morning, re-provisioned and ready, *Constitution* weighed anchor. Together with the sixteen-gun brig *Argus* and twelve-gun schooners *Enterprise* and *Nautilus*, the squadron sailed for Tripoli to reunite with *Philadelphia* and *Vixen*. The four men-of-war, each under full sail to take advantage of the favorable easterly winds, were halfway to Tripoli when a lookout on Preble's flagship spotted the masts of a vessel on the horizon sailing toward the squadron. As she approached, another lookout called down to the quarterdeck:

"Ship approaching is *Vixen!*"

Preble heard the lookout. "What in the name of Christ?!" he exclaimed to Captain John Rodgers, *Constitution's* commander, who was standing with him on the weather deck. Rodgers, a younger version of the fiery Preble, scanned the horizon with his spyglass.

"I don't see *Philadelphia*, sir," he declared, "but she's *Vixen* all right."

The schooner was making exceptional speed as she tacked toward the flagship. Rodgers thought of raising signal flags to see what Smith was doing here, but waited until *Vixen* was in speaking distance. The vessel passed the flag ship, came about and then alongside, fifty yards of *Constitution*'s starboard. Preble could see Smith, two of his officers, and Lieutenant O'Bannon standing at the rail.

"Ahoy the flagship!" called Smith over the wind through his trumpet.

"Ahoy *Vixen*!" responded Rodgers. "What news!"

"*Philadelphia* has been captured!" cried Smith, scarcely believing the words as he shouted them.

"Say again!" called Rodgers, sure he had not heard Smith correctly.

"*Philadelphia*! She's been captured! In Tripoli!"

Preble's face drained of color. Rodgers, dumbfounded, could think of no reply. Sailors on the deck were suddenly chattering about what they'd just heard. Finally, after a long minute of silence, the two ships sailing on parallel course, Preble looked at Rodgers.

"Tell him to come aboard," said the commodore, almost to himself. "Meet me in my cabin when he gets here. I want a full report. Maintain course for now."

Preble's cabin was silent save for the usual creaking of timbers and footsteps on the quarterdeck above. The ship pitched slightly as she sailed on an east, southeast heading. Smith, Rodgers and O'Bannon stood to attention before the commodore.

Preble's first reaction was to explode when he'd seen Smith, but he knew whatever had happened to *Philadelphia* was not the lieutenant's fault.

"Sit," the commodore ordered, gesturing to the dining table surrounded by chairs.

All the men took seats, Preble at the head. Without ceremony, he asked Smith, "What happened?"

The young lieutenant briskly gave his report.

"So she ran aground on Kaliusa Reef," Preble summarized with a taught voice, inwardly enraged at Bainbridge's stupidity. "Then what?"

"Sir, when we arrived, Reis, er, Lisle, demanded I come ashore. I didn't think it was advisable to leave *Vixen* without a commander, should I be taken prisoner, sir, so Lieutenant O'Bannon went ashore to meet Lisle instead."

Preble looked at O'Bannon. "Lieutenant?"

"I was taken to see that Scotsman, sir," O'Bannon replied in a firm voice. "But first they showed me some American sailors. They are being worked like beasts of burden, sir, reinforcing the breakwater."

Preble shuttered at this news. He knew the pirates mistreated prisoners, but he never for a minute thought that men of his squadron could be enslaved. He said nothing as he motioned for O'Bannon to continue.

"The bast...I mean Lisle, he demanded a three hundred thousand dollar ransom for officers and crew. He also wants powder and shot for *Philadelphia's* guns. Said he was going to keep the frigate as his new flagship and rename her *Fatima* or something. Paint her blue, sir."

Preble stared at O'Bannon, marveling at Lisle's audacity until Smith spoke up, "Sir, Lieutenant O'Bannon and I were able to speak to the Danish consul in Triploi, a man called Nissen. He came aboard *Vixen* to see us after the lieutenant's meeting with Lisle. The officers and midshipmen are being held in our old consulate and Nissen says he has the bashaw's ear. He told us he would do all he could to make sure our men aren't abused during their captivity."

"What's this Nissen want in return?" asked Preble.

"Nothing, sir," replied Smith. "He said he's a friend of a man named Eaton, the former American consul in Tunis. He said Eaton helped him many times so I reckon he's returning the favor."

"Yes, Eaton, I've heard of him," replied Preble thoughtfully.

"One more thing, sir," Smith said as he pulled a sealed envelope from inside his jacket. "I have this letter from Captain Bainbridge. Nissen said the bashaw encourages his captives to write because it gets him his ransoms faster. Nissen said it might be a good idea to read this letter by candlelight. Not sure what he means, sir."

Preble took the letter and set it down before him. "Anything else?"

Smith and O'Bannon looked at each other. O'Bannon finally spoke up.

"Sir, permission to speak freely?" O'Bannon asked.

Preble gave a curt nod.

"We can't let Lisle and that bashaw have *Philadelphia*, sir."

Preble's eyes bored into the marine lieutenant's. "I have no intention of letting that happen, Mr. O'Bannon!"

After the officers left, Preble read Bainbridge's letter. It was a full account of what had happened. He read the letter a second time and was disgusted Bainbridge had surrendered his command without a fight. His excuses for doing so translated to criminal dereliction if not outright cowardice. It was all Preble could do contain his temper. First the fool had lost *Retaliation* to the French. Then he'd allowed *George Washington* to be converted into a sea taxi by Bobba Mustapha, Algiers' regent. As angry as he was, Preble knew there was nothing he could do about Bainbridge for now.

He went to a cupboard, found a candle and lit it. He held the letter to the candle and new words began appearing on the page between the lines in ink. Bainbridge had written in lemon juice, the words appearing when the letter was heated.

The commodore read the secret message and considered its contents before finding he agreed completely with Bainbridge's recommendations.

The former United States consulate was a one-story house on a hill overlooking the harbor. In the front garden was the stub of the flagpole Yusuf chopped down when he declared war on America.

The American officers' quarters were cramped, but the men made do. They were permitted by the bashaw to roam the city because escape was out of the question. The city was surrounded by a trackless wasteland and the harbor was heavily guarded by the bashaw's soldiers and janissaries. Nissen was a frequent visitor and reported to Bainbridge that his crew was being held in a warehouse near the waterfront.

Nissen was able to prevent the bashaw from forcing the American officers to perform slave labor, but every dawn the *Philadelphia's* enlisted men and warrant officers were marched off to the quarries, where they cut stone and dragged it to the waterfront until sunset.

"Your ships' surgeons and most of your artisans like the carpenters and sail makers have been excused from this labor but they have been put to work tending the royal family or repairing and refitting Reis' ships," Nissen told Bainbridge.

"Is there nothing you can do for my crew?" the captain pleaded. "For innocent white men to be worked as black slaves…"

"I am afraid not, my dear fellow," the Dane replied as he placed a sympathetic hand on the American's shoulder. "I tried. But this is how they are. We must pray for your men and hope your navy soon comes to their rescue."

Bainbridge could do nothing for the crew, so he tried to keep his men in the consulate busy, especially the young and energetic midshipmen. Boredom was their chief torture so the captain continued classes in navigation, mathematics, rhetoric and other subjects under the direction of the ship's officers and chaplain.

Meantime, Bainbridge had time to ruminate on his own future. He knew his naval career was likely over. Losing a man-of-war without a fight, regardless of his reasons, was inexcusable. Several of his officers were cool but respectful toward him and he knew when the incident was investigated, they would probably not support him when asked about what happened on Kaliusa Reef.

But Bainbridge comforted himself with the knowledge he'd done what needed to be done, placing his men's lives ahead of his career. Now captive, he was determined to see to it that as many officers and enlisted men as possible survived their ordeal.

Bainbridge was presently writing a report that he planned to send to Preble through Nissen when one of the midshipmen dashed into the small room he used as his office.

"Sir! Sir!" the boy cried, "Ships! Our ships, sir!"

Bainbridge bolted from his seat and followed the excited youngster outside. Three new vessels had appeared and he instantly recognized the *Constitution* escorted by *Vixen* and three brigs. They were five miles offshore, but the Stars and Stripes could be clearly seen flying from *Constitution's* aft lines. At that moment, the flag ship fired her bow chasers in unison, the dual report rolling over the swells to the city. On the waterfront, a Tripolitan gun fired a response. Bainbridge smiled grimly. Preble had arrived.

❧ 15 ❧

Murad Reis glassed the scene before him. The forty-four gun *Constitution* appeared to be signaling her escorts. If things went as they always did, the Americans would lower a boat and approach the harbor under a white flag. Then, they would all sit with Yusuf and negotiate a ransom price. But no boats were lowered. The four ships merely sailed back and forth before the harbor, well away from Kaliusa Reef, which had been marked with buoys dropped by an American cutter.

"What's happening?!" the bashaw called to Reis. "Are they coming in?!"

Reis turned to his father-in-law. He was sitting on a plush chair of blue velvet surrounded by several ministers. They were all perched on a shaded veranda high above the harbor.

"No, Excellency," Reis replied. "It doesn't appear they are coming ashore."

Yusuf Karamanli made a face that conveyed deep displeasure. "They always come ashore to bargain!" he whined. "I have more than three hundred of the Christian dogs! Do the Americans know how much it costs me to feed them?!"

Reis ignored Yusuf's petulance. He went back to watching the Americans and tried to read their signal flags. They were too far away, so he gave up and joined Yusuf.

"This Preble impressed me as one who doesn't care about his men," he said.

"Then you should go see him Grand Admiral! Persuade Preble to come to me!" Yusuf growled irritably. "I want my gold!"

"Your Excellency," Reis replied, "I would be taken prisoner. They would want to trade me for some or maybe all of their men. It is best we wait to see what Preble has in mind first."

As he turned his attention back to the American ships he saw them all slowly tack away from Tripoli on a northerly course out to sea.

"They're leaving!" Lieutenant Porter cried. "Where the hell are they going! They just got here!"

Bainbridge looked up at Porter, who stood on the roof of the house with a telescope.

"Pull yourself together, Lieutenant!" Bainbridge ordered, annoyed at the young officer's loss of self-control. "They'll be back! We have to be patient, sir!"

Inwardly, Bainbridge wondered if Preble *would* be back. The plan had been to blockade Tripoli and, as long as they did that, *Philadelphia* wasn't going anywhere. She'd be shot to pieces by the four American ships before she ever cleared the harbor. But with the Americans gone, Reis was free to rearm and man the frigate then take to the open sea. Once there, the pirate admiral could make murderous mischief on shipping while evading American men-of-war bent on sinking him.

"While you are up there, Mr. Porter, see how far along the repairs and refitting are on *Philadelphia!*" Bainbridge called up to his second in command. "After you complete your survey, meet me in my office. I want a full report!"

Porter appeared a half hour later with notes in his hand.

"Shut the door," Bainbridge ordered. The officer obeyed and stood to attention before the captain. "In future, I want you to comport yourself in a dignified fashion, Mr. Porter! You cannot panic in front of your fellow officers like a frightened midshipman!"

"Sir!" acknowledged Porter, his face burning red at the rebuke. He was among of the *Philadelphia* officers who once had a warm relationship with Bainbridge. He now displayed only cool contempt for the captain.

"Your report, if you please."

"Yes, sir," said Porter, glancing at his notes. "All deck guns appear to be remounted. Likewise cannon on the gun deck. It looks as though they are adding guns fore and aft. I could see carriages in place, but no cannon as yet, sir. Any damage to the hull has probably been repaired by now. I think all they are waiting for is sufficient powder and shot. I reckon she'll be ready to sail by late February or early March, sir."

Bainbridge knew Porter was right. Lisle would wait for fair weather. January was cold and stormy, with frequent rain and unfavorable winds.

Bainbridge's face softened as he regarded Porter. "David, I would like to speak with you informally. Please sit down."

Porter silently obeyed.

"I know you are angry with me," Bainbridge began, "but I really wish you would consider the situation we faced…"

"I have, Will," Porter interrupted, anger edging his voice. "There were officers that knew about *Retaliation;* how you surrendered her without firing on the frogs. I spoke up for you when others wanted no part of shipping out with Captain Bainbridge in command of *Philadelphia!*"

It was Bainbridge's turn to be stung. Porter hadn't been there off Guadeloupe when the two heavily armed French frigates surprised him and bore down on his fourteen-gun brig four years earlier. As with the surrender of *Philadelphia*, fighting the enemy then would have been suicide, a bloody massacre of American sailors to no purpose.

"David, we would have been butchered out on that reef," Bainbridge patiently replied. "Every last man would have been murdered if I'd chosen to fight them."

"Then we would have died honorably as men, Will!" said Porter bitterly. "And they wouldn't have an American frigate. Now we are

bloody hostages and our men slaves! And they have a real man-of-war!
Our man-of-war!"

Bainbridge knew the young officer saw it only one way. Fighting and
dying were part of the adventure for Porter and men like him, Bainbridge
supposed, part of the lore. There was no doubt the loss of *Philadelphia*
was a cruel humiliation for the young American Navy. Now all he could
do was hope Preble would act on his recommendations, the sooner
the better.

16

The commodore led his squadron to Syracuse, where the five ships anchored in the Sicilian harbor. The senior officers took rooms at a hotel and the junior officers were left in charge of the ships. Most of the tars had shore leave.

Preble's war council gathered in a spacious suite of rooms provided by the hotelier where the officers dined well, the plates and silverware now gone, replaced with cognac, snifters and cigars. Preble asked O'Bannon to post a marine at the door to ensure their discussion would remain private.

"Gentlemen," began the commodore as he looked over the officers seated at the table, "*Philadelphia* will never leave Tripoli's harbor. We're going to burn her."

The officers stared back at him in astonishment as Preble continued, "All of us here tonight must devise a plan to accomplish that mission. I have my own thoughts on the matter but I wish to hear other ideas."

There was a silent pause of a minute before Lieutenant Issac Hull, commander of *Argus* asked, "Could we not throw hot shot into the harbor, sir?"

This was an obvious plan that Preble had already dismissed. Cannon balls heated in braziers until they glowed red before they were fired from cannons often worked well in close combat with other ships.

"The range is too great," answered Captain Rodgers. "We'd hit some ships, but I doubt we'd do much damage to *Philadelphia*. They have her tucked in there pretty well."

"What if we had a small force go ashore disguised as Tripolines," offered Lieutenant Smith. "They might be able to capture a small boat, row out to *Philadelphia*, get aboard and set her afire."

"From what I saw, the quays are heavily guarded," replied O'Bannon, who was smoking a cigar thoughtfully. "There were guards aboard *Philadelphia* as well." He exhaled a plume of smoke. "But did you notice that little felucca anchored in the harbor when we arrived yesterday? The pilot who brought us in said she was a prize taken by one of the Sicilian captains."

"Yes!" declared Lieutenant Stephen Decatur, the commander of *Enterprise*, one of the squadron's schooners. "I saw her! We could get into the harbor aboard her!"

"How would we do that, Mr. Decatur?" asked Preble.

The young lieutenant thought for a moment. "A small force of volunteers disguised as Tripolines sail into the harbor late at night..."

"We don't know how to navigate the harbor," Rodgers interrupted. "And I'm not aware of anyone in the squadron who speaks their language. Even if we found our way into the inner harbor, we might not get anywhere near *Philadelphia* if we were challenged."

There was more silence, cigar smoke hanging in the still air. Then O'Bannon spoke up again, "The pilot who pointed out the felucca speaks English pretty well. Told me he used to sail merchantmen in and out of Tripoli quite often, so he knows the harbor and he probably speaks the lingua franca."

Preble recalled that, because of the many languages spoken throughout the Mediterranean, the captains and most of the crews of trading vessels spoke a hodge-podge language of Spanish, English, French, Italian, and Arabic.

"Go on Lieutenant," the commodore invited.

"We will wear robes and turbans and get up alongside *Philadelphia*, slip aboard, kill the guards, place fire bombs, ignite them and escape." Decatur eagerly looked around the table. The expressions meeting him were skeptical. Only O'Bannon appeared to like the idea.

"I think it would work, sir," the marine officer finally said. "First, the heathens won't expect it. We'll have surprise on our side. If we move quickly, even if other guards are alerted, they may not understand what's happening. When the Tripolines think of us, they think only of frigates and cannons, not a small band of attackers moving swiftly and silently."

Preble was nodding.

"That's right, sir," continued Decatur. "The ship is highly flammable, as we all know. If we get the fire bombs placed properly below deck, *Philadelphia* will go up like a barn full of straw. They'll never be able to save her."

The faces were no longer skeptical.

"What about escape?" Rodgers finally asked.

"Mr. O'Bannon is right. Speed is of the essence," replied Decatur, "but if we are successful in burning her, then the fate of the raiders will matter little."

Preble regarded Decatur closely. He was, like the others, young, maybe twenty-five. He'd heard a rumor that Decatur's wealthy father had acquired a midshipman's berth for his son when he was eighteen or nineteen after the boy impregnated a servant girl.

Decatur was quite handsome, with a chiseled, clean-shaven jaw, a head of long curly black hair and slate blue eyes that now peered at the commodore intently. There was something else about Decatur beyond his good looks, Preble realized, something intangible he'd often seen in other good officers during his career.

"We should pursue this plan," he finally declared.

"Sir, I request the honor of leading the attack," Decatur quickly responded.

Preble gave the officer a wry smile, had expected nothing less. "Very well, Lieutenant, the mission is yours to command."

"Sir, I request permission to join the lieutenant as his second," O'Bannon said, smiling over at Decatur. "I reckon a few marines would be useful on this here adventure."

Preble hoped O'Bannon would volunteer. The marine officer appeared to be a little older than Decatur and might help steady the Navy officer if things went awry in the harbor.

The admiral commanding the navy of the Kingdom of Two Sicilies, also at war with Tripoli, readily agreed to part with the captured felucca. Preble told him through an interpreter that her use would need to be kept secret but that, calculating the odds for success, the small ship might not be returned. When he asked about the multi-lingual pilot, the admiral told Preble that he could not order the man to join Decatur since he did not serve in the admiral's navy.

Decatur and O'Bannon found Salvador Catalano at the Syracuse customs house the next morning. The Sicilian was about thirty and had a cheerful, eager-to-please demeanor. Catalano told the officers he could speak not only the lingua franca but some Arabic as well.

"I cannot tell you anything about what we are doing," Decatur explained to the pilot. "Only that we are going to Tripoli and we need your help. What we plan is dangerous but we will pay you well if you help us."

"*Si, si, si,*" the diminutive Italian replied. "But *what* you want me to do?!"

"You come with us. Once we are at sea, Commodore Preble will explain the plan," O'Bannon told Catalano. "If you do not wish to help us, then you must stay aboard the flagship until our mission is completed. We will pay you, but not as much money as you will get if you agree to help us."

The felucca, now christened *Intrepid* by Decatur, was towed to the coast of Tripoli by *Constitution*. The crossing from Sicily was stormy, rain falling the entire way. With time to reconsider, Preble thought of cancelling the attack. But after gauging his limited options, he finally decided there was no other choice.

Word spread among the squadron that something very dangerous was planned to "singe the tyrant's beard" so Decatur had more volunteers than he needed. He'd carefully selected twenty-five men he considered the most intelligent and capable in the squadron including a pair of marines recommended by O'Bannon.

After hearing the details, Catalano balked. Preble offered an even bigger bounty, but the Italian shook his head.

"Sir, it is not money! This is madness!" he exclaimed to the officers gathered in Preble's cabin aboard *Constitution*. "The harbor, she is always crowded with ships and there are soldiers and cannons everywhere!"

The commodore, who was growing impatient, decided to appeal to the man's patriotism.

"See here, Catalano. If the bashaw has *Philadelphia*, then he will most assuredly attack the Kingdom of Two Sicilies. There will be *nothing* to stop him from invading Syracuse and you know what that will mean!"

Catalano thought for a moment of his wife and six children. "But... but the British..." he replied doubtfully.

"The British are at war with France and Spain, man!" snapped Preble. "Admiral Nelson has more important things on his mind at the moment then to protect Sicily from the damned Barbary pirates! Once *Philadelphia* is free in the Mediterranean with Murad Reis in command of her guns there will be no end to his bloody depredations! He will lay waste to Syracuse!"

Catalano wasn't sure if Preble was right, didn't even understand everything he'd just heard, but he did know Murad Reis and the man's reputation for violence, so after a few moments he said, "I will help you."

O'Bannon and Decatur were on the lower deck with the *Constitution's* gun captains and the ship's carpenter constructing thirty fire bombs, or incendiaries as Decatur was now calling them. They'd stretched three-foot-square sections of tarred and oiled canvas on the deck then spread two pounds of gunpowder on each canvas section. The carpenter, a squinting old man, prepared two wooden boxes containing quart glass jars filled with whale oil, capped and sealed with bee's wax.

"The fire, she gets hot 'nough, sirs," the grinning carpenter explained to the officers, "them there jars'll blow! That oil catches, you'll have a blaze Lucifer hisself'd be proud of!"

The gunners rolled a jar into each sheet then loosely tied off the canvas bombs with heavy twine before the carpenter painted each with another coat of flammable pitch. Fuses would be stuck into each incendiary and lit by the man carrying it, the loose powder burning furiously rather than exploding as it did when it was compressed. The American raiders would have less than a minute to escape before the fires started.

They brought *Intrepid* up alongside the *Constitution*. The felucca looked even smaller next to the mighty man-of-war, her pitching deck reaching three-quarters of the way to the flagship's waist. There was a steady wind carrying a misting rain over the deck as Decatur, O'Bannon and their two dozen volunteers assembled, all dressed in the robes and turbans Catalano found for them in a Syracuse market. Each raider carried a brace of three pistols inside his robes and a cutlass and dirk in his belt.

The carpenter carefully packed the incendiaries in a water proof cask that was lowered to the pitching deck of *Intrepid*. Two tars placed it in the little craft's hold as Catalano, dressed in robes like the Americans, directed them. The felucca's two bow guns, small five pounders, were charged with langradge and ready to fire if needed.

When all was ready, Preble, face wet from drizzle and sea spray, shook Decatur's hand. James Decatur, Stephen's younger brother, an ensign assigned to *Constitution*, gripped the elder Decatur's arm and silently looked him in the eyes for a long moment.

Then the lieutenant was over the side with O'Bannon, the rest following.

The felucca was rigged with a pair of lateen sails and a set of oars. Laden with too many men as she was, the craft proved difficult to row in the swells, Catalano fighting the tiller but managing to guide *Intrepid* toward Tripoli.

So as not to alert Reis, Preble kept the squadron well away from the harbor. Thus *Intrepid* was obliged to navigate more than five miles along the coast before the lights of the city appeared. The inky darkness was broken only by the flash of phosphorescence in the breaking waves. Catalano steered *Intrepid* toward the lights, her shallow draft letting her slide over the same reef that had trapped *Philadelphia*.

Intrepid rounded the sea wall, where a menacing gun emplacement at the end of the mole remained silent. Catalano gestured for the oars to be shipped and all but the mainsail to be struck as *Intrepid* entered the harbor. Lanterns burning on the quay formed a semi-circle of light around the harbor. O'Bannon saw some figures, guards most likely, wandering along the waterfront but otherwise there was no activity.

Decatur soon pointed at the silhouette of *Philadelphia* looming above them two hundred yards away. Catalano expertly guided the *Intrepid* around anchored fishing boats and corsairs as the Americans of the raiding party stayed as low as they could. The wind slackened considerably and the surface of the harbor was calm as the felucca drew up to *Philadelphia*.

"Stop there!" called a voice in Arabic from the frigate's deck. Catalano heaved to and waved toward the voice. A lantern appeared above them, but its light didn't spill as far as the deck of *Intrepid*, so the Americans appeared to be sleeping forms in the dim light.

"Ahoy!" called Catalano in Arabic. "We are an olive oil trader from the Levant! We lost our anchor in a storm. Sir, may we tie up alongside?!"

"No! Move off!"

Catalano looked at Decatur, his eyes wide. "They won't let us near!" he hissed.

"Get alongside her anyway." the lieutenant whispered.

The pilot did as directed, pretending he didn't hear the order and letting the felucca drift to the port side of *Philadelphia.*

"Fool! I said move away from this ship!" the voice called angrily as O'Bannon, positioned in the bow, seized a cleated step and hauled himself up onto the side of the frigate, scrambling toward the rail. The others followed as a second lantern appeared above the deck of *Intrepid.*

"Americani!" a voice cried in alarm. By then, O'Bannon was over the rail and onto *Philadelphia's* deck. One of the guards charged him, but O'Bannon parried his sword thrust and plunged his dirk into the man's chest. Another guard tried to take aim with his musket at the men climbing aboard, but O'Bannon was there before he could pull the trigger, cutting the man's throat and stifling his cry.

The Americans were aboard. They met the frigate's five surviving guards converging on the scene of the commotion. Cutlasses clashed against pikes and muskets in a short, sharp fight. When it was over, the outnumbered Tripolitans lay slaughtered on the deck, their blood pooling in the scuppers.

"Move!" Decatur ordered the raiders. A line was thrown overboard and the cask containing the incendiaries was hauled aboard and broken open. O'Bannon passed a bomb to each man who scurried off to his pre-assigned target below deck, the incendiaries to be laid wherever there was fuel for a fire.

With the last bomb, O'Bannon made for the fo'castle. He found a lantern and scurried down the companionway to the sail locker tucked beneath the bowsprit. He placed his fire bomb on top of the sails stored there and pulled a fuse and tinderbox from beneath his robes. He struck the flint and the charcloth in the box flared. O'Bannon lit one end of the fuse and slid the other end into the incendiary.

He waited to make sure the fuse remained lit, then O'Bannon dashed for the deck where he paused to listen. Above the slight breeze humming through the rigging he heard some anxious voices and footsteps on the quay. To his astonishment, the killing of the guards seemed to have gone mostly undetected by soldiers on shore and even the sleeping sailors on the ships surrounding *Philadelphia.*

He made for the waist and was joined there by Decatur and the rest of the raiders. After a hasty headcount, they climbed silently down to *Intrepid.* The last man dropped onto her deck as she was pushed away from the frigate's hull. Sails were raised, oars were manned and, once again, Catalano, navigating by the harbor lights, guided the felucca through and around the slumbering ships and out toward the breakwater.

Decatur held his breath. As he watched, clouds of white smoke began seeping from hatches on *Constitution's* stern, waist and bow.

"Come on darlin'," whispered O'Bannon.

In a few moments, the quiet was broken by a rapid series of muffled *whumpf*s as the glass jars containing the whale oil burst inside *Philadelphia.* Just as the old carpenter predicted, crimson flames suddenly billowed from the frigate's lower gun ports and leapt from her hatches. Voices were now crying out ashore and muskets fired. The Americans dropped to the felucca's deck before they realized the shots were alarms. In less than a minute, the fire reached *Philadelphia's* rigging and masts, rising ever higher into the night sky and casting a lurid red glow over the harbor.

Intrepid reached the gun embrasure at the end of the mole where a figure appeared out of the darkness on the rocks, just thirty yards away. A voice called out to them and when no answer came, the soldier fired his musket at the vessel, his ball clipping the main mast. O'Bannon took aim with one of his pistols and returned fire. The man pitched forward onto the rocks before rolling into the sea.

"Good God!" cried Decatur as he turned back to the burning ship. If the raiders didn't know it before, they now understood why fire aboard a wooden ship like the *Philadelphia* was a sailor's worst terror. Scarcely fifteen minutes after lighting the incendiaries, flames fully engulfed the frigate's deck and masts while fire poured from the gun ports. Then her cannons began firing.

"Sweet Jesus and all the Saints!" cried O'Bannon, "her guns were charged!"

In addition to arming the cannon, Murad Reis had neglected to empty the frigate's magazine of the dozens of undamaged kegs of gunpowder salvaged the day *Philadelphia* was captured. The inferno soon reached more than a ton of gunpowder stored deep in her hold.

The Americans looked on in awe as the burning ship seemed at first to shudder then slowly rise out of the water in two ragged sections, the massive explosion in her bowels reducing the frigate to scorched timbers and spars.

The roar of the blast and its concussion reached the *Intrepid* a moment later, violently rocking the little vessel and the celebrating Americans cheering on her deck.

17

Quaking with rage, Bashaw Yusuf Karamanli stood in the early morning mist atop his castle wall overlooking the smoking remains of *Philadelphia* and the collateral destruction her explosion had wrought. The fire burned five other ships anchored around her to their waterlines, including the merchantman *Integrity*. At least ten other vessels in the harbor had been severely damaged by the fire and subsequent explosion.

What remained of the bashaw's grandest prize had sunk and now only her ribs were visible above the surface, the charred hulls of the other vessels half submerged or capsized, surrounding *Philadelphia's* blackened skeleton. Debris littered the quay and the stench of burned human flesh hung in the still air. A shattered mizzen yard from *Philadelphia* had been shot into the air by the blast and was now protruding like an arrow from the façade of a chandler's shop on the quay.

Yusuf tore his eyes away from the scene and glared at Murad Reis, who stood silently next to him on the rampart. The bashaw tried to speak to the grand admiral, but only spittle flew from his lips as he sputtered incomprehensible words.

Reis was deep inside his moaning Fatima when the alarm from the quay went up in the early morning hours. He'd pulled on a robe and raced to the roof of his villa where he watched in horror as the flames ripped unchecked across *Philadelphia's* deck, the dried wood impregnated with pitch burning like cedar shavings. The fire scurried up her tarred rigging and out onto her spars, the crackling and snapping of the blaze clearly audible a half mile away.

At that moment Reis knew there was no chance of saving *Philadelphia*. He'd once seen a fire aboard a sloop off Ireland and was well aware of how fast a ship could be consumed by flames.

Philadelphia became a giant torch in the center of Tripoli's harbor, flames swirling hundreds of feet into the night sky creating their own wind. He could feel the blasts of heat as nearby ships ignited. Their crews made half-hearted attempts to extinguish the flames before leaping overboard, swimming for their lives after realizing they'd be roasted in the firestorm.

The frigate's eighteen port guns were charged and pointed seaward in case the harbor was attacked by Americans. As Murad Reis watched in disbelief, *Philadelphia's* anchor broke away. Free of her mooring, the ship swung around, the port cannon now aimed at the city. The fire reached the guns' touchholes and one at a time they fired, their twenty-four-pound balls randomly smashing into buildings along Tripoli's waterfront. A ball clipped the corner of a tower above Reis, sending chunks of stone and a cloud of mortar cascading onto the grand admiral.

The explosion in the powder magazine threw Reis to the rooftop. He'd managed to get to his feet in time to see flaming wreckage falling from the sky onto the anchored ships and quay, where guards were cowering behind any cover they could find. As furious as he was at losing *Philadelphia*, Reis knew as he watched the catastrophe that his own rage would be no match for his father-in-law's.

"How did this happen, Grand Admiral!" boomed the bashaw, his pudgy fists clenched and his face ashen as we wandered about the rampart.

"It appears the Americans managed to get aboard her, Excellency," Reis explained stiffly with an awkward gesture at the remains of the frigate. "We found several of the guards floating in the harbor this morning. They were burned, but some had sword and knife wounds. They were murdered."

"I shall slaughter every American dog I hold captive! I will have my revenge!" bellowed Yusuf as he blindly stomped around. "Bring that son of a jackal Bainbridge to me. I shall cut off his balls and I shall feed his balls to him!"

Reis ignored the bashaw.

"And…and, bring, bring all his officers with him…they shall watch as I cut off Bainbridge's balls! Then I shall cut the throats of each of the Christian dogs one by one! I shall *have my revenge!*"

Reis, eyebrow cocked, glanced over at Sidi Mohammed Dghies. The bashaw's foreign minister was visibly trembling under Yusuf's tirade. Reis felt no apprehension, having witnessed many such tantrums. To murder the Americans, he knew, meant losing any chance of collecting ransom.

"Then…then…bring that Danish cunt here to me…he is part of this treason! I shall jam a pike up his arse and break it off at the hilt!" screamed Yusuf in frustration. He held his clenched fists above his head and roared his frustration and impotence to the sky, knowing full well he could not harm his prisoners or the Dane, "Ahhhhhhhhh!"

Spent, Yusuf fell to his knees and pounded the rooftop with his fist, tears falling from his eyes, mucus dripping from his nose and collecting in his luxurious black beard.

Two Turkish janissaries stood by, eyes wide in shock and horror, uncertain if they should do as Yusuf demanded and bring the American prisoners to the roof.

Reis stayed them with an outstretched hand. He walked over to the bashaw and gently raised him to his feet. "Come, Babu, come," he said quietly. "Let us go to your apartments. We shall talk all this over after you rest and you've had your tea. I will have a girl massage your back. Then we will decide how you will make the Christians pay for their crimes."

Sobbing now, the bashaw allowed the grand admiral to steer him toward the stairs.

The worsening weather during the night forced *Constitution* and the rest of the squadron to sail further out to sea, where the commodore waited through the night, anxiety twisting like a worm in his gut. A little after the start of the middle watch – about two o'clock - a lookout reported a red glow on the horizon, but Preble choked down the initial optimism he felt, refusing to believe it was *Philadelphia* ablaze.

The morning hours passed with no sign of Decatur. By noon, Preble began wondering if the mysterious glow had in fact been *Intrepid* burning. He sat alone now in his cabin imagining the worst and questioning the wisdom of sacrificing more than twenty brave men and two fine officers like Decatur and O'Bannon.

Captain Rodgers, ignoring the standing order to knock first, burst into the commodore's cabin.

"A lateen sail, sir!"

Feeling his heart leap, Preble raced with Rodgers to the quarterdeck. An officer handed the commodore his spyglass and pointed south. "Is... is it Decatur?!" Preble asked excitedly.

"Not sure, sir. It's a triangular sail for certain," the officer replied.

Preble's stomach churned as *Constitution* and the ships of the squadron sailed south to close with the approaching vessel.

Thirty minutes later a lookout on the top called down, "*Intrepid* approaching!"

Rodgers immediately ordered signal flags raised: "Have you completed the business you were sent on?"

Preble anxiously watched the approaching ship for an answer. He saw the flags being raised then felt a rush of relief and joy as he read the return signal, "I have completed the business I was sent on."

"What happened, sir?!" Lieutenant Porter asked Bainbridge as the captain entered the house in Tripoli holding the American officers.

Bainbridge broke into a wide grin. "They burned her!"

All of *Philadelphia's* officers crowded around their commander chattering excitedly. "It looks as though our men got aboard and set her alight! The guns we heard were *Philadelphia's* cannon the bastards loaded! The fools left powder in her magazine. That was the explosion! There's nothing left of her!"

The men cheered wildly. Porter slumped into a chair, tears in his eyes, the stain of disgrace for losing the man-of-war to a petty tyrant wiped away by the flames, at least for everyone but Bainbridge.

The captain held up his hands for quiet. "Lisle told me the gorilla is apoplectic," he continued. "I'm afraid he plans to take his rage out on all of us and our enlisted men as well."

"It doesn't matter, sir," declared Porter, wiping away his tears. "As long as he doesn't have *Philadelphia!*"

Bainbridge had met Reis on the parapet an hour earlier and gazed in bittersweet satisfaction at the shattered remains of his command. The grand admiral promised that his crew would suffer more than ever for the temerity of the attack.

"My countrymen were bound to prosecute the war your king started!" Bainbridge protested angrily. "They had to burn my ship!"

"It wasn't your ship, you ass! It was mine!" the Scotsman angrily retorted.

A messenger arrived at the consulate bearing a note from Nicholas Nissen shortly after Bainbridge announced the news of *Philadelphia's* burning.

"*Dear William,*" it read. "*I am sorry to report that as punishment for the burning of the frigate, your crew has been placed on half rations and ordered to work two more hours every day. I persuaded Yusuf to exclude you and your officers from these labors but he has confined you to your house. He told me he has increased the ransom for the officers and crew to half a million dollars. He has also forbidden me to visit you as he believes I was somehow responsible for what occurred.*"

Bainbridge had seen his men pulling the bashaw's sledges heaped with boulders. It was work unfit for lowly beasts let alone American seamen. He swore under his breath and walked to the garden gate. Sure enough, six armed Turks stood guard in the street outside. He strode back to the house where he sat down to write a letter of protest to the bashaw, demanding his men be released from the torturous labor. When he was done with that letter, he wrote another to Preble, explaining Yusuf's cruelty and pleading that his men be ransomed. After he signed it, he summoned a midshipman.

"Sir?" the boy asked, standing at attention.

"Mr. Abernathy," replied Bainbridge. "Please pick me a lemon from one of the trees in the garden and bring it here."

Jefferson finally received the shocking news of the *Philadelphia's* capture in March, 1804. The delay was due to the oldest reason in the military: bureaucratic incompetence. The civilian naval agent in Leghorn responsible for forwarding Preble's dispatches simply let all the squadron's mail pile up.

The president became physically ill when Secretary Smith told him that the five-year-old frigate, commanded by one of the navy's most senior captains, ran aground a couple of miles off Tripoli and been surrendered to the enemy without a fight, all officers and hands taken hostage. It seemed incomprehensible to Jefferson, simply impossible.

But the look on Smith's face told him it was true.

The president decided there and then to relieve Preble and redouble the prosecution of the war with Tripoli. Congress needed little convincing to provide the necessary funding once the news of *Philadelphia* became public. Americans were universally outraged, demanding that their leaders take action.

18

William Eaton paced the hallway outside Jefferson's office, unsure why the president had summoned him for a second meeting. It was possible Jefferson objected to the vigorous, maybe even forceful lobbying Eaton had been conducting to find support for his plan to topple Yusuf and place Hamet Karamanli back on the throne of Tripoli.

Through his close friend, Representative Samuel Lyman of Massachusetts, Eaton arranged meetings with any number of congressmen and senators. Most of these meetings ended politely but without the commitments of support he needed for the overland march and attack on Derna. Treasury Secretary Albert Gallatin, Jefferson's taciturn, Swiss-born financier, flatly told Eaton his idea was absurd.

"Men like you - soldiers - you think war is the solution to every dispute," Gallatin declared with a patronizing smirk. "You always underestimate how much money war will cost and then you overestimate the actual value of any success you claim to achieve. I prefer negotiations and paying tribute to fighting a war. You know what it costs and you also know the outcome."

Eaton's temper was mercurial. It was all the former consul could do to not call the secretary a coward to his face. Now, standing in the foyer of the president's house, he was glad he'd held his tongue.

Jefferson's secretary presently joined him and motioned Eaton into a meeting room down the hall from the president's office.

"Mr. Eaton arrives!" the president cheerfully called as he entered.

Jefferson met him and shook his hand as Eaton bowed slightly. "Thank you for inviting me, Mr. President."

Jefferson turned to the men seated around a gleaming maple table. "I think you have had occasion to become acquainted with most of these gentlemen. Secretary Smith you know, Secretary of War Dearborn, Mr. Madison and Mr. Gallatin, of course. And, this is Captain Samuel Barron. I don't believe you two gentlemen have met."

Eaton shook each hand in turn before taking Barron's. Captain Barron wore an ornate naval uniform and was about Eaton's height. His sallow face was long with pinched, plain features beneath a head of thin brown hair going to gray. The captain offered Eaton an indifferent handshake and a weaker smile as the president invited everyone to be seated.

"Thank you for joining us, Mr. Eaton," Jefferson began. "The loss of *Philadelphia* has changed the complexion of our business with Tripoli, as you may have read in the newspapers."

"Yes, sir, I have seen the reports," Eaton replied. "A new naval squadron is to be dispatched to the Mediterranean as soon as possible under captain, or should I say, Commodore Barron."

Barron gave a slight nod.

"Exactly," Jefferson continued. "Now that this barbarian Karamanli has *Philadelphia*, there's no end to the trouble he'll make for our shipping. His grand admiral – this Murad Reis - will also be in a position to attack our blockaders with *Philadelphia* as heavily armed as she is."

"I have met both the bashaw and the Scotsman, Lisle," Eaton said sternly. "They are nothing more than a pair of common criminals! You are quite right about them Mr. President!"

Ignoring Eaton's interruption, Jefferson went on. "Along with sending out the new squadron, we have been giving your enterprise new consideration."

Eaton brightened and sat forward.

"Perhaps you might help us better understand how you would go about executing it," Jefferson said with a gesture to his secretary who unveiled a map of North Africa that had been hanging hidden on the wall.

Eaton hesitated. His plan up to this moment was an ever-evolving abstract concept. Now Jefferson wanted meat on the bones. During his days in the Ohio Valley, Eaton had distinguished himself as an officer unafraid of risk and possessing a talent for improvisation. He had also been a schoolteacher. Eaton knew he must now call on all these skills.

He took the proffered pointer from the secretary and turned to his audience.

"Hamet Karamanli, as I have explained, is the despot Yusuf's elder brother. He and I became friends during my tenure in North Africa. At this time he is...here," Eaton pointed at the Egyptian coast, "in Alexandria or nearby. In his last letter to me dated January, he told me Yusuf tried to lure him back to Tripoli from his exile in Leghorn on Malta. Hamet feared he would be assassinated, so he fled to Egypt where he is now in hiding."

He looked at the others. All appeared attentive with the exception of Albert Gallatin, who was cleaning his finger nails with a penknife.

"What I propose is to sail to Egypt, find Hamet, recruit a battalion of volunteers and march cross country from here," he pointed at Alexandria, "to here." The pointer tapped a place on the coast called Derne.

"Derne is the easternmost city of Tripoli. I was there three years ago and saw that it is weakly defended by a garrison of fewer than one hundred soldiers. Turks mainly, who are not particularly motivated or well trained. The city can be stormed by a relatively small and well-armed force attacking from land. Once taken, Derne would become our base of operations. With Hamet at the head of our column, the Tripolines will undoubtedly rise up against Yusuf. I would then propose a coordinated land and sea attack on Tripoli itself. When he is returned to the throne, Hamet will declare eternal peace with America and free our captives and property. In fact," Eaton lied smoothly, looking at Gallatin as he did, "he guaranteed me he will refund from his treasury all of the tribute and ransom America has ever paid Tripoli as well as the cost of my enterprise."

Gallatin suppressed a yawn without looking up from his finger nails.

"Is Hamet trustworthy?" asked James Madison. "What are our assurances he won't betray us after we help him?"

"Hamet is not a bloodthirsty pirate like his brother, Mr. Secretary," replied Eaton. "He is educated and articulate. Most important, like each of us here, he loves his wife and children. This monster Yusuf, Hamet's own brother mind, holds Hamet's family hostage in Tripoli and our friend wants nothing more than to be reunited with them. He has sworn we will have his allegiance if we help him bring about that happy outcome."

"Why would the people of Tripoli rally to Hamet's banner?" asked Jefferson.

"Because, sir, the Tripolines hate Yusuf," Eaton said angrily, recalling the barbarity he'd witnessed in Tripoli, the public crucifixions, dismemberments and beheadings. "He's a cruel and selfish tyrant who brutalizes his own people as well as his captives. Most of his citizens live in squalid poverty, while the hairy baboon wallows in his luxury and perversions."

Secretary Dearborn was a distinguished veteran of the Revolutionary War. He wore long gray side whiskers, closely cropped hair, and was presently rubbing his chin, lost in thought. After a moment, Dearborn shifted in his seat and eyed Eaton.

"How far is that march, Mr. Eaton?" he asked.

"Five hundred miles, Mr. Secretary."

"That is desert, is it not?" asked Smith.

"Along the coast the terrain is desert steppe, sir," Eaton said, turning back to the map. "There are frequent winter rains and considerable vegetation, not the endless sea of sand you would find in the Sahara further south. My army would march along or near the coast during February, the coolest month. Because this is a caravan route, I am reliably informed there are numerous water holes and many cisterns and wells along the way. We would rendezvous here at the Bay of Bomba with a ship, resupply the column, and complete the march to Derne. I estimate four weeks from departure to attack."

"This...this column you are talking about," Dearborn interjected. "What is its number and composition? We cannot send Americans..."

"Five hundred volunteers, sir," Eaton interrupted. "More than ample to overrun Derne's defenses."

"What is the motivation of these *volunteers*? Certainly not patriotism!" Dearborn declared with a bark of laughter.

"No indeed, sir," Eaton smiled indulgently. "Money would be their motivation. I will hire mercenaries in Alexandria...soldiers of fortune, if you will."

"How much will all of this cost," asked Gallatin irritably. Eaton had already told him, but he answered the question anyway.

"Forty thousand dollars, Mr. Secretary," Eaton replied.

Gallatin gave Jefferson a peeved look and said, "We can buy peace for forty thousand dollars, Mr. President! Why should we give this man..."

"You know my sentiments on that score, Mr. Gallatin," the president gently chided the secretary before looking back at Eaton.

"Mr. Eaton, what makes you believe you can hire these mercenaries?"

"Hamet has already recruited two hundred Tripoline exiles, sir," Eaton lied again. "And there may well be hundreds more like them we can recruit or even persuade at no cost to join my enterprise. There are also Bedouins, Arabs, as well as assorted Europeans for hire. I would only need a small force of American marines to assist me in organizing my army and to keep order during the march."

"Jesus Christ, man!" Dearborn swore with a wave and good natured smile. "This plan is preposterous! How in God's name will you control a column of that size speaking a dozen different tongues?"

"Because I speak them, sir," Eaton replied. "And those I don't speak, I can learn quickly. I have a gift for languages, you see."

Dearborn was looking at Eaton with a puzzled expression because the consul had answered not in English, but in fluent Arabic.

He repeated his comment now in English, producing smiles from everyone but Gallatin and Barron.

"And what are your own qualifications for leading this battalion, sir?" Dearborn asked.

"As a very young man, I was a private soldier in the Continental Army, Mr. Secretary. In fact," he added, "I held your horse outside a tavern near Saratoga while you and some other officers took refreshment."

Dearborn smiled and Eaton continued. "I worked briefly in the Vermont House of Delegates after my graduation from Dartmouth, but that service was, well, boring. I rejoined the army and served with General Wayne in Ohio country as a captain in the American Legion."

Dearborn's eyebrows went up at this. Eaton's unit was a kind of elite regiment that had distinguished itself as guerilla fighters and scouts during Mad Anthony's campaign against the Miami.

"You asked about my qualifications, Mr. Secretary," Eaton went on. "Do you recall the battle at Fort Recovery?"

"I certainly do! Eighty or so of our men repelled repeated attacks by many hundred savages!"

"I commanded there, Mr. Secretary."

Nodding, Dearborn glanced at the others. "That was a very impressive piece of soldiering, gentlemen."

"I don't like it, Mr. President," declared Captain Barron in a high-pitched, raspy voice as he looked at Eaton with contempt. "I think I will be far more successful directing my squadron in attacking and reducing Tripoli."

Jefferson glanced at Barron. "I take your opinion under advisement, but Commodore Preble has endorsed Mr. Eaton's plan and I believe it is worth the attempt."

He waved a hand at Eaton now. "Please be seated, Mr. Eaton." Jefferson looked around at the others. "I do not see a great deal of risk here, gentlemen. When Mr. Eaton gets to Alexandria, if he is unsuccessful recruiting this army of his then little is lost. If he is successful, and his march proceeds as planned, we may well have a friend in the region once and for all."

Jefferson was working at his desk three days later when his secretary entered and silently laid an envelope on the president's desk. A few minutes later, Jefferson opened what appeared to be a formal dispatch from the British Admiralty, a highly unusual communication to say the least.

"*My Dear President Jefferson,*" read a sheet of heavy paper with an elaborately embossed crest of gold, "*I must commend the actions of your heroic Naval forces off Tripoli and most especially, the courageous attack on her harbor and the burning of the captured United States frigate* Philadelphia *without the loss of a single man. This was truly the most bold and daring act of the age. Your Humble Servant, Adm. Horatio Nelson,* HMS Victory."

Astonished, both at the news and at its esteemed messenger, Jefferson leapt from his seat and let out a whoop. His secretary immediately appeared, an anxious look on the young man's face. "Are you alright, Mr. President?"

"Mr. Burwell!" cried Jefferson holding out the letter. "This is from Lord Nelson! He reports *Philadelphia* has been burned at Tripoli!"

Burwell took the letter, read it wide-eyed.

"Please...please, Mr. Burwell," the president said excitedly, "you must get me more news as quickly as you can!"

A wave of relief flooded over Jefferson. The loss of *Philadelphia* was a humiliation to all associated with her capture, including the president. It was too late to recall Barron and he doubted that he would have changed his mind had he learned earlier that the frigate was destroyed. More ships were needed in the Mediterranean, Congress had approved the necessary appropriation, and Barron was senior to Preble on the Navy's sacrosanct list of captains. There was also Eaton's secret mission to consider, and just to make certain, Jefferson had also ordered his ambassador Tobias Lear to accompany the squadron to Tripoli should the opportunity for a diplomatic solution present itself.

19

After *Philadelphia* was burned, the American blockade continued in the hopes the bashaw might decide it was time to negotiate a peace. But Yusuf made no move. After six weeks off Tripoli, crews bored and water and provisions running low, Preble ordered the squadron to Syracuse, leaving *Vixen* and *Siren* behind to keep Reis' corsairs at bay.

In a letter to Secretary Smith, the commodore recommended Lieutenant Decatur for promotion to captain and thought of doing the same for O'Bannon but he knew the president would only be able to push one promotion through the Navy's byzantine chain of command.

For his invaluable service, Preble gave Catalano two hundred dollars in gold. The rest of *Intrepid's* raiders were each awarded a bonus of ten dollars and two weeks shore leave on Sicily.

When the squadron dropped anchor in Syracuse, the celebration was loud and drunken. It was a warm evening in late April as Preble sat in his hotel suite considering the next move against the bashaw. Out on the streets, he could hear some of his men singing and carousing in the city's *osterias*.

While an all out naval bombardment of Tripoli seemed the obvious way to bring Yusuf to his knees, such an attack on the city, Preble knew, would have limited effect. His flagship or any other frigate for that matter, would be unable to get their guns close enough to shore. And while his brigs and schooners could sail in nearly to the breakwater, these vessels lacked sufficient firepower to do much damage.

In his most recent lemon juice message, Bainbridge proposed gunboats as the solution. But Preble had no gunboats, fifty-foot-long, shallow draft barges, fixed with traversing cannons. Preble had seen batteries of these anchored off the Syracuse harbor, positioned there, the Sicilian admiral told him, to ward off marauding pirate ships.

As he pondered the problem, somewhere outside a fiddle played an Irish jig. O'Bannon. Preble smiled to himself as he rose and left his room in search of the lieutenant.

On the cobbled street before the hotel, tables and chairs were set out under lanterns. Preble seldom wore anything but his full dress uniform, regardless of the weather, but it was so uncomfortably warm this evening he was in shirtsleeves.

O'Bannon was sitting with a pretty raven-haired girl at one of the tables, a bottle of wine and his fiddle between them. The *senorina* was clearly entranced with the handsome American officer, but Preble knew her father would have a fit of rage if he saw his un-chaperoned daughter in the company of a strange man in a public place.

"Lieutenant? A word?" Preble called. O'Bannon turned, saw the commodore and stood to attention. Like Preble, he was in shirtsleeves.

"Sir!" the marine replied as the young lady came out of her spell and realized where she was and what she was doing. She flashed O'Bannon a brilliant smile and hurried off into the night.

"At ease, Mr. O'Bannon," Preble ordered as he took the seat just vacated by the girl. "I'd be careful with the ladies of good character, sir... and even some with questionable character! Their fathers and brothers don't take kindly to such attentions."

O'Bannon, still standing, wore a sheepish smile. "Yes, sir, I am aware of the social customs hereabouts," he replied, "but that young lass, well, sir, she was so very beautiful..."

Preble laughed and said, "Join me in a drink?"

A waiter put a bottle of cognac and glasses on the table. O'Bannon sat and poured for them both. The two officers touched glasses.

"I never thanked you for volunteering to accompany Mr. Decatur," Preble remarked, sitting back in his chair. "I wished to promote you as reward for your courage, Mr. O'Bannon, but I fear that isn't possible at this time."

"Politics, I reckon, sir," O'Bannon replied with a shrug and resigned smile. "What matters is that Scotch son of a bitch – begging your pardon - he won't have *Philadelphia*. That's reward enough for me."

Preble sipped his liquor and eyed O'Bannon over the glass then said, "I need your advice once again, lieutenant. It has been suggested we use gunboats to attack Tripoli. What are your thoughts?"

O'Bannon recalled the armed barrages outside the Syracuse harbor. "They'd work, sure enough. You can place big guns on them. A lot of men, too. With enough of 'em we could get close to the breakwater with your flagship and the rest of the squadron providing the cover fire. If the Tripolines want to come out looking for a hand-to-hand fight, we have enough marines and tars aboard to oblige 'em, sir."

This had been Preble's thinking but he appreciated the lieutenant's confirmation.

"I believe I can buy or borrow some of the admiral's unused gunboats," Preble replied thoughtfully. "He has eight or ten of them tied up at the quay. But rowing and sailing them across the Mediterranean? They're shallow drafted and heavy, fit for in-shore duty but not really seaworthy. Our men wouldn't know how to handle them. We're bound to lose some or all of the boats if we encountered a storm in the open sea."

"Maybe the admiral would loan us some of his sailors," replied O'Bannon. "One's who know how to sail the gunboats, sir."

That possibility hadn't occurred to Preble and it was precisely why he'd sought out O'Bannon's counsel. "That's an excellent thought. It'll be slow going, no matter what."

"Aye, but worth the time, expense and effort, even if one or two of them were lost. Once we get to Tripoli, sir, we'd be able to attack and lay siege to the city."

Preble was naturally risk averse. If he went into battle, he wanted to know that victory was certain. But the marine officer's reasoning was sound.

"Very well," he finally replied after a sip of his drink. "I'll pay a visit to the admiral in the morning. You should go see if you can find your lady friend."

It took almost a week to make the crossing from Sicily, but Preble's squadron, now included six gunboats and a couple of bomb ketches, small vessels armed with heavy mortars, on loan from the Kingdom of Two Sicilies, along with fifty sailors to man them, plus a contingent of Sicilian marines.

Cautious as always, Preble ordered the squadron to conduct maneuvers with the vessels before departing Syracuse. Combat with the Tripolitan gunboats would be unlike anything his crews were used to, so for more than a month they practiced their gunnery but also drilled in repelling boarders and assaulting the enemy's barges from the boats.

Constitution was trailing four of the cumbersome gunboats while *Enterprise* and *Siren* each towed a ketch and a gunboat. Aboard the barges and ketches, Sicilian sailors were struggling to keep the vessels steady in the light swells.

O'Bannon was back aboard his brig, *Argus*, commanded by Lieutenant Issac Hull. He was exercising his marines in close quarters combat under the hot June sun when the coast of Tripoli came into view. O'Bannon knew the squadron had been fortunate not to encounter a storm, and now that they were finally closing on the African coast, Preble was no doubt breathing a sigh of relief that none of the borrowed gunboats had been lost.

Small and speedy Tripolitan scout craft scurried around the American flotilla for days, veering off in haste if *Argus* gave chase, racing back to the city to report what they saw to Grand Admiral Murad Reis. When he heard that Preble was bringing gun boats, Reis had ordered his own fleet of armed barges arrayed in a defensive line before the harbor.

Late the next afternoon, the American squadron dropped anchor* three miles off Tripoli and Preble ordered all senior officers to *Constitution* for a war council.

"Gentlemen," Preble began. "You no doubt saw the harbor is defended by Yusuf's own gunboats. He looks to have almost twenty of them plus assorted corsairs in a line of about two miles across the harbor, all ready for action."

The stifling cabin was crowded but the sweating officers listened intently to Preble.

"We won't disappoint him," Preble went on, his steely eyes flashing. "We shall attack on the morrow. Captain Decatur will command."

Several officers shook the smiling Decatur's hand. Preble then presented his order of battle and dismissed the excited officers. Decatur waited for O'Bannon to join him on the waist. Next to the new captain stood his younger brother James Decatur, assigned by Preble to command one of the American gunboats. O'Bannon would be aboard James' barge leading his marines off *Argus* as well as a platoon of Sicilian marines.

"This is what we've been waiting for Presley!" declared Stephen with a grin. "If we give a good show, the men of *Philadelphia* will be free this time tomorrow."

"Aye, sir!" replied O'Bannon excitedly, shooting his thumb at the bashaw's distant castle. "Jamie here will put one of his shot right up that fat bastard's arse! And my boys can't wait to slaughter the savages!"

---

* *The Mediterranean Sea has virtually no tide, which makes anchoring possible.*

The beaming James Decatur was the spitting image of his brother. In fact, when he'd met them, O'Bannon had thought they were twins.

Under a cloudless azure sky, the line of American gunboats and the two bomb ketches slowly approached the Tripolitan vessels, laying in a long line two hundred yards from the harbor's entrance. The cannons on the American boats were primed, with fifty armed men aboard each vessel. Behind the line of American gunboats, the brigs and schooners waited, ready to swoop in and provide fire support to the vulnerable gunboats.

O'Bannon and James Decatur stood on the bow of the gunboat designated number five next to the muzzle their twenty-four pound cannon. They were joined by Ensign Henry Wadsworth, a close friend of James', who was glassing *Constitution* a mile behind the flotilla, waiting for the signal to attack.

A few of Reis' nervous gunners had already fired at them but the balls splashed into the sea well short of the advancing American battle line. The rowers on the gunboats strained at the oars, the distance between the enemy fleets gradually closing. There was nervous chatter from the armed men on the boat as the enemy crews came into view.

The red signal flag ordering the attack shot up *Constitution's* main top gallant mast. James turned to the gun crew and cried, "Fire!"

Almost simultaneously the gunboat fleet's six cannons roared, their concentrated fire aimed at the Tripolitan boats clustered around the harbor entrance. The well-aimed balls sliced through the pirate crews, decapitating and dismembering several and panicking others. James ordered his gun loaded with langradge. The American crew, far more skilled at their deadly trade than the Tripolitans, instantly obeyed and fired on James' command at the nearest enemy gunship. The chunks of scrap metal and grapeshot cut the pirate boat's crew to pieces. A poorly aimed return shot went over the Americans.

"Close! Make ready to board!" James ordered.

"Here we go lads!" O'Bannon called, drawing his sword with one hand and cocking his pistol with the other. His men were ready, muskets primed, bayonets fixed. The Sicilians were right beside them, their own officer translating the American's words. O'Bannon knew that among these men, there were scores to settle with the Tripolitans and they appeared as ready as his men to bleed the enemy.

Reis was aboard *Meshouda* behind his line of gunboats watching the incoming Americans and wearing a smug expression of confidence. His fleet outnumbered the enemy by at least three to one. He expected the Americans to fire and retreat, but the oars and square rigged sails kept pulling the attackers toward his boats. No matter, he thought to himself. This was the sort of combat he preferred and the Americans were falling right into his trap.

Through the thick cannon smoke, Reis could see his boats moving out to meet the enemy, his men ready with grappling hooks, a horde of fighters on each of Tripoli's gunboats preparing to board the American vessels.

"Admiral! Look!" said Reis' second in command pointing to the right.

Several Tripolitan gunboats were already making for the inner harbor. There were dead and wounded on their decks, but the boats otherwise appeared to be capable of fighting.

"Cowards!" screamed Reis, his words lost in the roar of the guns and now, musket and pistol fire. "Turn back! Fight!" he cried, waving his arms furiously.

The boat commanders ignored the grand admiral who was forced to return his attention to the unfolding battle.

Siren, under full sail, and her gun ports open, swept in close and blasted one of his gunboats with a full broadside from a hundred yards. The clumsy craft capsized and immediately sank taking most of her crew with her. *Siren* sailed on for another quarter mile, came about, quickly took aim on another Tripolitan boat with her eight starboard guns and fired again. This time, two shot struck an enemy craft, one of them holing the gunboat at the water line. The crippled boat's commander beat a hasty retreat toward the breakwater, his vessel severely listing.

Behind the American gunboats, the bomb ketches were methodically lobbing their thirteen inch explosive shells into the city where they randomly fell among the warren of streets, killing few civilians but terrifying everyone. The Tripolitan shore batteries not yet silenced by the covering fire of *Vixen, Siren, Argus, Enterprise* and *Nautilus* were trying to hit the two mortar ketches, but their shells were falling everywhere except on the American vessels. Reis cursed the miserable gunnery as he ordered a signal flag raised. Attack.

The grappling hooks flew over gunboat five's rail. The ropes went taught as the pirates hauled the two vessels together.

"Marines! Skirmish line!" bellowed O'Bannon over the cannon fire. The Sicilian officer translated. In moments there were two ranks of marines aiming their muskets at the rail, the kneeling Americans in their blue coats with red facings, the Sicilians standing above them in short green jackets trimmed with black and gold.

A score of screaming pirates brandishing pistols, scimitars, pikes and hatchets appeared out of the smoke on the rail, ready to board the American gunboat and slaughter her terrified crew.

"Fire!" cried O'Bannon.

The precise volley of musket fire cut down every attacker in sight. "Forward!" O'Bannon cried. In an instant, the American and Sicilian marines, joined by tars armed with swords and tomahawks, were swarming over the Tripolitan gunboat's deck.

Reis watched the melee before him in shock. This was not expected. Americans never closed for hand-to-hand combat! And there, leading the assault was that son of a leprous whore O'Bannon!

The Tripolitan crew was stunned as the marines and sailors rushed them, screeching like banshees. O'Bannon fired his pistol into the back of a fleeing pirate then swung his sword cleanly slicing off the arm of another.

James Decatur was fighting a Turk with his blade, the sharp clash of steel rising above the din of shouting voices, the cries of the wounded and the staccato of musket fire. One of the Sicilians went down and screamed as he was run through with a pike. An American sailor saw the killing, swung his cutlass and struck the pirate in the neck, producing a torrent of arterial blood that splashed over the deck.

O'Bannon slipped in gore as he went after a Tripolitan officer and was nearly chopped in half by a battle axe. The brutal blade struck the wooden deck inches from O'Bannon's head. He rolled over and plunged his sword into the chest of the Turk wielding the weapon.

Seven or eight Tripolitans and Turks were on their knees begging for their lives while a crowd of vengeful Sicilian marines surrounded them near the stern. Despite their pitiful pleas they were butchered with bayonets and swords.

Terrified pirates saw the massacre of their comrades and began to flee in panic before the savage and merciless attack, leaping headlong over the rails and swimming desperately away from the blood bath.

Reis, stunned, looked to his left. The scene was the same. His boats were either retreating under the fury and accuracy of the American cannon fire or were being overrun by the murderous enemy. As he watched, *Argus* fired her two bow chasers into a fleeing enemy gunboat, the five-pound balls ricocheting around inside the craft killing or maiming a half dozen of his men.

Reis had seen enough. "Raise the retreat flag," he angrily ordered just as he saw the tall marine officer emerge from the smoke drenched in blood, his chapeau bras gone. Reis watched him run his blade through another pirate who'd fallen to the deck on his hands and knees. O'Bannon swung the sword and lopped off the man's head in one stroke. Another American officer stood beside him, priming his pistol and looking about for a victim.

"Give me a musket!" snarled Reis. One of the pirates handed his weapon to the grand admiral, who took aim at O'Bannon from one hundred yards, the limit of the gun's range. He fired. The smoke cleared, but the marine officer was still standing, now looking Reis' way.

The ball struck James Decatur in the head as he fired his pistol. The young naval officer fell to the deck, his eyes open, his mouth twisted.

"Don't try to speak," O'Bannon said to him as he knelt down. "Wadsworth!" he called to the ensign who was standing nearby. "Guard him!"

O'Bannon rose in time to see the gaudy Tripolitan flagship enter the harbor, the grand admiral standing on the quarterdeck wearing an evil grin and pointing at him.

Gunboat five's cannon had just been fired and *Meshouda* would be gone before it was reloaded so O'Bannon snatched a musket away from one of his marines. He took a deep breath, steadied his aim and pulled the trigger. The ball went wide, *Meshouda* now well out of range as she cleared the breakwater. Reis tilted his head back and laughed as O'Bannon threw the weapon to the deck in frustration.

Gunboat five fired another charge of langrage at the last of the fleeing enemy vessels, killing and wounding pirates that hadn't taken cover. O'Bannon found the wounded James Decatur sprawled on the bloody deck, Wadsworth holding his head and sobbing.

"He's frightful hurt, sir!" the young ensign moaned looking up at the marine officer, the tear tracks washing lines down his powder-blackened cheeks.

"The surgeons'll try to help him, lad," O'Bannon gently replied. "You should order the boat to return to the squadron. You're in command of her now."

Preble watched the battle from the quarterdeck on *Constitution*. Through the smoke and confusion of the fight he was disappointed with what he saw. The two mortar ketches had done their work, blasting the city and frightening the civilians. Both their crews had emptied their racks of shells and smoke rose from fires in dozens of buildings throughout Tripoli. Preble could also see some damage was done to the bashaw's castle. But most of the enemy gunboats along with Reis's flagship appeared to have escaped the attack.

Preble hoped the battle would move into the harbor and then the streets of Tripoli. If it did, the war might end by sundown. But Decatur had failed to press his advantage during the assault. Murad Reis and his surviving gunboats disengaged at the height of the battle and retreated. Preble knew his hope for a quick ending to the conflict with Tripoli was probably unrealistic; still, the seasoned warrior in him had seen the opening and was frustrated the inexperienced Decatur had not exploited it.

The six American gunboats approached *Constitution*, Stephen Decatur standing on the bow of the lead barge that was towing three captured enemy vessels. As he came alongside, unaware of his brother's condition or Preble's mood, Decatur proudly called up to the quarterdeck, "I have brought you three of the enemy's gunboats, sir!"

Preble glared down from the quarterdeck, "Three, sir?! Where are the rest of them?!"

Stung at the rebuke and not understanding its source, Decatur climbed to *Constitution's* main deck while Preble returned to his cabin where he would await Decatur's full report. Meantime, junior officers greeted Decatur as he came aboard, crowding around their hero and excitedly asking him questions. While they spoke along the rail, the last gunboat came alongside. One of the officers glanced down at the new arrival and silently tapped Stephen on the arm.

Decatur turned and his face went ashen when he saw his younger brother lying on a litter in the bow of gunboat five, O'Bannon and Wadsworth comforting him. There was silence among the junior officers as they watched the still form of James carefully lifted aboard *Constitution* by tars. Sailors met them at the rail and quickly moved the wounded officer to the surgery below.

O'Bannon came aboard, saluted the quarterdeck and was met by the stricken Stephen.

"I'm sorry, sir," O'Bannon said, placing his hand on the captain's shoulder. "He was shot by that bastard Lisle from the quarterdeck of *Meshouda*. I think he was aiming at me. Your brother was hit in the head. Coming over he was in and out of consciousness."

Stephen had tears in his eyes as he patted O'Bannon's blood-streaked sleeve. "Thank you, Pres." With that, Decatur disappeared down the companionway that led to the sick bay.

Knowing Preble was waiting, O'Bannon reported to the commodore.

"Where the hell is Decatur?!" demanded Preble, his face flush.

"Sir, Captain Decatur's brother James was grieviously wounded in the attack," replied O'Bannon. "Shot in the head, sir. Mr. Decatur is with him in the surgery."

Preble took a deep breath and calmed himself. "Do you have any idea why Captain Decatur didn't press the assault?"

"No, sir, but it was awfully confusing what with the smoke and gun fire," O'Bannon replied. "The Scotch bastard was out there in his yellow brig – he's the one who shot Jamie – so maybe the captain thought there might be a trap waiting in the harbor."

"Very well, lieutenant," Preble said, deciding his briefing would have to wait. He now eyed the officer's blood-soaked uniform. "Good God, man, you look like you were in a slaughterhouse."

"I was, sir," O'Bannon said grimly.

James Decatur died in his brother's arms during the night. All hands were assembled at first light for the burial service, Stephen weeping piteously throughout Captain Rodgers' reading of the scriptures. O'Bannon had his arm around the young captain's shoulders. Stephen looked up only when the weighted canvas bag containing James' body slid out from beneath an American flag and plunged into the sea. The *Constitution*'s marines fired a salute from the quarterdeck and the ship's company was dismissed.

❧ 20 ❧

Licking his wounds, Grand Admiral Murad Reis kept his battered gunboats anchored in the harbor while keeping his distance from the bashaw. Now unopposed, day after day, *Constitution* closed to within a mile of the city where she fired volley after volley of twenty-four-pound shot at the gun batteries on the city's walls.

The mortar crews on the two ketches picked up where they had left off, firing accurately on the bashaw's castle and destroying scores of buildings in the city. Meantime, the American schooners and sloops sailed in unopposed, blasting the breakwater and quay.

As if the pounding Tripoli was already receiving wasn't enough, the six American gunboats along with those that had been captured were anchored near the breakwater and fired on Reis' ships and barges in the harbor.

Hordes of civilians fled Tripoli into the surrounding countryside. But hidden with his immediate family deep inside the bowels of his castle, Yusuf frantically pawed his worry beads as he listened to the dull thump of the exploding shells and the crash of solid shot that struck his city again and again. The bashaw's own surviving gunners gamely fired back at the Americans but, as usual, their marksmanship was atrocious, the shot splashing harmlessly around the American gunboats and ketches.

One afternoon a week into the siege, Reis positioned himself atop a minaret overlooking the harbor where he helplessly watched the

American cannon fire chop his anchored gunboats, corsairs and xebecs into kindling. *Meshouda*, tied up on the quay and shielded by other ships, had even taken hits in her hull and rigging. Reis thought about meeting the Americans as he had on the day of the gunboat battle, but he knew his men. They were unaccustomed to victims that fought back and lacked the stomach for clashing hand-to-hand with this ferocious and determined enemy a second time.

Reis believed it was past time for the bashaw to sue for peace, but his father-in-law was nothing if not obstinate. As long as he held *Philadelphia's* crew, Yusuf knew he had the upper hand, so Reis could do little more than watch the shot and bombs rain down on Tripoli.

Near five o'clock one afternoon, just as the Americans appeared to be withdrawing for the day, Reis heard one of his guns at the end of the breakwater suddenly fire. The grand admiral thought the battery long since silenced, but the shot penetrated an American gunboat's hull and struck her powder magazine. The blast enveloped the barge in a wall of fire. When the wind carried off the last of the smoke, the vessel was gone and so was her crew. Reis could hear cheering from the quay and city's walls but the victory was hollow. Out on the horizon, through his looking glass, he spotted another American frigate approaching.

After securing the bombardment, all hands were called to attend a service for the twelve enlisted men and two officers of the obliterated American gunboat. Shortly after the prayers, *John Adams* dropped anchor a quarter mile from *Constitution* and her commander, Master Commandant Issac Chauncey, was rowed over to report to Preble.

The commodore was excited to learn that *Adams* would soon be joined by four more frigates, *President, Congress, Constellation* and *Essex*.

"Finally, we can bring this damnable business to a close!" Preble declared as the two men sat at the table in his cabin. In return for his news Chauncey was delighted to hear that *Philadelphia* had been destroyed by Decatur and his raiders.

"We can expect the rest of the squadron within the month, sir," Chauncey said as he concluded his report. "I have been ordered by Secretary Smith to give you this letter."

Chauncey saluted and left Preble alone. The commodore opened the envelope, fully expecting a rebuke over the *Philadelphia* debacle. The news was even worse. In the disingenuous political language Preble detested he was ordered to relinquish command to Captain Barron.

"*Be assured, Sir,*" Secretary Smith wrote, "*that no want of confidence in you has been mingled with the considerations which have imposed on us the necessity of this measure.*"

Preble was certain that if the news of the *Philadelphia's* burning had reached Washington faster he would not have been relieved. But for now, he was still in command and he had one last idea to secure the victory over Tripoli before Barron arrived.

Captain Decatur reported to Preble an hour later. He wore a black armband as he saluted. The once gregarious and enthusiastic young officer was now a stoic, unsmiling veteran, Preble could see. He knew the captain swore revenge on Lisle, but his chances of having satisfaction were slim if the Scotsman refused to meet the Americans.

"I have been relieved of command," Preble said flatly.

Decatur looked shocked at the news. "But...but why, sir?!"

"The usual reason," Preble replied with a wry smile, "politics."

"But we burned *Philadelphia*..."

Preble held up his hand and said, "It's done, Mr. Decatur. That is how things work when civilians are in charge. Take note and don't make the mistakes I made."

"Sir."

"Now, we have one last opportunity to defeat the bashaw," Preble replied, getting down to business. "Where is *Intrepid?*"

The admiral of the Kingdom of Two Sicilies awarded the felucca to the Americans after their success burning *Philadelphia* ("It is not a good trade," the old officer told Preble through an interpreter, "a felucca for a frigate, but she is yours.")

"Anchored at Leghorn, sir," replied Decatur, wondering how the little vessel figured into the commodore's plans to finally defeat Tripoli.

"Good," replied Preble. "Dispatch a sloop and have her sailed here immediately. We shall convert her into a fireship."

William Eaton had come to loath Samuel Barron in their time together, made worse by contrary winds that slowed crossing the Atlantic Ocean to a crawl. Officious and condescending, the new commodore hadn't missed any opportunity to let Eaton know what he thought of his clandestine mission during the voyage aboard Barron's forty-four gun flagship *President*. When she finally anchored in the harbor at Syracuse at the end of the summer, Eaton immediately disembarked, taking rooms at a hotel rather than tolerate Barron's belligerence any longer.

Constitution and three escorts including *Argus* arrived in Sicily. The meeting between Preble and Barron was awkward, the two officers acquainted but not friendly. Still, Barron felt sympathetic as he shook Preble's hand.

"My most sincere congratulations, sir," Barron began stiffly as the two sat opposite each other in the new commodore's cabin. "You cannot imagine the public outrage when we received news of *Philadelphia's* capture."

Preble shrugged indifferently. Barron continued, "When I was told in Gibraltar you had burned her, well, you can well imagine my relief."

Preble smiled thinly and said, "And you can imagine mine."

"Yes, yes, of course!" Barron interjected. "Well done! Well done!"

There was a clumsy silence as Preble gazed at Barron who appeared momentarily distracted before he asked, "You know this man William Eaton?"

"Know him? No," Preble replied. "Know of Eaton, yes."

"He accompanied me on the voyage here," Barron continued. "The president approved his plan to make an overland attack on Derne. He is to be taken to Alexandria."

Preble brightened. He knew the general outlines of the mission and regarded the plan as audacious and unexpected, exactly the sort of tactic he favored.

"Preposterous, of course!" Barron declared dismissively. "We now have ample naval assets to crush the bashaw, but for whatever his reason, the president acquiesced to Eaton and his supporters in the cabinet."

"Perhaps President Jefferson's reason is to win this war," remarked Preble.

Barron was beginning not to like his predecessor. He made a sour face and said, "That is what I intend to do, captain."

Preble nodded, not really caring anymore. He had already decided to resign from the Navy when he reached Washington and then return home to his wife and farm in Maine.

Lieutenants Issac Hull and Presley O'Bannon stood to attention before Barron in the commodore's cabin the following afternoon. A man neither of them knew dressed in simple civilian clothes stood silently to one side.

"These are your written orders, Mr. Hull," Barron said as he handed an envelope to *Argus'* young commander. "You are to sail to Alexandria and convoy American merchantmen."

"Yes, sir," Hull replied, taking the envelope.

Barron gestured to the man standing next to his desk. He was of medium but solid stature with a pugnacious, impatient bearing.

"Those are your covering orders, Mr. Hull. Your actual orders are verbal and as follows," Barron continued. "You are to deliver Mr. William Eaton here to Egypt. When you are under sail, Mr. Eaton will provide you with the details of his...enterprise, which are presently secret. You will cooperate with Mr. Eaton in every way."

"Yes, sir," Hull repeated glancing at Eaton.

Barron now fixed his eyes on O'Bannon. "Lieutenant, you are to select six of your best men. You will detach from *Argus* when you reach Alexandria and you and your marines will be temporarily assigned to Mr. Eaton. You are to follow his orders until you are relieved."

"Aye-aye, sir," O'Bannon acknowledged peering more closely at Eaton. He guessed the man's age at forty, which O'Bannon thought old for somebody carrying out a secret mission. But Eaton had a handsome, boyish face. He wore his dark blond hair in a queue and was dressed in a non-descript black jacket and britches.

Barron dismissed the two officers, then sat back in his chair and regarded Eaton who took a seat without asking permission.

"You know I have very little confidence in what you are about to embark on," he finally said. "It's insane in my opinion."

"Yes. You've repeatedly expressed that opinion. It is one I have heard many a time from naval officers who believe theirs is the only means of waging war. But your opinion, Commodore Barron, is somewhat less important than that of President Jefferson's," Eaton said, his tone barely disguising contempt.

"I know it is," Barron replied, anger edging his voice. "But out here, thousands of miles from Washington, I have considerable leeway in the execution of my orders, sir. And one of those orders is to assist Mr. Lear in negotiating a peace with Tripoli if the opportunity presents itself."

"Talk instead of fighting," Eaton sarcastically replied. "Until Captain Preble demonstrated otherwise, talk was something the bashaw came to associate all too well with the American Navy."

Barron glared at Eaton, said, "I've called off any more attacks on Tripoli for the time being. Since the pointless tragedy with the fire ship we'll blockade only."

Eaton learned earlier in the day that after the series of bombardments had failed to wring surrender out of Yusuf, the frustrated Preble slipped *Intrepid* under the command of Henry Wadsworth into the harbor at Tripoli as a fire ship. She had been packed with explosives and sailed in under cover of darkness in much the same way Decatur had attacked.

The plan was for the crew to light fuses and escape before the devastating explosion aboard *Intrepid* ripped apart every Tripolitan ship at anchor in the harbor. But something went terribly wrong. Before she reached the harbor *Intrepid* detonated. The massive explosion rocked the city and was seen aboard the American ships waiting for the escaping crew miles off shore. All men aboard were lost, including Wadsworth.

"I'm sure chatting with Yusuf will bear about as much fruit as our previous diplomatic talks with him have," Eaton said caustically. "I've met that disgusting baboon, commodore, and the only talk he understands is about money, gifts, ransom and tribute. It's a God damned outrage that our nation has been pathetically reduced to bargaining with a son of a bitch like Yusuf! A God damned outrage, sir!"

Barron, now accustomed to Eaton's angry outbursts, waved a hand and replied, "Mr. Eaton, you will have the support I have been ordered to provide you. However, anything else you require will need my personal approval. Mr. Hull is so instructed. Frankly, I don't think much of your game nor do I think much of you. But I have my orders and you have yours, so there it is."

Eaton felt like striking Barron. How in God's name had such a buffoon advanced so far in the Navy, he wondered. He knew the answer, of course. During his career he'd met many an officer like Barron, little men who clung to their little desks, seldom understanding the deadly nature of their business, satisfied to reach retirement unscathed by combat or politics and collect their little pensions.

"Very well, commodore," Eaton said at last as he stood. "I shall join Mr. Hull aboard *Argus*. Thank you for your hospitality and your opinions during the crossing. I shall look forward to seeing you again. In Derne - after I take the city."

It was a little before dawn when they arrived at the remote rocky stretch of beach below a lighthouse on Leghorn's outskirts. O'Bannon and Hull accompanied Eaton to the duel along with several of *Argus'* junior officers. The British captain in his scarlet uniform jacket and cocked hat was already waiting, laughing in seeming indifference with a half-dozen of his fellow officers as the Americans approached.

The affair had begun innocently enough after *Argus* reached Malta to deliver the squadron's mail to the naval agent there. O'Bannon and Eaton dined together at a café before stopping at a tavern frequented by naval officers from many nations. There, Eaton entertained the lieutenant with stories of his days fighting alongside Mad Anthony.

The two men took an instant liking to one another, O'Bannon enthralled with the older man's military exploits and urbane charm and Eaton impressed by O'Bannon's easy going personality and the stories he heard of the young lieutenant's leadership and courage in the burning of *Philadelphia* and the gunboat battle at Tripoli.

As they were leaving the tavern to return to *Argus*, several British officers were entering. One saw O'Bannon's uniform and stepped before him. When O'Bannon attempted to go around, the officer again stepped in front of the marine.

The man was tall, like the lieutenant, but not as solidly built. He was handsome, with long brown hair tied off loosely in a queue. He appeared to be drunk, his eyes bleary and his speech slurred.

"I believe the exit for inferiors is at the rear of this establishment, my good man," the Englishman drawled.

"And I believe if you won't kindly stand aside, I'll knock you on your arse, my good man," O'Bannon replied with a grin.

"Ah ha!" the officer exclaimed to his companions. "This chap wishes a bout of fisticuffs!"

"Not if you stand aside," O'Bannon smiled. "But if you'd like yourself a fist fight, you sure found one!"

The officer laughed. "You American bumpkins are all the same. Gentlemen in name only."

Eaton peered at the British officer and remarked, "You may have heard we bumpkins slaughtered quite a few of you British gentlemen over in the colonies not so very long ago, captain. I killed a few myself, as matter of fact. Perhaps you'd like to join their number?"

The officer stopped smiling. His own father, a colonel in the British Army, had been killed in the battle at Princeton. "How dare you?!" he angrily replied.

"Listen, friend, just step aside and we'll be on our way," O'Bannon said quietly. "We've no truck with you."

"This fellow has insulted my family's honor. I shall have satisfaction!"

Two of the British officers standing behind the captain were appealing to him to let the slight go, but the man would hear none of it.

"No, no!" he cried, glaring at Eaton. "On the morrow at the beach beneath the lighthouse! Pistols! Be there at dawn or I shall come find you!"

Now they all stood on the gravel beneath a dull gray sky. Seabirds wheeled overhead screeching, the north wind chilling the air.

Eaton appeared completely at ease, but O'Bannon was afraid for his new friend. Dueling was common among British officers, and no doubt this young captain was handy with a pistol.

Another British officer came forward with a pair of weapons, handed one to the captain and held the other out to Eaton who took it and passed it to O'Bannon. The marine looked it over carefully.

"It has been charged," the officer told O'Bannon.

"We'll reload her anyway," O'Bannon replied, as he fired weapon over the ocean then re-primed it with ammunition he had brought for that purpose.

"Gentlemen trust other gentlemen!" the officer declared indignantly.

"Well I'm no gentleman, mister. I'm an American marine," said O'Bannon as he finished charging the weapon.

"Ten paces?" Eaton asked the captain mildly.

The British officer gave a curt nod. He removed his jacket and hat and handed them to his second. The bareheaded Eaton drew off his overcoat and handed it to Hull. The British and Americans stepped back and the two gunmen faced each other. Sweat appeared on the captain's forehead as he nervously fingered his weapon. Eaton wore a blank expression, holding his pistol at his side.

One of the British officers said, "On the count of three, raise and fire."

The British duelist swallowed and stared at Eaton, who gazed impassively at his opponent.

"One...two...three!"

Each man leveled his weapon while turning his body to the side in order to present a narrower profile. The British officer took careful aim and fired, just as Eaton pulled his trigger. The muzzles of the flintlock pistols gushed flame and thick, acrid smoke concealing the shooters for a moment before the breeze carried it away.

The British captain stood motionless for a moment before his pistol fell to the gravel. He dropped to his knees and rolled over onto his back. The ball struck him between the eyes, a thin trickle of blood oozing from the hole

"Fredrick!" cried one of the other British officers as he raced to the dead man. "Oh God!" the man wailed as he held the lifeless body. "Oh, my dear brother!"

As the smoke that enveloped Eaton lifted, O'Bannon and Hull could see the British officer's ball had struck his bicep, blood soaking the arm of Eaton's white shirt. They rushed forward with a bandage as the British officers gathered around their dead comrade and his grieving brother.

"Your friend was brave but he was foolish, gentlemen," Eaton said as Hull dressed the slight wound. "I have fought and won many duels with pistol and sword. I advise all of you young officers to know your adversary before you challenge him in deadly combat. You will live longer."

Eaton pointed at the corpse with his pistol and gazed at the weeping officer. "I am sorry your brother is dead. But it is he who wanted it that way. *C'est la guerre.*"

Silently, the British officers lifted the dead man and carried him from the beach.

21

"My enterprise is unprecedented and dangerous, gentlemen," Eaton began as he stood before Hull and O'Bannon. They were all crammed into Hull's tiny cabin, the ship rolling through rough seas, water dripping through chinks in the deck above their heads. Eaton wore a military-style uniform he had designed himself that featured the epaulettes of a general.

"We will proceed to Alexandria," Eaton continued, pointing to a map on the table before him. "There, we will learn the whereabouts of a man named Hamet Karamanli and find him."

"Karamanli?" replied O'Bannon. "That's the bashaw's name, isn't it, sir?"

"Yes it is," Eaton said nodding. "This man we're looking for is Yusuf Karamanli's elder brother. We're going to locate Hamet, put him at the head of a column of volunteers we recruit, and we march overland to attack Derne, Tripoli's easternmost city. Once seized, Derne will become our base of operations against Yusuf. Our aim is to help Hamet retake his rightful place as regent of Tripoli."

"Mr. Eaton," said Hull gesturing to the map, a look of disbelief on his face. "That's...that's hundreds of miles..."

"General Eaton, if you please Mr. Hull. And it's five hundred miles," came the stiff reply. "We must march in the coolest month, so I wish to begin the enterprise by mid-February at the latest. That leaves about seventy-five days to recruit, equip and train our force."

"Force?" O'Bannon asked with a frown. He was having trouble masking his incredulity.

"Yes, Lieutenant O'Bannon," Eaton replied, his tone vexed. "You and I will recruit a column of Tripoline exiles along with local Arabs and any European mercenaries we can find. We will arm and train them. We will march from here," he stabbed the map forcefully, "to here, Derne. I expect we will have a difficult journey. At the Bay of Bomba here, Mr. Hull will meet us. That's two or three-day's march from Derne. We will re-supply the column and then continue on. Once at Derne we will give Governor Mustapha the opportunity to surrender before we attack. If we must fight, Mr. Hull will support our assault from the sea."

It was the most outlandish scheme O'Bannon had ever heard. He knew next to nothing about North Africa, but he was reasonably sure an endless wasteland lay just beyond the beach. The Tripolines and Arabs he'd encountered so far were nothing more than greedy and bloodthirsty savages unlikely to join an American-led army. How in God's name had Eaton ever conceived such a plan, O'Bannon wondered as he pretended to study the map. And how had it ever been approved by President Jefferson? Was this self-appointed "general" a madman?

O'Bannon finally looked up at Eaton's face, which was bright with anticipation and remembered that, first and last, he was an officer in the United States Marines and he had his orders, no matter how crazy he thought they might be. He said finally, "Well, General Eaton, what do you require of me, sir?"

Smoke from a thousand fires hung over the squalid city, where scores of minarets and a hundred towers jabbed the hazy morning sky. The calls to prayer, the braying of asses and camels, and the clamoring of countless merchants serenaded Eaton, O'Bannon and the six American marines as they marched through a stinking alley in search of Hamet Karamanli.

At their first stop, the gated home of a prosperous Tripolitan merchant Eaton knew they learned that Hamet, fearful of assassination, had fled down the Nile toward Cairo. Where he'd gone, the merchant had no idea. Eaton wasn't sure if the Tripolitan was lying, perhaps protecting the rightful bashaw, so he continued the search.

At the British garrison camped near the river, a major in command said he knew of Hamet but he was not sure of his whereabouts. The Americans then marched to the custom house, where Eaton said he knew a Frenchman who worked there.

"This fellow, Dutourd, is not really a commercial agent," Eaton explained to O'Bannon as they walked through the crowded streets. "He's a spy who works for Bonaparte."

If it was possible, the scene in the vast brick and stone barn that served as Alexandria's custom house was more chaotic than its streets and alleyways. Crates, bales of cotton, and all manner of containers, clay jars and baskets were piled everywhere as bare-chested black stevedores unloaded or loaded the lighters ferrying goods to and from ships anchored in the harbor. Arab and Turkish merchants, bawling at each other, jammed the narrow corridors created by the stacked freight.

In a corner they found a small man at a desk dressed in plain white robes. "*Bon jour, mon ami!*" called Eaton as he approached. "*Como talle vouz?*"

"Ah, *Monsieur* Eaton!" the man cried as he hugged the American and kissed his cheeks. "My good friend! How are you? It has been two, three years, no?"

"Three, I think," replied Eaton who patted the man's shoulders. "In Tunis."

"I see you are a soldier again and you bring the American army with you!"

"This is Lieutenant O'Bannon of the United States Marines and these are his men," Eaton replied with a wave of his hand. "And this, gentlemen, is my dear friend Citizen Francois Dutourd...commercial agent," he spoke the last two words with his eyebrows raised.

"*Oui!* A humble agent of commerce in the service of the emperor," agreed Dutourd. "And sometimes a pair of eyes and pair of ears for him as well, eh?" he added touching the side of his nose. "*Café?*"

O'Bannon ordered his men to wait as he and Eaton went across the alley with Dutourd to a coffee house thick with blue tobacco smoke and incomprehensible chatter. Equally thick coffee was poured into tiny cups by Dutourd.

"Hamet Karamanli?" the Frenchman replied to Eaton's question. "No, he is not in Alexandria. I believe he is among the Mamelukes in the desert, somewhere between here and Cairo. He's something of a wanted man by the Turkish rulers of Egypt. The Mamelukes are their enemies and Hamet has sought refuge among them. Guilty by association I believe you would say, no?"

Eaton cursed his luck. Hamet could be anywhere in the desert and they might never find him. Dutourd interrupted his thoughts.

"I do know a man who might be able to help you find him," the Frenchman remarked thoughtfully. "A most unusual person. A Tyrolean. Rather colorful, I must say, but a man who can get things done."

Eaton brightened at this news and asked that Dutourd arrange a meeting. The next morning, Eugene Leitensdorfer appeared at Eaton's hotel. He was of medium height and completely bald. Hatless, he wore simple black britches and stockings and a red jacket. A saber scar decorated his left cheek and he seemed to be nervous, his blue eyes darting about as if in anticipation of some unpleasant surprise.

Eaton invited Leitensdorfer to join him at a table with O'Bannon. Port was brought and poured. When the innkeeper disappeared, Eaton outlined his need to find Hamet but didn't explain why.

"I know the Mameluke leader," Leitensdorfer finally declared in good though accented English. "At least I have met him. I believe I can find him in Minyeh. If this Hamet fellow is with the Mamelukes that is where he will be, sir."

Eaton regarded the man more closely, unsure if Leitensdorfer was trustworthy. "Tell me about yourself," Eaton invited.

"Well, there is not much to tell, General Eaton," Leitensdorfer replied with a nervous smile before sipping his port. "I was a soldier once. In the Austrian army, then in the French army and then in the Turkish army. But I didn't like the army, or armies so I, um, left. I was also a thespian in a theater in Venice. Then a novice Capuchin monk at a monastery in France. But that life was rather lonely. I lived among the Bedouin for awhile. I once owned a theater and another time I owned a coffee shop…."

"Not much to tell!" Eaton laughed. "You've had enough careers for six men!"

Leitensdorfer looked at the Americans sheepishly. "Yes, I suppose so," he said. "My travels have made me fluent in many tongues. I speak the Turk, German, French, English of course, several Arab dialects and a bit of Italian and Spanish."

"You say you were a soldier once," O'Bannon said. "We need soldiers. A lot of them. But first we need to find Hamet. Can we trust you to help us?"

The man was nodding his head vigorously before the marine had finished speaking. "Yes, yes, of course!" he declared. "But, I am afraid I have a bit of difficulty here in Alexandria. I owe a man some money. He wants to be paid."

Eaton now knew his initial skepticism wasn't misplaced. No doubt this miscreant owed cash to everyone in Alexandria. "How much?" Eaton asked, his tone one of resignation

"About fifty American dollars." Leitensdorfer replied, then added quickly, "I know this is a lot of money, sir, but if you might advance me a little of it, this man would probably leave me alone and I can help you."

Startled at the trifling sum, Eaton smiled. "I will tell you what, *Herr* Leitensdorfer," he proposed. "I shall give you twenty-five dollars now and twenty-five dollars when you deliver Hamet Karamanli to me. I shall pay you another fifty dollars to join our enterprise and fifty dollars more upon the enterprise's successful conclusion."

Leitensdorfer appeared to be near tears, relief washing over his wide, beardless face.

"I am your humble servant, *Herr* Eaton. And yours, lieutenant."

To be on the safe side, Eaton ordered O'Bannon and his marines to accompany Leitensdorfer when he left to deliver the money to his debtor. They walked for more than a mile through the souk and the slums, then along the Nile before they finally arrived at a large gated house on a hill overlooking the river. The Tyrolean knocked on the gate and exchanged some words with a servant who answered through a small screen. Presently the gate swung open and before them stood a middle-aged man wearing green robes and a menacing expression.

In fluent Arabic, Leitensdorfer spoke to the man and produced from his pocket the gold coins Eaton had given him. He handed them over to the man who placed them in a purse hanging from his belt. They spoke a few more words before the Egyptian disappeared behind the gate.

"My former father-in-law," Leitensdorfer explained to O'Bannon as they walked back to Eaton's hotel. "I am permitted under their laws to divorce my wife or wives any time for any reason, but that gentleman took exception to my divorcing his daughter."

O'Bannon, no stranger to jilted women, replied with a wry grin.

"She frankly wasn't very good at her, shall I say, marital responsibilities," he went on. "But her father is a powerful man in Alexandria. He promised to remove a certain part of my body with a dull blade unless he was paid for the disgrace of a daughter defiled by an infidel."

"Some fellas back home in Virginia have been known to take such notions when their daughters had difficulties like that with menfolk," O'Bannon remarked. "It's the same everywhere. But I reckon fifty dollars is a small price to pay to keep your balls!"

The next morning, with expense money of ten dollars in gold and a letter from Eaton to Hamet, Leitensdorfer departed for Minyeh aboard a river trader. Eaton had his doubts about the man but he had little to lose. He decided to give the Austrian two weeks and if Leitensdorfer didn't return to Alexandria by then, he would go to Minyeh himself.

Tobias Lear strolled through the streets of Syracuse, pausing occasionally to admire his own reflection in shop windows. He was tall and bore an uncanny resemblance to George Washington, the man who had served as Lear's mentor when he was the commanding general of the Continental Army and later as president. He wore an impeccably tailored suit of clothes, preferring modern trousers to britches and stockings. On his head was an expensive and fashionable beaver skin top hat he'd purchased during a stop in London. An ivory walking stick inlaid with silver filigree completed the ensemble. Lear couldn't resist one last look at the distinguished American emissary reflected in a baker's window before engaging in the unpleasant task of once again lobbying Commodore Samuel Barron.

Lear visited the commodore nearly every day of his confinement, which began a month earlier, shortly after Eaton's departure for Alexandria. Ostensibly, Lear played the role of concerned friend and trusted confidant, but he deeply disliked the socially inferior naval officer. With Barron now seriously ill, the diplomat Tobias Lear understood his advantage. Today he had a piece of news he was certain would convince the commodore to abandon support for Eaton and allow him to pursue a diplomatic end to the struggle with Tripoli.

Lear entered the commodore's small hospital room. The window was open to a pleasant, breezy morning, overlooking the harbor full of ships riding at anchor, their crews scurrying about, performing their endless chores.

The commodore, his face pale yellow, lay half asleep beneath a thin sheet. Despite the fresh air, Lear detected the rancid odor of the man's unwashed body. The British doctor attending Barron explained to Lear during an earlier visit that the officer had a disease of the liver.

"I'm afraid his illness is getting progressively worse," the physician said. "There is not very much I can do for him. He may or he may not recover."

The commodore stirred and opened his eyes, which, like his skin, had a yellowish cast.

"Colonel Lear," he croaked, "would you kindly hand me that glass of water."

The diplomat picked up the glass from a nearby table and handed it to Barron, who had risen up on an elbow. He drank the water down in two gulps and handed the glass back to Lear.

"How are you feeling, sir?" Lear asked.

Barron slowly shook his head in answer before he placed it back onto the pillow. Lear eyed him and decided the time was right to press his case.

"I understand Lieutenant Hull returned to Syracuse last night to report that Eaton had been successfully delivered to Alexandria," he began.

"Yes," sighed Barron, his eyes closed.

"This adventure of Eaton's is destined to fail, of course. Any man in his right mind can see that," Lear continued. "It must be terminated and we must press Bashaw Yusuf to negotiate now that he has been humbled."

Barron said nothing in reply. Lear wondered if he had drifted off to sleep. "Sir?"

"Aye, I am listening," Barron said in a reedy voice.

"Before he left, do you know Eaton had a tailor here make a general's uniform for him? Then, in Malta, he stupidly killed a British officer in a duel. We need the support of the British Navy, not its animosity!"

"Mmm," Barron replied.

"Eaton's vanity and ambition appear boundless. He seeks for himself personal glory while *Philadelphia's* pitiful captives suffer every day in Tripoli. We - I mean you - have the authority to end this madness and I have the authority to negotiate with the bashaw's emissaries if only you will allow me to do so, commodore."

Barron stirred but said nothing. From his inner coat pocket, Lear removed sheets of paper folded together and held them up.

"I have received a letter this morning from the bashaw's foreign minister, this Dghies chap," Lear declared. "He claims to be the only member of Yusuf's cabinet to vote against declaring war with America. He also believes the time is ripe for a diplomatic settlement. He goes on to suggest the bashaw is afraid we will bombard Tripoli again."

"Mmm," Barron mumbled.

"Dghies is worried that if we mount an all-out assault on Tripoli, Yusuf will flee into the desert to a stronghold miles from the coast. He will take the officers and men of *Philadelphia* and hold them beyond our reach. God only knows what will happen to Captain Bainbridge and his crew then, sir."

"No, no, no," the sick man moaned. "Cannot let him…"

"With your permission, Commodore Barron, I wish to sail to Tripoli and open negotiations immediately. Certainly I can do no harm by talking to Yusuf. If Dghies is right, we can deliver all the *Philadelphia's* captives at an acceptable cost."

Barron, exhausted and only half listening, felt a sudden stabbing pain in his side as though a white hot knife had been plunged deep into his organs. Sweat broke out on his face and he groaned and then shivered.

"Sir!" an alarmed Lear cried as he clasped Barron's hand. "What can I do to help you?!"

"Doctor!" came the reply through clenched teeth. Then Barron opened his eyes and stared at Lear. "Go…go to Tripoli."

22

The Napoleonic War swept through Egypt four years earlier and left in its wake hundreds of ex-soldiers from all over Europe. It proved far easier to recruit an army of them than Eaton had ever imagined.

For ten dollars each, three meals a day, and the promise of a two to three month-long adventure that might also yield plunder, they were able to enlist Greeks, Turks, Frenchmen, Spaniards, and Portuguese, along with Europeans from a half dozen other nations and kingdoms. Through his friend Dutourd, Eaton also found and recruited a cadre of Irishmen who had deserted the ranks of their British units and were now hiding out in Alexandria, some married to Egyptian women.

Most all of the mercenary recruits were destitute and desperate, stranded in Alexandria with no means of returning home. Along with food and arms, many needed decent clothing. At a vendor's stall in the souk O'Bannon found large bundles of uniforms, French and British, looted from the bodies of dead soldiers after the Battle of Alexandria. The merchant had cleaned and patched the uniforms as best he could, but faded blood stains were still visible. The merchant was eager to rid himself of the inventory so, for the equivalent of five dollars, O'Bannon bought the lot along with several dozen hats, helmets, breastplates and other soldiers' accessories.

Eaton moved the mercenary army to an encampment on the outskirts of Alexandria, near a beach beneath the ruins of a lookout tower, where O'Bannon and his marines began drilling them. Along with food, spirits, powder and shot, Eaton purchased arms and ammunition for those men who needed them.

"Get your arses up here you bloody dago bastards!" cried Sergeant Arthur Campbell at the Spanish soldiers, who were proving to be less than inspired at the prospects of a long march followed by a battle. Satisfied to be regularly fed, the thirty or so soldiers were lazy, lagging behind in the close order marching drill and driving the impatient Campbell mad with rage.

"Easy, there, sergeant," O'Bannon called from his horse as he rode up on the scene. "We don't need them to march pretty."

"Aye, lieutenant," Campbell replied, his face red. "But you seen 'em yerself, sir. They won't do as ordered!"

"They have no officers nor sergeants of their own to discipline them," O'Bannon remarked. "And I don't speak Spanish. Neither do you, so we'll have to make do. It's hot. Dismiss the men and we'll pick it up when it gets cooler."

O'Bannon wheeled his mount and rode from the dusty makeshift parade ground surrounded by scores of small dun colored tents to the large white marquee set up a hundred yards away as Eaton's headquarters and regimental office. The sun was low in the early winter sky, but waves of heat still shimmered off the hard pan desert floor.

A few hundred yards away, past a series of low sand dunes cloaked in clumps of thick grass, the sea shimmered and next to Eaton's marquee there were men washing clothing and pans in a fresh water lagoon shaded by towering palm trees. Feeling the sweat and grit trickling down his back as he approached the headquarters, O'Bannon reminded himself to bathe when he had the chance.

He tied his mount to a palm and walked into the tent. It was cooler under the canopy, a light sea breeze wafting through the marquee's open sides. Within Eaton had partitioned the space off with canvas walls so he could have privacy during his discussions with O'Bannon and the other officers. He also managed to furnish the headquarters with chairs and tables and had even purchased for himself a feather bed.

"General?!" called O'Bannon.

"Lieutenant!" Eaton called brightly from behind a canvas wall. "Just the fellow I seek!"

O'Bannon smiled. He couldn't help it. General Eaton's impetuosity was matched only by his endless enthusiasm and boundless optimism. Eaton appeared from one of the chambers clad in flowing white Arab robes and wearing a checkered burnoose on his head, a curved scimitar at his belt, and a brace of charged pistols on another belt worn across his chest.

The marine officer was shocked when he'd first seen Eaton in native dress, but he had come to understand over the days since meeting him that he should never be surprised by anything General Eaton did or said.

O'Bannon made a sharp salute and said, "Sir! Reporting as ordered!"

The two men had agreed that the column should always bear some semblance of military discipline so they constantly demonstrated it, even if it was just before a couple of British clerks Eaton had hired who were working at nearby desks. When they were alone, their relationship was friendly and informal.

"Fetch your fiddle, if you please," Eaton replied. "We're going on a recruiting mission."

An hour later, the tall marine in his blue uniform and the general in his Arab robes rode up to a Bedouin encampment set out among Roman ruins near the sea. Goats and sheep scattered as they dismounted and led their horses through crowds of veiled women and clamoring children who emerged from the low tents to eye the strange visitors.

"*Aasalaamu Aleikum,*" Eaton called out cheerily as he handed bits of hard candy to some of the children. "Hello! Good afternoon, madam!"

Three men in black robes appeared from a marquee and approached.

"Aasalaamu Aleikum!" Eaton said to them touching his hand to his chest as they approached.

"Ahlan wa-Sahlan!" replied the eldest looking of the three. "Welcome to our humble camp, sir," the man continued in Arabic. "Your messenger told us you would be visiting. You honor us. I am the village chief, Abbud. Come, we have arranged hospitality."

Abbud, like his companions, was short, his neat goatee flecked with gray, his eyes a remarkable greenish gray, which contrasted sharply with his bronze skin.

Eaton bowed deeply then motioned O'Bannon to follow Abbud. They were led to the marquee, somewhat smaller than Eaton's, but more lavishly appointed. A blue carpet had been spread on the sand and large pillows were arranged across the floor. The Americans' horses were staked outside and a boy watered them while the Bedouin motioned for the Americans to sit.

A water pipe was produced and ceremoniously passed around to each man. Then, a bitter tea was poured by a cloaked young woman. The men drank, Eaton making exclamations to his hosts on the quality and flavor of the beverage while O'Bannon tried hard not to show his disgust as he choked it down, his eyes watering.

Small talk followed with Eaton asking Abbud a flurry of questions about the size of the village and its flocks. O'Bannon watched and listened, as always fascinated by Eaton's command of the Arab tongue. The general laughed, smiled, gestured and replied to questions as though he'd known these particular Bedouin his entire life.

O'Bannon suddenly realized all eyes had fallen on him. Eaton smiled and asked, "How about a tune, lieutenant? I've told them you are an exceptional musician and master of an instrument they have never seen nor heard."

Nodding, O'Bannon rose and retrieved the fiddle and bow from his saddlebag. Standing, he tuned the instrument first, producing shouts of excitement from his wide-eyed hosts. There were far better players in

Fauquier County, O'Bannon knew, but right now he was probably the best fiddler in this corner of the Sahara Desert.

He began the concert with a Virginia reel followed by a pair of Irish folk tunes his father had taught him. As he played, he tapped his booted foot on the carpet. The Bedouins clapped in time and laughed as a delighted crowd of men, women and children crowded outside the chief's tent to listen.

Sweating, O'Bannon finished the last note and bowed to the men. Abbud exclaimed something excitedly to Eaton.

"Abbud says he's never heard such wonderful music before," Eaton translated. "He wishes to learn to play the fiddle! I think we've got him, Mr. O'Bannon!"

Confused, O'Bannon mopped his face with a kerchief. "How's that?"

"Give him the damned fiddle and teach him to play, of course!" Eaton declared. "Then we'll have his village's one hundred men in our column!"

"Well, General, I can't give him this fiddle. It was my grandfather's. He brought it from Ireland," O'Bannon explained. "But I can probably buy one for him in Alexandria and I'll teach him as best I can during the march."

Eaton translated this to Abbud who appeared utterly ecstatic. He chattered something to his two friends, then rose and Eaton followed suit. The two solemnly embraced. Then the chief embraced O'Bannon, the marine's chest at the level of the man's head. He said something to O'Bannon and Eaton again interpreted:

"You are Abbud's ally and friend until the day he dies," Eaton said quietly.

"Then Abbud is my ally and my friend for the rest of my life, too," O'Bannon smiled, patting the man's shoulder.

Eugene Leitensdorfer rode into Eaton's camp the next morning on a camel. It had been nearly three weeks since he'd left to find Hamet Karamanli and Eaton was about to give up on him and depart for

Minyeh himself. At the news of his arrival, Eaton raced from his tent to greet Leitensdorfer.

"I found your friend, sir. He is well, sends you his greetings and expresses his undying gratitude…"

"Yes, yes, yes!" Eaton interrupted impatiently. "Where is he now?"

"He is being held in custody by a Turkish admiral in Alexandria."

"For the love of Christ!" Eaton swore bitterly. "Why?! Why is he being held?!"

"The admiral is unhappy that Hamet and his retinue were consorting with the Mamelukes, Sultan Selim's sworn enemies," replied Leitensdorfer as he dismounted. "He had his men arrest us when we entered the city. I was released. *Monsieur* Dutourd told me you were here at the Arab's Tower. The admiral said he is deciding if Hamet should be taken to Constantinople and punished."

Facing the end of the enterprise before it had begun, Eaton's face fell at the news.

"Sir. General," Leitensdorfer continued, placing his hand on Eaton's shoulder. "Do not despair. I know this man, the Turkish admiral. He can be bought."

Eaton knew bribes were the way most things got done in this part of the world, so he wasn't surprised by Leitensdorfer's revelation.

"How much?"

"For me or for the Turkish admiral?" Leitensdorfer replied, almost apologetically.

Lips pursed in a tight smile, Eaton thought of his limited supply of American gold coins in the chest buried beneath his tent and guarded by O'Bannon's marines around the clock. Then he thought of his dwindling timetable. Finally, Eaton sighed.

"Lieutenant O'Bannon will accompany you to meet with the admiral," said Eaton, his tone resigned. "I can authorize up to five hundred dollars, *Herr* Leitensdorfer. We'll determine *your* fee when we know if that is acceptable to this Turkish thief."

The man bowed. "As you command, *mon general.*" His apologetic smile returned. "Sir, um, one final detail...might I have the balance of my payment, sir, now that I have found your Mr. Hamet? I have that... little problem..."

Eaton burst out laughing. "Yes! By all means, *Herr* Leitensdorfer! By all means! Let us go find Mr. O'Bannon. Then I shall pay you your twenty-five dollars so you and the lieutenant may leave immediately for Alexandria! No time to lose, sir! No time to lose!"

Anchored off Tripoli aboard *Constitution*, Captain John Rodgers was fuming. He had been awaiting orders from Barron, but instead Tobias Lear appeared on his ship that morning.

"You shall continue your blockade," Lear explained in the privacy of Rodgers' cabin. "I shall begin negotiations with the bashaw."

Like William Eaton, Rodgers had a short temper.

"Are you mad, Lear?!" he cried. "This is a frigate of the United States Navy and my orders come from Commodore Barron, not some damned civilian!"

Lear decided to indulge the captain's outburst, knowing it was difficult for fighting men to comprehend the business of diplomacy. He reached into the leather folio on the table before him and withdrew a letter. With a genial smile he handed it to Rodgers.

It was written by Secretary Smith and addressed to Barron. It contained the usual florid declarations of support, but it essentially left the entire war and its settlement or prosecution in the hands of Barron. *"The subject is committed entirely to your discretion,"* Smith's letter concluded.

Rodgers placed it on the table, regarded Lear then said with a sneer, "And Commodore Barron has decided to negotiate."

"Indeed he has," Lear said with an unctuous smile. "You and the rest of the squadron have shown Karamanli that America will no longer be cowed..."

"*Yet*," interrupted Rodgers, "we'll pay him ransom for the men of *Philadelphia*. That's rather a confusing message, is it not Mr. Lear? Fire cannon at him with one hand and give him money with the other?"

"Colonel Lear," the diplomat corrected before sitting back in his chair. His tone became expansive. "You don't understand the nature of this enemy, captain. Yusuf Karamanli won't be defeated. He will hole up in his citadel and withstand your bombardments. He cares not a wit for the citizens of Tripoli who might be killed or wounded or displaced. He only cares for himself and his riches. He will do whatever is necessary to protect those, even if that means hiding behind the *Philadelphia* hostages."

"That may be so," Rodgers angrily countered, "but we have Eaton and his men moving on Derne. When the tyrant has learned he has lost the city that anchors his eastern flank, he will begin to recalculate the value of holding our men."

"Posh!" sniffed Lear with a dismissive wave. "Eaton has as much chance of succeeding on his ridiculous adventure as he has of sailing your ship around the world by himself! Why President Jefferson would give that silly peacock two minutes of his valuable time I cannot imagine. In any event, Eaton can play soldier in the desert if that is what the president desires. Meantime, sir, you shall reinforce the blockade and I will approach the bashaw's foreign minister. Am I clear?"

"Abundantly," Rodgers muttered.

Admiral Safak's headquarters was a small dingy house in an alley near Alexandria's quay. He was short, with thick black hair and mustaches and wore a crimson tunic and fez. He smoked a clay pipe constantly as he listened to Leitensdorfer introduce O'Bannon and explain their business.

"No. Hamet Karamanli must be sent to Constantinople to face Selim's justice," Safak declared flatly in Turkish before sucking on his pipe and exhaling a plume of aromatic smoke. "He allied himself with those filthy Mameluke dogs. He must be punished."

"I understand, Excellency," the Tyrolean replied, his two hands clasped before him like a supplicant. "But...but perhaps we can arrange to pay a bail for the prisoner."

Safak's face softened at this suggestion so he gestured for Leitensdorfer to continue.

"I think if we pay bail, we can all agree on some future date for Hamet to travel to Constantinople to submit to the will of the sultan. Say five hundred United States dollars?"

It took a moment for the admiral to calculate the exchange but after he had, he realized the figure represented a small fortune. It was all he could do to contain his excitement.

"I would say one thousand is a more appropriate bail for an enemy of Selim," Safak sternly replied.

Leitensdorfer swallowed nervously as he glanced at O'Bannon.

"What does he say?" the marine asked impatiently.

Leitensdorfer translated.

"Does the damned bargaining never end with these people?!" O'Bannon snapped. "Tell him five hundred. That's it."

Leitensdorfer translated but before he finished, Safak was shaking his head.

"The Admiral says he might permit a bail of eight hundred dollars..."

O'Bannon had heard enough. His fist crashed down on the admiral's desk. "Tell this son of a bitch to release Hamet Karamanli immediately! If he does, I will give him one hundred dollars! If he refuses, I will be back here tomorrow at first light with my mercenaries to rescue Hamet!"

Realizing he had overplayed his hand, Safak's alarmed eyes were darting between O'Bannon and the Austrian.

"I...I can't say that to him..." Leitensdorfer sputtered.

"Tell him, damn you!" O'Bannon cried.

Leitensdorfer did his best to temper the lieutenant's words. To his surprise, Safak's face went white as he shot out of his seat and held out his small hand to O'Bannon, jabbering some words.

"Admiral Safak says America and Constantinople are eternal friends!" the relieved Leitensdorfer said as O'Bannon shook the offered hand. "He says he is most sorry for this unfortunate misunderstanding. Please come back tomorrow and Hamet and his party will be ready to leave on transportation provided by the admiral. The small gift you mentioned is unnecessary but would be most welcomed."

Unnerved by O'Bannon's sudden anger, Safak scrambled to a cupboard from which he produced a bottle of Scotch whiskey and glasses. He poured and then offered a toast. As they all tapped glasses O'Bannon looked at Leitensdorfer with a grin.

"Misunderstanding my arse," he said as he touched glasses with the grinning Safak. "This bastard heard about what we did at Tripoli and he's worried we'll do the same to him!"

Early the next morning O'Bannon and Leitensdorfer were at the Turkish fort near the breakwater where Safak had told them they could collect Hamet. The iron gate swung open and a dozen men mounted on camels and another ten on foot emerged. They all wore white robes and burnooses and appeared excited at the prospect of their sudden freedom. Safak followed them out and greeted O'Bannon deferentially.

"The admiral again apologizes for the confusion," Leitensdorfer said. "As you can see, Hamet and his men have been well treated in his custody."

The man on the lead camel trotted forward and gestured to the American. His camel knelt and the rider dismounted. He was short and like his brother Yusuf, he had penetrating eyes of onyx. Unlike Yusuf he was lean, a neatly trimmed beard decorating his jaw and chin. He stood before O'Bannon, bowed and then took the lieutenant's hand and kissed it.

"I am Hamet Karamanli. Thank you, sir, for delivering us from the Turk's prison. The admiral was about to send us all to Constantinople."

"I'm Lieutenant Presley Neville O'Bannon, General Eaton's second in command, Mr. Karamanli," O'Bannon replied with a slight bow. "The general is camped near the Arab's Tower. If you are ready, we will go to him. I know he is looking forward to seeing you again."

"And I him," Hamet smiled warmly. "Yes, we are ready. The admiral made a show of feeding us a large breakfast and then provided us with these camels. I don't think the beasts belong to him."

"I am sorry to say it took a threat to win your release, sir, but the admiral decided he'd rather be our friend than our enemy," O'Bannon said with a smile.

Leitensdorfer nudged O'Bannon. Safak stood nearby, his greedy eyes bright with anticipation. O'Bannon gestured and the Turk trotted forward like an excited child. The admiral snatched the purse O'Bannon offered and secreted it in his tunic.

Two hours later, the little column reached the American encampment, a sprawling tent city now that Abbud's entire Bedouin village had joined the enterprise. Upon word of their approach, Eaton galloped out on his white gelding to greet his friend.

The American and the deposed regent of Tripoli enthusiastically embraced, kissing each other's cheeks and then shaking hands.

"My friend, my dear friend!" cried Eaton. "I told you we would come!"

"You did and you have! My humble thanks, William!" smiled Hamet, displaying his fine white teeth.

"President Jefferson sends you his most warm salutations!" Eaton declared. "He has ordered me to help you remove your brother Yusuf from power and to return you to your family and your rightful place!"

There were tears in Hamet's eyes. He could think of no words so he again embraced Eaton, who, after a moment gently broke away but held Hamet by his shoulders. "We have much work to do, friend," he said earnestly. "We have men and we have arms, but we need more of both."

Hamet turned and gestured to his men. "These are my loyal subjects who have been in exile with me since Yusuf forced us out of Tripoli. All of them will fight and, if necessary, die to see my brother removed and punished."

Eaton smiled. "Come, let us dine and then you should rest. Later, we will talk and I will show you my plans."

O'Bannon found Abbud in his tent smoking a water pipe. Upon seeing the marine officer, the Bedouin chief leapt to his feet. Under his arm, O'Bannon carried a violin and bow he'd found in a pawn shop the day before. It had cost one dollar and was in reasonably good condition. Wrapped in a chamois clothe, O'Bannon held the gift out to Abbud. The Bedouin's eyes grew large as he carefully took the violin from O'Bannon and unwrapped it.

Women and a few men looked on as Abbud imitated O'Bannon, placing the violin under his chin and holding the neck as he'd seen O'Bannon do. He held the bow awkwardly and drew it across the cat gut strings, producing a raspy note. Abbud gasped. O'Bannon demonstrated the correct way to hold the instrument and bow then he began Abbud's first fiddle lesson.

"Are there more men of Tripoli we might recruit in Alexandria or Cairo?" asked Eaton anxiously.

As Hamet considered his answer, a bonfire crackled cheerfully. Eaton, Hamet, O'Bannon and Leitensdorfer sat cross legged on the beach, some distance from the camp for privacy sake. A full moon hung in the star spackled night sky above the calm sea.

In the distance they heard an occasional shout, the bellow of a camel, and songs sung in different tongues. Abbud was happily sawing away on his fiddle somewhere, producing whoops of delight from his audience.

"Perhaps fifty," Hamet finally replied tentatively, his statement more a question than an answer.

Eaton bit his lower lip. With Abbud's men, there were two hundred and thirty or so foot soldiers in his column, certainly not enough to make an effective attack on Derne. He hoped there would be at least several hundred Tripolitan exiles in Egypt ready to join the enterprise. That is what he had told President Jefferson, after all. But fifty men? Perhaps?

O'Bannon threw a chunk of drift wood on the blaze and a cloud of sparks flew above them. The marine then turned to Hamet.

"Your English is very good, Mr. Karamanli," he said. "Where did you learn to speak it so well?"

"I have always been interested in learning," Hamet replied. "My father and my younger brother didn't care about such things but as a boy I read every book I could find. When I was fifteen, I begged my father to send me to Europe to study."

"And he agreed?" asked O'Bannon.

"In a way, yes. I wished to attend university in England but Father didn't trust infidels. He was afraid they would teach me bad things," Hamet said thoughtfully. "So, he took me to Constantinople. We found a scholar there whom my father hired to tutor me in the Koran but also to teach me English and French and mathematics. I spent five years with him." He sighed, adding wistfully, "I was very happy in those days."

"What happened when you returned to Tripoli, if I may ask?" O'Bannon inquired.

"You may ask," Hamet quietly replied, gazing into the fire. "Along with knowledge, I had acquired many books and maps during my years in Constantinople. When I returned home I began teaching my young cousins who wished to learn what I knew. I was not interested in ruling Tripoli after my father died, since my elder brother Hassan was his successor. Hassan was a kind and generous man and he would have made a good ruler."

"Was?" Leitensdorfer asked.

"Yusuf, my younger brother, murdered him with a pistol in the presence of our mother," Hamet said. "I was away when it happened. I learned that Yusuf wished me dead too so I didn't go home. I went to Tunis with some of my followers and friends and that is where I met

General Eaton."

Hamet paused as the men watched a meteor shower streak through the night sky.

"My wife and three children along with the families of my men are being held by Yusuf in Tripoli," Hamet went on sadly. "He has told us we may return anytime to reunite with them, but I fear he will put us all to death if we do."

"You shall return, friend, and you shall turn the tables on your accursed brother," Eaton said as he patted Hamet's back reassuringly.

Karamanli replied with a thin smile, "I would not harm him. Revenge and violence is not in my nature. I wish only to be with my wife and children again and, if we are successful, to rule Tripoli peacefully."

The fire was burning down to embers. Leitensdorfer silently stirred them with a stick. There were fewer voices from the camp as men settled down to sleep, but noise from Abbud's abused fiddle continued.

"Jesus Christ, lieutenant!" Eaton suddenly exclaimed. "Why did you give him that infernal thing?! What awful sounds!"

"You ordered me to, general, remember?!" laughed O'Bannon. "Leastways, he can't go anywhere now. I've got to teach him to play it!"

"Yes, well, another hundred men is good, but we must have more," said Eaton, returning to the business at hand.

Leitensdorfer had been sitting with his arms around his drawn up knees, gazing into the dying fire. He had satisfied the debt to his former father-in-law and his assistance in freeing Hamet had earned him the job as Eaton's adjutant along with a bonus of fifty dollars.

"I know a man," he now interjected. "A Bulgarian cavalry officer who fought in Napoleon's army here in Egypt. He was cashiered. He opened an apothecary shop and married an Egyptian woman – a very beautiful one, I might add…"

"And?" Eaton interrupted.

"Well, this Bulgar, his name is Fedor. He loves to ride horses and is quite friendly with a band of Arabs who share his passion," Leitensdorfer

23

Yusuf awoke depressed each morning to see what was left of his navy bottled up in Tripoli's inner harbor and fearful at the prospect of another devastating bombardment at any time. The damage Preble's earlier attack had done to his corsairs had mostly been repaired by the carpenters, caulkers and sail makers of *Philadelphia*, but now, day after day, the American war ships lurked off his coast, preventing any vessel other than little silks or fishing boats from leaving or entering Tripoli.

An occasional shallow draft felucca loaded with grain or fruit would make port by hugging the shoreline, but these were few so Yusuf was forced to bring supplies and food to the city overland from Benghazi hundreds of miles away, a far more costly proposition for the bashaw. This drain on his treasure had the effect of further deepening Yusuf's depression and rage. He began drinking forbidden brandy and beating his wives, servants and slaves for any slight or for no reason at all.

For his part, Grand Admiral Murad Reis made himself scarce, staying aboard *Meshouda*, powerless to break the American stranglehold. From the quarterdeck, he took some small pleasure watching the American slaves building the breakwater one giant rock at a time, their guards brutally driving them to and from the quarry.

Bainbridge wrote letters. Every day he begged Barron to intervene and win the release of *Philadelphia's* officers and crew, the former growing

continued. "I understand these particular Arabs are ⟨
love battle."

Ignoring all of the possible complications and dan
horde of mounted and armed Arabs joining his colun
already nodding. "A cavalry, eh?" he said thoughtfully. "
many of these Arabs there are?"

"Why was this Fedor cashiered?" interrupted O'Banno

"Oh, lieutenant, for the usual thing," Leitensdorfer r
shrug. "Drunkenness. He has a taste for a spirit called vc
that is what he makes and sells in his apothecary. Believers a
alcohol, but they may take small amounts for medicinal
would seem many in Alexandria have illnesses that only Fed
because he does a good business."

more despondent by the day, the latter growing weaker and sicker under the bashaw's relentless lash. He had learned that one of his men was thrown from the city wall as punishment for the accidental killing of a Tripolitan guard. If they could execute one American, Bainbridge reflected, it would be an easy thing for Yusuf to murder every *Philadelphia* man he held.

New Year's Day, 1805 passed mirthlessly for the captives, who could do little but watch the squadron of American ships lying off the harbor and hope that soon a cutter would emerge from among them under a white flag of truce.

Then one cool afternoon it happened.

Bainbridge and his officers watched an American brig join the blockade fleet shortly after sunrise. Through his glass he saw a boat lowered and what appeared to be a civilian climb aboard. They were rowed over to *Constitution*, Rodger's flag ship, where the passenger disembarked.

An hour later, *Constitution* lowered one of her boats and the same civilian boarded. The boat began rowing toward the harbor as a white flag was raised. Bainbridge's officers gathered around their captain and excitedly watched the scene unfold. They gave a lusty cheer at the sight of the flag.

"Men! Men!" cried Bainbridge. "This means nothing! Let us wait patiently. You midshipmen and junior officers, get to work on your studies. I did not dismiss you!"

There was some grumbling but also bright smiles and excited chatter as the young men resumed their book work. Lieutenant Porter joined Bainbridge as he glassed the inbound boat. Along with the eight men rowing her, it contained Rodgers and a tall, well dressed man the captain did not recognize. It entered the harbor, where a Tripolitan cutter escorted the Americans to the quay.

"What do you think, sir," Porter asked.

"It's Captain Rodgers and another man," Bainbridge replied. "They could be here to negotiate. There is nothing to be done but wait, I'm afraid." Bainbridge folded up his glass and looked around. "See to it that the quarters are thoroughly cleaned and that those drying clothes on the wall yonder are taken down. If we are to receive Captain Rodgers, I want us to look presentable."

"Aye, Will," Porter said with a smile, the first genuine affection his second had displayed toward him since the loss of *Philadelphia*.

"Let them wait," Yusuf mumbled through a mouthful of rice pilaf. He glanced up at his foreign minister Sidi Mohammed Dghies who had just announced the arrival of the Americans, Captain John Rodgers and American Consul Tobias Lear. Dghies, always terrified of Yusuf and particularly so since he had begun drinking spirits, simply nodded and withdrew from the suite.

"The bashaw is currently occupied with important matters, gentlemen," Dghies explained as he rejoined the Americans. "Please, come, we have refreshments prepared for you…"

"We'll just wait for his Excellency, thank you," declared Lear. "Our business is urgent. Our men are being worked to death out there and we wish to begin negotiations to win their release. The sooner the better, minister."

"Yes, yes, yes," replied the nervous old man. "I understand this. But, Bashaw Karamanli, he does not like to be hurried. I beg you to be patient." Dghies gestured to a pair of chairs. "Please, sit here and I will do what I can to help get the bashaw in the correct frame of mind. Meantime, please, allow me to serve you wine, at least."

Lear shrugged and seated himself. Rodgers followed suit and shortly, a bottle of Madeira and glasses were brought by a boy. As the wine was poured, a door opened and Murad Reis entered the room.

"Greetings, infidels!" he called. "I am Grand Admiral Murad Reis, commander of the bashaw's naval forces."

Rodgers eyed Reis but said nothing. Lear stood and held out his hand which the grand admiral shook. "I am Tobias Lear, Commissioner of the United States here to negotiate peace with Tripoli." When he noticed that the captain had not gotten to his feet, Lear shot Rodgers a look.

"I'm sorry, Colonel Lear," Rodgers angrily declared, "but I'll not shake this bastard's hand!"

"Captain Rodgers!" snapped Lear. "We are here on a peace mission! You shall stand and greet this man or Secretary Smith will hear of your insubordination!"

Red faced, Rodgers stood and took the smirking Reis's hand then sat down, casting his eyes to the floor in humiliation.

"So it's peace ye seek, is it?" Reis asked with a bemused smile. "Peace is expensive!"

"Yes, we understand that," Lear replied. "But so is continued war, admiral. It seems to me we are at a stalemate. You cannot sail from your harbor and we cannot liberate our countrymen that Tripoli holds captive. It has been my experience that negotiations can break such impasses."

"Aye, they can," Reis agreed. "My father-in-law, the bashaw, can be most reasonable when his enemies seek peace. But he can be most ruthless when they choose war."

"There is an interesting coincidence," said Lear. "You just described President Jefferson's attitude about this entire conflict."

Reis considered this. The American attacks and blockade had done much to shake Yusuf's confidence in his grand admiral. Their relationship had grown cold and distant since the bombardments. At times, Reis wondered if he might be blamed and punished for the turn the war had taken against Tripoli.

"I think ye will find Bashaw Karamanli receptive," Reis finally said. "We are civilized men. Further bloodshed and destruction are pointless."

"Civilized!" Rodgers spit the word at Reis. "You call what you are doing to our men civilized?!"

Lear snapped, "Captain Rodgers! Silence!"

Another door swung open and Mohammed Dghies appeared. "Come, gentlemen! Bashaw Yusuf Karamanli is most eager to meet you! This way," he gestured excitedly, "this way, please!"

Eaton was mounted on his agitated gelding waiting for the signal. A pistol shot rang out, the rope dropped and thirty horses sprinted from the starting line. Eaton spurred his mount and raced across the sand toward a pole that marked the finish a mile away.

His Arab hosts were shouting and screeching, slapping out at competing riders with their crops to gain an advantage. Somebody grabbed Eaton's robes and tried to pull him out of the saddle. Eaton drove his spurs into his horse's flanks and, despite the heavy sand, the gelding responded with a burst of speed.

He found himself wedged between two riders, one tried to strike him with his crop but he seized the man's wrist and with a sharp tug, the rider fell from his saddle. If this race was without rules, Eaton was happy to oblige.

He found himself in the lead, the pole just a half mile away now. The horse's powerful legs drove into the sand and he seemed in command until Fedor was suddenly at his side, his white stallion flying past as though Eaton's mount was walking.

Sheikh Kazim was right behind him aboard a black Arabian stud.

Fedor let out a bellow of laughter as he crossed the finish line, Kazim a half length behind. Eaton finished third. Kazim was grinning broadly at the antics of Fedor, who galloped around the finish pole, standing in his stirrups, his arms raised above his head in triumph.

"Surely that was blind luck!" called Kazim to the Bulgarian in Arabic.

"Blind luck?! Balls!" mocked Fedor. "This little stallion is faster than any wretched nag you own, Kazim!"

The sheikh waved a hand dismissively at the jibe as O'Bannon, Hamet and Leitensdorfer rode across the finish line, far back in the pack aboard their inferior horses.

"So, you see General Eaton," Kazim declared, "we Arabs are far better horsemen than you Americans! Even a drunken Bulgar is better!"

Eaton good naturedly laughed as he reached out and shook Kazim's wrist. The horse race had been the sheik's challenge when they arrived in the Arab camp that morning and now Eaton understood the real reason for the race had been to test the Americans.

Kazim seemed satisfied to have seen whatever he needed to see. He looked about at all the horsemen. "Come!" he cried happily, "let us feast and find out what these Christians want of us!"

Fedor had a tin plate filled with roasted mutton and a bottle of the clear spirit he called vodka. He joined Eaton, O'Bannon, Leitensdorfer and Kazim and some of the camp's senior men beneath a wide silk canopy that shaded them from the afternoon sun.

The Bulgarian was tall and lean, with a wide florid face, a broad forehead and receding brown hair. Eaton thought he might be close to his own age. Like the Arabs, Fedor wore flowing white robes and a white burnoose, which he removed now that he was in the shade. Fedor took a long pull from the bottle and offered it to Eaton who sipped.

"Excellent!" he declared, passing the bottle to O'Bannon who, like his Arab hosts and Hamet, abstained. He passed the bottle to Leitensdorfer, who drank deeply.

The mutton was delicious, seasoned with pungent spices O'Bannon had never tasted. Veiled women in vivid blue robes brought them apricots, oranges, lemons and nuts while the vodka bottle continued to circulate. Coffee was served in small silver urns and then water pipes were lit.

Sated, Kazim leaned back on his pillow and took in his guests. The American called Eaton who spoke excellent Arabic was clad in robes like his own. The tall soldier with long black hair was dressed in a handsome blue uniform and white britches. The Tripoline called Hamet had dark skin and eyes and said very little. The German was wearing a red jacket, black britches and a black fez with a silver tassel on his bald head. Taken together with Fedor, surely this was the oddest group of foreigners to ever visit Kazim's nomadic camp. Always careful not to give offense to his guests, the sheikh waited patiently to hear what it was his guests wanted.

Finally, after an eloquent speech that flattered Kazim's hospitality, Eaton got down to business.

"I have been sent here to meet with you, Sheikh, by President Thomas Jefferson," Eaton began, "the ruler of America."

Kazim had never been to America nor had he heard of this Jefferson but he smiled indulgently.

"Yusuf Karamanli, the illegitimate ruler of Tripoli, has demanded tribute and gifts in return for allowing America's merchant shipping to trade unmolested in the Mediterranean Sea," Eaton continued. "Until two years ago, my country disgracefully paid him whatever he demanded."

Piracy was not news to Kazim, who saw nothing wrong with plundering Christians. Again he offered a silent smile in reply.

"President Jefferson decided that it was a disgrace to our national honor to continue to pay Yusuf. He ordered a halt to tribute and built a navy to defend our merchant shipping. My country is today at war with Tripoli."

The sheikh had no idea what "national honor" meant, but he remained silent and attentive.

"I was sent here to mount an attack Derna, Yusuf's eastern stronghold, Sheikh Kazim. We are gathering an army at the Arab's Tower. We need more men, sir. Your men, if I may be blunt..."

Kazim was beginning to comprehend Eaton. He abruptly held up his hand.

"A Muslim is forbidden to make war on another Muslim and, most especially, to ally himself with a non-believer to make war on another Muslim," Kazim explained. "It is written."

An awkward silence hung in the still air broken only by the buzz of a fly. Hamet cleared his throat. Knowing Kazim understood and respected the sanctity primogeniture, he took a different tack.

"Yusuf is my brother, Sheikh Kazim," he began. "He is a cruel and dishonest lout, the youngest son of our father, Ali, whom, before he died, designated my elder brother Hassan as his heir."

Kazim and his retinue were listening.

"Yusuf disrespectfully argued with Hassan over our father's wishes for succession, claiming he should rule Tripoli, not my elder brother. One day, Yusuf lured Hassan to our mother's villa on the pretext of making peace. When Hassan arrived, Yusuf shot him in the head while my poor mother watched," Hamet continued.

The sheik's face darkened at this revelation.

"I was traveling when this terrible murder took place. I never went home. Now, Yusuf is bashaw of Tripoli and holds my wife and children hostage as well as the families of my followers, hoping some day we will return so he may slay us," Hamet explained, looking intently at the Arabs. "I ask you, is this how a believer treats the wishes of his father?"

"Is...is this outrage true?!" Kazim indigently asked, his dark eyes flashing. "Yusuf murdered his own brother in order to disobey his father and seize the throne of Tripoli?!"

Grateful for Hamet's timely intercession, Eaton picked up its theme.

"I am afraid it is so, Sheikh Kazim," he began. "My nation's ruler is also an honorable man who wishes to reunite Hamet Karamanli with his family and to help our friend here retake his rightful place. Like you, he also wants to see Yusuf punished for his bloody crime. Hamet needs more honest men to achieve this. If it is possible, sir, we humbly beg that one hundred of your best horsemen join us. You will all be well paid by President Jefferson for your service and you will have America's friendship forever."

Kazim said something to his lieutenants, several of whom nodded. "I must convene a council, friends," he said, looking at the

Americans. "We would like to speak privately to Hamet. Will you please excuse us?"

"Of course, sheikh, as you wish," Eaton replied as he stood. He gestured to O'Bannon, Leitensdorfer and Fedor to follow and the three left Kazim's pavilion.

The next morning, a deal struck with Kazim that paid the sheikh five hundred dollars and each of his armed horsemen twenty dollars plus any plunder captured in Derne, Eaton proudly rode out of the sprawling Arab encampment alongside his new ally.

Behind rode a column of one hundred and ten mounted and armed cavalry. Fedor, always one for an adventure, joined the enterprise as an officer, closing his apothecary until he returned to Alexandria.

O'Bannon, once again amazed at Eaton's audacity and resourcefulness, trotted up alongside his commander. "This'll give us nearly four hundred men, general," O'Bannon declared. "You reckon that's enough?"

"No, but Hamet says we can recruit more on the march to Derne," Eaton replied. "What we really we need now are camels to move supplies. As many as we can hire."

24

L ear swallowed the bile rising in his throat as he smiled at Bashaw Karamanli and then sipped the tea that had been set before him. He carefully placed the cup on the saucer and looked again at his host who sat across the table, Mohammed Dhgies to Yusuf's right and Murad Reis to his left.

"I'm afraid three hundred thousand dollars is out of the question, Your Excellency," he said. "I have explained why in our previous meetings. I am prepared to offer you one hundred thousand and no more. I may be able to add some arms and ammunition as tokens of our appreciation."

Yusuf listened to Dhgies' translation then, glaring at the American, sat his bulk back in his chair and folded his thick arms over his belly. After several long moments, he slammed his heavy palm down on the table.

"You come from a rich country Mr. Lear!" Yusuf cried. "I have read that your finance minister is able to raise one million dollars with just the stroke of his pen! Three hundred thousand is only one thousand dollars for each Christian I hold! Your offer is an insult!"

Dhgies wore an apologetic expression as he translated Yusuf's words.

Lear had learned to bide his time during his many years as an ambassador no matter how despicable he found his interlocutors. He casually crossed one of his legs over the other and looked Reis' way.

"We appear to be at loggerheads again, grand admiral," he said quietly.

"Look what your navy did to our city," Reis angrily declared, "and to my ships in the harbor. Were it me, Lear, I would be demanding a million dollars for the damage and the hostages. So three hundred's really a bargain looked at that way, eh?"

The American made a face. Lisle had been useless in the negotiations, which had now been going on for two weeks as the blockade continued.

The ambassador stood and walked to a large window. He pointed at the frigates and brigs patrolling a few miles out, their great American flags serenely fluttering as they sailed along.

"We can certainly resume the bombardment if that is what it will take to encourage the bashaw to be flexible," he said mildly. "We are expecting gunboats and at least two more frigates to join the blockade within the next few days. I am a patient man, but the officers aboard those ships? Well, I think you know their preferred solution."

Dhgies finished translating. Karamanli sat, arms crossed and lips pursed beneath his thick beard, considering his options. He liked none of them. Finally Yusuf lifted his bulk out of the chair.

"Mr. Lear, I must take some time to consider what you have said," he replied pleasantly. "But remember, also, I hold three hundred of your countrymen. Should you decide to attack the city, I shall leave with all the prisoners to a castle I have many miles from Tripoli and hold them there."

Lear had heard this threat before. It was a potent argument, but the American merely shrugged.

"We may well have means of preventing you from doing so," Lear bluffed. "We have surprised you before, have we not?"

Reis bitterly recalled the Americans swarming the decks of his gun boats and slaughtering his panicked men, then the merciless pounding Tripoli had received, all unexpected. The room was silent. Finally, the bashaw turned and walked through a door, Dhgies following, the meeting concluded.

Lear gave Reis a menacing look and said, "I think you should talk some sense into your father-in-law."

Reis sat alone with Yusuf in an ornate salon bedecked with colorful carpets and tapestries. The bashaw was lounging on a sofa, meditatively sipping brandy from a goblet that a black slave girl kept filled. "This army Hamet and his infidel friends are preparing in Alexandria is a problem," Yusuf finally declared without looking at Reis. "After they attack Derne, they will come here."

Reis nodded his agreement, taking a swallow of his own brandy as he did. He had not been alone with the bashaw since the bombardments, but Yusuf summoned him after the meeting with Lear.

"My enemies in Derne will probably join them if they are successful in taking the city from Governor Mustapha," the bashaw continued. "Maybe even some from Benghazi. This is dangerous."

Reis had heard that a cousin of Yusuf's living in Alexandria and loyal to the bashaw discovered that an American was assembling Tripolitan expatriates and mercenaries in Alexandria for an attack on Derne. Worse, the cousin learned Hamet Karamanli was with them, intending to take back his throne with the help of the Americans. The loyal cousin had sailed to Tripoli, the speedy felucca successfully eluding the blockade. Yusuf had listened in stunned silence as his kinsman delivered the news, then rewarded the man's loyalty with fifty gold sovereigns.

"This army was probably what that whoreson Lear was talking about when he said he might have a way of stopping us from taking the Americans into the Nafusa Mountains," Reis observed. The bashaw had a castle there with ample room for the prisoners set high among the foothills of the desolate inland range.

Without acknowledging the grand admiral, Yusuf nodded as the servant girl poured more liquor. He finally turned his gaze to Reis, his expression dark.

"You must go to Derne and ready the defenses there," Yusuf said with a tone of finality. "This is your fault. You must correct your errors."

Reis stared at the bashaw in disbelief. "My fault!?" he finally sputtered at Yusuf's sudden accusation.

"You should have defeated the dogs when they attacked with their accursed gun boats. You outnumbered them but they defeated you instead!" growled Yusuf. "Now my corsairs cannot go to sea to replenish my treasure while you sit there pretending nothing has happened!"

Reis saw Yusuf was drunk, but the tirade continued. "Yes, you, *grand admiral*!" he spit the last two words at Reis. "You have failed to protect my throne and now I am under assault by sea and land!"

Reis tried to reply.

"Silence!" cried Yusuf. "You leave in the morning for Derne! Then wait for the hyenas to attack and defeat them there! Bring any captives to me alive! They shall suffer the torments of the damned for their insolence!"

Stung and now comprehending his own peril if he should fail this time, Reis rose, bowed deeply and said, "As you command, Excellency."

The negotiations for the camels began on friendly enough terms the day before with a distant uncle of Sheikh Kazim's. But the haggling dragged on all afternoon, into the night, and now the next morning.

Eaton had become frustrated more than once, leaving his tent to vent his frustration with el Taiib the camel dealer, then returning to resume the dickering. Impatient as he was, Eaton knew more than most that this was how business was transacted in North Africa.

The old Arab's face was the color and consistency of a walnut and he could flawlessly perform any emotion the situation called for. At the moment, he was playing the role of indignant benefactor.

"Mine are the finest camels in all of Egypt, General Eaton!" el Taiib declared when the American again protested a rental fee of twenty-five dollars for each of the beasts. El Taiib brought a pair to show Eaton and one of them, lying outside the tent, belched as if to second the endorsement. The wily old dealer clutched his hands as though begging Eaton. "How, sir, *how* can I let them to you for only eight dollars apiece?"

Eaton wasn't listening. He was instead calculating how he was going to rent the camels with his dwindling funds. At the twenty-five dollars each el Taiib was demanding, the two hundred camels Eaton needed to move his army would cost five thousand dollars.

Recruiting along with the food and supplies his army required had been far more expensive than he estimated. Certain things, rice for instance, was cheap. But gunpowder, shot, muskets, medical supplies and boots were far more costly because they were scarce. When they were located by Leitensdorfer or O'Bannon, the merchants selling them demanded scandalous prices.

Eaton was also forced to pay bribe after bribe to various "officials" who showed up at Arab's Tower under one pretense or another and, when some of his mercenaries threatened to leave, Eaton promised to pay them more after they took Derne.

Hamet and his followers required several large marquees and furnishings, for which Leitensdorfer paid more than he should in Alexandria. When Eaton made an accounting of his remaining gold coins two days earlier, he discovered he had less than three thousand dollars left of the twenty thousand he'd brought to Egypt.

"I shall pay you nine dollars for each animal when we reach Derne..."

El Taiib was vigorously shaking his head. "Twenty now!" he demanded stabbing a grubby forefinger into his even grubbier open palm, now playing the mistrustful merchant he really was.

Eaton had reached the breaking point. "Enough!" he barked, his face flush with anger. "You think you are the only dealer hiring camels in Alexandria, old man?! You think me a fool who would pay you twice what your sorry beasts are worth?!"

One of el Taiib's camels let out a loud groan.

El Taiib's face mutated into that of a hurt child. He bit his lower lip and, tears welling in his eyes said, "Sir, I have given offense. I shall leave..."

Angry at himself for his outburst, Eaton held up a hand. "Eleven dollars for each camel, el Taiib. I can pay you no more than that. Half now, half when we reach Derne."

El Taiib considered the bargain. It was at least five dollars more than he could make if he let the camels for two months to a believer. This infidel looked desperate and he was also right. There were other camel dealers in Alexandria like that viper Nasib who always undercut el Taiib's price when he had the chance. Perhaps eleven dollars was all the money this American actually had. The old man finally decided it was the best he could get so he agreed - for now. He made a show of vigorously shaking Eaton's hand and then hugging the general warmly and kissing his cheeks.

"Very well, General Eaton," he said with a genial and toothless smile, "two hundred camels at eleven dollars each. I shall take half of my money now, please. When shall I deliver the camels?"

Argus was riding at anchor in Alexandria's harbor when Eaton and O'Bannon boarded her. Hull had returned from Syracuse for a final war council with Eaton and ordered his steward to prepare a proper American meal for his guests. Fried chicken and greens were served along with biscuits, butter and gravy, followed by a cobbler made with fresh pears, all accompanied by a good Italian red wine.

"Very thoughtful of you, lieutenant," remarked Eaton with a pleasant smile as he offered the others cigars. "We've been eating mutton and rice and drinking Fedor's dreadful vodka nearly every day since we got here."

"My pleasure, general," Hull replied. "Always good to get a home cooked meal...or at least an attempt at a home cooked meal!"

The old black steward appeared to clear the plates. "Well done there, Miller," O'Bannon remarked with a smile. "Finest victuals I've had in weeks!"

"Thank ye, sir," Miller replied with a nod before disappearing from Hull's small cabin.

Eaton sat forward and began the meeting. "Lieutenant Hull, we're ready to advance on Derne. Camels will be delivered the day after tomorrow, so I reckon we depart on March the seventh or eighth."

"Aye, sir," Hull replied.

"We should be at Bomba Bay in four week's time if we can make twenty miles a day," Eaton continued pointing at the chart before him. "But it could be longer. Hamet has promised me we can recruit more Bedouins during the march, so that might require additional time. When we get to Bomba we will need to be resupplied on or about the first of April with food, ammunition and…more money."

Hull stared at Eaton. As ordered, he had given the chest filled with twenty thousand dollars in gold coins to Eaton scarcely two months before. When Commodore Barron had taken the receipt for the funds from Hull he sarcastically remarked that there would not be another penny for Eaton's "fantasy."

"I don't think there will be any more money, General Eaton," Hull said with a nervous glance at O'Bannon. "The commodore was quite clear on that point."

Eaton already knew Barron's attitude about the enterprise. He broke into a wide smile, sat back and drained his wine glass.

"Oh, I am sure he was, Mr. Hull!" Eaton declared with a barking laugh. There was no need for him to be politic here so, fueled by the excellent wine, he continued. "You see, sir, the commodore has never *actually* been in battle! He's never *actually* had to organize men to fight! That son of a…that *gentleman* has advanced through the ranks unsullied by combat! Can you imagine?!"

O'Bannon and Hull were now smiling at Eaton's good natured diatribe.

"Yes, when eighty-six of us were fighting for our lives at Fort Recovery, we could have used an officer like Commodore Barron! While we were trying to keep our scalps, he would have kept account of the powder and ball we expended!"

O'Bannon and Hull were laughing now.

"Commodore Barron and Secretary Gallatin think of war as something that can be accurately estimated beforehand, the fools!" Eaton exclaimed, wide eyed.

"Still, general, I don't know how I will be able to get you more money," Hull said, "especially now that the commodore is sick and in the hospital."

Eaton was watching the smoke from his cigar, considering the dilemma.

"The enterprise has been allocated forty thousand dollars," Eaton replied. "Barron has no choice but to make the balance of twenty thousand available to me."

"Aye, sir," Hull replied doubtfully. Eaton understood Hull's hesitance. The young officer didn't want to jeopardize his career for something he probably didn't believe in himself.

"Lieutenant," Eaton declared with a chuckle. "Captain Barron doesn't know much about war, but I know he understands politics. I expect he will provide the funds when he considers the consequences of refusing my request."

Reis had waited two weeks for the right conditions. Now he had them. Fog rolled in off the sea at sunset obscuring the moonless night sky. *Meshouda* was prepared days before and his fighters were now aboard, armed and ready to defend Derne.

Reis ordered six boats to tow *Meshouda* beyond the breakwater and then eastward along the coastline. With her lights doused, Reis' flagship would be invisible in the mist and darkness. The primary danger was sand bars. If he should ground *Meshouda* she would be at the mercy of the Americans when the fog lifted. But Reis decided he had no choice if he was ever to leave the harbor.

It was nearly three o'clock in the morning when the rowers reached the end of the mole and turned east. The going was slow, but the men at the oars knew these waters and, more important, no Americans were sighted.

Once Reis felt *Meshouda's* keel graze a reef, but now the boats were leading her out into deeper water. An hour later, Reis quietly called for the tow lines to be cast free, the sails raised into the light wind, and an eastern heading.

25

The hostility between Eaton's Greeks and the Turks, simmering for weeks, broke into an all out brawl the night before the column was to depart Arab's Tower. It started over a lamb.

A young Greek soldier purchased the animal from one of Abbud's Bedouin herders and then led it to a grove of palms where he slaughtered it.

As he was dressing the carcass, a pair of Turks happened upon the scene and claimed the lamb. Insults quickly followed. The Greek was kicked and punched and the lamb stolen.

Word of the theft reached the Greek contingent, which marched to the Turk encampment. There, Lieutenant Ulovix, the Greeks' officer, demanded the return of the lamb which the Turks were roasting over a fire. More insults were thrown and the fistfight broke out. Swords and pistols were drawn just as O'Bannon came dashing into the camp.

"Stop!" he cried, pulling a Turk up off a fallen Greek. "Enough!"

The Greeks and Turks, some bleeding, pulled back at the sight of O'Bannon's armed marines who followed their lieutenant to the fracas. They all began jabbering at O'Bannon and pointing at one another.

O'Bannon sent one of his marines for Leitensdorfer, who shortly appeared and explained the situation to the lieutenant after he spoke to officers from each side.

"A lamb?!" O'Bannon asked incredulously. "They were ready to kill each other over a lamb?!"

"It is not so simple as that Pres," Leitensdorfer answered. "The Greeks and Turks hate each other. It goes back many centuries. You probably have seen how the Christians are camped over there and the Muslims over here. This is no accident."

O'Bannon had not noticed, but Leitensdorfer was right. The many languages spoken among the soldiers and cavalry created confusion, but Eaton's mercenary army was really divided along religious lines. The lieutenant now understood this was cause for concern. Would the Muslims and Christians work as a unit when they attacked Derne? Had Eaton considered that they might not?

"This is why I gave the British uniforms to the Muslims," Leitensdorfer continued, "and the French uniforms to the Christians. So we could distinguish them quickly."

O'Bannon hadn't noticed this detail either, but it made perfect sense. The blue French uniforms reasonably matched the blue uniforms of his marines while the red was close to the crimson tunics many of the Turks wore.

"That was good thinking, Eugene," O'Bannon finally said. "Uniforming the men like that never occurred to me. We had better divide them up into companies. We'll keep the Christians together and apart and I will command them. You had better take charge of the Muslims, since you speak their tongues. Fedor can assist you. We'll keep them separated, but when the time comes we'll all have to work together."

O'Bannon turned to the Greeks. Most wore pleated white skirts they called *foystanellas* over white woolen trousers. A white shirt, blue waistcoat and red fez completed the uniform. "How much did they pay for the lamb?" the lieutenant asked.

Leitensdorfer spoke to Ulovix in French. "He says two sequins, about one dollar."

O'Bannon reached into his pocketbook and removed some coins. He held them out to the Greek officer, who smiled and took them. "The Greeks can buy another lamb."

He turned his attention to the Turkish officer who wore a British major's tunic, white britches and, curiously, a French cuirassier's brass helmet. "And tell this bastard to keep his men under control or by God I will."

El Taiib appeared in the camp the next morning at eight o'clock, his two hundred camels in tow. He brought with him one hundred camel drivers, mainly teenaged boys and old men to handle the animals. Leitensdorfer greeted him and began directing the drivers to their cargo but el Taiib told him no camels would be loaded until he spoke to Eaton.

The general and his officers had been up since dawn striking the camp while O'Bannon and his marines prepared the army for the long march.

"I must have more money, sir," el Taiib demanded as he approached Eaton. "We did not negotiate a price for the drivers."

Eaton, who was distracted by some detail, turned to el Taiib. "What did you say?"

"I must be paid for the drivers as well as the camels!" El Taiib demanded. "Our agreed price is for the camels only. We will not load the camels until I am paid!"

Eaton's money was nearly gone and there would be no more until they reached Bomba Bay, and maybe not even then if Barron was not in a generous mood when Hull visited him in Syracuse.

"How much more?"

"Five dollars for each driver," el Taiib eagerly replied. "I brought one hundred drivers. This is a bargain."

Eaton knew five dollars for a lowly camel driver for two months work was anything but a bargain, but he broke into a kind smile anyway, determined not to let the greedy camel dealer ruin this august day.

"Why, of course, el Taiib!" he laughed. "Five dollars?! Is that all?! Are you sure?!"

El Taiib wasn't fooled. He eyed Eaton warily. "Yes, just five dollars and I want my money now!"

Laughing, Eaton patted the Arab's shoulder. "I can't pay you now, my friend! I will have no more money until we meet our ships at Bomba in four weeks. Surely, you can wait that long, can you not?"

El Taiib considered this. "Very well," he finally agreed before stalking off, gesticulating and swearing at the drivers who hustled with their camels in different directions.

Three hours later, with Eaton and Hamet Karamanli at its head, the mercenary army was on the march. O'Bannon placed the most experienced and disciplined European foot soldiers at the head of the column to set the pace. Between the Christians and Muslims rode O'Bannon, Fedor, Kazim and Leitensdorfer. Behind them, Kazim's Arab cavalry in their white robes followed by Abbud's Bedouin horsemen wearing their black and navy blue robes. The Turks and the other Muslim foot soldiers and the baggage train took up the rear. Clouds of dust rose into the clear sky as Eaton's mercenaries marched west on an ancient trading track that paralleled the coastline.

Within a few hours, the column stretched out for over two miles. By the time the lead elements made camp at sunset, it took two hours for the rest of the column to catch up. It wasn't until nearly midnight that everyone was fed and bedded down.

Eaton and his exhausted officers gathered in his marquee to discuss the day. "We marched, what, ten, eleven miles today?" Eaton asked. "At that rate it will take us nearly two months to reach Derne! We need to pick up the pace!"

O'Bannon considered this. "I'll disperse my marines and some of those Irish and French lads through the column. They can help keep everyone moving."

Eaton nodded as he looked around. "Where is Hamet?"

"He and Kazim are tenting together," Leitensdorfer replied, "over in the Arab camp."

Since Kazim and his cavalry joined the army, Eaton had seen far less of Hamet, who seemed to prefer the sheikh's company. He didn't know what to make of this, wasn't sure there was even any significance beyond their shared religion and culture. Perhaps Hamet simply felt more comfortable with Kazim and his tribesmen. Dismissing thoughts of Hamet, Eaton rose.

"Let us get some sleep, gentlemen," he said as he stretched his frame. "We ride at dawn."

The sun rose over the placid sea but nobody other than the Americans and Europeans was moving. Gradually Muslims began emerging from their tents and some began to leisurely collect driftwood along the beach for breakfast fires. For fifteen minutes, all of them stopped for the morning prayer, prostrating themselves in the sand, facing east. Fires were then lit and tea was brewed as laughter and chatter rose from their camp.

Meantime, the Americans and Europeans had eaten breakfast, extinguished cook fires, struck their tents, fed, watered and saddled their horses and were now standing around watching the Muslim's prepare for the day.

"Jesus Christ, they look like a hunting party, not a military column!" barked Eaton impatiently. "What the hell are they doing?!"

Fedor looked at Eaton, "Sir, haste is a thing they cannot understand."

Eaton gestured at O'Bannon, said impatiently, "Lieutenant! Go find Hamet!"

It took O'Bannon and Leitensdorfer a half hour to locate their ally. He was seated alone on the beach a quarter mile from camp writing in a tablet.

"Sir, we are ready to move," O'Bannon declared. "General Eaton is growing impatient!"

Hamet continued to gaze out over the sea before writing something down. He turned and smiled at O'Bannon. "A glorious morning is it not, lieutenant?" he asked. He looked out over the water and pointed. "Watch that white seabird out there, how he holds his place without moving his wings. It is magical, is it not? I am writing poetry so I might remember this moment."

O'Bannon glanced at Leitensdorfer who shrugged. "That's fine, Mr. Karamanli, but we must leave now or we will never reach Derne."

With a sigh Hamet slowly closed his tablet, placed a stopper in his ink bottle and stood. With one more wistful look at the bird, he followed O'Bannon and Leitensdorfer back to the camp.

Eaton was furious after he heard O'Bannon's report. He abruptly motioned to Hamet and the two walked off alone toward a dune. When they were out of earshot, Eaton turned on Hamet.

"This is unacceptable!" he scolded. "It is past nine o'clock and your people are dawdling about as though they are on holiday. This won't do, sir!"

Hamet glanced back over his shoulder at the Muslim camp where just a few tents had been struck, the camels were half loaded, a group of Kazim's horsemen were examining mounts and discussing the merits of their animals, while others sat before their tents eating breakfast. The Turks appeared to playing some sort of game with their daggers. All the while, the Americans and Europeans looked on.

"Yes, I see what you mean, William," Hamet replied with an embarrassed smile.

"You are their leader, are you not?" Eaton asked.

Hamet thought about this and finally said, "Yes, I suppose I am."

Eaton could contain himself no longer. "Suppose?!" he roared. "Suppose?! Hamet! Why do you *suppose* we are here today?!"

Stunned, Hamet stared at Eaton. Nobody but his brother Yusuf had ever spoken to him thus. He cast his eyes to the ground and mumbled a reply.

"I shall remind you why we are here, Hamet!" Eaton cried. "To place *you* back on the throne of Tripoli! Do you not understand you have an obligation to help me bring that about, sir?!"

Hamet was overwhelmed with shame. Tears fell from his downcast eyes into the sand. Eaton realized he'd gone too far. Arab men were all too cognizant of their pride and Eaton had abused Hamet's. He took a deep breath and placed his hand on Hamet's shoulder.

"I am sorry, friend," he said calmly. "I anger too quickly. But certainly you can appreciate my frustration."

"I do, William," Hamet replied without looking up. "I shall hasten the departure and I shall not allow this to happen again." He looked up at Eaton. "But please, remember, I am not a soldier. I am a scholar. I know nothing of war, marches or such things. I am also not American."

It was Eaton's turn to be embarrassed. In his rage, he had forgotten all he had learned about the Arab mind. He understood that he had failed to properly prepare Hamet or the Muslims for the march. The delay was his fault, not Hamet's.

"Come," Eaton said, patting Hamet on the back. "Let us work together with Lieutenant O'Bannon to get our army on the march again. We have far to go and only a little time to get there. You must lead your men to Derne and victory. I will show you how. Please forgive my words."

Hamet said nothing in reply.

26

WASHINGTON
February 20, 1805

The dispatch reached Jefferson's desk just before noon. It was from Tobias Lear. Once again the diplomat had ignored his immediate superior, Secretary of State Madison, to communicate his opinions directly to the president. Jefferson thought Lear an egotistical fop who leveraged his father-son relationship with the late George Washington for political advantage. Jefferson knew Madison would be angered by the latest display of disrespect but he read Lear's letter anyway.

It contained the usual self-aggrandizing prose Jefferson found so annoying, but the president also agreed with its gist. *"Captain Bainbridge believes the time is right to make an overture to Bashaw Karamanli and I concur with his informed opinion. Mr. Bainbridge is most fearful that the regent will not surrender the good men of Philadelphia unless he receives a ransom and that if this does not occur, the prisoners will be removed to some stronghold deep in the desert from which we will have little prospect of rescuing them."*

All along Jefferson and most of his cabinet had believed that, through a demonstration of America's overwhelming new naval power and the will to use it, Karamanli would come to realize he'd chosen to declare war on the wrong country.

That was the conventional strategy at least.

But what was becoming painfully obvious was that Yusuf was anything but a conventional foe. Preble blasted his capital city yet the tyrant was no closer to surrender than he had been when Preble's squadron had arrived in force before Tripoli. Why should he be? He was unconcerned about his citizens and he held the men of *Philadelphia* hostage, prepared to use them as human shields if Jefferson forced his hand. This was an unintended consequence the president and his advisers had never anticipated, he thought to himself as he continued reading.

"I am certain I can convince the Bashaw to release the prisoners if we simply agree to pay him a reasonable ransom. He understands now his demand of three hundred thousand dollars is not viable. I believe I can persuade him to accept less money, perhaps far less, while winning from the Bashaw a pledge of permanent peace. He has been wounded and humiliated, but he is immensely prideful. Yusuf cannot accept defeat without some form of recompense. This is the mind of the Mohammedan, Mr. President."

There were so many other matters before Jefferson as he began his second term that the conflict in the Mediterranean had ceased to be a priority for him. Gallatin was constantly at him about the high cost of maintaining a navy far from home waters while the nation's other financial obligations were being neglected. In the end, the decision was easy. Jefferson drew a sheet of writing paper from a drawer and addressed a letter to Tobias Lear.

All morning the column traversed a moonscape of rubble strewn across the desert floor while the temperature rose to ninety-three degrees. Flies descended in swarms on the horses and men and fine white dust penetrated clothing and equipment.

But a week into the march and Eaton's army was now moving along at an acceptable average of twenty miles each day.

They stopped for a mid-day meal amidst the ruins of some forgotten fortification, its stone walls crumbling with age. The decrepit fortress also offered water, drawn from a well drilled thirty feet through solid rock.

"Can you imagine the determination it took to do that?" Eaton asked O'Bannon, pointing down at the well as his soldiers pulled up leather buckets to fill stone troughs for the animals.

O'Bannon glanced down at the handiwork of the long-dead engineers. "At least as difficult as marching an army like this one five hundred miles," he remarked with a rueful smile.

The horses were unsaddled and watered by boys from Abbud's Bedouin contingent. Meantime, the soldiers and camel drivers lined up to fill their goatskin water bags.

As they sat in the shade of a wall eating cold mutton, O'Bannon pointed. "A rider," he announced as the figure neared the halted column. The horseman hesitated, looked about then headed toward Eaton.

They had passed other wayfarers, camel trains and eastbound pilgrims mostly, but this one rode straight for the officers as though he were expected. Eaton, Hamet and O'Bannon stood and greeted the rider as he reined in his mount. His name was Ghazi and he claimed he was a messenger from Derne.

"Word of your army's approach has reached the city!" he exclaimed. "The people have risen up against Yusuf and are ready to join you! Governor Mustapha has run away!"

Hamet was delighted at this unexpected news, Eaton immediately suspicious. Was this a ruse, he wondered, concocted by Yusuf who hoped Eaton would disband the army if no attack was required to capture Derne?

As Eaton questioned the messenger, Kazim and some of his men joined the officers and Hamet excitedly repeated Ghazi's announcement. The Arabs began cheering and firing their pistols and muskets in celebration. As the news reached the rest of the Arabs and Bedouins they joined the noisy celebration and the column quickly dissolved into a dusty swirl of confused revelry.

El Taiib, a half mile behind with the baggage train, heard the gunfire but mistook its meaning. He excitedly gestured to the nearby drivers.

"The infidel swine are being attacked by bandits!" he cried. "They shall be slaughtered! Come, let us join them, kill all the Christians and share the plunder! Then we return to Alexandria!"

Seizing their weapons, the drivers ran toward the shots. Lieutenant Ulovix, the Greek officer, happened to be at the rear of the column with a company of his men when he saw el Taiib and fifty of his drivers charging forward brandishing guns, swords and daggers looking for all the world like mutineers. He quickly formed his twenty men into a skirmish line, muskets pointed at the approaching Arabs.

"Find Eaton!" Ulovix ordered one of his men. "Tell him there is an uprising by the camel drivers!"

El Taiib, seeing the Greeks at the ready, stopped in his tracks.

Up ahead, Eaton found discrepancies in Ghazi's report. "You say the people rose against Yusuf?" he asked.

"Yes, yes!" Ghazi replied too quickly.

"We have only been on the march a week. It would have taken you at least three weeks to ride here from Derne, you lying son of a poxed whore!" Eaton growled, cuffing the man. "We are more than a hundred leagues from Derne! Who sent you here?!"

The man was rubbing his cheek, his lips trembling. Before he could speak, the Greek runner was in front of Eaton. In broken English he delivered his message as he pointed to the rear, "Sir! The...the camel men! They attack!"

Eaton ran to his horse and leapt aboard bareback. He raced to the rear and found the line of Greeks holding off the mob of drivers. Eaton wasn't surprised to see el Taiib leading the treachery. Drawing his scimitar, he steered his horse around the Greeks and into the milling crowd of Arabs.

"Silence!" he cried as he wheeled his mount around glaring at the camel drivers. "I will cut off the head of any man who dares fire a shot!"

El Taiib dashed forward crying, "General Eaton! Praise Allah you are not hurt! We heard the shooting and thought bandits were attacking! We were coming to defend you!"

KEVIN EMMET FOLEY   187

Lieutenant Ulovix presented himself to Eaton and saluted. "They looked as though they had murder in mind, General Eaton," he said in French as he pointed at el Taiib. "They stopped when we met them but this old man appeared to be leading them."

Eaton glared at el Taiib who offered a nervous smile. "Get your men back to the camels!" he finally ordered. "If I need your help, I will summon you!"

O'Bannon rode up as el Taiib and his drivers were trotting back to the rear. "Are you alright, general?!"

"Aye, Mr. O'Bannon, I'm alright," Eaton replied. "But that bastard el Taiib had some sort of scheme in mind just now. We'll have to watch him."

Back at the head of the column the premature celebration was winding down. Kazim continued the interrogation of the messenger Ghazi using his knife to extract the truth. Kazim had severed one of the man's thumbs and was preparing to slice off the other.

"Governor Mustapha sent me!" the man cried out in pain and terror. "He knows about your army! He…he is frightened!"

"How many soldiers are at Derne?!" asked Eaton as Kazim placed the blade on the joint of Ghazi's thumb.

"No more than two hundred!" Ghazi screamed.

"Stop!" O'Bannon cried as he came upon the scene. "I want no part of torturing this man!"

Eaton glanced at the lieutenant then said something to Kazim who lifted the blade. "Sometimes this is necessary, Mr. O'Bannon," Eaton said calmly nodding at the weeping man who had fallen to his knees, clutching his wounded hand.

Angry now, O'Bannon glared at Eaton. "That might be *their* way, general, but God damn it, that ain't *our* way!"

"You are being naïve lieutenant," Eaton harshly replied pointing at Ghazi. "This son of a bitch would have had us continue on to Derne without the army. Can you imagine what would have happened to us if we had?!"

"That doesn't make it right!" exclaimed O'Bannon as he lifted Ghazi to his feet. One of his marines appeared with bandages and started dressing the horrible wound.

"I agree with the lieutenant," said Hamet with a look of disgust. He had walked away, refusing to watch Kazim torture the messenger but rejoined the officers now that the barbarity was over. "There is no reason for us to behave like animals. This fellow is simply a pawn. He has suffered enough. Let him go."

"You two have no stomach for what must be done here!" snapped Eaton. "We are at war with these villains!"

"Aye, sir, at war…but there are rules to war," O'Bannon said quietly. "This here is against the rules."

"Tell that to the men of *Philadelphia*, lieutenant," Eaton snarled before turning on his heel. As he walked away he looked back over his shoulder. "The messenger stays with us until after the attack on Derne."

Bashaw Yusuf Karamanli was ready to accept two hundred thousand dollars for the *Philadelphia* captives, the exact figure Jefferson had authorized in his most recent letter to Lear. But the counsel already decided Yusuf would get no more than sixty thousand. After all, what was to be gained returning to Washington having merely delivered the president's settlement when he could attain even more of a reputation as a skilled diplomat by forcing the bashaw to accept less? If the crew of *Philadelphia* had to suffer for a few more days or weeks, so be it.

"Please tell the bashaw that sixty thousand is as high as I will go. He will also receive the arms I promised," Lear told Nicolas Nissen, the Danish envoy. The two men stood on the deck of *Constitution* riding at anchor off Tripoli under a bright sun.

"Very well, Mr. Lear…"

"*Colonel* Lear."

"I mean Colonel Lear," replied Nissen, "but your men, they are in very bad condition. The bashaw is angry about the delay in negotiations. He continues to needlessly punish them."

"The delay is his fault, not mine," Lear sniffed.

"Yes…but the men…"

"Our men shall endure, Mr. Nissen," Lear declared. "They are American tars, tough and durable. After they are delivered, they will be heroes and they will be rewarded. Sixty thousand. Tell him!"

Angry as he was at Lear's indifference to the well being of his own countrymen, Nissen bowed slightly and said, "As you wish."

The Dane was led to the roof of the palace where Yusuf was taking the afternoon air. Mohammed Dhgies sat nearby. They could hear the sound of hammers and saws around them as carpenters continued to repair the damage caused by the American bombardment. The bashaw greeted Nissen and offered him a chair next to his beneath an awning. They exchanged pleasantries before Nissen finally got around to mentioning Lear's ransom offer.

"*Sixty* thousand?!" Yusuf barked irritably when he heard the number. "I have already made a big concession…all I want is *two hundred* thousand."

During his career, Nissen had met many men like Lear, ambitious and cunning without scruples or souls. They never made a move unless there was some profit or advantage to be gained for themselves. But Nissen had also seen the bedraggled American sailors slouching back to their stinking warehouse, dirty, naked, thirsty and nearly starved and his heart ached for them. If Lear had seen them at all, he'd chosen to ignore their plight spending all his time ashore with only Bainbridge.

"Your Excellency, if I may speak plainly, Lear is not going to pay you what you ask. He might be able to but he won't," Nissen explained, his expression one of sorrow. "He is too full of pride and selfishness and he cares little for the captives you hold."

"Is he a beast, this Lear?!" the bashaw asked, bushy eyebrows raised in disbelief. "How could he let his countrymen suffer so?!"

Nissen almost laughed in Yusuf's face at the irony of the question. Instead, he nodded thoughtfully then made a proposal. "Sir, I advise you to accept the sixty thousand. I am afraid that if you choose not to, Captain Rodgers will begin bombarding the city very shortly and when the bombardment starts, it won't end for some time."

"Let them bombard the city!" Yusuf cried. "I shall take my prisoners to the mountains. They will be my slaves forever more!"

Nissen waved a hand at the bashaw's impatience and continued. "But after you receive the money and the captives are released, Your Excellency, I will personally negotiate a gift for you with the American president that will make up the difference between what you demand and what Lear will pay you now."

Nissen was a bloody Christian crusader, to be sure, but the bashaw also regarded him as a useful tool who was usually as good as his word. This might be a solution. He slowly rose from his chair. "I shall consider this proposition."

"Your Excellency, if I may…perhaps as a goodwill gesture you will let some of the Americans go."

Yusuf gave this some thought and said, "You may take those young boys with Bainbridge – midshipmen I think he calls them – with you. Also, take the sick men. We cannot care for them."

His heart racing, Nissen bowed. "You are most merciful and benevolent, Your Excellency."

The bashaw nodded his agreement. Dghies, smiling broadly now that the impasse was nearing a settlement, patted Nissen's arm before he followed Yusuf to the stairs.

Lear was dining alone in Rodger's cabin when he heard excited voices on *Constitution's* deck suddenly turn to cheers. Curious, he wiped his mouth and walked out onto the deck where the first of the *Philadelphia's* midshipmen were coming aboard. They were greeted at the waist with embraces and slaps on their backs by *Constitution's* own midshipmen and junior officers. Captain Rodgers, who was tending to business on the gun deck, heard the commotion and raced up the forward companionway. His jaw dropped at the sight of the freed Americans.

By now, the ship's senior and warrant officers were greeting the midshipmen but the cheering subsided as *Philadelphia's* sick and injured were lifted aboard. Surgeons and their mates appeared and rushed about examining the condition of the two dozen men on litters. All of the sick were filthy and skeletal. Some of them were weeping while others happily shook offered hands.

Nicolas Nissen, the Danish consul, climbed aboard and was greeted by Lear who warmly embraced him. Rodgers met the two and heard Nissen deliver the good news. "Yusuf is considering the new offer," the Dane told the Americans with a smile. "I think he will accept. He has released the midshipmen and sick as a token of his good will."

Rodgers felt tears in his eyes as a wave of relief flooded over him. Lear wore a thin smile. The captain motioned to the ship's chaplain and strode with him to the quarterdeck where a lieutenant called for attention.

"Let us pray to our Lord God Almighty! Let us thank Him for the deliverance of our shipmates!" announced Rodgers, emotion clutching his voice. "And let us humbly beg Him for the speedy delivery of the other brave men of *Philadelphia!*" Rodgers finally looked down at Nissen, extended his hand toward the diplomat and cried, "And let us all thank God we have such a friend as Nicolas Nissen!"

The men removed their hats as the chaplain led them in prayer.

27

I ssac Hull came ashore at Syracuse and was delighted to learn he had been promoted to master commandant. His joyful mood didn't last long.

Hull found Commodore Barron at his temporary office near the quay. Barron's condition was improved enough for him to resume his duties but Hull was appalled at the commodore's appearance. He had lost twenty pounds from an already lean frame, his uniform hanging from his body as though from a scarecrow. His skin and eyes were a light shade of yellow. Barron sat behind a desk and lethargically shook hands with Hull, congratulating him on his promotion.

"Thank you, sir," Hull replied as he stood to attention. "Are you feeling better?"

Barron wore a resigned expression and shrugged weakly. "As best a man can feel when he is on death's door, Mr. Hull," Barron said in a raspy voice. "Please sit. What is your report?"

"Mr. Eaton and Mr. O'Bannon are on their way to Derne, sir," replied Hull. "I am presently loading supplies I'll deliver when we rendezvous at the Bay of Bomba around the first."

Barron slumped down in his seat and nodded.

"Um, Commodore Barron, Mr. Eaton also requested seven thousand dollars as he is out of funds and requires that figure to complete the enterprise," Hull continued. "He asked that I bring the money to Bomba."

"Seven thousand dollars," Barron repeated flatly. "I told him there was no more money."

"Yes, sir, I understand you did, but the enterprise has cost more than Mr. Eaton estimated. He has had to pay bribes and encountered other unexpected expenses…"

"God *damn* that man!" cried Barron with a level of fury that startled Hull. "There *is* no more money! Not a penny, not a farthing for Eaton's bloody *enterprise!*"

The commodore spit the last word at Hull who reflexively jumped from his chair and stood to attention.

"That vainglorious bastard sent you here to ask for money, is that it, Hull?!" Barron boomed, the color of his face visibly changing from pale yellow to pale white.

The new master commandant swallowed, said, "Yes, sir."

"No! No! No!" bellowed Barron. A moment later his office door opened a crack and a clerk peeked in.

"Shut that fucking door, Walters!" Barron boomed. The clerk instantly obeyed.

Hull stood rigid before the commodore, could think of nothing to say.

Barron's sudden anger, like a summer thunderstorm, was quickly ebbing. The British doctor treating him had ordered the commodore to stay quiet, but Eaton's outrageous request was more than he could stand. He fixed his eyes on the hapless Issac Hull and forced himself to take a deep breath, remembering there was no news from Lear since the consul had left for Tripoli weeks earlier.

Eaton's attack on Derne, in the unlikely event it ever succeeded, might still be a necessary gambit to force Yusuf to the bargaining table. More important, Barron remembered, Eaton's mission was supported by President Jefferson and Secretary Smith. If he refused the money, the commodore might well be held to account later if he somehow survived his liver disease. He tapped the desk until his breathing returned to normal.

"Master Commandant Hull," he said finally. "This is not your doing. You are following your orders. Please excuse my temper."

Hull blinked at Barron. "I understand, sir."

"Kindly see my clerk Mr. Walters outside," Barron continued. "He will draw up the necessary paperwork and give you the seven thousand dollars," Barron said, his voice rising again. "But, by God, you tell Eaton for me, this is the *last* money he will see from me this side of judgment day!"

O'Bannon sat in Abbud's tent as the rain drummed down. He took the old fiddle from his friend, tuned it and played several simple bars of a tune he knew. Eye's bright, Abbud watched O'Bannon's fingers on the bow and fingerboard as his several wives tapped their hands on their thighs in time to the music. O'Bannon handed the instrument back and made a gesture. Abbud licked his lips and played. It wasn't perfect, O'Bannon thought to himself, but it wasn't bad either. He nodded and smiled at the Bedouin who grinned in reply, showing teeth stained by kaat. He continued to play the ditty over and over and with each try, it got a little better.

Abbud paused and O'Bannon gestured for him to continue practicing. Outside, torrential rain pounded the desert. They stopped two days earlier when it began and moved the camp to higher ground after their first site flooded. There had been no let up since.

Smoky fires glowed beneath dripping tents while thunder roared and lightening ripped across the night sky. O'Bannon walked through the camp to Eaton's marquee. Inside, he found the general sitting alone on in a camp chair writing in his journal with the help of a sputtering candle that dripped wax onto the sand.

"We can't move in this," Eaton said without looking up at O'Bannon. "Impossible."

"It would appear so," the marine remarked as he shook the water off then lit a cigar. "Nothing to be done but wait, I'm afraid."

Since the afternoon when Kazim had cut off the messenger's thumb, the relationship between O'Bannon and Eaton had cooled. The marine followed orders, but he had avoided Eaton's company, deeply disappointed in a man he had come to respect so much.

Eaton finished writing and closed the journal. He regarded O'Bannon for a moment then asked, "Got another one of those cigars?"

O'Bannon handed him the cheroot and lit it for Eaton. The general blew the smoke into the air and then looked intently at O'Bannon.

"Out in Ohio country we once captured five Miami warriors," Eaton began. "We tracked them from a farm they'd attacked and burned. They killed the man who lived there, raped and killed his wife, murdered all the children save two babies. We figured they killed them too, but we couldn't find their bodies, so we decided they'd taken them; planned to bring them up Miami, I suppose."

O'Bannon smoked in silence, listening.

"Anyway, these braves didn't have the babies," Eaton went on. "But they knew where they were so we…questioned them. When they saw what we did to their leader, the others decided to speak up."

O'Bannon didn't ask, but Eaton told him anyway. "We had an old French trapper with us so I ordered him to skin that Indian alive. It's something I hope you never live to see, lieutenant."

O'Bannon shuddered as he exhaled smoke.

"We took the rest of the Indians back to their village where they told us they left the babies. It was small, maybe twenty lodges, miles from the Ohio River, hidden in a deep ravine. We'd have never found it nor the babies if the Miami hadn't led us there. We marched right in with our captives at gunpoint and demanded the children. They were alive and well and we eventually returned them to the dead farmer's sister," Eaton said.

"The Indians and village?" O'Bannon asked.

"We hanged the four we'd captured and burned all the lodges," Eaton replied.

O'Bannon stared at Eaton as though seeing the man for the first time.

"If I had not done what I did, those babies would never have been found," Eaton explained. "I am not proud of what we were forced to do, but there it is. That is how war is fought, Lieutenant O'Bannon."

The rain stopped during the night. The sun crept up over the sea where a fresh breeze whipped up white caps beneath a cloudless sky. Eaton stepped from his tent and took in his command. A couple of hundred drenched tents of all sizes and descriptions hung limply in the dim light. Out in the distance, camels and asses were sleeping next to supplies that were piled on the ground beneath canvas tarps. Some sheep and goats were grazing on thin grass while a few wet and sleepy guards wandered around the camp's perimeter.

"General, you're up," said O'Bannon, appearing from behind a bush hiking up his trousers.

"Indeed I am, Mr. O'Bannon," Eaton replied with a smile. "Looks like we finally have a dry day."

"Yes, sir," O'Bannon replied as their eyes met briefly and an awkward moment followed. "I was thinking about what you told me last night. I understand your point, but we are civilized men…"

"Yes, and war is an uncivilized business, Pres," Eaton interrupted. His face softened and he added, "But since you are crucial to our success we shall refrain from any more of…that."

In the silence that followed, some unspoken message passed between them. Finally, Eaton pointed west.

"Hamet claims there are some friendly Bedouin up ahead. Says we may be able to recruit some more men. We have lost too much time here so let's get moving."

Before they could depart, tents and bedding had to be dried, which didn't take long under the warm sun. By noon, the army was ready. Just as Eaton and Hamet were preparing to mount their horses, el Taiib came scuttling toward them trailing a half dozen of his camel drivers. O'Bannon and Leitensdorfer saw the old man approach and walked over to see what it was he wanted.

El Taiib stood before Eaton, frowning, arms crossed over his chest. The general smiled and waited for the old man to speak. The silence hung for more than two minutes, the Arab glaring at the American who returned an indulgent smile. Finally, some of el Taiib's drivers began jabbering so their leader spoke up.

"These men do not trust you Mr. Eaton!" he declared. "They want more money and they want it now."

Eaton, still smiling, was shaking his head. "No, no I am afraid not, el Taiib. We have an agreement."

"Then we shall go no further!"

Eaton looked at Hamet. "Will you please speak to this fellow?"

Hamet appeared confused. "What about, William?"

Eaton felt a bolt of anger but checked it. "About getting his damned people moving, that's what! I agreed to a price and I agreed to payment terms already."

"These merchant people change their agreements all the time, William," Hamet said with a wave of his hand. "I suppose we have to make a new agreement with el Taiib."

O'Bannon, who had been listening to the exchange, saw Eaton's face go red and decided to step forward.

"Mr. Karamanli, we don't have any money to pay el Taiib," he said. "And we can't stop to negotiate with him every time he takes a notion to ask for more money."

"Well, I am not a merchant, lieutenant" Hamet replied with a shrug. "I have no understanding of the minds of men like el Taiib…"

"Yes, but you are the leader here," O'Bannon reasoned. "You need to tell el Taiib to live up to his end of the bargain."

Hamet thought about this for a moment. "I cannot do that…"

"Very well!" Eaton roared, his patience at an end. "We return to Alexandria *right now!* The enterprise is *over!*" With that, he turned, mounted his horse and rode off toward the beach.

El Taiib said something in Arabic to Hamet who replied angrily. At first, the camel merchant appeared defiant but his face slowly melted into one of regret, then remorse and finally grief. He was owed half his fee but it appeared now as though he would never see it. In a pleading tone he said something to O'Bannon.

"He begs forgiveness for any offense he has given," Leitensdorfer translated.

O'Bannon suspected Eaton was bluffing so he shrugged. "The general always says what he means," he told Leitensdorfer. "If he says the enterprise is over, then it's over. El Taiib can leave with his camels and drivers and good riddance, I say."

Hamet's face fell. "We cannot simply end the march on Derne, Mr. O'Bannon!" he cried.

"We sure can and we sure will, Mr. Karamanli," O'Bannon replied matter of factly.

Hamet stepped forward and slapped el Taiib hard across the face. The old man crumbled into a pile at Hamet's feet as his frightened camel drivers stepped back. "You silly old ass!" cried Hamet. "You have ruined everything! Now I will never see my family again!"

Tears were falling as el Taiib looked up at Hamet, clutching his hands before him in supplication. "Please, please! I beg forgiveness, Your Excellency! We want no more money...we only wish to continue to Derne!"

Leitensdorfer was translating but O'Bannon was shaking his head.

"Lieutenant, please, speak to General Eaton. Tell him there has been a terrible mistake," pleaded Hamet. "This dog shall ask for no more money!"

O'Bannon saw tears welling in Hamet's eyes. He looked down at el Taiib, who was copiously weeping into the sand. "I will try," he finally replied. He mounted his own horse and rode out after Eaton.

The general was some distance down the beach when O'Bannon caught up with him.

"What did they say?" asked Eaton. He was casually smoking a cigar as he rode along.

"Hamet begs you to continue the enterprise," O'Bannon said with a smile.

"Put the fear of God in him, did I?" Eaton asked. "I should have done that a long time ago."

"Probably."

"Well, let Hamet stew for awhile," Eaton replied. "It is high time he started pulling his weight. Anyway, this day is gone. We'll camp here and leave before dawn. And if el Taiib shows his face, I'll slit his skinny throat, I swear on all that is holy!"

After a leisurely ride with Eaton along the beach, O'Bannon trotted back to the column. Already tents were being unpacked and re-pitched. Kazim's Arabs were conducting horse races out on the muddy plain below the camp. Somewhere Abbud was playing the tune he'd learned the night before. O'Bannon thought it sounded good.

He found Hamet waiting in his marquee working his worry beads, anxiety etched on his bronze face. He got to his feet as O'Bannon entered.

"The general has changed his mind," the lieutenant said sternly. "We are to camp here tonight and ride before sun up tomorrow."

Hamet smiled at the news but he said nothing in reply.

"I would advise you, sir, to help General Eaton," O'Bannon added. "You can start by telling el Taiib to not bother him again about money."

Grand Admiral Murad Reis sailed *Meshouda* into the harbor at Derne and was quickly reminded how much he loathed the place. The drab little city made Tripoli look like Paris. The harbor was really just a shallow indentation in the coastline, a breakwater stretching a few hundred yards into the sea guarded to the east by a low fortress with turrets on either end. There appeared to be twenty nine-pound cannons arrayed on the battlements. On the western edge of the city was the governor's palace several stories high and surrounded by a low wall. The city itself was bisected by a dry riverbed. There appeared to be no plan to the layout of buildings, dingy one and two story houses and shops comingled in a confusing labyrinth of narrow streets and alleys stretching to the ridges and hills that surrounded the city to the south.

As he stood on the quarterdeck, Reis observed a flurry of activity on the quay. He saw the governor hastily climb down to a boat with the help of his attendants before he was rowed out to *Meshouda*.

Mustapha climbed aboard and bowed deeply. "Welcome grand admiral!" he said. "I trust the bashaw is in good health?"

As always, Reis was startled by the man's resemblance to Yusuf. Heavy and hairy like his brother-in-law, Mustapha lacked the bashaw's brains and ruthlessness.

"He is and thank you for asking," Reis replied with a quick bow of his own. While he didn't consider the governor an equal, he was still Yusuf's relation and, more important, Arab. "What news of the infidel army?"

"We dispatched a runner to intercept them and report that the people of Derne had risen against me, but the man has not returned," Mustapha replied. "That was two weeks ago."

"Why would you do that?" asked Reis.

"Because the bashaw thought it might cause the Christian dogs to abandon their attack on the city," Mustapha replied before nervously adding, "And because that is what the bashaw told me to do!"

Reis nodded at Mustapha's prudence then said, "I was able to find a hundred men in Benghazi to reinforce the defenses here," Reis remarked. "How many have you?"

"Two hundred more or less, grand admiral," Mustapha eagerly replied, "but a messenger from Tripoli arrived yesterday to say that the bashaw is assembling an army there and sending it here! It should arrive in a few weeks!"

This news surprised Reis. Did Yusuf now believe the grand admiral incapable of defending Derne? Had the bashaw received more information about the size and disposition of the American army?

Feeling himself growing depressed again, Reis motioned his second-in-command to begin unloading men and supplies then looked at the governor. "We have brought extra cannon, arms and ammunition. The Christians won't attack without support from the sea, so I shall deal with any men-of-war they send while you repel the ground attack."

"Excellent!" declared Mustapha with a smile visible through his thick black beard. "We shall crush the Christians ourselves and have Yusuf's eternal gratitude!"

Reis stared at the governor. Maybe Mustapha wasn't as stupid as Reis thought he was. If he could defeat the American jackals here, Reis might well win back Yusuf's favor.

Mustapha suddenly threw his arm around the grand admiral. "Come! I have prepared for you a suite of rooms and comforts after your long voyage!"

❦ 28 ❦

The money was gone, the food was in perilously short supply, now water was not to be found. And always the heat, dry, penetrating, suffocating even now in the early spring. Eaton spurred his mount up a craggy hillside and saw that another vast plain of brown desert flecked with vegetation lay before his army. He had moved the march several miles inland to avoid sand dunes, so the sea was no longer visible to his right.

Eaton removed his hat and wiped his forehead as the column moved by below. He tugged at the collar of his woolen jacket, but refused to open it lest he appear in anything but full military bearing. He watched as the men trudged past, glassy eyed with fatigue and thirst. The inescapable dust rose around them, clogging their eyes and noses and ears and everywhere the flies, buzzing and biting.

O'Bannon swatted one on his leg as he approached on his own horse. He joined Eaton gazing out over the great expanse of waste.

"Did you know the Roman Legions marched through here, Lieutenant O'Bannon?" asked Eaton cheerfully with an expansive wave of his hat. "Can you imagine their great columns? Tens of thousands of sturdy soldiers in bronze breast plates and helmets armed with pikes and spears, defending and expanding Caesar's vast empire! The Carthaginians saw them coming and shit themselves, I'll wager!"

"Well, we could sure use some of those boys now," O'Bannon replied dryly as he slapped away another fly, unimpressed with Eaton's impromptu history lesson. "And water, too. We should have found the villages by now."

It had been twenty-six days since they'd left the Arab's Tower, the European's uncomplaining and stoic, accustomed as they were to the hard marching of the French and British armies. Even the Spanish and Portuguese soldiers of fortune had shaken off their initial lethargy and were now at the front of the column. To the Arabs and Bedouin, the desert was home, trekking though it for days on end nothing unusual. But they all needed water.

Hamet and Kazim rode by but appeared not to notice the Americans on the rise. Leitensdorfer passed by with a quick wave, his round face sunburned as red as the fez he wore. Fedor was next to him aboard an unruly stallion, the ever present bottles poking from his saddlebags.

"At least Fedor brought enough to drink," observed O'Bannon.

"Yet he never appears or sounds drunk," Eaton replied dryly. "A remarkable trait I wish I shared."

Sergeant Campbell strode by amidst some of the Arab foot soldiers and saluted O'Bannon and Eaton. The other six marines, their blue jackets covered with a layer of brown dust, were scattered among the remaining Arabs.

Finally the camel train loaded with equipment and supplies passed, the animals bawling and snorting as their riders drove them along. When he saw Eaton, el Taiib shot the general an angry look before swatting his camel with a crop and darting off into the dust cloud raised by hundreds of big hooves.

"Let's move before they leave us behind," said Eaton.

They found a large cistern carved in stone at sunset. Built into the ground and designed to collect rainwater, it was covered by a stone roof.

It contained ample water but also two decaying corpses. The stench was overwhelming.

"Maybe pilgrims on their way to Mecca," Leitensdorfer observed as he peered down into the shallow well, a kerchief over his face. "They were probably robbed and murdered by bandits and then thoughtfully dumped in there."

Eaton considered the dilemma for a moment then looked around at the other officers and said, "We've no choice. Let's fill the bags and canteens, water the animals and pitch camp."

Each man ate a cup of rice for supper. The evening chill descending as it always did, they were seated around a fire exhausted by the day's ride. O'Bannon dozed off after the food, not bothering to pitch a tent, his head on his saddle. Eaton and Leitensdorfer shortly followed suit. Sometime after midnight, shots rang out on the southern edge of the camp.

"Bandits!" cried Eaton, jumping to his feet and seizing his pistols. O'Bannon snatched up his own weapons and the two were off toward the sound of the shooting, Leitensdorfer just behind.

A fire fight was underway when they reached O'Bannon's marines who were deployed as guards with some of the Europeans along the column's southern flank, just for this reason. Eaton found Sergeant Campbell who had just fired his pistol at a pile of boulders on a low hill fifty yards away.

"In them rocks!" Campbell cried as he saw the officers arrive.

In answer, there were muzzle flashes from among the boulders. Eaton guessed ten to twenty bandits were shooting. Balls whizzed and ricocheted around them so Eaton and O'Bannon dropped to their bellies.

There was no moon, but brilliant starlight illuminated the scene. Eaton looked over his shoulder and made out a few more Europeans arriving. They all concentrated their fire on the rocks.

"Hold!" bellowed Eaton. To his right, he saw mounted men burst from the camp. Kazim appeared to be in their lead. The riders raced to the south then disappeared behind the hill. The attacker's shooting stopped moments later.

"Kazim's outflanking them," Eaton remarked. "Smart."

Muffled shots from the far side of the hill were heard, then high pitched screams. O'Bannon shivered at the awful sound and glanced at Eaton, who was slowly getting to his feet.

"Reload and advance!" O'Bannon ordered. "Hold fire until I give the order! Our own men are out there!"

The skirmishers stayed low and raced toward the rocks. More screams were heard, then silence.

"Friends! The fight is over!" cried Kazim. He had climbed to the top of one of the boulders, holding a scimitar in one hand and a man's head in the other.

A moment later, Eaton and O'Bannon were looking down at a dozen bodies sprawled in the sand.

"Bandit scum," Kazim remarked indifferently as he joined them, gore dripping from the head he held. He threw it onto a body. "They are everywhere out here. These were probably after our camels and horses. We must remain vigilant."

After crossing fifty more miles of featureless desert, they turned toward the sea and crested a low rocky hill. There, spread before them, were several hundred tents surrounding what appeared to be a large one-story villa made of mud bricks encircled by a shoulder-high stone wall.

Hamet rode up alongside Eaton. "This place is called Massouva. These are the people I told you about, William," Hamet said excitedly. "They are Bedouin. A sheikh lives in the house there."

The men in the column saw the village and cheers rose from their ranks.

"I reckon Bomba is just over those ridges, sir," O'Bannon said looking up from a map and pointing at high hills to the northwest.

"That looks like two or three days march," Eaton replied, scratching his stubbled chin. "Let's rest here for a couple of days and let the men get their strength back."

The local sheikh turned out to be an ancient Arab named Wazir. One of his minions was sent out to greet the approaching army and bring its leaders to the house.

Eaton and Hamet rode with the messenger to the villa and were met by the sheikh at his gate. He invited them into a pleasant garden where they all sat while tea was served.

"A Christian who speaks our language!" Wazir exclaimed when he discovered Eaton spoke Arabic. "Finally, a civilized one!"

"I have spent many years among your people, Sheikh Wazir," Eaton smiled, "and with the help of my friend Hamet here, I have learned to understand and respect your language and your ways."

The old bearded man smiled at this, displaying worn teeth.

"Sheikh Wazir," Hamet began. "We humbly beg you to allow our men to camp here for two or three days so we may rest before we continue our march."

"What is mine is yours," the sheikh said. "Where are you going?"

"To Derne," Hamet replied. "We will demand that the city surrender or we will attack."

Wazir looked confused, asked, "Why?"

Hamet hesitated so Eaton spoke up, "Bashaw Yusuf is not the rightful regent of Tripoli," he declared. "Hamet is. He is Yusuf's elder brother."

"Your father was Ali Karamanli?" Wazir asked looking at Hamet, eyes wide. "He was a great man! I traded with him for many years!"

"My father wished for my older brother to succeed him as bashaw," Hamet continued. "But my younger brother Yusuf murdered him."

"In truth?!" Wazir cried.

Hamet nodded. "I fled and have never returned to Tripoli. Yusuf holds my family hostage there to this day."

This was more than the old sheikh could stand. Tears fell from his eyes as he reached out and gripped Hamet's shoulder then sat back, wiped his dripping nose with a clothe while he looked earnestly at his visitors. "So you are righting this terrible wrong."

"Yes," Eaton said. "My country wishes peace with Tripoli, but there can be no peace as long as this treacherous dog Yusuf demands tribute and makes my countrymen slaves. Hamet's interests and my country's interests coincide, Wazir, so we are going to attack and defeat Yusuf and help Hamet take back his throne."

The sheikh was nodding throughout this. It appealed to his own honorable sensibilities. "How may I help you?"

"We need more men to ensure victory at Derne," Hamet explained. "Once we have the city, the American Navy can use it as a base to attack Tripoli and capture Yusuf."

"There may be men here who will join you," Wazir replied standing. "But before we speak anymore, you must rest and have refreshment. You both look tired."

"You are too kind, Sheikh Wazir," Eaton said standing.

"Please join me this evening for a feast," Wazir said.

"May we bring three or four of our officers?" asked Hamet. "One of them plays a musical instrument you will enjoy."

"Of course!" Wazir exclaimed. "And I wish to know more about your country, General Eaton!"

The baths had been built by the Romans two thousand years earlier. The original tile was gone and so was the roof, but the recent rains had filled the pools nearly full of remarkably clear water.

Under the warm afternoon sun, Eaton floated on his back enjoying his first bath in more than two months. O'Bannon and his marines splashed nearby with some of the Europeans and Turks. The modest Arabs including Hamet had declined to communally bathe with the Christians after the pools were discovered among ruins on the other side of the village.

"Lieutenant O'Bannon!" Eaton called out, his voice echoing off the surrounding rocks. "In all your life in Virginia did you think it was possible you would one day wash yourself in the same bathes used by Antony and Cleopatra?!"

"No, general," O'Bannon laughed, standing up to his waist, water dripping off his bare shoulders. "This is better than our swimming hole back home!"

"I daresay you needed a bath, Mr. O'Bannon," Eaton called, "you were beginning to smell like el Taiib!"

"And you were beginning to smell like his camel!"

Eaton and the marines roared with laughter. They heard giggling and looked up at a collapsed stone column. Standing behind it, their head and shoulders just visible were three veiled Bedouin women watching the naked Americans.

O'Bannon waved at the them. "Come on down here, ladies!" O'Bannon called out. "The United States Marines will show you the manual of arms!"

This produced a gale of bawdy laughter and cat calls from the men. The women took one last look, giggled again then disappeared behind the column.

"At ease Campbell!' O'Bannon laughed at the red-faced sergeant who had gone erect. "One of those Turks over there might take a notion to get better acquainted with you!"

There was more laughter as Campbell ducked under the water with a sheepish grin.

They returned to the camp shaved, wearing clean, dry uniforms they had washed in the baths. O'Bannon ordered his men to tend to their weapons, polish their boots and brush their hats and then posted them as guards between the army's encampment and the village.

"We want no trouble here," Eaton told him as they walked to Wazir's house with Hamet, Leitensdorfer, Kazim and Fedor. "We're days from resupply at Bomba and almost out of food. I am out of money altogether, but the sheikh is sympathetic to our mission and inclined to help us, so we mustn't abuse his hospitality."

A servant admitted the men into the same garden where they had met Wazir earlier. It was illuminated by lanterns now and carpets and pillows had been arranged on the ground around a feast of lamb, figs, rice and condiments. In the Arab style, the men sat cross legged and ate with their right hands from the large pan of food. Fedor poured vodka into cups and passed them to those who imbibed. After they finished eating, a servant appeared to light a brazier that warmed the garden against the chill night air. An endless sea of stars lit the night sky above as the men smoked and chatted.

"Our sheikh is a man named Jefferson," Eaton told Wazir. "He lives in a palace the size of which you cannot imagine."

"What is your country like?" Wazir asked.

"There are trees there as numerous as the grains of sand here," Eaton replied. "We have mountains that touch the clouds in America, rivers wider than the Nile, and cities that dwarf Tripoli. The ships that brought us here are twice the size of any trading vessel you have ever seen."

Impressed, Wazir rubbed his shaggy gray beard and remarked, "Yusuf is a fool for making war against America, then. Why would he do such a thing?!"

"He is an evil man," Hamet replied. "And because America is across a sea thousands of leagues wide, Yusuf believes the Americans cannot fight him."

"But we did fight him," Eaton said. "We fired cannons on his city and slaughtered his soldiers by the score while Yusuf hid like a eunuch with his women."

Wazir shook his head, either in disbelief at Yusuf's audacity or disgust at his cowardice.

"Enough about war and killing, Sheikh Wazir," Eaton said. He looked over at O'Bannon. "We must sing for our supper, lieutenant! Or, in your case, fiddle for it!"

"Aye, sir," said O'Bannon who rose and retrieved his instrument. He tuned and began playing. Wazir's wives were in the house but rushed out into the garden at the sound of the strange music. The old sheikh stared in wonder as O'Bannon, hunched over slightly, working his fingers furiously, played "*Hogs in the Corn.*" Only the eyes of the women were visible behind their dark veils but Eaton could see their delight anyway.

Outside the walls of the house, the Americans heard anxious voices above the music. The people of the village had no idea what they were hearing. O'Bannon paused, picked up a lantern and climbed onto the top of the low wall where the villagers could see him. He placed the lantern at his feet and began playing again. There was an excited cheer of approval from the audience beyond the wall.

Wazir, grinning now, stood and was doing an awkward dance, shuffling his feet and waving his arms feebly. Seeing their host, Hamet and the others leapt to their feet and joined him. The wives, uncertain at first of the protocol, decided to dance too, joyfully keening all the while.

O'Bannon began another reel to more cheers and dancing, producing the most festive evening Massouva had seen since Cleopatra consorted there with Marc Antony.

A half hour later, exhausted, O'Bannon played one last slow tune called "*Starry Night.*" He finished to wild cheering outside and inside the walls, bowed deeply, then jumped down to the garden. Eaton pounded him on the back. "A most excellent concert, Pres!" he declared with a wide smile. "I'll wager they will rename this place after you!"

Eaton drank more of Fedor's vodka than he should have after O'Bannon's impromptu performance. The Americans and Europeans, leaning on one another, left Hamet, Kazim with Wazir and made their way back to their tents.

The general slept late and now his head ached as he walked out into the bright midmorning sunshine. Seated before his marquee, waiting patiently, were five camel drivers. One stood as Eaton appeared and bowed before the general.

"What is it?" Eaton asked irritably in Arabic, shading his eyes against the painful glare.

"We have come for the balance of our money, sir," the man replied without meeting Eaton's eyes.

"What money?"

"For the camels and drivers," he replied, gesturing to the others. "Our contract was to bring you to Massouva. We are here. We wish to be paid so we may return to Alexandria."

O'Bannon had seen Eaton emerge from his tent and walked over to discuss the orders for the day. "Good morning, sir," he said cheerfully.

"Please bring Hamet here right away, lieutenant," Eaton ordered in reply.

Five minutes later Hamet stood before Eaton, who addressed him in English. "This lad is looking for his money. He says his agreement was to come only as far as Massouva. What is going on?"

Hamet regarded the driver for a moment then looked at Eaton. "I think he is right, William."

Eaton could scarcely believe his ears. He stared at Hamet, who continued.

"You see, I believe the agreement was that el Taiib and his men would come as far as Massouva because, by now, we would have enough men rallied to our cause with their own animals…"

"Wait, Mr. Karamanli," O'Bannon interrupted. "You are saying you agree with el Taiib?"

Lips pursed, Hamet thought about the question as though it were a mathematical problem. "You see, lieutenant, el Taiib *does* have a point although I know it is hard to comprehend," he began. "He may have agreed to go to Derne but we also *did* believe more men would have joined us by now. At some point, we would have enough camels to carry the equipment and supplies and el Taiib and his drivers would have been paid and dismissed."

Eaton started to say something but Leitensdorfer, who had joined them, spoke up.

"There are many camels and asses here," he declared. "We can pay el Taiib and his men and let them go."

"That is not possible," Hamet said shaking his head. "Wazir told me these people are peaceful and want no part of a fight with Yusuf."

"But yesterday Wazir said..." Eaton began.

"Wazir wished to give you no offense in his home yesterday, General Eaton," Hamet explained. "It is rude to do so."

"Good God, Hamet, you told me we could expect to find more men here!" exclaimed Eaton.

"Not *here*, William," Hamet replied calmly as he pointed west. "Out there. We will find more villages of Bedouin who I know will join us."

Seeing Eaton's murderous expression, O'Bannon quickly asked, "What do you propose, then?"

Hamet considered this then said, "Pay el Taiib to take us as far as Bomba. We will find men who will join us by then."

"I *have* no money," said Eaton stiffly.

"I do," replied O'Bannon. "So do most of the men. I'll take up a collection. We'll have more cash at Bomba and we can repay them there."

"And I shall be the first to contribute!" declared Hamet before opening his purse and pouring its content into O'Bannon's hat. Leitensdorfer dropped more coins in the hat and Fedor followed. In thirty minutes,

O'Bannon collected nearly eight hundred dollars. Sergeant Campbell had written out IOUs to each man who contributed.

El Taiib, fearful of the general's threats, was summoned. He appeared with several body guards and O'Bannon gave him the money after Hamet explained the terms.

"As far as Bomba?" asked el Taiib suspiciously. "Then we shall be paid in full?"

Hamet nodded.

"Very well!" exclaimed el Taiib with a leer, grabbing the bag containing the money from O'Bannon.

Before daybreak the next morning, O'Bannon was shaken awake by Campbell. "Sir, come quick!"

In bare feet and wearing only his britches, O'Bannon ran with Campbell through the sleeping camp. They found Privates Owens and Thomas on guard duty standing where the camel drivers and their animals were supposed to be. The supplies and equipment were still there covered with tarps, but el Taiib, his camels and his drivers were gone.

❧ 29 ❧

Wazir's village held market days each Wednesday so it was that a merchant named Farid was selling cotton cloth of a fine quality, which he had purchased in Tunis six months before. He was a middle aged Algerian, cautious and wanting no trouble. His goal was to obtain the best profit possible then continue on to Alexandria to purchase goods to sell in Algiers. There were many buyers for his cloth, Bedouin women who paid him in sequins. Some wished to barter, but Farid had no interest in the goats or dates they offered, cash his exclusive tender.

When he had passed through Tripoli three weeks earlier, he saw something he'd never seen before. There were soldiers camped on the plain outside the city gates. This was not in itself unique but their numbers were. An observant man, Farid guessed there might be as many as five hundred men, perhaps more, judging by the number of tents and cook fires he saw.

At the inn where he stayed, there was much excited conversation about the recent bombardment of the city and the bashaw's castle. Someone said that an army of Americans was marching on Derne and that Yusuf was sending his soldiers there to meet them. None of this had anything to do with Farid's business, which was selling his cloth, buying goods in Alexandria and returning home to Algiers and his family.

As he sold his last bolt of cloth and prepared to move on, a messenger arrived from Kazim with an invitation to dine. Never one to give offense, Farid happily agreed.

He arrived at Kazim's pavilion after prayers and greeted his host graciously. He had one small bolt of cloth left over, so he presented this to Kazim who gratefully accepted the gift. Presently, another man joined them and was introduced by Kazim as Hamet Karamanli. The name meant nothing to Farid.

The men sat. Tea was poured by a servant and then pipes were lit.

"I trust the market day was profitable for you, Farid?" Hamet asked.

"Indeed it was," Farid replied, exhaling smoke and feeling the pleasant weariness of a successful day of business. "I sold all of the bolts of my Spanish cotton cloth, so I am on to Alexandria."

"Your accent tells me you are from Algiers," Hamet observed.

"I am!" the Arab acknowledged with a smile. "I have been traveling now for nearly ten months."

"Is it not dangerous to travel alone?" Hamet asked, thinking of the corpses in the cistern.

"I have traveled this route for years as my father before me and his father before him," Farid replied. "I have body guards with me, but the local Bedouin know me and leave me alone."

Hamet nodded at this. Traders had crossed back and forth over North Africa for the millennia. It was dangerous work, but a man could amass a fortune provided he wasn't murdered in his sleep.

"You must have passed through Tripoli then?" asked Kazim as he sipped his tea.

"I did indeed," Farid replied, "and there was something most curious there. I saw many soldiers at Tripoli. I was told they are going to Derne. Apparently the Americans plan to attack the city and Bashaw Yusuf's men are bound to meet and defeat them there."

Hamet's eyes grew wide at this. During the silence that followed, a servant appeared with platters of food. Kazim gestured at the fish and rice before them and said, "Come, let us dine."

Farid, oblivious to the effect his news had on Hamet, tucked into the meal. Kazim joined him, but Hamet had lost his appetite. The men ate in silence and when they'd finished, more tea was poured as a plate of sweets was presented. Farid gobbled several of these before finishing his tea. He rose, patting his belly.

"Many thanks, Kazim," he smiled. "You are a generous host. Please forgive me. I must retire as I have a long journey tomorrow."

Kazim stood and bowed but Hamet remained sitting, staring out into the night. Farid glanced at him and then at Kazim who shrugged at Hamet's rude behavior. Host and guest embraced and a moment later, Farid was gone. Kazim resumed his seat and re-lit his pipe. As if seeing him for the first time, Hamet's lip began to tremble.

"Yusuf *is* sending an army after us!" he moaned. "We shall be massacred at Derne!"

"We have an army, too, Hamet," remarked Kazim, frowning at his friend. "Let your brother send soldiers. We shall butcher them like sheep!"

"But...I never...this is not..." blubbered Hamet.

Like Eaton, Kazim was a soldier, a hardened veteran of many battles. He had personally slain scores of his enemies. He leaned forward staring at Hamet.

"You sound like an old woman, not the rightful bashaw of Tripoli!" Kazim hissed, keeping his voice low lest others hear him. "Did you think Yusuf would run away and just give you the regency without a fight?! Don't be a fool!"

Hamet hung his head, tears falling. Kazim sat back against the pillows, worried now about his payment. If Hamet lost his courage and ran, Kazim would never see the gold he'd been secretly promised by Hamet after they took Tripoli. This journey with the crusaders would be for naught.

Kazim inhaled the fragrant smoke and considered this new dilemma as el Taiib entered the marquee, sat and poured tea without asking permission.

"I entertained a cloth trader from Algiers this evening," Kazim said to his uncle with a cocked eyebrow. "He enjoyed a profitable day in the market. He leaves at dawn for Alexandria."

El Taiib nodded his understanding. Before the Algerian merchant traveled a league, his body guards would be murdered, Farid's throat cut, and his gold shared between the el Taiib and Kazim.

"Where are you camped?" asked Kazim.

"Not far," el Taiib replied, pointing west. "Perhaps three leagues. Far enough away so they believe we are gone."

"Eaton is angry," said Kazim with a wry smile. "But he is also nearly to Derne and has no camels to pack his supplies. He can't go forward and he can't go back…"

"*And* he has no money!" el Taiib angrily reminded Kazim. "He had to beg sequins from the other Christians!"

"He seems confident he will receive more cash when we meet the Christian ship at Bomba and we are almost there," observed Kazim. "You have your half of the payment we received from O'Bannon. Bring the camels and drivers back tomorrow and let us continue on. I am sure you shall be paid even more."

El Taiib considered this. He was already ahead, could return to Alexandria now and stop worrying about Eaton's mad quest to conquer Derne. But el Taiib was also greedy, so the promise of still more profit proved irresistible.

"I don't own all the camels," he said. "But the drivers who do own them might listen to me if I offer each a few more sequins."

Kazim glanced at Hamet who was sitting back on his pillows, eyes closed, his face a mask of consternation, apparently trying not to listen to what was being said.

"You shall have those sequins," said Kazim with a wink. "That Algerian gentleman I referred to…"

El Taiib drew his extended thumb across his throat while he grinned his toothless grin.

❧ 30 ❧

"Send a rider to the Bay of Bomba?" asked Eaton. "Why?"

"I received a report that Yusuf is sending an army to Derne to meet us!" Hamet declared, desperation in his voice. "I must know we will have the support and reinforcements you promised before I travel any further!"

"So, you no longer trust my word?!" snapped Eaton, hands on his hips, disgusted at Hamet's obvious fright.

"It is not that, William!" Hamet replied anxiously. "It is that I know my brother. If we assault Derne with too few men or not enough support from your ships and we are defeated…and if I am captured…"

"You will be tortured and executed by your brother!" Eaton angrily interrupted. He had come too far and now that el Taiib's camels and drivers had returned to the camp it was time to move again. He needed Hamet with him.

"That was always the risk you ran, was it not Hamet?! It is the risk I am running being here with you! And the risk Lieutenant O'Bannon is running! It is the risk we all run!"

Hamet, eyes wide and face pale, nervously ran his hand over his mouth. Eaton could see this talk only served to make his ally even more fearful.

"Very well," Eaton finally declared. "We'll send one of the Arab's ahead to have a look. But I know my countrymen will be there."

Lear was finally growing impatient with Yusuf's dithering. It had been days since the midshipmen and sick were freed, but still no response to the offer of sixty thousand dollars. Nissen visited the bashaw on at least three occasions, but either Yusuf refused to speak to him or Dghies reported that he was ill.

As the days drifted by, they watched the *Philadelphia's* men labor on the bashaw's breakwater. Rodgers was livid and demanded Lear allow him to at least throw some shot into the city.

"He's delaying because he wants his damned mole finished!" Rodgers had argued.

"Perhaps," Lear replied mildly. "But if you open fire on the city, the lives of those poor men will be endangered, captain. I won't allow that."

Lear had been to see Bainbridge and the *Philadelphia's* captain was like minded. With the bashaw close to accepting a reasonable ransom, now was not the time to antagonize him. But time was also running out, Lear knew. If the prisoners weren't released soon, Barron would likely order the bombardment resumed.

The morning was warm and nearly windless. Lear sat in a chair on the quarterdeck writing in his journal when *Nautilus* came alongside. The schooner had been dispatched to Syracuse to fetch more water, rations and the squadron's mail. As the supplies were being unloaded the ship's commander, Master Commandant Peter Dent, was rowed over to *Constitution*. Rodgers greeted him at the rail and the two went to the captain's cabin. Ten minutes later they emerged, Dent returning to his vessel and Rodgers, wearing a wide smile, climbing to the quarterdeck.

"Good news?" asked Lear.

"Very. I have been made commodore of the squadron," Rodgers said. "Captain Barron has relinquished his command to me due to his failing health."

This was a development Lear hadn't expected. It now placed Rodgers in charge of prosecuting the entire war. He could overrule anything Lear wished to do. Nevertheless the diplomat rose to heartily shake Rodgers' hand.

"I shouldn't have wished to take command under such unfortunate circumstances," Rodgers said, his face revealing otherwise, "but poor Captain Barron simply cannot continue. Master Commandant Dent reports that he is in hospital again and near death."

"You are the right man, John, of course," Lear reassured him. "You have done splendidly managing the blockade here."

Officers who had overheard the conversation came forward to offer Rodgers congratulations while Lear returned to his chair and gazed out at Tripoli considering his next move.

Master Commandant Issac Hull was frustrated. He arrived as planned at the Bay of Bomba on the morning of March 31st. Entering the bay had been tricky. The narrow channel ran between two spits of land that sheltered the bay from the open sea. The bay itself was nearly oval and calm, protected on all sides by high hills. It was one of the better anchorages Hull had seen in the Mediterranean.

He sent his marines ashore and they returned at nightfall to report they had gone to the top of a ridge and searched the horizon to the southeast with their spyglasses but had seen nothing that looked like Eaton's mercenary army.

After a few days, the young officer weighed anchor and sailed northwest along the coast in case Eaton had overshot the rendezvous. Other than some caravans, no human life was spotted so he reversed course, cruising along the eastern shoreline. Perhaps Eaton was waiting at some bay further down the coast, mistaking it for Bomba. His search yielded nothing.

Worried, Hull sailed back to his original anchorage and waited five more days. On the sixth day, a sandstorm was seen approaching from the south, great red clouds of dust were lifted off the desert floor and carried north by hot howling winds. *Argus* quickly made for the open sea lest she be overwhelmed.

The following evening, *Argus'* officers sat glumly in Hull's cabin as the ship cut through the swells ten miles off the coast.

"Most anything could have happened to them," remarked Ensign Miles. "They could have gotten lost or the Arabs might have turned on them…"

Knowing Hull and Lieutenant O'Bannon were close friends, Lieutenant Warren interrupted, "Or, they could simply be delayed, Mr. Hull. No one has ever attempted to do what they are doing. Who knows what they encountered? Like that sandstorm for instance. You wouldn't be able to march in that. You would have to stop and wait it out."

"Aye," agreed Hull sitting back against the bulkhead. "I suppose there could be high mountains or other obstacles they didn't know about."

"Exactly," agreed Warren. "We all know Mr. O'Bannon."

This last comment made Hull feel more optimistic. While he was not well acquainted with Eaton, Hull knew if there was any man in the Navy who could see something like the Derne enterprise through, Pres O'Bannon was he.

The officers were silently smoking their pipes when they heard a lookout's call. They couldn't understand what he said, so they climbed up to the deck where the night sky was full of low hanging clouds. The schooner was bounding along through the chop, sea spray and drizzle soaking the officers who hadn't bothered to don their oilskins.

"What did the lookout say?! Hull asked the helmsman.

"Fire on shore, sir!" the sailor replied pointing to starboard.

It took a moment for Hull's eyes to adjust but when they did, to the southwest he detected a distinct red glow reflected off the clouds.

"That's a fire, all right!" cried Ensign Miles over the wind.

Warren added, "Might be a house or a field, sir!"

"Set course for that fire!" ordered Hull. "I'll wager that's the general and Pres!"

Riding toward the Bay of Bomba, Eaton watched Hamet's apprehension grow with each passing day. As the prospect of battle became more real, Hamet became more racked with anxiety.

Eaton was growing irritated with his ally's timidity and the situation wasn't helped when the scout sent to the Bay of Bomba failed to return after several days. Then it was further exacerbated when the column encountered a trading caravan whose leader confirmed Farid's earlier report. Not only had Yusuf raised an army, it was on the march to Derne.

"I wish to stop now until the rider you sent to Bomba returns," Hamet demanded after the caravan departed.

"Stop?!" Eaton cried. "Are you mad?!"

O'Bannon tried to reason with Hamet, "Mr. Karamanli, if your brother is sending soldiers to meet us, we should hurry to Derne, not delay. We've gone on half rations and we will soon be out of food. We have no money and water is getting scarcer."

Hamet knew all of this. Over the last week, wells and cisterns were nonexistent, dry or full of poor water. His own horse hadn't been watered in two days and was growing lethargic. Likewise, the men were hungry, subsisting on a daily meal of a handful of rice and some dried dates.

"We are just a day or two from Bomba, sir," O'Bannon pleaded. He showed Hamet a map and pointed to a spot on it, "I reckon we're right about here. Please, let's keep moving."

Hamet glanced at O'Bannon and nodded.

The march took them to the top of a ridge separating the sea from the desert. The climb was exhausting for the weary army, the men and animals struggling through the afternoon heat and dust until they reached the crest, where the land flattened out into a narrow plateau. They found a spring with good water and pitched camp.

The Bay of Bomba was visible now through the late afternoon haze, perhaps twenty miles away, and as the soldiers and cavalry realized their destination with its promised relief was in sight, an excited buzz rippled through the army.

"I don't see any ship, general," O'Bannon commented as he stood on a rock scanning the bay with his glass. But we're still too far away to be sure."

Eaton peered through his telescope and then folded it. "We need to preserve what little food is left, then. We'll stay on half rations."

Their thirst slaked, the men cheerfully set up tents while the horses, camels and asses foraged on the thin grass and shrubs. With Bomba finally in view, most of the soldiers assumed a full ration would be provided for the evening meal, so there were noisy complaints when Leitensdorfer and his helpers began doling out the half rations of rice as O'Bannon and his armed marines stood by the commissary tent.

"Our men must eat!" cried Sheikh Mohamet, one of Kazim's officers. "We meet the supply ship tomorrow! Give us a full ration!"

El Taiib jostled through the angry crowd standing around the tent and pointed at the few remaining muslin bags of rice. "There is plenty of food!" the camel trader yelled over the growing commotion. "These Christians are holding out so they may eat their fill!"

The Muslims in the crowd pushed forward, driving the helpless Leitensdorfer back into the tent.

"Halt!" cried O'Bannon over the tumult. "Halt I say!"

By now the men around the tent were pushing and shoving one another. There came shouts in a dozen different languages as O'Bannon and his marines surrounded the tent, pointing their weapons at the mob, gleaming bayonets fixed. O'Bannon had drawn his pistol and sword and stood impassively, staring down el Taiib who continued to point at the food and demand the men take it. Presently, Kazim and a dozen of his horsemen rode up on their mounts.

"You see what they do!" cried el Taiib to the riders. "They threaten us with their guns! Show them what a real fight is!"

Eaton's tent was on a rise overlooking the encampment. Hearing the shouts, he emerged from his marquee and was astounded to see a crowd of angry Muslims and even some of the Christians surrounding O'Bannon and his marines.

"What in the name of God...?!" he mumbled to himself just as the Arab cavalry surged forward, scimitars drawn. As if the scene wasn't appalling enough, to Eaton's astonishment, there, right alongside Kazim was Hamet Karamanli.

The mob pulled back to make way for the horsemen and now O'Bannon placed his men and himself between the tent and Kazim's cavalry. Leitensdorfer had found his musket and joined the marines to defend the remaining food.

Screaming, the Arab cavalry charged. But the marines stood their ground.

"Steady, men!" O'Bannon calmly ordered. "Fire only on my command!"

The charge stopped ten paces short of the American line before the Arabs wheeled their horses away. Kazim and Hamet led another bluff charge, the mob urging them on. Still, the marines did not waver so, again, the Arabs broke off.

Suddenly Eaton, mounted on his horse, was between the Arabs and the marines waving his own scimitar.

"Stop!" he cried in Arabic. "Dismount immediately!"

"Go to hell!" replied Kazim.

"What is happening here, Mr. O'Bannon?!" Eaton called over his shoulder.

"General, these men are unhappy about half rations!" O'Bannon shouted. "El Taiib whipped them into a frenzy!"

Eaton now understood but before he could speak, the crowd on foot as well as more horsemen closed in behind him. He was surrounded.

O'Bannon helplessly watched Eaton disappear into the mob and the dust. His only option was to fire but he knew all of the Americans would be massacred if he ordered a volley. He could hear Eaton's voice above the clamor.

"He'll be murdered, lieutenant!" Leitensdorfer cried. "We must save him!"

O'Bannon bit his lip, could still hear Eaton cajoling the Arabs. "Let's wait one more moment!" he finally said.

Eaton dismounted and, glaring at Hamet, Kazim and the others, walked in a circle yelling at the top of his lungs in Arabic, "You old women! You buggerers of sheep! How dare you challenge my command of this army!"

"We need more food!" Kazim angrily replied.

"Shut up! All of you girls dressed as fighting men! I thought you had courage and honor, but you cry like little children for some food! I have heard of the fearsome reputation of Arab horseman and fighters! But now I find you are just a bunch of cunts!"

Kazim had never been spoken to this way. But instead of anger, he felt a wave of shame because he knew Eaton was right.

"Hamet!" cried Eaton. "You! You are with them?! Get off that horse and face me like a man!"

Hamet meekly did as ordered and walked over to Eaton, who slapped the would-be bashaw across the face. This produced gasps from some of the Arabs and few shouts of protest, but Hamet hung his head and then broke down completely. Nearly everyone could hear his weeping.

"I am sorry, William," he moaned through hands that now hid his face. "I...I become too heated..."

O'Bannon and the marines pushed through the now silent mob and joined Eaton.

"Are you all right, sir?!" the lieutenant cried. "I nearly soiled myself when they surrounded you, general! I thought they would tear you apart!"

"Thank you for your concern, Mr. O'Bannon," Eaton replied. "But I believe I have shamed them. These Arabs have a highly tuned sense of honor and propriety and they know they violated both."

O'Bannon could see that Kazim had hung his head and the others mounted on horses were riding shamefaced from the scene. The crowd was slowly dispersing as Hamet, who had fallen to his knees before the Americans, continued to cry.

"Wait!" Eaton bellowed looking at the retreating soldiers. "You think nobody will pay for this transgression?!"

Alarmed, Kazim looked up. Was Hamet about to be punished?

"Bring that son of a diseased dog el Taiib to me instantly!" Eaton demanded.

The old camel trader was slinking away, but was seized by two of Kazim's men and dragged before Eaton.

"You, old man, have been at the head of every commotion since we left Alexandria," Eaton said, his voice cold with fury. "And now you lead a mutiny of my soldiers!"

The camel trader began to protest his innocence, but Eaton ignored him. All eyes were fixed on the curved scimitar in Eaton's hand. Hamet rose to his feet and started to say something, but before he could the blade flashed, the blood red setting sun glinting off the polished steel.

El Taiib's head flew from his shoulders, his body toppling back into the dust. Blood pulsed in gouts from the neck and pooled on the hard packed earth as Eaton wiped gore from the sword on the camel merchant's robe.

Hamet's eyes went wide at the sudden killing. Kazim had never liked his uncle, so the execution meant nothing to him. In fact, he wondered why Eaton had taken so long to rid himself of the annoying old man. Kazim also reminded himself to plunder el Taiib's body and belongings for Farid's gold the moment he had the chance.

"Let no man in my army dare break military law again!" Eaton called as he looked about at the shocked faces while pointing at el Taiib's corpse. "*This* will be the consequence!"

He turned to O'Bannon. The lieutenant was staring at el Taiib's head, which had landed upright, eyes blinking reflexively, mouth twisted in a grotesque parody of his toothless leer. He tore his eyes away and looked at the general.

"Damn you, sir!" O'Bannon said sharply. "You could've been killed!"

"Maybe," Eaton replied mildly with a shrug. "In any event, well done, Mr. O'Bannon. So this was about the food?"

"Aye, sir," O'Bannon replied. "They want a full ration."

"Very well, give it to them," he said before turning his attention to Hamet who had stopped crying and now met Eaton's eyes.

"This shall never happen again," Hamet meekly promised. "You are my friend and my protector, William. I don't know what I was thinking... these are my people...they...they influenced me, I suppose."

Eaton's expression softened. He had little choice but to accept the explanation.

"If these are your people, you cannot let them rebel again or you may never see Tripoli or your family. You understand?!"

Hamet nodded weakly, looking uncertain and fearful.

"What about the Bedouin?" Eaton asked. They had yet to come upon the nomads Hamet had insisted they'd find.

"Tomorrow? Perhaps?" was all Hamet could say.

Eaton shook his head in anger at the reply. "Hamet," he finally said, "if I live through this, I shall return to my wife and home in Connecticut knowing I exerted myself to the fullest on your behalf. Whether you become the rightful bashaw is now up to you, not me. I have gotten you this far, close enough to touch the throne. You must lead the rest of the way."

The next morning as the column drew nearer to the bay, the advance scout finally returned.

"There was a ship!" he declared breathlessly as he rode up to Eaton and Hamet at the head of the column.

"What did it look like?" asked Eaton.

"Square sails!" the man replied eagerly. "It flew the red and white flag..."

The leaders broke into smiles and, as the news pulsed through the army, there were cheers and shouts.

Rejuvenated, the column picked up the pace but as they neared the coastline, a sandstorm bore down on them from the south.

Kazim galloped up to Eaton. "We must stop and shelter before it arrives!" he cried.

The camels were unloaded and the tents were going up as the storm enveloped the column in thick, choking dust driven by fierce winds. In a moment, visibility was reduced to a few feet as the men struggled to erect the tents in the howling gale. When finally all of the men were under shelter, Eaton and O'Bannon met in the general's marquee, the wind battering the canvas.

"Damn our luck!" Eaton said over the screaming wind. "Let's dispense the rest of the food. That should keep everyone's spirits high!"

The storm subsided during the night but the tents were nearly buried in the fine sand. By nine o'clock, the column was re-assembled and marching. A little before noon, Eaton reached the top of the last sand dune, the glittering Bay of Bomba stretching before him. O'Bannon and Leitensdorfer rode up alongside the general and stared in disbelief.

"Sweet Jesus and all the Saints!" O'Bannon exclaimed. "Where's the ship?!"

"Ship?! Where's the port?!" cried Eaton looking desperately to the east and west and seeing only miles of deserted beach. "I thought there would be at least a settlement here! There's nothing!"

"Where are the Bedouin Hamet told us we'd find?!" wondered Leitensdorfer.

Kazim and Hamet appeared, looked out over the empty bay and began jabbering angrily at each other.

"What has happened William!?" Hamet cried, desperation in his voice. "Where is your ship?!"

"It's not here!" Eaton snapped. "Hull probably had to move off shore because of the sandstorm! Make camp. We're out of food, so slaughter a camel and pass out the meat to the men! Tonight we will build a bonfire on that ridge yonder. Mr. O'Bannon, find us water, if you please!"

"Aye, general!" O'Bannon replied, spurring his mount and calling for his marines.

Eaton glared at Hamet. "You have been promising me for weeks we'd find Bedouin. Take Kazim and find them now!"

Hamet glanced around with a confused expression.

"Now!" Eaton cried.

"Yes, yes, of course, William," replied Hamet before saying something to Kazim and riding off over the dunes.

Eaton looked at Leitensdorfer and said, "Make camp and post men on the beach to keep a lookout. Use driftwood and seaweed to make a great smoky fire."

31

A thousand Bedouin were camped three miles to the south. It had taken Hamet all afternoon to find them. Forever on the move, they drifted like shadows across the desert from one oasis or water hole to the next. They knew nothing of city states like Tripoli or countries like America, their lives governed only by the seasons and the moods of the desert.

Luck was with Hamet. He had once met the leader of this particular band in Tripoli, a man called Sheikh Emir.

"We usually spend the winter," Emir explained after warmly greeting Hamet and Kazim. "There are many date palms here and the fruit is ready about this time so the women gather it."

Hamet explained his purpose and Emir agreed to meet with Eaton. Hearing the army was out of food, Emir had several camels loaded with dried dates and some lambs slaughtered. That evening, as dusk fell, they were seated in Eaton's tent dining.

"I have men who will join the attack," Emir declared after listening to Hamet explain the plan. "Governor Mustapha is as terrible as Yusuf! His janissaries murdered my brother when we were camped near Derne last year and he poisoned the well we were using!"

Hamet smiled at Eaton. "Can you give us a hundred men, Emir?" Eaton asked.

"I can give you three or four hundred!" Emir said proudly. "All of my people shall move with you!"

This was thoroughly unexpected and Eaton could scarcely hide his delight. They would have nearly a thousand soldiers and cavalry when they attacked Derne, all but assuring victory *if* they got there before Yusuf's army.

Hamet spoke up, "We must make haste, Emir. My brother is sending an army from Tripoli to meet us at Derne."

Sheikh Emir smiled at this. "We Bedouin take but one hour to move," he said. "I also know a short cut to Derne. We can be there in two days."

Finally, Eaton thought to himself, things were beginning to go their way. But where was *Argus*? Had Barron refused to support the march? Perhaps Hull decided to return to Syracuse when the army hadn't shown up on time? It didn't matter how many Bedouin he had if resupply and, more importantly, the money he needed didn't arrive.

He excused himself and walked to the top of the ridge where O'Bannon and Fedor were overseeing the bonfire. Flames roared fifty feet into the air as men continued to bring driftwood up from the beach to feed it. The weather had closed in during the day. It was blustery with a cold, teeming rain.

"If they are out there, they should be able to see this," O'Bannon remarked as several French soldiers threw the trunk of a tree into the blaze.

Eaton was silent as he peered out over the dark water.

Argus sailed into the bay just before sunrise, the fire Hull had seen now clearly visible on the ridge. They heard shouts and musket shots so Hull ordered cannons rolled out and loaded with langradge. He scanned the shore and could make out forms running up and down the beach waving their arms, but Hull thought they could be anyone so he decided to wait for more light before sending in a boat.

As the sun climbed, a mounted figure appeared atop a sand dune. He carried a banner on a staff. Hull adjusted the focus on his glass and saw a grinning General William Eaton on his white horse holding the American flag aloft.

"Lower a boat!" he ordered Lieutenant Warren. "It's them!"

The jubilant reunion of Americans took place on the sun dappled beach where O'Bannon greeted Hull and his officers with back slaps and handshakes. "Look at you lieutenant!" cried Hull in mock rebuke. "You're filthy and unshaved, sir! Most unmilitary!"

"That's because I don't live the soft life aboard yonder ship, Mr. Hull!"

Eaton watched the first lighters bring supplies ashore then returned to *Argus* on one of them with the new master commandant.

"Well done Mr. Hull," Eaton said as they were rowed to the ship. "I appreciate your diligence."

"We were getting worried, general," replied Hull. "But we knew you would appear sooner or later."

"I encountered repeated delays," Eaton remarked. "I underestimated the effort and expense of moving an army such as mine."

Hull presented a letter to Eaton when they sat down in the officer's cabin.

"*I cannot but applaud the energy and perseverance that has characterized your progress,*" wrote the former Commodore Barron, shortly before he had resigned his command. "*I did not lose a moment sending you the resupply and money you requested.*"

Eaton smiled to himself at this, knowing full well Barron's real thoughts.

"*You will have enabled to form a correct opinion as to the prospect of ultimate success and thence to estimate the advantages likely to result,*" Barron continued. "*Should you have encountered unexpected difficulties which place the chances of success upon more than precarious grounds, your own prudence will suggest the propriety of not committing these supplies and money uncontrollably to the power of Hamet Karamanli.*"

"What an old woman!" Eaton bitterly exclaimed, throwing the letter onto the table before him. Barron had no doubt made a copy of the letter to present to Secretary Smith when he returned to America. If the enterprise achieved its aim, Barron could take the credit. If it failed, Barron would blame Eaton.

Hull said nothing. Instead, he retrieved the chest containing the seven thousand dollars in gold hidden beneath his bunk and brought it to the table with three copies of a receipt.

Tobias Lear returned to Syracuse to look in on his wife, who was staying with her servant woman at a pleasant villa on a hillside that Lear had rented for her. He also checked on Barron, who was back in the hospital under the care of the British surgeon. Barron was semiconscious and incoherent. When Lear asked about the prognosis for recovery, the doctor sadly shook his head.

Lear returned to the villa where the American naval agent was waiting for him. He handed Lear a letter from President Jefferson written seven weeks earlier and delivered as a priority by the captain of a swift schooner.

"Your recent account of the situation there leaves us with few options," Jefferson wrote. *"I hereby invest in you full power and authority to negotiate a Treaty of Peace with the Bashaw of Tripoli in order to gain the release of the men of Philadelphia."*

Of course, Lear had already taken steps to secure such a treaty, but Yusuf had still not accepted and Eaton was no doubt closing on Derne. If Eaton took the city, Lear now realized, that might provide the catalyst needed to push Yusuf to accept the sixty thousand dollar offer. As diplomats are wont to do, Lear found himself suddenly reversing his position and supporting Eaton.

After four days of rest and food, Eaton's army was refreshed and ready to march. With the addition of Emir's entire Bedouin village, the column stretched out over two miles and would have appeared from a distance as a great host descending on Derne.

So it was that Mustapha's lookout, sitting atop a high hill overlooking the eastern approach to the city, watched the Americans and their mercenaries approach, his eyes growing wider in alarm by the minute. He was instructed to look for a few hundred or so men on foot and on horses. This looked like an army of thousands.

Murad Reis, the grand admiral of the navy of Tripoli, decided Allah had intervened and caused the Americans to meet with some disaster out in the desert. He knew if Eaton had left Alexandria at the beginning of March, as Yusuf's spies there claimed, they should have reached Derne by now.

Still, the city's guns were ready, Mustapha's soldiers prepared. The governor sent lookouts to the southeast with orders to return at the first sight of anything that resembled a column of invaders. Meantime, Reis wiled away his time with an Egyptian courtesan who lived under the protection of Mustapha. Reis was engaged with the young girl when a messenger rapped urgently on the door of his apartment in the governor's palace.

"What?!" cried Reis as he was thrusting, nearing climax.

"Americani!" the messenger exclaimed.

Any ardor Reis felt immediately went cold. He dressed and raced to the governor's suite. There he found Mustapha questioning one of the lookouts.

"What is it?!" Reis anxiously asked.

Mustapha looked at him irritably, "There are thousands of men approaching from the east, fool!" he cried. "And you believed the Americans were dead and gone!"

"Thousands?!" cried Reis.

"Five leagues from here!" exclaimed Mustapha. "A day's march!"

Reis felt panic and then fear. How in the name of the Prophet had the Americans recruited an army of thousands? There had to be some mistake but it was too late to do anything but prepare for battle.

He left Mustapha and raced to the waterfront, intent on preparing *Meshouda* for combat. He was rowed to his ship and as he came aboard he saw his second-in-command pointing seaward where three American war ships had appeared a mile off the breakwater.

After leaving the Bay of Bomba, *Argus* sailed on to Derne to rendezvous with *Hornet* and *Nautilus*. There, Hull was surprised and pleased to discover Murad Reis' flagship was anchored in the harbor.

Reis understood his predicament. He would have to sail out to fight the Americans once the attack on the city began. The prospect of three ships against his own was daunting, but he reckoned his advantage in manpower might improve the odds if *Meshouda* closed with one or more of the Americans and his men boarded and slaughtered the crews.

Lear arrived aboard *Constitution* and immediately showed Rodgers the letter from President Jefferson. The new commodore once again found himself taking orders from a civilian.

"I forbid you to fire on the city," Lear declared when the two men were alone. "We will negotiate peace with the bashaw. Is there any word from Eaton?"

Rodgers shook his head.

"Very well," he said, "we must know what is happening at Derne."

"Nissen reports that Yusuf has sent an army there under his general, Hassan Bey," Rodgers replied. He couldn't help but smirk at the look of shock on Lear's face.

"An army?!" Lear exclaimed. "When? When did he send this army?"

"Two weeks ago," Rodgers replied.

"How far is it to Derne?"

"Seven or eight hundred miles, more or less," Rodgers said, pointing at a chart of the coastline on the table.

"So…"

"Thirty days," the commodore replied flatly pointing at the chart. "They will likely move their army by ship across the Gulf of Sidra, here, to Benghazi. That would shorten the march by maybe ten days."

Lear took this in and decided there was little he could do about it. He now understood that Yusuf's delay in accepting the ransom offer was a ruse aimed at giving him time to raise and deploy his army. Eaton had a march of five hundred miles, but he had many weeks head start on Yusuf's column. If Eaton got to Derne first and took the city, Lear was sure he would have the leverage he needed to secure a deal. On the other hand, he realized, if Eaton was defeated, the bashaw would have the upper hand.

William Eaton stood triumphantly on a ridge overlooking Derne, O'Bannon and Hamet standing next to him. They all gazed down on the city where guns were aimed seaward atop the waterfront fortress on the east side of the city. Across the *wadi* to the west, was Governor Mustapha's walled palace.

The two Americans looked at each other and exchanged brief, wordless smiles.

"No sign of your brother's vaunted army!" Eaton declared, glancing Hamet's way.

Hamet nodded anxiously and asked, "What now, William?"

"We'll offer the governor a chance to surrender the city, of course!" Eaton replied cheerfully. "If he refuses, we attack. You will lead us!"

Hamet's face twitched. He licked his lips and gave a nervous laugh while Eaton turned his attention to the sea.

Argus and her two small sister ships prowled off shore, just out of range of the batteries. Hull saw the army's arrival through his glass and signaled that the squadron was ready to send ashore the two cannons Eaton requested at Bomba.

O'Bannon suddenly struck Eaton's shoulder. "Look!" he cried. "They have that Scotch bastard trapped in the harbor!"

"*That's* Murad Reis' flagship?!" asked Eaton, looking in wonder at the garish yellow ship. "Good God! What horrible taste he has! And how the hell did he ever get out of Tripoli?"

"I don't know!" O'Bannon replied grimly. "But I've a score to settle with the son of a bitch!"

"Patience Lieutenant O'Bannon," ordered Eaton. "First things first. Let's convince Mustapha to surrender – with or without a battle. Then you can have your vengeance."

"Aye," O'Bannon muttered.

A party from the sloop-of-war *Hornet* rowed two cannons ashore along with their carriages, powder and shot. The plan was to manhandle them up a sheer rock cliff to the top of the hill that commanded the view of Derne. It took most of the afternoon to get the first gun in place so Eaton, concerned Yusuf's army might appear at any minute, abandoned the second gun. Once the first cannon was mounted on the ridge, a gun crew from *Hornet* aimed it at Mustapha's palace.

While O'Bannon prepared the artillery, Eaton composed a letter to be delivered under a white flag to Governor Mustapha:

His Excellency the Governor of Derne,

Sir, I want no territory. With me is advancing the legitimate Sovereign of your country. Give us passage through your city; and for the supplies of which we will need you shall receive fair compensation. Let no difference of religion induce us to shed the blood of harmless men who think little and know nothing. If you are a man of liberal mind you will not balance on the propositions I offer. Hamet Bashaw pledges himself to me that you shall be established in your government. I shall see you tomorrow in a way of your choice.

Eaton

He handed the letter to Kazim and several of his horsemen who delivered it to the gates of the palace. They returned less than an hour later to the camp Eaton ordered pitched on a broad field behind the hill. Kazim handed the general a piece of paper on which Mustapha had scrawled his reply.

Eaton read the message and could not help but smile at both its imagery and brevity.

My head or yours.

32

Issac Hull, commanding the three-ship squadron, joined the war council in Eaton's marquee after the evening meal. O'Bannon, Hamet, Kazim, Abbud, Emir, Leitensdorfer and Fedor were sitting or kneeling on the ground beneath a lantern looking down at a reasonable model of the city Eaton had constructed using stones and sticks.

"The local Bedouin told Sheikh Emir that Mustapha has between five and six hundred men ready to fight us," Eaton began with Leitensdorfer translating in Arabic. Hamet looked startled at this news but the general continued. "As you saw today, many of the citizenry are fleeing into the countryside before the battle begins."

Indeed, late that afternoon people began streaming out of the city and into the hills to the south, their belongings on carts, camels and asses. While the exodus was underway, the governor's soldiers were seen barricading streets and alleys with whatever they could find. Leitensdorfer, Kazim and Fedor scouted and reported loopholes had been cut into the walls of houses facing east and south. At the fortress near the waterfront, more soldiers were seen scurrying around its ramparts, preparing guns and ammunition for the coming assault.

Eaton calmly pointed at the model of the waterfront fortress with his sword and addressed his officers.

"Lieutenant O'Bannon, you shall lead your marines and a company of European and Arab foot soldiers in the assault on the fortress from the south and east. It is imperative that fort be captured."

"Yes, sir," replied O'Bannon.

"Bashaw Hamet Karamanli," Eaton declared in Arabic so his Muslim allies would understand. "You shall lead the Arab cavalry attack on the palace, here," Eaton said pointing with his scimitar at the pile of rocks representing the building.

Hamet, who had never heard the word bashaw in front of his name before, glanced up at Eaton wearing a weak smile and blinking.

"Bashaw Karamanli?"

"Yes, of course!" Hamet blurted anxiously. For his part, Kazim broke into a smile when he understood the assignment. He knew the governor's palace was sure to be packed with booty and maybe even the governor's treasury.

"Our gun here will support your attack on the palace," Eaton added.

"Master Commandant Hull," Eaton continued in English. "Please send ashore all the marines from the squadron to join Lieutenant O'Bannon's assault."

Hull eyed Eaton then said, "I am afraid that is not possible, sir. Commodore Barron was most specific when he told me none of my marines were to be part of any land combat."

"What the...?" Eaton began before stopping himself. Of course Barron would make sure Eaton had no more assistance than was absolutely necessary. The young officer had no choice but to obey Barron's command or risk his career.

Hull looked uncomfortable so Eaton smiled at him. "Very well, sir. When Mr. O'Bannon and the bashaw are in place, I will fire our gun. That will be your squadron's signal to commence your bombardment of the fortress ahead of Mr. O'Bannon's assault."

"Aye, aye sir," Hull acknowledged, relieved that the general understood his predicament.

"Are there any questions?" Eaton asked looking around. O'Bannon and Hull both thought the plan sound, but Fedor spoke up.

"What of prisoners?" he asked.

"We shall afford enemy who surrender full quarter," Eaton said with a glance at O'Bannon. "We're not barbarians after all!"

Following the meeting the men gathered around a fire, where O'Bannon and his pupil Abbud presented a fiddle recital. During their weeks on the march, the Bedouin had practiced nearly every evening and could now play a passable version of *Hogs in the Corn*, which he performed and which earned him enthusiastic applause from the men who'd gathered around to listen.

Later, as he lay awake, O'Bannon heard men praying in nearby tents, Muslims and Christians, imploring their Gods for protection. He joined them whispering, "Sweet Jesus and all the Saints, please be with me tomorrow."

Murad Reis waited until three o'clock to weigh anchor. He first ordered all the lights along the waterfront extinguished to prevent the American lookouts from seeing *Meshouda's* silhouette. A waxing moon hung in the sky, but the grand admiral decided he would have to risk being seen. If his flagship were caught in the harbor when the American attack began, she would be pulverized.

Meshouda rounded the breakwater without incident. Reis knew there were sandbars everywhere, so to reach deep water he was forced to stay in a quarter mile long channel marked by buoys. His luck held as an off-shore breeze pushed the brig rapidly through the channel.

An American lookout aboard *Nautilus* spotted *Meshouda's* sails in the dim light. He called an alarm, but Reis ordered more sail as the flagship cleared the channel. Before the Americans could react, Reis and his ship disappeared into the darkness.

Hamet Karamanli came to Eaton's tent at dawn and asked that he and his followers be allowed to return to Alexandria.

"I don't think I can do this," Hamet explained in a plaintive voice.

Eaton wasn't completely surprised by the sudden announcement. Hamet had been anxious during the entire march balancing precariously between his old life of quiet scholarship and his new one as a regent fighting for his rightful place.

"Every soldier has this feeling before battle, my friend," Eaton replied. "We all fear death. But the enemy fears death as well, so battle is always a test of wills. The question is, who is more afraid of dying than defending his country and cause?"

Hamet cast his eyes to the ground.

"Your rightful place – your destiny – is as the ruler of Tripoli, Hamet," Eaton continued in a reassuring voice. "Yusuf dishonored your father, murdered your brother, and stole what was yours. Surely, you want to do as your father commanded. Now you have the means. You do believe in your country and your cause?"

Eaton had struck a nerve by invoking Hamet's father. The young man's eyes brimmed with tears of shame as he continued to stare at the ground. Without looking up at Eaton and in a barely audible voice Hamet finally said, "Yes, I believe in my country and my cause, William. Our cause."

Eaton stepped forward and embraced Hamet. "Then lead us to victory today, Hamet," he whispered. "This is your moment."

Under a clear sky and hot sun, O'Bannon and his company scrambled down the hillside, through scrubby trees and bushes toward the fortress. He selected his assault team carefully. He needed numbers, but he also needed disciplined fighters when the shooting started.

He deployed his six marines into a skirmish line ahead of the assault force that included Lieutenant Ulovix and most of his Greek contingent, twenty Europeans in blue, and forty handpicked Arab and Bedouin foot soldiers led by Leitensdorfer. Those not wearing red tunics wore red kerchiefs around their necks so they would not be mistaken for the enemy.

They passed some farmers tending plum trees, but encountered no resistance as they reached the edge of the city, the fortress looming to the west.

The attackers knelt in a thicket of reeds while O'Bannon glassed the objective. Now that they were within a hundred yards, the fortress guarding the harbor entrance looked far more imposing. Just ahead, the governor's soldiers had barricaded the streets leading to the fort with wagons, carts, casks, baskets and logs. As Leitensdorfer reported, loopholes were cut in the walls facing east. O'Bannon looked to the north, thinking his men might try to outflank the houses and barricaded streets, but the fortress anchored the northern edge of the enemy line, a sea wall just beyond. There was no choice but to attack the barricade blocking the street closest to the fortress.

Hamet, Kazim, Fedor and two hundred mounted Arab and Bedouin cavalrymen rode west along the road that defined the southern outskirts of Derne. Hamet, his throat dry, his bowels churning, was silent as he rode at the head of the cavalry while Kazim and Fedor, excited at the prospect of a fight and plunder, exchanged bawdy insults.

They crossed a crude bridge over the *wadi*, rode another hundred yards then turned into a wide, dusty lane to face the palace, a quarter mile to the north. The houses and streets were less dense here, so no barricades had been erected. Instead, Mustapha assembled half of his soldiers behind the low walls surrounding his palace while the other half of his men were deployed in the waterfront fortress and behind the barricades on the eastern side of the city.

"We wait here for the signal," Hamet ordered.

Eaton stood on top of the ridge with his reserves ready to join the attack if and where they were needed. Through his telescope he watched O'Bannon's team hunker down in reeds on the eastern edge of the town then turned his glass on the cavalry. They were poised on the road to the south of the palace, a squat three-story stone structure with two towers jutting above the main building.

Outside the harbor, Hull's squadron was moving into position, forming a line of three ships ready to open fire on the fortress's gun embrasures. Eaton could see the enemy gunners loading their cannon on the ramparts.

He glanced at his watch. It was a little after two o'clock. "Prepare to fire," he called to *Hornet's* gun crew.

Eaton took one last look at the battlefield then, seeing the ships were ready, he cried, "Fire!"

The gun's roar echoed off the surrounding hills as the ball crashed into the palace's eastern façade. In answer, *Argus* let loose a broadside on the fortress. *Nautilus* and *Hornet* followed, the balls blasting the battlements and showering the enemy gun crews with rubble.

"Forward!" cried O'Bannon.

The attackers burst from their hiding place, howling like fiends, their bayonets glittering as they raced toward the barricade closest to the fortress. Scores of musket barrels bristled from the loopholes and fired a volley, dropping three of O'Bannon's men.

"Keep moving!" O'Bannon shouted over the gunfire. "Keep moving to the barricade!"

Hamet drew his sword, stood up in his stirrups, turned to his cavalry and cried, "*Allahu Akbar!*" The screaming Arab and Bedouin riders raced toward the palace as musket fire erupted from behind the walls knocking several men from their saddles. Fifty yards before the palace's main gate as planned, Kazim and Fedor broke to the right with half the cavalry while Hamet cut to the left leading the other half. The palace wall was less than four feet high so several of the Kazim's men leapt their horses over it.

Seeing it was an easy obstacle, others followed them, firing pistols from their saddles and then savagely slashing the defenders with their scimitars.

From his position, Eaton saw immediately that most of Mustapha's soldiers had no interest in fighting. Once they fired their muskets, many of them dropped their weapons and fled rather than reload. He watched Kazim cut off the head of one defender, while Fedor drew one of his six pistols and shot an officer who was trying to rally his men.

Eaton scanned the scene for Hamet and found him inside the palace walls. Several enemy fighters had him surrounded but Hamet was slashing at his attackers with his sword as his mount reared and lashed out with its hooves. The governor's soldiers fell back when Hamet charged forward, his horse trampling a man on the ground. Another tried to pull Hamet from his saddle, but he swung his blade and cleaved the soldier's head open.

"By God, he's found his courage!" Eaton bellowed with delight.

Argus had come about and let loose with another volley on the fortress from her port guns. The expertly aimed balls found the mark, crashing into the battlements and sending the crews scattering for cover. The enemy cannons returned fire, but as in Tripoli, the gunnery was poor with balls falling short or wide of the targets.

Eaton glassed O'Bannon's attack and saw it was stalled. The assault force had reached the barricade and taken cover from the fire pouring down on them from three directions.

"Gun captain!" called Eaton. "Load with shot and fire on the houses ahead of Mr. O'Bannon! Fire at will!"

"Aye, sir!" the gunner cried. The big gun was levered into place and quickly charged. The gunner aimed the weapon and fired. The first ball blasted through the façade of the house where most of the enemy infantry had taken cover. Another ball quickly followed the first and then another. The *Hornet's* gun captain adjusted the aim and fired into the buildings and houses behind the barricade. The salvo cut the defenders to pieces and those who weren't hit by the shot ran when they saw the mangled bodies of their comrades.

Nautilus and *Hornet* sailed past the fortress again and fired their broadsides once more, but the enemy had already cleared the ramparts, abandoning their guns before the ferocious American onslaught.

O'Bannon's assault force was still pinned down at the barricade as another ball sliced through Mustapha's retreating soldiers. The screaming of enemy wounded could be heard above the steady musket fire.

On the hill, Eaton mounted his horse and rode down the hillside to join O'Bannon's attack. As balls whizzed past, he raced across the open ground to the barricade where he leapt from his saddle and found O'Bannon and Leitensdorfer sheltering behind a cart. Eaton looked around and could see fear and doubt on the faces of the mercenaries and even some of the marines.

"Bugler!" Eaton cried. "Sound the charge!"

The Belgian soldier who served as the bugler licked his lips and blew a note, then tried again.

"Mr. O'Bannon, I don't care how you do it, but get around this barricade and attack!"

"Aye, sir!" O'Bannon yelled. With that, the assault team pushed through, over and around the debris. The enemy's gunfire intensified as the Americans and mercenaries began fighting their way up the narrow street. "Keep moving to the fortress!" cried O'Bannon through the smoke, shots pinging off the nearby buildings.

Mustapha's men outnumbered O'Bannon's but they began to panic as the maniacal attackers advanced. To them it appeared Satan had flung open one of his gates, releasing a horde of demons from every black corner of hell.

Two howling Americans, one tall and one short, led Bedouin fighters with tattooed faces, shrieking Turks wearing brass breastplates, Arabs brandishing scimitars, and Greeks in skirts wielding axes and pikes. Still, some of the enemy found the courage to fight back.

Private Edward Stewart, one of O'Bannon's marines, knelt, prepared to fire but was struck by a ball, his blood and brains spattering the mud wall of a house.

One of the Greek soldiers fell in front of Eaton, shot in the chest. The general fired his pistol at a retreating gunman, dropping the man in his tracks.

Leitensdorfer fought two enemy swordsmen expertly with his own blade, running one through and slashing the other across the face. Another marine turned up the alley leading to the fortress gate. While he sheltered in a doorway reloading his musket, a ball struck him in the belly. As O'Bannon raced to his man's aid, a Turkish janissary came at the lieutenant with a pike. O'Bannon sidestepped the weapon and smashed his fist into the soldier's face. Stunned the Turk fell to his knees. Before O'Bannon could finish him off, Ulovix shot the man with one of his pistols.

When he reached the fortress gate, Eaton saw a flash to his left and turned to face a wide eyed enemy solider who could not have been older than fifteen. The boy blindly fired his pistol at Eaton before throwing his weapon to the ground and joining the retreat into the city ahead of the determined charge. The ball struck Eaton's wrist, shattering a bone. Eaton fell to his knees clutching the wound. Leitensdorfer quickly reached him and bound the bullet hole with his kerchief. Seeing the general down, O'Bannon ran to Eaton and knelt next to him.

"Keep moving, lieutenant!" Eaton growled through clenched teeth.

The gate was made of iron bars that O'Bannon could see opened into a narrow courtyard. The attackers put their shoulders to the gate. Others joined them and the lock snapped. With shouts of triumph, the mercenary force burst into the fortress.

The vibration of *Hornet's* guns dislodged a cross beam that supported the schooner's deck. Master Commandant Samuel Evans raised flags signaling *Argus* and *Nautilus* he was unable to fire. The distraction was all the time Reis needed. *Meshouda* swept in from behind a finger of land a half mile to the east where she had been lurking since daybreak.

Too late, one of the lookouts aboard *Argus* saw the brig approaching and called a warning to the deck. Issac Hull, whose attention was on the fortress and then the damaged *Hornet*, spun around just in time to see Reis fire his two bow carronades from five hundred yards, the balls striking *Nautilus* amidships and slicing through her gunners.

Reis ordered his helmsmen to steer toward *Nautilus* and called for his boarding parties to prepare. Hull, stunned by the sudden appearance of the enemy flagship, shook off his surprise and ordered his helmsmen to come about and his gunners and crew to prepare to meet *Meshouda*.

The fortress defenders threw down their arms and were crowded into a corner of the courtyard. Some of the Arabs and Bedouin, twirling their swords and loading pistols looked as though they were about to massacre the captives, but Leitensdorfer and Emir ran before them, their arms raised. "The American general said to spare those who surrender!" cried Emir. "We will obey!"

O'Bannon and his surviving marines and some of the Europeans were already up the stairs that rose from the courtyard thirty feet to the ramparts. There they found a few wounded and dead gunners.

"These guns are charged!" cried O'Bannon as he inspected several of the nine-pounders. "Turn 'em on the enemy!"

While the cannon were readied, O'Bannon glassed the scene unfolding on the sea before the fort. That morning he noticed *Meshouda* gone and damned his luck, but now here she was again, bearing down on *Nautilus* a mile off shore. *Argus* appeared to be plowing toward the enemy vessel to intercept her, Hull's gun crews readying their cannons.

He looked around the rampart and saw the flag of Tripoli fluttering from a standard above one of the embrasures. He drew from his tunic the American flag he'd brought and strode over to the flagpole.

The marines and mercenaries preparing the enemy cannons paused to watch the lieutenant haul down the Tripolitan flag then tie on the Stars and Stripes. While his men cheered, O'Bannon raised the American flag over Derne.

Cannon thundered across the water. Reis expected Hull to run but instead, the smaller brig came at *Meshouda*, her guns firing as quickly as her crews could reload them. *Nautilus* cleared her decks of dead and wounded and came about to join *Argus'* attack.

"Look at that, boys!" cried O'Bannon pointing at the American ships.

Reis brought his port guns about to face the two oncoming attackers. He waited until they closed to three hundred yards before firing.

It had been months since Reis' crew was at sea. Their gunnery was poor to begin with, but now, out of practice, it was truly horrible. Her fourteen port guns fired langradge and shot at the Americans. Some of the grape shot hit men on *Argus* while a ball smashed into *Nautilus's* fo'castle. The rest of the volley splashed harmlessly into the sea.

Reis violently cursed the gunners as the two American ships passed, *Nautilus* off *Meshouda's* bow and *Argus* off her stern. As they slid by, both ships sent raking fire into the flagship. The balls crashed thorough *Meshouda's* lower decks while marines on both ships fired at Reis' men.

"Close to board the bastard!" screamed Reis pointing at *Nautilus*.

"I can't, sir," the helmsman replied. "She's too fast!"

Reis drew a pistol and shot the man in the head then seized the helm.

On the fortress rampart, O'Bannon's men turned the enemy guns and began firing them on Mustapha's soldiers fleeing into the city. Despite his painful wound, Eaton managed to climb to the rampart where he and O'Bannon turned their glasses on the palace. Through the smoke and dust, it appeared the battle there was over. The flag of Tripoli had been struck and Kazim's riders were circling the walls waving their swords.

Eaton lowered his telescope, glanced over his shoulder at the American flag fluttering in the late afternoon breeze above them and then looked at the marine officer. "I believe we have done it, Lieutenant O'Bannon!"

As punctuation, an explosion reverberated off the sea. One of Murad Reis' gunners near the bow pushed a heavy bag of powder into the mouth of his cannon. The barrel had not been completely sponged so the powder bag touched a glowing spark. The blast vaporized the gunner and his mates. The cannon, its barrel peeled back, was driven lengthwise down *Meshouda's* crowded main deck, butchering any man in its way. Reis watched in horror as the gun hurdled toward the helm.

Eaton and O'Bannon saw the smoke pouring from *Meshouda's* waist. Eaton wondered if one of the American balls had found her powder magazine, but the fire appeared to be on her deck.

They watched *Argus* and *Nautilus* break off their attack on *Meshouda* to rejoin *Hornet.* The damaged schooner lowered her sails and dropped anchor a half mile from the fortress.

"Send a boat out, Mr. O'Bannon," Eaton ordered. "We need any surgeons they can spare. And please have Eugene bring the reserve force down here."

They heard a rider enter the courtyard. Kazim dismounted and raced up the steps to Eaton.

"Governor Mustapha has surrendered the city!" he cried. "He is hiding in his harem!"

"Bring him here!" Eaton demanded.

Kazim was shaking his head. "The harem is sanctuary," he explained. "It may be violated for any reason."

Eaton recalled that harems were the rooms set aside by Muslim noblemen for their wives and daughters. To enter a harem without permission was against religious law. But if Mustapha was now a prisoner, he was a valuable pawn Eaton could use against Yusuf when the time came.

"I don't care," Eaton finally replied. "I want Mustapha."

33

Surgeons and their mates from the three ships came ashore along with twenty armed sailors and Lieutenant Warren from Argus, who reported to Eaton.

"Commodore Barron didn't say anything about armed Navy volunteers coming ashore to help out," Warren told the general with a smile.

The former treated the wounded while the latter fanned out across the city with Eaton's reserve force finding and silencing any resistance. Occasional musket shots rang out, but the city was mostly silent as dusk fell, the thick smoke and dust that had hung over Derne all afternoon carried off over the sea by the wind.

Abbud lay on a litter holding his bowels in with his hand. He had been cut open by an enemy swordsman in the fight on the street. The Bedouin's face was pale, his eyes glassy as he looked up at O'Bannon. Dr. Arnold off the Argus came by and gently pulled back Abbud's robe exposing the ghastly wound.

"I can't do anything, Mr. O'Bannon," he said quietly. "Is he a friend?"

"More than a friend," O'Bannon replied, his eyes misting.

Abbud's shallow breathing suddenly stopped. His back arched and he died as O'Bannon gripped his hand.

The lieutenant stood, wiped his eyes with the back of his filthy hand and moved over to where Campbell lay. He had been shot in the foot.

"It ain't bad, sir," the sergeant reported. "Just took me big toe off is all. Hurts like the devil, though."

The lieutenant patted Campbell on the chest then moved over to look down at the bodies of Privates Edward Steward and John Whitten, the two marines killed in the assault. He gestured to a surgeon's mate in a bloody apron and pointed at the corpses. "Have their bodies prepared for a burial at sea tomorrow," he told the man.

"Yes, sir," the mate said as he carefully covered the bodies with blankets. He looked at O'Bannon sympathetically. "I'm sorry, lieutenant. I knew Steward and Whitten. They was fine lads."

O'Bannon nodded and moved on.

A few tables were found in nearby houses and brought over to the makeshift hospital in the fortress's courtyard. Eaton lay on one as a surgeon O'Bannon didn't know treated the general's wrist.

"Looks like you'll live, general," O'Bannon remarked.

"The ball broke his wrist, but it went through cleanly," the surgeon said as he wound a bandage around the wound. "No danger of putrification."

"I'm lucky," Eaton observed as he got off the table. "If the boy knew what he was doing, he'd have put one in my heart, he was that close!"

Hamet and Kazim came through the gate and spotted Eaton. They wore expressions not of triumph but of deep consternation.

"What is it?" asked Eaton as the surgeon placed his arm in a sling.

"Yusuf's army approaches!" Hamet exclaimed in a panicky voice. "The officer in charge of the governor's soldiers told me Hassan Bey is one day's march from Derne!"

Eaton wasn't particularly surprised at the news. His mercenary army won the race to Derne, but he was certain Hassan Bey was close behind.

"And so we shall prepare to defend your city," Eaton replied sternly.

Hamet stared at Eaton.

"You have taken back one-third of your regency," Eaton went on. "After Benghazi, we shall attack Tripoli if need be. Now, let us reorganize your forces and prepare to defeat Hassan Bey and any other filthy dogs your brother sends here to do his fighting for him."

Hamet considered this. If he was honest, he had surprised himself during the battle at the palace. After Eaton shamed him that morning, he decided if he was to die it might as well be in defense of his father's wishes. He swallowed his fear and somehow led his Arab and Bedouin cavalry to a rout of the governor's army. Only eleven of his men had been wounded and none killed.

After the captain of Mustapha's men had surrendered on the steps of the palace, Hamet questioned him.

"The governor is in the palace hiding in his harem," the captain angrily told him. "While you were leading your men, Excellency, the coward Mustapha was nowhere to be found."

The captain, a man named Mohammed, went on to explain that of the five hundred men under his command, more than half were slaves or Turkish janissaries who had no wish to die protecting Yusuf.

"They were ordered by Governor Mustapha to fight or they would be tortured," Mohammed said, disdain dripping from his voice. "But there are real soldiers here who will fight for you. Men of Tripoli, Your Excellency. I am one of them. If you will allow me, I shall speak to my soldiers and convince them to join you. I think you will need us soon. Hassan Bey will be here tomorrow or the day after at the latest."

Hamet stared at the man. "What?!"

"The bashaw…I mean Yusuf Karamanli is sending an army here, Excellency," the officer replied. "One of his men arrived yesterday with a message to expect them any day."

"How…how many men?"

"One thousand, Excellency," Mohammed replied.

Hamet now understood Kazim and Eaton were right. They had captured Derne but Hamet had no reason to expect his brother would concede the city without a serious fight.

"Yes, William," Hamet said finally. "We should prepare."

"I agree," Eaton replied. "I dispatched *Nautilus* to Tripoli this evening to deliver news of your victory and to request more ships, men and arms. *Hornet* has been sent to Syracuse for repairs and to bring back supplies."

The idea of more ships and men raised Hamet's flagging spirits. He managed a smile at his friend who clapped him on the back with his good hand. "You should be happy, Hamet! I watched your attack on the palace from the hill. I am proud of you!"

"Thank you, William," Hamet said with a look of embarrassment. "I'm afraid it was an easy victory."

"Easy?!" exclaimed Eaton with a look of astonishment. "You and your men were outnumbered yet you attacked an enemy who was dug in behind cover. Those you didn't slaughter ran away like terrified old women!"

"Perhaps so," Hamet replied.

"And you! Lieutenant Presley Neville O'Bannon!" Eaton exclaimed turning to the marine. "Magnificent, sir! Truly magnificent!"

O'Bannon offered a thin smile in response but said nothing thinking instead of young Steward and Whitten, now aboard Argus bound inside canvas bags with iron shot at their feet. Both had been good marines, excellent marksmen and indispensible during the march to Derne. Tomorrow they would be dropped into the Mediterranean Sea where their bones would reside forever. O'Bannon also thought of Abbud whose corpse was claimed by several of his tribesman, washed and immediately buried in a nearby cemetery in accordance with Islamic law. Eaton might be flush with the victory, but all O'Bannon thought of was the dead men.

"General," O'Bannon said. "I suggest we wait until tomorrow to decide the disposition of forces. It has been a long day. Everyone is tired."

"Good idea," Eaton replied, eyeing the lieutenant. "But we need lookouts posted."

"Aye, sir."

Exhausted but unable to sleep, O'Bannon left the rope bed he found in a house whose owners had fled the city. He walked to the fortress and climbed the steps to the rampart where Fedor and Eaton were drinking from a bottle of vodka alongside a lantern. He joined them and they sat silently on the battlement wall enjoying the cool breeze and the sound of the waves lapping against the sea wall.

Eaton looked at the other two, smiled and said, "Barron will shit himself when we hears what we did here," he chuckled.

"It hasn't exactly succeeded yet," O'Bannon absently remarked. "Mr. Karamanli isn't bashaw."

Eaton lit a cigar. "You're right. Not yet he isn't, but I do believe we have seized the initiative."

O'Bannon took a pull off the bottle Fedor offered and wiped his lips with the back of his hand. "I don't know," O'Bannon shrugged. "Now we're going to march on that other city…Benghazi? And then Tripoli?"

"Maybe," replied Eaton. "But with the capture of Derne and after we defeat this Hassan Bey, Barron might decide to resume bombarding Yusuf and quit negotiating with the scoundrel. If it goes the right way, Yusuf will quit Tripoli and Hamet can take the throne unopposed."

O'Bannon yawned, then rose and drew a chunk of white chalk from his pocket. "You know more about these things than I do, general," he said as he scrawled something on the battlement's stonework.

Eaton watched him, trying to divine the younger man's mood. Fedor interrupted his thoughts.

"We made wager today, Kazim and I," the Bulgarian announced.

"You did?" asked Eaton.

"Yes. We had race to see who could kill more men. I won."

"That's wonderful!" Eaton said with a glance at O'Bannon. "Congratulations Fedor. And what was the score?"

"I kill ten men, Kazim kill eight," Fedor said proudly. Then he frowned. "Kazim say I cheat because I shot three of the men and he killed all his with sword. He won't pay me my twenty sequins!"

"That doesn't seem fair. I would say you won the wager, Fedor. A dead man is a dead man. It doesn't matter how he got that way. You may tell that to Kazim for me!"

"Thank you, General William."

"You are most welcome, my friend."

Shaking his head and hiding a smile, O'Bannon rejoined them for a final drink then silently left the rampart.

Eaton, unsteady after the vodka but temporarily relieved of the pain in his wrist, walked over to the place where O'Bannon had been writing on the wall.

There, in large block letters, Eaton read the words, *Fort Enterprize.*

Meshouda limped into Benghazi's harbor four days after the battle at Derne. The explosion had ripped out planking in the bow near the waterline so the crew was forced to man her pumps the entire way.

More than fifty of Meshouda's men were dead, either by the explosion on the deck or by the cannon fire from the two American ships. But Grand Admiral Murad Reis had survived, dropping to the deck as the shattered cannon that had become a projectile flew over the helm before crashing through the stern rail and falling into the sea.

Reis sent word to his father-in-law of the battle at Derne by a speedy pink that could slip the blockade. He didn't know the outcome of the fight on land, but he knew not to return to Tripoli until he did. Carpenters began repair work on his flagship while Reis sulked at the local governor's palace.

Master Commandant Dent saluted the quarterdeck as he came aboard *Constitution*. He saw that another American frigate had joined the Tripoli blockade in his absence. *Constellation* was anchored a few hundred yards from Rodgers' flagship.

A midshipman saluted Dent and led him to Rodgers cabin, where the commodore sat behind his desk while Tobias Lear occupied the meeting table.

"Welcome, Mr. Dent," Rodgers said, standing and shaking the junior officer's hand. "You've a report?"

"Yes, sir," Dent replied, trying to contain his excitement. "General Eaton has captured Derne!"

"No?!" exclaimed Rodgers.

"Yes, sir, four days ago!" Dent said, trying not to smile. "He and Mr. O'Bannon seized the fortress and the governor in his palace. *Nautilus*, *Argus* and *Hornet* supported the attack. The squadron also exchanged fire with *Meshouda*. She was damaged but got away. The fight took less than three hours, sir. Our nation's flag flies above the fortress in Derne as we speak."

Jaw agape, Rodgers dropped back into his chair and looked over at Tobias Lear who seemed unimpressed. The diplomat eyed the young officer then asked curtly, "You're certain of this Dent?"

The young officer looked at Rodgers who gave him a nod.

"Yes, I am," Dent replied. "General Eaton sent me here to report the news and request more ships, men, arms and supplies to secure the victory."

Lear made a face and said derisively, "General Eaton sent you."

"That's right, Mr. Lear, General Eaton sent me!" Dent snapped testily.

"Easy, Mr. Dent," Rodgers warned.

"Sorry, sir," Dent said, glaring at Lear.

"We need to discuss the situation," Lear said to Rodgers. "This changes the equation."

Rodgers stood. "Congratulations, Mr. Dent. Well done. I shall have your orders for you shortly."

Dent saluted, shot a last look at Lear and left the cabin.

"So, he managed it after all," commented Lear, almost to himself. He calculated the advantages and disadvantages and decided now was the time to press Yusuf Karamanli. Lear would never have better leverage once the bashaw confirmed Derne had fallen. "Please arrange a boat and marine guard for me under a white flag," he ordered Rodgers. "I'm going ashore to meet with the bashaw."

Yusuf already knew what had happened at Derne. The captain of the pink Reis dispatched to Tripoli evaded the Americans and reported to the bashaw the afternoon before.

Yusuf's tantrum was epic, even by his own lofty standards. As he wailed over the loss of his city, furniture and vases flew out windows before the bashaw savagely beat his chest, vowing revenge. The hapless messenger feared for his life but quickly slunk from the room after Mohammed Dghies made a furtive gesture at him.

Almost twenty-four hours later, Yusuf had come to accept the capture of Derne, wrestling as rationally as he was able with his two remaining options while he lay on a divan in his apartment, eyes closed.

He could wait for Hassan Bey to recapture Derne and bring Hamet and the American dogs back to Tripoli where, along with ex-Governor Mustapha and ex-Grand Admiral Murad Reis, they would all curse their own mothers for giving them life.

But if Hassan Bey failed, then Hamet and his American allies could march on Benghazi and then Tripoli, picking up supporters along the way. If that happened, it would be Yusuf who wished he had not been born. The bashaw never believed the American jackals and their mercenaries would take Derne. How difficult would it now be for them to crush Hassan Bey then topple Yusuf, especially with the help of the American squadron that lay off Tripoli's harbor? More ships joined the blockade every week and Nissen told him gunboats were coming.

He felt his bowels heave as he thought of his severely depleted treasury. Every day, filthy merchants appeared at Yusuf's back gate demanding payment for the goods they'd sold his chief steward. Sixty thousand American dollars were still on the table along with Nissen's promise to negotiate with Jefferson for more. If he made peace now, the Americans would disappear. Yusuf could once again send out his corsairs in search of plunder. He could demand tribute and gifts. Things would be better.

Yusuf opened his eyes and looked up at Dghies, who stood silently before him like a statue.

"What?!"

"Mr. Tobias Lear is here to see you, Your Excellency," the old foreign minister replied with a deep bow and hopeful tone. "Shall I send him in?"

34

Hassan Bey's army was camped on the same hill Eaton's army had occupied the week before. Yusuf's general was in his forties and handsome, with a neatly trimmed beard adorning a chiseled chin. He wore white silken robes and a white turban as he surveyed Derne. There were many Bedouin camped on a wide field on the eastern edge of the city while Eaton's mercenary army appeared to be occupying houses around the fortress, where, disgracefully, the American flag flew above the parapet.

He called for his telescope and peered out at the palace. More Bedouin and Arabs were encamped outside and inside the walls there. Other than the activity at the palace and the fortress, the city looked deserted.

Hassan Bey called his lieutenants and presented his plan. "Encircle the city," he ordered them, "let no one enter it or leave it."

He glassed the palace again then motioned to the captain of his cavalry. "Prepare to attack the palace in one hour's time. We must relieve Governor Mustapha."

Eaton watched the arrival of Hassan Bey's army from the ramparts of *Fort Enterprize* and estimated his force to be close in number. In fact, Eaton guessed he probably had more cavalry. Beyond leading his army to the top of the hill overlooking the city, the general had done nothing for several days.

"Sir!" O'Bannon called. The marine was pointing south at scores of horsemen riding down the face of the hill. "They're moving!"

At the palace, Hamet had taken over Mustapha's plush apartments. His cavalry was now reinforced with Mustapha's former soldiers as well as a company of mercenary infantrymen.

Hamet also watched the arrival of Hassan Bey and his army but the fear he had once felt did not grip him this time. He merely sized up the numbers and began to feel as confident as Eaton that Hassan Bey could be defeated.

Kazim had already seized Mustapha's treasure. A Moroccan eunuch who despised the governor was happy to lead the Arab to a store room in the palace basement. There he pointed at a block of marble the size of a dining table and said, "Beneath that."

Kazim waited until the middle of the night before he returned to the basement with ten of his most trusted lieutenants. They sweated and strained but finally slid the giant block off a manhole in the floor.

Kazim dropped down into the shallow recess and someone passed him a lantern. Stored there were casks of gold sovereigns, drachmas, sequins and francs. Several chests held diamonds, sapphires, pearls and rubies. Kazim choked down a cry of joy and quickly climbed out of the hole where his men waited wide eyed with anticipation.

"Nothing!" Kazim spit, his face a mask of rage. "He must have emptied it when he heard we were coming! Never fear, friends. Before we leave Derne, we'll torture Mustapha and find out what he did with the treasure!"

The disappointed Arabs filed out of the basement and returned to their beds. After his men were asleep, Kazim snatched a lantern and returned to the hole where he worked the rest of the night moving the treasure to another hiding place he'd found behind a wall at the far end of the basement.

"They are coming!" called the lookout on the palace roof. Hamet looked up at the man who was pointing east. "Many riders!"

Hamet followed the man's gesture and saw enemy horsemen descending the hill.

"Prepare to receive the attack!" Hamet cried.

Kazim's men were already mounted while foot soldiers armed with muskets and pistols readied themselves behind the palace walls.

Hassan Bey's cavalry thundered over the *wadi* bridge and then, without pausing, raced down the lane leading to the palace.

Hamet mounted his horse and led Kazim's men forward to meet the enemy assault. The two armies crashed into each other, swords clashing, men crying out and horses screaming. Thick dust rose from the melee and Hamet had trouble identifying friend from foe. Still he slashed out with his blade while he forced his horse to move forward. Kazim wheeled his mount swinging his scimitar blindly at an enemy. Hassan Bey's cavalry captain didn't see the sword, but it severed his arm cleanly. The stunned officer fell from his mount to the ground where he was trampled.

Five of Hamet's horsemen including Fedor were surrounded by a score of screeching Tripolitans. Too late to help, Hamet watched as the enemy closed and slaughtered them. Fedor, run through with a scimitar, tried to grab the blade, but was beheaded by another stroke.

Kazim watched his friend fall from the saddle and disappear into the churning dust. He let out a bellow and charged into the enemy who had killed Fedor. He sliced one man open before another stabbed Kazim in the arm. He turned on his attacker and thrust his sword into the man's chest.

This was the sort of battle that favored the Arabs. Indeed Kazim's men were winning it, their horsemanship and fighting skills vastly superior to those of the Tripolitans. Hamet watched in horror as Kazim, bleeding profusely from his wound, fell from his mount. His untrained eye didn't see the advantage he had over the attackers so he cried over the din of the battle, "Retreat to the palace! Retreat!"

Some of his men heard him and broke for the gate. Others saw the retreat and disengaged.

Hamet and his horsemen raced past the palace with the enemy riders, sensing victory, in pursuit. Before they realized their mistake, a volley fired from fifty muskets brought down twenty of Hassan Bey's riders. The enemy cavalry broke off the attack and raced away as another fusillade dropped ten more of them.

"There's too much dust!" screamed Eaton as he watched through his telescope from the rampart. "I can't see what's happening!"

On the hill, Hassan Bey saw his men attack and was certain they would win the day when Hamet's riders suddenly and inexplicably retreated. His cavalry gave chase but, leaderless, they rode right into Hamet's infantry. Gritting his teeth, he watched his men shot from their saddles. The survivors were already riding over the bridge, returning to the hill.

Eaton and O'Bannon along with fifty heavily armed men and Dr. Arnold raced on foot to the palace a half mile away. When they got there they found Hamet, his robes splattered with blood, kneeling over Kazim where he had fallen. The Arab was severely wounded, his face pale from the loss of blood. Dr. Arnold applied a tourniquet to Kazim's arm while his surgeon's mates attended the other wounded.

The road was filled with corpses and wounded men screaming for help. Eaton saw Fedor's headless body lying in a ditch. Furious, he stormed into the palace, intent on dragging Mustapha out of the harem.

Hamet ran after him. "No! William! You mustn't!" he begged. "You may not violate the sanctuary! It is forbidden under our law!"

Eaton wasn't listening. He found the ornately carved wooden door leading to the harem. It was locked from within so he pounded on it with the hilt of his sword.

"Come out of there coward!" Eaton cried in Arabic. "You hide with your women! What real man would ever follow you again?!"

He heard the cries of women and children then a man's voice silencing them.

Hamet seized Eaton by the collar and yanked him back from the door. The American spun and their noses almost touched.

"He assisted Hassan Bey!" Eaton growled. "He somehow got word to him and told him to attack the palace!"

"I don't care!" Hamet snapped. "I order you not to enter that harem. I shall put you to death if you do!"

They stared at one another, neither blinking. After a long moment Eaton pushed past Hamet and went outside.

A week went by, then another. The mercenary army had become an occupying force while Hassan Bey surrounded the besieged city intent on starving the Americans out. But *Hornet* returned from Syracuse in the middle of the third week repaired and carrying badly needed supplies and ammunition as well as news.

"Captain Barron is no longer commodore?" Eaton asked, not sure he'd heard correctly.

"No, sir," Lieutenant Evans reported. "He's deathly ill. He turned command of the squadron over to Captain Rodgers weeks ago."

The men stood on the ramparts of *Fort Enterprize* with O'Bannon. From this vantage point, Eaton could keep an eye on Hassan Bey. Since the attack, the palace had been reinforced with men and cannons and the streets around the fortress barricaded and manned, each side waiting for the other to make a move. Hamet commanded at the palace, but the two men hadn't spoken since their confrontation.

"And Rodgers is still blockading Tripoli?" Eaton asked.

"Aye, sir, but Mr. Lear is there now too," Evans replied.

Eaton knew Rodgers wanted Bashaw Yusuf bombarded into submission, but with Lear in Tripoli that was less likely to happen. Eaton looked at O'Bannon and said, "We need to attack Benghazi, so we will first have to fight our way out of here on a battlefield of our choosing."

"What about holding Derne?" O'Bannon asked.

"We have a stronghold right here at *Fort Enterprize*," Eaton smiled. "We will leave a force behind with cannon and soldiers under the command of *Herr* Leitensdorfer. If Hassan Bey wants to attack a heavily armed fortification filled with determined defenders and fire support from our ships, let him try."

O'Bannon nodded. On a table before them was a chart of the coastline. Benghazi lay one hundred and fifty miles to the southwest.

"The road that leads south from the city will take us to Benghazi," O'Bannon observed. "We could be there in a week to ten days. But I reckon they'll try to stop us up yonder."

He pointed at the hills to the southwest. Hassan Bey would see Eaton's army moving, guess its destination and take the high ground before Eaton could. He would then force the Americans and mercenaries to fight uphill. It was an unappealing prospect that could prove disastrous if they failed.

O'Bannon, rubbing his chin, spoke up, "It might be possible to sail the army around to Benghazi and go ashore just north of the city."

It was an audacious idea and Eaton broke into a wide smile. "Move the army by boat! An amphibious landing!" he exclaimed. "You are a genius, lieutenant!"

"*Argus* has room for maybe two hundred men," Evans declared. "I could take half that on *Hornet*."

"We'll need cavalry support and more soldiers," Eaton replied. "That will mean at least one more big ship. Mr. Dent is due back here any day. Let's wait."

The longboats were waiting on the quay, two dozen of them, ready to take the men of the *Philadelphia* away from Tripoli. Yusuf ordered his soldiers to clear the waterfront and citizens to remain in their homes and shops. Now scores of American marines stood to attention guarding the boats and their crews against any treachery.

Tobias Lear sat with Yusuf Karamanli and his divan in the castle and signed a peace treaty shortly after nine o'clock. With great formality, the bashaw signed his name to the parchment copies, one in English, the other in Arabic. Lear then signed with Captains Rodgers and Bainbridge, Mohammed Dghies, and Nicolas Nissen witnessing each document. There were smiles on everyone's face as the bashaw gave a great bear hug to Lear, who returned the embrace and customary kisses on the cheeks.

"This has been a great misunderstanding between our two nations," Yusuf unctuously declared, still holding Lear. "But now we have pledged our eternal friendship, one to the other."

Lear smiled his diplomat's smile, patted Yusuf's fat shoulder and stood back. Two marines came forward with a chest and placed it on the table.

"You wish to count it?" asked Lear.

"No!" cried Yusuf after he heard the translation. "We are brothers! I trust you now and forever!"

"Then, if I may, Your Excellency, I wish to go to our men and take them home to America," Lear replied.

"Of course, of course! This is what I have always wanted!" Yusuf declared, tears of regret in his eyes. "Please, Mr. Lear, take them home to their families with my kindest wishes!"

Lear, Bainbridge and Rodgers were led to the dank warehouse where the captives lived. They entered and found the stench overwhelming. Seeing the American officers, the ragged men got to their feet. There were questions and cries.

Bainbridge couldn't contain himself. He broke down completely upon seeing his pitiable crew. Through his hands he moaned over and over, "I am so sorry men, I am so sorry!"

Rodgers patted the captain's back as Lear held up a hand for silence and addressed the men. "You are going home today, my good fellows!" Lear announced. A weak cheer went up. "I most humbly regret that it took this long to win your release. This enemy has been pernicious and greedy, but I finally convinced him to release you. Each of you has done honor to our country and yourselves and each of you shall be rewarded for your faithfulness!"

With that, Lear gestured to the surgeons and their mates who had followed them to the prison. They came forward to look after the sick and injured. Marines appeared and began leading those who could walk down to the boats. Despite their condition, there was excited talk among the captives who began to comprehend they were at last free after nearly two years.

Bainbridge recovered his composure and left the stinking prison. As he made his way to the quay, there was a tap on his arm. Bainbridge turned to see a filthy, nearly skeletal man standing before him. The sailor knuckled his forehead and said, "Beggin' your pardon, sir."

"Yes?" asked Bainbridge, peering at the man.

"It's Jilton, sir...your steward!"

Bainbridge's face went pale. Jilton had been a jolly rotund man with a clump of unkempt white hair and a rosy complexion. This fellow looked like a corpse.

"Oh dear God," mumbled Bainbridge seizing Jilton's shoulders. Tears welled in his eyes again. "Of course. Jilton, my good man. I am sorry."

"I understand, Cap'n Bainbridge," Jilton replied. "None of us looks too good. 'Ceptin them what turned Turk."

Bainbridge heard rumors that come of the *Philadelphia's* crew converted to Islam in order to be spared enslavement.

"Who? Who turned Turk?"

"Oh, six maybe, Cap'n. Most of 'em English, no surprise there, sir," Jilton replied.

"Which Americans?"

"Just Wilson," Jilton reluctantly replied.

"Quartermaster John Wilson?"

"Aye, sir," Jilton angrily spit. "He was the worst. Took to wearin' robes around and even beat one of our lads. Told the guards who was hordin' food, who was pretendin' to be sick, that sort o' thing, sir."

"That's an outrage!" cried Bainbridge. "Where is he?! I'll have him hanged!"

"Oh, he's under the ape's protection now, cap'n," Jilton replied. "He's outta reach, believe me, sir. A few of us were gonna cut his throat if we ever got us the chance."

"Very well, Jilton, thank you," Bainbridge said. "Go on down to the boats. We're taking you to Syracuse for care and rest. I cannot tell you how sorry I am this happened to you and your shipmates."

Jilton nodded, shrugged, said, "Nothin' to be done about it, sir. We be tars and every tar knows he takes risks when he takes a berth."

Through tears, Bainbridge watched Jilton shuffle down the cobbled street toward the quay.

Constellation appeared off Derne ten days later. Eaton could scarcely contain his excitement at the sight of the majestic thirty-six gun frigate. She was one of the newest, fastest and best armed men-of-war in the Navy.

"*Now* we can move on Benghazi, gentlemen!" he exclaimed to O'Bannon and Leitensdorfer as he watched the man-of-war drop anchor. "And we can give that bastard on the hill a taste of her guns before we leave here!"

They watched as a boat was lowered and a half hour later they met Captain Hugh Campbell on the city quay.

A tall, gregarious man of thirty-five, Campbell enthusiastically shook hands with Eaton and O'Bannon.

"Congratulations, Mr. Eaton! By God, well done, gentlemen, well done! We saw our flag flying over the fort from five miles out! Your victory here will live forever!"

"Thank you, captain," Eaton proudly replied. "The city is secured. Now if you please, I would like to discuss my plan for moving on Benghazi with you."

The smile instantly disappeared from Campbell's face. "Have you a place we might speak privately, Mr. Eaton."

Leitensdorfer rode to the palace to summon Hamet. "General Eaton would like to meet with you, Your Excellency," he said. "I don't know what it is about."

The Tyrolean led Hamet to the armory off the fort's courtyard where Eaton had made his quarters and office. The general, his face expressionless, closed the door of the small, windowless room and stood before Hamet holding out his hand. It was the first time the two men had seen each other since their clash over Mustapha.

"I am sorry I offended you," Eaton said, his voice flat as the men shook hands.

"I am sorry too, William. Of course I could not kill you. A stupid thing for me to say," said Hamet as he embraced Eaton. He held Eaton's shoulders, smiled and said, "We are hot blooded, we warriors, eh?"

"Yes, hot blooded," Eaton replied without expression. "Hamet, I have received terrible news…"

"Not my family!" cried Hamet.

"No, no, Hamet, not your family," Eaton said gesturing to a chair. O'Bannon was already sitting at the other, staring at the stone wall, his face blank.

"What…what is it, William?"

"My country has…has signed a peace treaty with your brother, Yusuf," Eaton said, almost in a whisper. "The war is over. I have been ordered to evacuate Derne."

Hamet stared at Eaton in confusion and disbelief then said, "But… but what of retaking my throne…"

Eaton, shaking his head, said simply, "No."

O'Bannon slammed his fist down on the table before him. "God damn Lear!" he cried bitterly. "We had the fucking war won!"

"Please, keep your voice down," Eaton warned. "We can't let anyone know what is happening."

"William…what of our friends…our allies?" Hamet asked, desperation in his voice. He pointed out the door. "We can't leave them…"

Eaton held a sheet of paper. He looked down at it again, hoping the message had miraculously changed since he'd read it the first time. It was a letter from Tobias Lear. Eaton read the gratuitous closing again, with a sense of disgust and shame.

"I pray you will accept and present to Mr. O'Bannon, and our brave Countrymen with you, my sincere congratulations on an event which you and your heroic behavior has tended to render so honorable to our country."

He placed the letter on the table and looked at Hamet.

"I am ordered to take you, your followers and the Christian mercenaries to Malta. My…my country will no longer support you or the enterprise."

Hamet blinked his eyes. O'Bannon slumped forward, his hands over his face, trying to contain his rage and hide his mortification at the betrayal of his friend. Eaton leaned back in his chair, defeated finally, he thought to himself, not by the enemy but by a loathsome diplomat.

"I don't know what to say, Hamet," Eaton mumbled. "I had the support of President Jefferson but…" his voice trailed off.

Hamet gazed at Eaton for many silent minutes before he reached out and placed his hand on the general's.

"We must trust in God's will, William," Hamet said. "It is written."

Eaton looked his friend in the eye and replied, "Yes, it *is* written, Hamet."

After the meeting, Eaton and Hamet rode to the palace to see Kazim. For their plan to work, they needed his help. They found the sheikh in one of Mustapha's apartments recovering. He lay on the bed, the stump of his missing arm wrapped in bandages. Dr. Arnold had done all he could after the cavalry battle to save it but gangrene had set in so he amputated Kazim's arm.

"I hear a big ship arrived today," Kazim said after they exchanged greetings. "This is good, is it not?"

Eaton nodded but for once found himself tongue tied now that he faced an ally who had lost an arm and his best friend in the service of an enterprise now void of any meaning.

Seeing that Eaton was too embarrassed to speak, Hamet stepped forward. "Word of our victory here reached my brother, Kazim. Yusuf sued for peace. Our American allies accepted. The war is over."

Kazim frowned at this. "But, your throne…"

"I accept the will of God."

"So it is written," Kazim replied mildly after a moment.

"Yes," said Hamet. "Now, we must leave Derne. That is why the big ship is here. To take General Eaton, Lieutenant O'Bannon and all our Christian allies to Malta. I will go with them. Yusuf promised he would not harm me or my followers, but I do not trust him."

Kazim nodded. "And we stay here?"

"Yes."

The Arab looked away, considered his options and thought of the treasure he would have to recover.

"Very well," Kazim said finally. "What is your plan?"

The story was circulated that an attack on Hassan Bey was being prepared. The Arabs and Bedouin were ordered to gather at the southern outskirts of the city late that afternoon and await orders. At the same time, the surviving marines, Christian and Turkish mercenaries along with Hamet and his followers were gathered under a similar pretext near the waterfront.

As soon as it was dark, the evacuation began. The boats ferried Hamet and his retinue to *Constellation* followed by the others. Lieutenant Ulovix was astonished when Eaton told him to take his Greeks aboard one of the boats but he quickly obeyed.

O'Bannon went to the ramparts of *Fort Enterprize* for the last time and struck the American flag, folding it carefully and carrying it back to the quay where he found his marines boarding boats. He silently joined them. Eaton took one last look at the city then dejectedly took a seat in his boat.

He didn't look back when he heard the cries of his Muslim allies who were beginning to discover they had been abandoned to their fates. Instead, Eaton stared into the night, thought about Tobias Lear's treachery and what he would do about it when he had the chance.

Captain Campbell greeted him at the rail as shots rang out and howls of rage rose up on the waterfront. The two men went silently to Campbell's cabin.

"I'm sorry, Mr. Eaton," Campbell said, pouring brandy into glasses. "I suppose things change and we must adapt."

Eaton shot back the brandy and let the liquor do its work. Campbell poured him another drink and Eaton gulped the brandy.

"Change. Adapt," Eaton said absently with a glance at Campbell. "The words of diplomats and politicians."

Campbell said nothing.

"We marched more than five hundred miles and defeated the enemy," Eaton went on, the alcohol spurring his anger. "We were going to take Benghazi and then Tripoli if Yusuf failed to surrender to the will of America. Our ships were in position to support us. We had an able friend ready to assume power and repay our country all of the tribute and ransom we ever paid his evil brother plus the cost of the campaign to restore him. This would have been a victory that all of the civilized world would have regarded with awe. Our nation would be feared and respected forever, Captain Campbell!"

"But Lear had other ideas," Campbell remarked.

"There will be an accounting of Mr. Lear's actions, I can assure you, Captain!" Eaton cried. "This...this *Judas* will be called to answer for what he has done to our nation's honor!"

After one more brandy, Eaton stood and excused himself. A midshipman led him to a small aft cabin on the gun deck. Eaton placed his saddlebag on the bunk, drew out his journal intent on recording his feelings.

"In a few minutes we shall lose sight of this devoted city," he wrote, *"which has experienced as strange a reverse in so short a time as ever was recorded in the disasters of war; thrown from proved success and elated prospects into an abyss of hopeless wretchedness."*

Eaton considered Hamet's plight, now without a country or even his family, disgracefully abandoned by his American allies for expedience sake.

"The man whose fortunes we have accompanied thus far experiences a reverse as striking," he continued. *"He falls from the bright flattering prospects of a kingdom, to beggary!"*

35

O'Bannon stood before Eaton, Hamet and Leitensdorfer on the deck of *Constellation*. A boat was ready to take the marine lieutenant back to his duties aboard *Argus*. In the distant haze, Derne was disappearing.

There was an uncomfortable silence and then Hamet stepped forward and warmly embraced O'Bannon.

"Thank you for all you did, my friend," Hamet said. "You are the brave American and I shall never forget you."

Hamet unbuckled his sword belt. He drew the blade and presented it to O'Bannon. "This was given me by the Mameluke chief in Minyeh. I wish for you to carry it now and always as a token of my eternal gratitude and friendship."

O'Bannon choked back tears and took the sword, admiring its jewel encrusted hilt. He could think of nothing fitting to say ashamed as he was of his country, so he stood to attention and sharply saluted. "It was an honor to serve you, Your Excellency."

Leitensdorfer smiled and pointed west. "I am sailing for America, Pres," he declared happily. "Mr. Eaton is going to obtain land for me from your government in payment for my service. We shall see each other there! I wish to hunt with you in those forests around your home in Virginia!"

O'Bannon shook his hand and said, "And so you will, Eugene. Thank you for all you did for us."

Finally Eaton offered his hand as he looked O'Bannon in the eye. "I will march and fight with you anywhere, anytime, Mr. O'Bannon," he said simply.

O'Bannon blinked back tears, snapped off another salute and was over the side and into the boat without a word.

Argus had orders to return to the Brooklyn Navy Yard, O'Bannon learned from Issac Hull as the brig sailed through the Mediterranean that sunny afternoon. The two officers leaned on the rail watching puffy clouds slide by overhead.

"There's talk that the Navy will decommission *Argus*," Hull explained, "along with a couple of frigates and some other ships. They say it is too expensive to maintain so far from America."

"I reckon the politicians decided it was cheaper to buy peace than defend our country's honor, after all" O'Bannon replied bitterly.

"We're simple sailors, Pres," Hull reminded him. "We just follow our orders."

Fog enveloped *Argus* the next morning. Hull stood at the helm near the compass reading a chart. O'Bannon posted his marines along the rail to keep watch for other ships then stood at the scuttlebutt, peering into the mist. The seas were calm, with only a soft wind to push *Argus* along.

"Sir! Voices!" hissed Sergeant Campbell from his place on the rail. The man's foot was wrapped in bandages and he was excused from duty, but he insisted on doing his part even if he had to walk on crutches.

O'Bannon listened and heard the eerie but unmistakable sound of Arabs speaking nearby amplified by the fog. He strained his eyes and caught a glimpse of yellow fifty yards from *Argus'* port side. He turned to the helm. "*Meshouda!*" O'Bannon whispered. "There!"

Hull hesitated. The war was over. He could not fire on the Tripolitan ship so Hull shook his head, "We cannot attack, Pres!"

"We must!" O'Bannon replied hotly. "That bastard Lisle is a criminal wanted in Washington. You heard Commodore Preble say so in Gibraltar!"

Hull, lips pursed, considered O'Bannon's argument. If it came to a board of inquiry, he would need a good reason to explain why he engaged a neutral ship. But O'Bannon had provided a plausible explanation.

"Very well," he said. "But we do it my way."

Hull picked up his speaking trumpet. "Ahoy," he called out.

Startled voices reached them through the fog.

"Ahoy!" came the reply. O'Bannon recognized Reis' accent. "Identify yourself."

"We are the American merchantman *Diligence* out of New Bedford! Who are you?!"

Muffled orders and excited voices were heard in response. Hull gestured to the first mate. "Roll out port guns and make ready to fire," Hull whispered. "And for God's sake, be silent! Mr. O'Bannon, marines ready to repel boarders."

Out of the fog three grappling hooks clattered onto *Argus'* deck as her gunners feverishly loaded their cannons. Arab chatter rose as the two ships were hauled together.

Two more grappling hooks snagged the rails and now *Meshouda* emerged from the mist, fifty or sixty pirates lined up on her rail ready to attack.

Too late, Reis on the quarterdeck saw the trap.

"Fire!" ordered O'Bannon to the marines lined up in two ranks on the waist.

The unexpected volley of musket fire dropped a dozen pirates while others fell to *Meshouda's* deck for cover. O'Bannon, sword flashing, ran down the deck slicing the grappling lines. As the two ships began drifting apart, the port gunners signaled the first mate they were ready.

"Fire!" bellowed Hull. The roar of the guns shook the brig's masts and rigging, the balls crashing through *Meshouda* at point blank range, ripping across the gun decks killing or maiming Reis' crews desperately trying to ready their own guns.

O'Bannon watched Murad Reis race along deck, rallying his men to throw more grappling lines, his only hope to close with the American brig and board her. The marines reloaded and stood ready. Most of the pirates understood the peril and hugged the deck, ignoring Reis' frantic cries

Another volley of cannon fire shattered what remained of Reis' gunners. Hull saw his advantage and decided to sink *Meshouda* rather than take her as prize.

"Depress your guns! Hull her at the waterline with the next volley!" The barrels were loaded and lowered. "Fire!"

Meshouda shook violently as the fusillade struck her timbers from a range of less than one hundred yards.

"Well done, gunners!" screamed O'Bannon.

Fire had broken out on *Meshouda* and, with water pouring into her, she began listing. Another volley, this time langradge, ripped through her rigging, tearing her sheets and cutting lines. *Meshouda* began drifting as her helmsman wrestled with her wheel.

Through the smoke and fog, O'Bannon could still see Reis in his red robes, screaming at his crew to fight back. *Argus* fired another broadside of shot and the crippled *Meshouda* shuttered violently. One ball broke the mainmast at its base. It swung about in a lazy circle for a moment then fell like a great pine tree over her starboard side, taking men and rigging with it.

"Let's close with her, Mr. Hull," yelled O'Bannon. The commander gave a quick nod and said something to the helmsman.

Argus moved in and this time, the grappling hooks went over *Meshouda's* rail. Reis' men, recalling the butchery during the battle of the gunboats, struggled to lower boats or dove into the sea to escape. Marines, joined by sailors armed with pistols, pikes, boarding axes and cutlasses, climbed aboard *Meshouda* after the two vessels were hauled together, rail to rail.

There was shooting and swordplay, but those who resisted were quickly overwhelmed and killed. Those who couldn't escape were already on their knees pleading for mercy.

"Quarter for them who surrender!" O'Bannon cried as he climbed aboard and looked around for Murad Reis. Smoke was pouring from *Meshouda's* main hatch and there were cries and screams from the wounded below. The ship was listing severely and, with the added weight of the toppled mainmast and sails dragging in the waves, she threatened to capsize. O'Bannon realized he had to abandon the ship quickly.

He glanced around one last time for Reis, but the grand admiral was nowhere to be seen.

"Off the ship with the prisoners and any wounded that can be saved!" he ordered.

The marines and sailors obeyed, disarming and herding the surviving pirates aboard *Argus*. As O'Bannon followed, he saw a movement out of the corner of his eye. He turned in time to see Reis scampering over the far rail, making for a boat lowered earlier. O'Bannon charged across the deck. Reis, the boat's only occupant, was rowing away from his crippled brig. He glanced up at O'Bannon and smiled.

With a roar, O'Bannon leapt off the rail splashing into the sea short of the boat. In two strokes he caught its stern and hauled himself aboard. The grand admiral stood, pulling a pistol from his robes but O'Bannon was faster. He dove forward and tackled Reis, who fell back, his head crashing against the bow seat. One of O'Bannon's fists broke Reis' jaw and the other crashed into his forehead. Through the pain and shock of the blows, Reis somehow found the grip of his pistol and brought it up to O'Bannon's head.

"Gotcha now, Paddy!" he snarled through broken teeth and blood. He pulled the trigger but there was only a fizzle, the powder soaked by water in the boat's floorboards.

O'Bannon stood over his foe, teeth gritted, and slowly drew the Mameluke sword. Reis seemed to shrink at the sight of the glinting steel. "Please…"

Before he could finish, O'Bannon had plunged the blade into Reis neck. The grand admiral's eyes grew wide with horror at the blood pulsing from the wound. He tried to speak but vomited blood instead. O'Bannon rinsed the blade in the sea and re-sheathed it then regarded his dying foe. "You asked once if I was a coward, Lisle. Now you have your answer."

Reis tried to speak again. He reached weakly for his sword and then went slack.

"Pres!" called Hull from *Argus* as the brig approached. "She might blow! We need to get away!"

O'Bannon gave a wave, dove back into the sea and grabbed the line his marines had dropped as *Argus* passed by. His men hauled O'Bannon aboard. After he had changed into dry clothing he found Hull at the helm watching *Meshouda* through the lifting fog. She had rolled onto her starboard side and was sinking. The rescued Tripolitans were huddled and shivering near the bow under the muskets of the marines.

"We're making for Benghazi to release these prisoners," Hull said. "Then we head home."

"What will you tell Rodgers?" O'Bannon asked.

"The truth," Hull said before adding with a smile. "Mostly. Reis mistook us for a merchant vessel and attacked, I had no choice but to fight back. We sank his ship and unfortunately killed the grand admiral in combat. He is dead…right?"

"Aye," O'Bannon replied as he watched the Meshouda's yellow bow sink beneath the waves. "And the devil's having his way with the bastard as we speak."

36

LOGAN COUNTY, KENTUCKY
September 11, 1850

U ncle Presley is not well this afternoon. I fear the reliving of his remarkable exploits with General Eaton has drained too much of his remaining strength. Still, his astonishing story needs to be retold, so I gathered my sheaves of notes together and prepared to depart *Derne* for home, where I will begin writing the story my late mother so earnestly wished told.

I found Lily sitting with Pres in his study. She rose and poured me tea. Pres had lost more weight, if that was possible, and his face was gaunt and pallid. He managed to open his eyes and a small smile crept to the corner of his lips.

"Are you going home?" he asked, his voice low and hoarse.

"Yes, Uncle Pres, tomorrow," I said. "I wish to begin writing the story of the enterprise."

He said nothing in response. I could see Lily had dosed him with laudanum and she now sat before my uncle, regarding his ravaged body with sadness.

"Take...take the sword, Harrison," Presley croaked, "it is yours."

"Thank you, Pres," I whispered. "It will always be displayed in a special place."

I could see this pleased him. He closed his eyes and Lily tugged the comforter up around his shoulders then gestured me to follow.

I had grown close with Lily over the previous weeks. She seldom left Uncle Presley's side and often filled in some of the areas of the story that Pres had skipped over.

We sat on the porch. The day had been warm, but with summer coming to an end, it was growing cooler in the shade of the hardwood trees.

"I am still puzzled about Eaton, Lily," I remarked. "Why did he go to such great lengths to destroy Tobias Lear? It seems as though his efforts were self-defeating"

"That's true, I suppose," Lily said as she rocked. "When General Eaton returned to America he spent all of his time telling any congressman or senator who would listen about Lear's betrayal. At first, he had their support because his enterprise was so widely celebrated. But he wore out his welcome when he began implicating President Jefferson."

"Well, the president did change his mind," I observed. "He authorized the enterprise and then decided to back Lear. It doesn't make sense."

"Remember, it took weeks and sometimes months for news to travel across the ocean," Lily said. "The president made his decisions based on what he knew at any particular moment in time."

"But Eaton was successful in convincing congress to denounce Lear," I interjected.

"Yes, he was," she said. "But the cost was hardly worth his exertions."

I knew the rest of the story. William Eaton returned to his wife in Connecticut where Aaron Burr, Jefferson's former vice president, approached him with a scheme to lead another mercenary army, this time against the Spanish in Louisiana Territory. At first, Eaton thought this a grand plan, especially because Burr wanted him to organize and command the army. But Eaton later discovered that Burr intended to seize the territory and form his own nation. The outraged Eaton sought Burr's trial and punishment for treason, but nothing ever came of the matter, Aaron Burr acquitted of wrongdoing.

Dejected and disgraced, Eaton retired to his home, drank too much, fell ill and died at age forty-seven in 1811.

"But Hamet Karamanli did reunite with his family," I observed. "At least something good came of the treaty with Yusuf."

"That almost didn't happen," Lily said. "Lear and Yusuf agreed secretly that the bashaw could hold Hamet's family hostage for at least four years after the treaty was signed - more treachery on Mr. Lear's part. Eventually, the American counsel in Tripoli did win their release and a small pension for Hamet, who lived in exile in Egypt for the rest of his days."

I shook my head sadly. How utterly dishonorable of Lear, I thought to myself.

The sun was setting by now behind the hills. Lily rose from her chair, intent on preparing our supper. She paused at the door and looked at me.

"The captain came here after he resigned from the Marine Corps," she said quietly. "He saw the slaves and recalled the men of *Philadelphia*. He freed every black man, woman and child, there and then."

My own attitude about Negroes had changed dramatically during my stay at Derne. If it was wrong to hold a white man in bondage, then what right had I to keep a Negro in servitude? Until I learned about the fate of the men of *Philadelphia*, I had never so much as considered this moral dilemma.

Lily was still looking at me. I felt tears of shame in my eyes. She offered me a kind smile, touched the side of my face gently and said, "Go home tomorrow and write your book, Harrison. I shall very much look forward to reading it."

After we helped Uncle Presley to bed, Lily and I dined in silence then retired. I slept fitfully and rose at first light. After I washed and dressed, I walked downstairs with my satchel. I found Lily in the kitchen, quietly weeping.

"He is gone?"

She nodded. "Will you help me dress him in his uniform?"

"Of course."

Presley Neville O'Bannon appeared to be sleeping when I entered the bedroom. Lily opened a window. Cool wind carried a slight drizzle, but the air was refreshing.

Lily found the Marine officer's uniform in a trunk and I helped her wash the body and dress it. I shined his boots and placed them on his feet, then positioned the handsome chapeau bras on his chest while Lily brushed his gray hair back off his forehead.

"Something is missing," I remarked. In the study I found the fiddle Pres carried across North Africa, the one he had used to instruct Abbud. I brought it to the bedroom and laid the instrument alongside Presley.

"Please ride to the village now and inform everyone the captain has passed on," she directed me. "Tell them to come here today if they wish to view him. There is an undertaker there. Ask him to come as well, Harrison."

Two days later, the entire town of Russellville turned out for Presley's funeral along with most of the inhabitants of Logan County. As we prepared to lay my uncle to rest in the little family cemetery under a great oak tree on *Derne*'s grounds, a strange old man arrived by private coach. He was helped down by his liveried driver and led to the burial plot. He wore simple black suit and, oddly, a red cylindrical hat with a gold tassel on his bald head. I met him and shook his hand. His face was withered and there was a faded scar on his cheek, but his blue eyes were lively and he flashed a smile as I introduced myself.

"I am Eugene Leitensdorfer," he said as his man steadied him. "I learned of Pres' death just a day ago and drove all night from Louisville to be here."

"We must speak after the funeral, *Herr* Leitensdorfer," I replied. "I have some questions I would like to ask you if you would permit me. About the enterprise, I mean."

He smiled again as he removed his fez and regarded the worn and faded flag draping Presley's coffin.

"Is...is that *the* flag?" he asked.

"It is," I smiled. "He kept it all these years and flew it proudly from the flagpole before his home."

"Such a story!" Leitensdorfer declared thoughtfully, gazing at the banner.

"I intend to tell it, sir, if you will help me."

All of the field hands from *Derne* were there (I had long ceased thinking of them as slaves) under the bright late summer sunshine. I stood next to Lily, my arm around her shoulders as Uncle Presley's coffin was lowered into the grave. After the brief service I hugged Lily tightly and she kissed my cheek before she silently walked with one of the hands to a buggy. Miss Lily was helped aboard, offered me a last wave and then rode back to *Derne*.

❦ Author's Notes ❧

Long before the Navy SEALS, secret agents, clandestine operations, and regime change there was the remarkable American enterprise to capture Derne and topple Tripoli's regent from power. That this exploit took place in Muslim lands is not a little ironic, since nothing has really changed since William Eaton and Presley Neville O'Bannon marched their marines and mercenaries across what is now Libya more than two hundred years ago. Christians and Muslims still misunderstand and mistrust one another and America remains at war with Islam's radical elements.

Students of the Barbary War know I have taken considerable license in telling this story. Lieutenant O'Bannon had no role in the *Philadelphia* disaster, nor did he fight in the Battle of the Gunboats, but I placed him in the middle of both events because I am certain this valiant United States Marine would have wanted to be in the thick of things.

The march from Alexandria to Derne encountered innumerable delays. I condensed these into representative incidents in order to keep the story moving along. The cunning camel dealer el Taiib was the cause of most of the trouble during the march, although he was not beheaded by Eaton.

After he signed the treaty with America, Yusuf Karamanli ruled Tripoli for fifteen more years. His brother Hamet, sadly, disappeared from the pages of history not long after he was abandoned by his American allies. Yusuf's son-in-law, the Scotsman Peter Lisle, aka Grand Admiral Murad Reis, was not killed by O'Bannon as I depict, but he was disgraced and eventually demoted by Yusuf to court interpreter.

Captain William Bainbridge's naval career did not suffer as he feared it would after he was freed and returned home, although his name will always be associated with the embarrassing loss of *Philadelphia*. Bainbridge did go on to distinguish himself in the War of 1812 as did Stephen Decatur, Issac Hull and the rest of "Preble's Boys" who served under the commodore in the Mediterranean.

Fatefully, it was the men and women of the *U.S.S. Bainbridge* who rescued the American captain of a container ship being held by Somali pirates off the coast of Africa in the spring of 2009.

Preble returned to America after he was relieved of command, retired due to poor health, and died in 1807 at the age of forty-six. His name stands alongside those of other United States Navy heroes at Annapolis, Maryland, where Preble Hall houses the U.S. Naval Academy Museum.

Lieutenant Presley Neville O'Bannon and the six enlisted men who accompanied Eaton were the early embodiment of the indomitable fighting spirit of the U.S. Marine Corps. O'Bannon was the first American to raise the Stars and Stripes over foreign soil and his heroism would be repeated through the years by the Marine Corps at Chapultepec Castle, Belleau Wood, Iwo Jima, Chosin Reservoir, Khe Sanh, Iraq, and Afghanistan. O'Bannon's life after he returned home was not as bucolic as I describe here, but he did receive a hero's welcome. Today, you may visit his grave in Frankfort, Kentucky.

Readers interested in this rather obscure but important chapter of our nation's military history will be happy to know there are a number of excellent non-fiction accounts of the war with Tripoli including, *To the Shores of Tripoli* by A.B.C. Whipple (Bluejacket Books), *Jefferson's War* by Joseph Wheelan (Carroll & Graf), and *Six Frigates* by Ian W. Toll (W.W. Norton). Along with his many talents, William Eaton was a dedicated journalist who faithfully recorded his own thoughts during and after the enterprise. His extensive papers may be viewed at Huntington Library in San Marino, California.

Kennesaw, Georgia

July, 2016

Kevin Emmet Foley was born in Indiana but has lived on the East and West Coasts, and in the Midwest and South. A graduate of the University of Connecticut, he studied journalism and history. Kevin began his career as a newspaper reporter before moving into public relations. He started his own firm in 1986, delaying his career as a novelist until he was well established in business.

Kevin is attracted to obscure but important historical events around which he can develop compelling real life and fictional characters who take readers into the time and place. His first novel, *Where Law Ends* (Pronghorn Press, 2008), is a retelling of the Montana Vigilantes legend. He is completing a novel about Ireland during the opening days of World War II and researching a little known battle that changed the complexion of the Korean War for his next historical novel.

Kevin lives in Kennesaw, Georgia and Bozeman, Montana. You can contact him at www.kevinemmetfoley.com.

CPSIA information can be obtained
at www.ICGtesting.com
Printed in the USA
LVOW10s0912081017
551661LV00010B/405/P